THE DEAD OF WINTER

Julie Solano
& Tracy Justice

The Dead of Winter

Interior design and formatting by Stacey Ryan Blake at Champagne Formats
Web Page Designer: Vianna Bailey
Editor: Marnia Brownell

Visit us on Facebook:
https://www.facebook.com/JT-Authors-342478559284742/timeline/?ref=aymt_homepage_panel

Visit us on Twitter and Instagram:
https://twitter.com/jt_authors
https://instagram.com/jt_authors/

Visit our Webpage:
http://www.jtauthors.com/

ISBN-10: 0986383635
ISBN-13: 978-0-9863836-3-2

Other Books

Seasons of Jefferson
When Fall Breaks, Book 1

DEDICATION

*For our husbands and four children who inspire us
every day. Thank you for your unending support and
understanding throughout this exciting journey.
We did it again!*

~ Like a snowflake on the wind, fate has a way of picking you up and setting you down right where you belong. Though you may not know where you're headed, sometimes it's best to enjoy the ride. Trusting that you are part of a larger plan. ~

PROLOGUE

S TILL ANCHORED TO THE FREEZING snow, I curl into a ball, shaking, shivering, and screaming in agony. The bitter cold bites at my fingertips, pierces through my soaking clothes, and stabs at my face, head, and ears. The pain of the frigid temperature does little to distract from the anguish that rips through my heart and soul. Trapped in an uncontrollable nightmare, I try to snap out of it, forcing myself to look up at my brother. His lifeless body lies unconscious on the ground in front of me. His face and clothes are covered in blood. A tourniquet has been tied around his arm. *Did this really happen? Did my brother just topple down an embankment in his truck? Peyton ... Where is she?* My mind is fuzzy. I can't think. *It's so cold ... so ... so cold. Warm up.* Trying to trap the heat from escaping my body, I wrap my arms around myself, clutching intensely at my soaked jacket. *This isn't working.*

Hesitantly, I unfurl my shaking arms from around my waist and begin to rub my hands together. It's too cold. Not even the friction of the rapid movement can create enough heat to bring the feeling back. Praying there is enough warm air left inside my lungs to defrost my icy fingertips, I pull my folded hands up to my mouth. I rock back and forth, huffing into them, and doing my darndest to understand the scene before me. With my vision anchored to my motionless brother, nothing breaks my fixed stare. Not even the sounds of screeching voices, intermittently streaking through my ears.

Howling winds shroud the hillside, muffling the voices. I don't understand them. *What are they saying?* Straining to focus on their shrill pitch, I track the screaming sound. The trail of desperate cries creates a path that leads just beyond my brother. My focus settles on the figure of a girl. She's huddled on the ground near Caden. Her long, blond hair fans out over a blue and black flannel jacket. I recognize her. She's my best friend, Jenna. *Jenna's here? That's right. She was with us in the truck. We were following Caden and Peyton when they went over the cliff.* Her head is raised in the direction of the embankment. She's screaming for help.

I pull my vision back to my brother's lifeless body. Brody huddles over him, slapping the sides of his face incessantly. He's gasping for air, panicked, "Caden, come on buddy. You can't leave us! You can't!" He pauses momentarily and arches into him. Turning his head, he rests his ear on Caden's mouth. I watch his hand slide up toward his neck. Quickly, he pulls away and yells to Mason, who's making his way toward me. "His breathing is shallow. I'm picking up a pulse, but I can't get him to wake up!"

Mason's movement quickens. "Kaitlyn! Snap out of it! You have to get up! We're going to try to get Caden up the embankment. Nobody's going to be able to see us down here. We don't have a choice. We have to move him. It's going to take all of us. We have to go, now. Come on!"

The scene before me begins to spin out of control. The wind is howling. The river is raging. There's so much screaming. So much movement. From everywhere and everyone. Except from my brother. He's still lifeless. Still unmoving. Panic erupts inside of me. I can't think straight. Shaking my head, I try to clear my mind. *What is he trying to get me to do? Move Caden up the ridge? We can't move him. He was just in a horrible car accident. What if he has a spinal injury? Come on. Be smart about this. What am I going to do?* My teeth audibly clap together from the intensity of the shivering. I look again toward my brother.

"Kaitlyn. Come with me. We need you," Mason begs, grabbing my arm. I look down at his firm grasp and see my ex-boyfriend's rough hand curled around my wrist. Reflexively, I recoil, balling my hand into a fist.

"That's enough! Don't touch me!" I scream, angry that he's coming after me again. *How could that insensitive bastard hurt me at a time like this?* "Get away from me, Pistol!"

"Kaitlyn, I'm not Pistol. It's me, Mason." His voice is calm, as he releases my hand and backs away. "Your friend, Mason. I need your help. I'm not trying to hurt you. Look at me, sweetie."

Not Pistol? I take a second look at the horror stricken face staring back at me. It is Mason. *If this is Mason, where's Pistol? Pistol? Oh, hell ...* In my mind, I replay the haunting image of Caden's truck swerving to dodge gunshots as it slides across the icy river road. *Pistol's truck went over the embankment too. He's the one who drove his truck into my brother's, pulling them both over the edge. Where's Pistol? And Peyton ... Where's Peyton? Peyton ... she's in the truck ... in the river ... Oh my God! Peyton is still in the river!*

I turn toward the raging Salmon River, and look for any visible sign of my brother's truck. "Peyton!" I scream, pulling myself from the snowy ground. Running down the riverbank, I scan the rushing water, searching for the truck.

"Stop, Kaitlyn! She's gone!" Mason's strained voice calls after me. "We need you back here! We need your help! You can't do anything for her. It's been too long. At least your brother still has a chance!"

I can't give up. I have to get to Peyton. Without looking back, I continue to run, stumbling over the icy rocks. Protruding brush and branches lash my frozen skin as I quickly wriggle my way through the thicket near the river. Discovering a possible opening, my desperate hands tear through the thick brush, pausing momentarily, when a small movement catches my eye. After moments of intense focus, I realize it's just the water rolling over a small rapid in the middle of the river. *If Peyton is out there, time is working against us.* The voices in my head are telling me to move quickly. *Keep going, Kait. You can do it. You're a lifeguard, a swimmer. If anyone can do this, it's you. You have to find her.*

My face burns and my skin stings. It feels like I've just run through a maze of blackberry bushes. Tears roll down my cheeks as I continue to run down the riverbank. When there's no shoreline left and a formation of boulders blocks my way to the rest of the river, I begin to climb. *There's no way in hell that I'm going to stop searching for that truck.* Clambering up the steep surface, my foot slides over the slick, icy face of the rock. My knee crashes down with a shattering thud. Shrieking in agony, my body momentarily freezes as I slide down the slippery surface, and land back on the ground. I'm stunned by the harsh impact on my icy, cold bones.

Mind over matter. Move it! Convincing myself to push through the pain, I begin to search for another way up. Hobbling to the backside of the formation, I find a new foothold in a crevice where I begin to climb once again. When I finally reach the top of the towering rock, I carefully pull myself up and find my balance. Beneath me, the river rages, spitting white foam up the sides of my icy perch. The truck is nowhere in sight. I decide to scan upstream, where my view had previously been blocked by the thick brush. The wild water gushes downstream, rushing below the boulder. *One slip and I'm as good as gone.* Tracing the path of the water as it pushes away from the base of the formation, I watch as it flows toward the bend.

Just yards downstream, something peculiar catches my eye. An oddly shaped rock rests partially submerged in the rushing water. There's something different about this rock. It's a dark shade of brown and navy blue. Yellow moss flows from the top. I pause, fixing my sight on the interesting hue. *Where have I seen that flowing shade of color before? Wait a second. Yellow moss?* Climbing back toward the river, I work to get a closer look. *My God, it's moving!* When I lie down on my belly to zero in on the object, the moving figure before me becomes quite clear. That's when I realize, it's not moss at all. *It's Peyton's hair!*

I roll over onto my bottom and begin descending rapidly toward the river. Thankfully, the smooth face of the boulder works as a much needed slide. Rolling over onto my belly, I release my hold, and slip down on my stomach until my feet find a flat protrusion. Closer to the water now, only a couple yards separate me from the icy water. Glaring over my shoulder into the rushing current, I pause momentarily, planning my strategy. *I've got one shot at this. I need to get to her fast, and I need to hit that water at the right angle.*

For a brief moment, I study the direction of the current before deciding to take the plunge. "I'm coming, Peyton!" My voice is barely audible, small, and winded from exhaustion. Launching myself off the rock, I leap toward my target. Within seconds the freezing, cold water wraps itself around me, punching me in the stomach and seizing my entire body. When I break the surface, my frozen lungs gasp for air. It's nearly impossible to fight the painful urge to curl up in a ball. But I've made the choice to fight for her, and with everything in me, I kick and claw toward my friend. She seems so far away. Too far. In my moment of panic, it becomes clear that if I can't pull myself toward the middle of the river, I'm going to miss her altogether. Strengthening my kick, I reach toward the brown jacket that has just come into view.

Just about a yard away, my feet give one good dolphin kick, propelling me beneath the surface. As I thrust forward, my entire focus is on the oversized, thermal jacket. A sense of hope washes over me when my hand wraps itself around the thick, drenched fabric. Peyton clings to the rock as I desperately grasp onto her anchored body. The water has chosen to put up a fierce battle. Another wave crashes down on top of my head, trying to sweep me away from Peyton. My legs pull away from my body, trying to escape downstream. The force is strong, but I'll be damned if I'm going to give up without a fight.

Desperately, I continue to cling to my stationary friend, alternating hands each time my grip fails me. My hands are so cold now, that it's only a matter of seconds before they lose their hold completely. "Peyton, I need you to let go. We have to get to the shore." Her head bobbles slightly back and forth as she continues to cling to the rock. With panic setting in, the desperation in my voice increases, "Peyton, we'll die in this water! It's too cold! You've got to let go! Now!" There's a sudden shift beneath me. Unexpectedly, I find myself submerged, carrying the weight of the two of us down river. Holding her head above water, I kick wildly, until my face breaks the surface.

Finally able to take in a much needed breath, I'm able to speak again. "We're going to let the wwwater take us. Just head toward the shore. Can you pppull your arms for me?" I feel the slight shake of her head as Peyton's arms begin to move. "Cccup your hands, okay?" She shakes her head *no* and slightly raises her left hand out of the water. Peeking over her shoulder, I spot an open pocket knife. She's gripping it tightly and won't let it go. "Drop it! We need both of your hands!" She shakes her head *no* again.

"Ssssaved mmmy llllife." I can barely understand Peyton's

faint voice. "It's Cccaden's. Cccut the bbbelt."

Realization hits me. *Holy Crap. She cut herself out of the truck with Caden's knife?* This is no time for sentiment, but I've got to get her to work with me and there's no way she's letting go of that knife. "Okay, give it to me. I'll hold it. We've got to stay up, and to do that, I need you to use your hands." Slowly Peyton releases the knife into my hand and she begins to pull water. "Tttoward the bank, Pppey. That's right. Don't fffight the current. Let it work for us."

This part of the river is narrow. "We're not far now." I continue talking her through the motions, not knowing if I'm trying to convince her or myself that we're going to make it. Peyton gives a couple more good pulls before her arms come to a rest. She calms as we begin to move closer to the bank. She's not fighting me at all, and it doesn't take long before I feel the rocky bottom beneath my feet.

"Okkkay, Pppeyton, you can ssstep dddown nnnow." I stutter in her ear. There's no response. "Hhhelp me out, gggirl. Ssstep dddown," I shiver. There is still no movement. She's heavy. So heavy it feels as though I'm pulling dead weight. Trying not to cut her with the knife, I pull and tug. The task grows more difficult as we near the shore. Not strong enough to pull her all the way out, I collapse in the shallow water, holding Peyton's head above the surface. She's not helping and my strength is all but gone. Cradling her helplessly, I begin to shake and cry. "Pppeyton, ppplease, wwwake up. I cccan't do this alllone. I'm not ssstrong enough."

Despite my loud, gasping breaths and the strong clapping of my clattering teeth, I hear water begin to splash wildly around me. Suddenly, Peyton's weight becomes lighter. Tipping my head back, I see Mason behind me. I watch as he lifts Peyton from my arms and drags her to the bank. He's leaning over her, with his ear to her mouth. "Kaitlyn, get over here. Was she breathing when you found her?"

"Ssshe just hhhelped me get her to the ssside," I cry.

Mason moves his hand from her wrist to her neck, shaking his head, "I'm not finding her pulse."

Panic overwhelms me. Closing the knife and stuffing it in my pocket, I stumble to Peyton. Mason moves to the side allowing me to check for breathing. It's hard to hear through my wheezing. I try to hold my breath long enough to listen for hers. There's nothing there. I don't hear it, and I don't feel it. I tilt her head back, and check her airway. It seems to be clear. Gasping for air, I begin CPR. "One, two, three, four, five ..." I whisper each compression, hoping to save enough oxygen to give her when the time comes. Shaking and shivering wildly, I desperately continue to perform the lifesaving operation. The cycle repeats until I can barely move. I have nothing left. I'm frozen. Depleted. Hypothermic.

Watching my struggle, Mason steps in. "I'll do the breathing, Kait. I've never done this before, but I'll try."

I nod in relief and slide down to her chest, giving Mason room to take over the breathing. We continue to work, hoping against hope that we can re-start Peyton's heart. When doubt begins to invade my mind, the tears come faster. *This isn't working.* With every compression, I send up a prayer, begging for help. My arms have turned to noodles, and I struggle to deliver solid compressions. We've been going at it for an impossible amount of time. Even if we can get her back, I know in my heart, it's been too long.

I'm shaking and ready to quit, when I hear a low rumbling sound off in the distance. *Give it another minute,* I convince myself when I've all but given up. Mid-compression, I wince, when a thunderous roar blasts overhead. As Mason breathes for me, I look up to see a helicopter descending upstream. I'm tempted to just give up and run to catch it, but I can't do that to Peyton. She's one of my best friends, and she means everything to my twin brother. I don't know if he's going to make it through this, but if he does and she doesn't, he'll never be the same. His world would fall apart without her. Mason and I continue to work on Peyton. Shaking wildly from fatigue, tears continue to stream down my face.

I don't know how long we labor. It could be seconds, it could be minutes. But we don't stop; not until we're nearly blown off the ground by the force of the landing helicopter. The door of the Forest Service chopper flies open and two firemen with bags and blankets jump out and run toward us. They are followed by Marissa. *Thank you, God, for letting her find help!* At their approach, I collapse in exhaustion, wailing at their feet.

CHAPTER I

POKER FACE

CADEN

MY BREATHING IS HEAVY. SWEAT pools beneath my overheated body and trickles down my forehead, finding its way beyond my small tragus bump and into the opening of my ear. My eyes flutter beneath my lids, trying to escape the vision that unfolds before me. There is no relief from this haunting scene. My eyelids seem to be glued shut. Trapped, I kick at the heaviness weighing me down. The water won't stop roaring around me. Screams. Water. Rolling. Twirling. Crunching. Flying. Dizziness invades my senses.

Wake up, Caden. Wake up. I know I'm stuck in that place halfway between sleep and awake, but I need to convince myself to wake up and make it stop. The same haunting nightmare has been on a continuous loop for days. I kick my feet wildly, finally freeing myself from the suffocating mountain of covers. Finally free to move, I shift my weight so I can roll to the edge of the bed. The shock of the searing pain in my arm instantly pops my heavy, swollen lids wide open, reminding me of why

I'm here, lying in a hospital bed. The light shining through the window pierces my sensitive eyes, blinding me momentarily. Looking away from the glare, I try to blink away the fresh black spot burning a hole in my vision.

As it begins to vanish and my vision clears, I notice I'm still here. Room 78B. I hear the rhythmic tick of the clock, mixed with the beeping and clicking of the machines behind me. Looking around the room, I find that I've been left alone. It's still early. Otherwise, my parents would be right next to me, asking more questions and trying to get me to talk. I read the clock on the wall. It's 6:30 a.m. My parents must still be home getting ready for another day of *Operation Hide Crap from Caden*. Focusing on the chart that hangs beyond the foot of my bed, I can just make out a few of the details. Caden Woodley. Dislocated Elbow. Liver Lacerations. Severe Hypothermia. The words are followed by a bunch of medical mumbo jumbo that I don't understand. And then I zone in on the date. It's December first.

It's been three days since the firemen found us and flew us into Jefferson Medical Center, and I still don't know anything about Peyton and her condition. The only question they've answered is how we were rescued. I guess the worst fire season on record was a blessing after all. Apparently, there were firemen doing a routine check on the fire damage in the Russians and Marbles. They spotted Marissa running down the snowy highway, frantically waving for help. She led them to the scene of the accident. If it wasn't for our new friend and the first aid skills of the firemen, I would've probably bled out, and the rest of us would've died from hypothermia.

Aside from the vague details of our rescue, Mom and Dad don't have any other answers they are willing to give me. Kaitlyn, Jenna, and Mason won't talk to me about anything related to the accident. Even my best friend Brody hasn't opened up. Nobody who was there with me will tell me anything. *Why won't they tell me the truth about what's going on with Peyton? How is she doing? How serious are her injuries? Is she going to make it? What are they keeping from me?*

The only comfort I have right now is knowing that she came in alive. She was lying beside me when I woke up in the helicopter. When my fingers curled around her icy hand, I swear I felt a tiny squeeze. *There's no way that was just a reflex.* We landed right afterward. They didn't even give me a chance to say goodbye. They rolled her off as soon as the door opened, and I haven't been allowed to see her or hear from her since. No updates. No communication. Nothing. *What are they hiding from me?* I know one thing. I'd better start getting some answers soon, or I'm going to break out of here. I don't care if they tie me down. I'll gnaw through the damn straps with my teeth. I will get out of this place and find my girl.

My arm is killing me from my injury. The pain temporarily shifts my mind away from scheming on how to get to Peyton, and slams it back into my throbbing body. I want to hit the call button to get that sweet nurse, Sarah, in here for some medicine, but I can't lift my arm. Thankfully she's good at her job. There's no doubt in my mind that she'll be stopping by any minute.

My parents keep repeating how lucky we are to be alive. *We? How can I believe there's a "we" when they're keeping me in the dark like this?* Maybe I'd be a little more convinced if they'd stop protecting me from whatever news they don't want me to hear about. How do I know *we're* alive when I haven't even seen her?

One more thing. Don't they understand that keeping Peyton's condition a secret isn't helping with all these damn nightmares? I'm afraid to close my eyes because I can't block out the continuously haunting visions. I keep seeing Mason, Kaitlyn, and Brody struggling to pull her from the truck before it's knocked loose and plummets down the raging river. She disappeared right in front of me. *How in the hell did they save her?*

Damn it! I need answers!

The door creaks open and I look up to see the friendly smile of Nurse Sarah standing in the doorway. She's holding a tray with a small paper cup, a bottle of water, and a tablet of paper. "Hey there," her soft voice floats through the room. "How's my number one patient feeling this morning?"

I push my gruff, unused voice from my body, "I'd be feeling a lot better if I knew the paper on that tray you're carrying had some answers on it."

"Well, I'm not sure what kind of answers you're looking for, but I do have a pretty potent pain reliever for you. I'm sure it's about time for this." She studies my angry face. "It should take the edge off a bit."

"Sorry, Sarah. I don't mean to be an ass, especially not to you. You've been so great with me. I'm just frustrated. I need to know if my girlfriend, Peyton, is okay. She was brought in with me, and nobody will tell me anything about her condition. I'm going crazy here."

A hesitant grin forms across her face as she walks toward me, bends in close, and begins to whisper, "The cute little blonde girl down in room 83A?" She lifts her eyebrows and crinkles her nose. "I really shouldn't say anything, but since you're my favorite patient, I will tell you that she woke up last night." She brings her finger up to her lips. "Shhh. That's our little secret okay? Now take this medicine and let's get rid of some of that pain."

My eyes grow wide, as I swallow the lump in my throat. *She's still here. She woke up. That means she's not dead. Not only that, but I know where to find her. I commit my new favorite number to memory. 83A. I don't know how I'm going to do it, but the first place I'm going when I get out of this bed is straight to her room. I've got to figure out how to get to her.*

Slowly sitting up, I thank Sarah for her willingness to let me in on the little secret. The pain of the movement has my head spinning, and I'm reminded that I'm still not strong enough to get out of bed and run down the hall like my heart is telling me to do. Instead, I take the much needed medicine from the paper cup on the tray and swallow it down with the refreshing water. I hadn't realized how thirsty I was until I found relief in that bottle. Being upright, even for a moment, has left me weak and nauseous. Sarah evidently sees the color leaving my face, and helps me lie back in the bed.

"Whoa there, kid. I can see you're not feeling so hot. Try to stay still while the medicine goes to work."

I do as I'm told and wait once more to feel the dizzy sensation I've come to expect from this pill.

"I'll see you in a bit," are the last words I hear from Nurse Sarah, before I drift back to sleep in room 78B, just five doors down from the love of my life.

I'm driving down the road in my pickup truck. Icy, cold winds gush through the open windows. I don't understand why the windows are down. When I push the button to roll them up, nothing happens. They're gone. Looking down, I notice shards of glass blanketing the floorboard beneath my feet. The windows have been broken out. Thank God Peyton is wearing my heavy thermal jacket, because it is bitterly cold. Not just the kind that can be fixed with a cup of hot chocolate, but the kind that bites the skin and makes one's eyes water. Peyton is snuggled in close to my side, shivering as we drive as fast as we can through the winding canyon. Four wheel drive is limiting my speed. I can't remember why I feel such an urgency to return to the cabin so quickly, but something is telling me to push this truck to its limit. The snow is coming down in strong gusts, and my windshield wipers are on full blast, trying to clear the muddy, snowy streaks from obscuring my vision. Off in the distance, the color red, zig-zags down the mountainside. It's weaving in and out between a cluster of tall cedars. It looks like it could be a truck making its way down to the road. Checking my rearview mirror to see my dad's truck carrying Brody, Kaitlyn, and the rest of the gang, I have to chuckle at the massive pile of Christmas trees in the back. They're blanketing the cab and hanging down over the front, slightly covering the windshield. I gently pump my brakes, trying to get Brody's attention. He should be aware that there could be another vehicle headed our way. It's a pretty narrow road, and the driving conditions are even more treacherous with the slick snow and ice. I continue to look back in the rearview mirror, trying to get their attention.

That's when I hear her scream. Adrenaline bursts through my body when Peyton shrieks, "Caden, watch out!" I pull my eyes back to the road to see that not only has the red truck made its way off the mountain, but it's coming straight for us. The driver behind the wheel seems to be waving his arm wildly. He's coming at us in a quick blur. Slamming on my brakes to avoid the impending collision, I lose control and begin to fishtail toward the embankment. As hard as I swing the steering wheel back and forth, I can't straighten it out. Simultaneously, several loud bangs ring through the canyon. They sound like gunshots! I can't tell where they're coming from. Is the driver waving his hand, or is that a gun? It all happens so fast. I hear the clanking of metal and feel the force of the impact. There's a loud pop, and the rolling begins. I pull Peyton in close with one arm, and hold onto the steering wheel with the other, ducking, spinning, rolling, crunching. Cold. Water. Heaviness.

"Caden, wake up. I think you're having that nightmare again."

I feel the gentle pressure of a wet washcloth streak across my forehead. As with every time I've had this dream for the last three days, I work with much effort to pry my eyes open. When my body finally allows me to peek through my heavy lids, I see Jenna standing over me.

"Hey Caden, sorry to wake you, but I couldn't handle watching you for one more minute. It's pretty bad, isn't it?"

Looking at Jenna, I take a deep breath, slowly releasing it as I swallow the freshly formed lump in my throat.

"The pain? I'm okay. I just took a pill."

"No, the nightmare. It's hard to watch my best friend go to battle every time he sleeps." Jenna's response is quiet and somber. She gently sits down on the edge of my bed. I cringe in pain, as it dips beneath me.

Jenna winces, "Sorry 'bout that." She scoots a little further from me, helping to relieve the dip that's pulling my weight onto my arm. "I understand your fear of going to sleep. Every night since the accident, I've fought to stay awake because I know I'm about to relive the worst day of my life." Jenna rubs her eyes, showing me that fatigue has set in. A pained expression spreads across her face, and I'm reminded that she's trying to erase the same shattering images that are plaguing all of us. I can't imagine what it was like for her to look over the precipice to find my truck in the middle of that raging river. I'll never forget how she stayed by my side when she found me lying there on that bloody bed of snow. I can only imagine what she sees every night when she closes her eyes.

Reaching out for her hand, I give it a thankful squeeze, "Are you going to be okay?"

"Don't worry about me, Caden. How can I help you? Anything. Just name it."

I look up at her sincere face, and her close-mouthed grin looking back at me. It's comforting to have Jenna here. In all of the confusion and pain of the last three days, I had forgotten my trusted friend is always someone I can count on to help me. She'd have my back, even if it meant sacrificing her own. She's pretty much filled in for my twin sister since I've been recovering from my injury.

My poor sister. Mom and Dad say she's having a tough time leaving the house. She's still working through her understandable fear of being out in the open, unguarded. It makes me feel better to know she's safe at home. Besides, Jenna is the person I need right now. She's strong. Brave. I don't need to protect her. The girl has guts. She'll take on any challenge. Thinking about her character gives me an idea. She's the one who can get me to Peyton.

With no time to waste, I blurt it out. "Take me to her. Take me to Peyton."

Instantly, the smile leaves her face. Staring at me like I've lost my mind, she shakes her head. Her tone drops to a serious murmur, "Anything but that."

Upset with her immediate, inconsiderate response, bitterness courses through my veins. *She didn't even think about it.* I allow myself a moment of silence so I can think this through. *How can I get her to help me? I have to get her on my side. I'm desperate.* I glare at her intensely, knowing there's no other choice but to lay it on thick.

"What happened to always having my back, Jenna? You can see this is torturing me. You're one of my best friends. We take care of each other. I'm there for you; you're there for me. Remember? I thought you'd always be my wingman." I squeeze her hand one more time before letting go. *Come on. How can I get her to do this for me? Think.* That's when the memories begin to roll.

"Remember the time you snuck out to meet Dante's band after the fair, and I covered for you? Or there was that time in biology when you were going to take an "F" instead of dissecting the frog. I made all the cuts for you when Mr. Pine wasn't looking. Oh, and let's not forget the time you were speeding down the road without a license. I switched seats with you before the officer got to the window. Did you forget? It's my turn to get some help here, Jenna. How about it?" I know I'm not playing fair, and my tone is conniving, but I have to get through to her.

A contemplative look flashes over Jenna's face as she leans in to whisper, "Caden, you know I am only looking out for you.

I know I owe you. I do, but please don't ask me to do *this*. Not right now. Not yet. You're not ready."

I'm furious that she's making this decision for me. Doesn't she see how critical it is that I get to Peyton? I'm going to have an aneurysm if they don't let me see her. I feel an intense surge of fury come over me as I muscle myself up in the bed. Shakily, I take a deep breath, gathering my composure before I speak.

"Jenna, I get it. I appreciate your thoughtfulness. I do. But I've realized something today. Being kept in the dark is the one thing that's tearing me apart. I *can live* with the fact that my truck is submerged somewhere in the Salmon River. I *can live* with the fact that I'll be in pain for weeks. I can *even live* with the fact that I can't play basketball this season. But do you know what I *can't* live with? Not. Seeing. Peyton! I *can't* live one more day without seeing her! Jenna, you're my only hope." I pause dramatically, hoping my desperate stare will pierce through her thick skull and find its way to her soft spot. "Why won't you help me?!?"

Silence momentarily settles upon the room. The slight pinch and pull of her lips, tells me that Jenna is about to fold. Her eyes are squinting now as she slowly leans toward me. I watch every minuscule twitch of her face as she struggles with her decision. Finally, she speaks.

"This is going to be tricky, but I'll figure it out. I won't let you down. I know where she is. When do you want to go?"

Relief overtakes me as I slowly release my breath. "I knew you wouldn't let me down." I light up inside with joy at the renewed hope of seeing my girlfriend. "It sure took you long enough to remember which pack you're running with." I raise my eyebrows, smiling at the return of my partner in crime. "Now, let's figure out a plan."

A quizzical look overtakes Jenna's face. After what seems to be five minutes of deliberation, her eyes narrow in on mine. "What time do you think your parents will be here today?"

"The last few days they've been coming about midmorning. The doctor makes his rounds close to lunchtime, and they like to have plenty of time to come up with questions before we see him. Last night, my dad said he was going to try to get me released. We don't think there's anything more they can do for me here that can't be done at home. I'm going crazy, Jenna. I need to get out of this place."

"Ok, I've got an idea."

"An idea to get me out of here?"

"No, we'll let your dad handle that. I have an idea to get you in to see Peyton before you're released."

I feel the frustration beginning to rise in my chest. I don't see why this should be so hard. She's like five doors down. "Just grab a wheelchair and take me down there. Nobody is stopping us," I snap.

My stern tone causes Jenna to draw away from me. She drops her eyes to the floor and releases an audible sigh. "Not on this end, at least."

What is the deal? Why the games? Why do we have to sneak in to see her? We were all in this together. It's been three days. They must know I'm dying to check on her. "What do you mean, not on this end?"

"Okay, listen. I can see you're frustrated, but you need to know something. Kaitlyn, Brody, and I have all tried to visit Peyton. Her parents won't allow it. We've followed them to the room, but they've stopped us every time. They won't let us in. They won't let us see her. None of us. We wanted to protect you. We didn't want to get you down there, only to be turned away. We knew it would crush you, but I can see it's just doing more harm than good. So I've got an idea, but it's not going to work unless we're here alone. We've got to make sure your family is not around. But we've also got to get Peyton's guard dog mother away from her room for a few minutes."

Desperate, I whimper, "A few minutes is all I need. I just

need to see her to make sure she's okay." I can feel the tightness pulling at the tendons in my neck. Images of Peyton screaming in the middle of the raging river invade my mind. It's the last thing I saw before everything went black. *I need to see her. I need to hear her voice. I need to touch her.* "What's your plan?"

"Well, whether you're released today or not, it's going to take a bit of time to process the paperwork. The Hanna Wedding is at two o'clock at the church down the street. I think the entire town is going, including our parents, so there's going to be a skeleton crew on duty at the hospital. I'll come up with an excuse to stay here with you. Don't worry. I'm going to figure this out. Give me some time. I'll be back soon, okay?"

I give Jenna a slight nod and smile as she rises from the bed and begins to walk toward the door. She glances back over her shoulder and winks, before leaving the room. At her absence, emptiness begins to fill me once again. I don't like being alone in the hospital, and the ache of knowing Peyton is just down the hall makes it even worse. I shrink back into my bed and try to flip through an old *Four Wheeler* magazine to take my mind off of my loneliness.

Time passes slowly, but just as I thought, my parents arrive at the hospital around 11:30. They've brought a change of clothes, just in case I get to leave today. When the doctor stops by to go over my blood work and give me the once over, I'm disappointed that I'm stuck here for one more night. He's concerned about my blood count and the amount of redness and swelling around my incision. My chest empties at my run of bad luck, and I can tell by the look on my parents' faces that they feel awful for me.

"I'm really sorry, son. But we don't want to get you home

and have something happen. I'm sure your healing might be a little slower with the tissue damage from the frostbite. I can stay here with you tonight if you'd like. Your mom can go to the wedding with Cinda and the girls."

Oh no. No, no, no. Parent patrol is the last thing I need. I have to get that alone time so I can sneak down to see Peyton. I can feel my head shaking before the words even leave my mouth. "Oh no, Dad. I'm all good. I'll just sit here with my mag …"

My words are interrupted when the heavy, wooden door creaks open. "Hi, guys!" Jenna bounces through the doorway with a soda in one hand and an overloaded grocery sack in the other. "I just passed your doctor in the hallway. What's the word? Are you coming home?"

I shake my head and close my eyes solemnly. "Not today." When I look back at her, Jenna's face is pulled into a frown. "I have a low blood count and if it doesn't go up, I'll need a transfusion. My incision doesn't look so good either. I'm stuck here tonight."

"Well, I've got your cure! This is for you." She hands me the soda, then sticks her hand in the bag, and pulls out a gigantic Gold Rush Burger.

A smile grows across my face. "Finally, someone who knows the kind of medicine a recovering patient needs. Thanks, Jenna."

"I knew your favorite food would cheer you up, and there's enough iron in that beast to get your blood count up. Eat it. We'll have you home in no time."

As I peel back the wrapper from the monstrous burger, Jenna pulls a poker set from the bag. "I've got big plans for us tonight, Cade Monster. You and I are going to play a little Texas hold 'em with this bad boy."

"Aren't you going to the wedding?" my mom interrupts.

"Nope, pretty sure I was uninvited when I dumped the

groom's best friend last summer. I'd rather hang out with Caden anyway. Don't worry about us. I'm on duty tonight, guys. Go have some fun with my parents. I've got this." Jenna smiles and waves my parents toward the door.

"So, you're going to hang out with our boy all day? That makes me feel so much better." My mom turns to me once more. "You're okay with this, son?" she asks hesitantly. "We don't want to seem insensitive, leaving you here while we go to a wedding."

I really do need this adult-free time. There's no way I'm getting to Peyton with my parents in the mix. I smile. "We're all good here. Go have fun. It's probably only one more night, and Jenna's *okay* company, I guess." Squinting my eyes, I shoot Jenna a devilish grin. "Besides, I plan on destroying her at her own game, just like I did last time." I raise my eyebrows wiggling them up and down.

Jenna rolls her eyes and looks at my parents, "You know he's a cheater, right?"

My mom and dad chuckle, heads bobbing up and down.

"Alright, get out. Enough of you ganging up on me," I laugh. My hamburger bun bobs up and down as I wave my parents off with my good arm.

"Alright, son," my mom bends down and gives me a hug. "We'll check in after the wedding. I guess there's really no need to worry when you've got your homey looking out for you." She giggles, proud of herself that she's picking up on some of the high school lingo she catches floating through the halls of Jefferson High. "Thanks for taking such good care of him, Jenna."

"That's what *homies* are for, Jacie," Jenna humorously mocks the word.

"Well, in that case, keep him in line, and make sure he follows the doctor's orders," she jokes as my dad opens the door and begins to escort her from the room.

"Really, Mom? You're asking *JENNA* to keep *ME* in line?"

My dad clears his throat. "Umm, Caden does have a point, honey. We might need to see how she handles today's challenge, before we go trusting her to babysit our boy again."

He winks at Jenna and chuckles as the door closes behind them.

"Speaking of homies," Jenna leans in close and lowers her voice, "I've got to call Kaitlyn. We're going to need her help on this."

Jenna grabs her phone and the grocery sack that carried my lunch, and she heads into the bathroom. "Why are you leaving? Can't you talk to her in front of me? Are you trying to hide something? Cuz you know I'm going to find out whatever it is."

"Oh no, silly. I'm not hiding anything, just killing two birds with one stone."

I will never understand girls. Even when they're not together, they still can't go to the bathroom alone. The bathroom door closes behind Jenna, and I find myself occupying my time playing with the poker chips. When the door creaks open, I look up to see a dark haired nurse standing outside of the bathroom. She's holding onto a wheelchair and smiling down at me. I jump a bit, not realizing the unfamiliar nurse has entered the room. When she wheels the chair toward me, the lady's gait is faintly recognizable. Then it clicks, "You're kidding me," I laugh. It's Jenna. She's standing in front of me wearing a nurse's uniform. The swaying, black, bobbed wig and glasses fooled me for a minute. I actually have to do a double take to make sure it's really her. She looks so different without her long, blond hair, but I know it's her because of her eyes. Nobody I know has those steel blue eyes. "Where did you get that uniform?"

"I snuck it in the grocery bag under your lunch. I hope I don't smell like onions," she laughs.

"No, *where* did you get it? It looks real."

"Oh, it's the costume I wore for *One Flew Over the Cuckoo's Nest* last year in the fall play. The wardrobe people took their jobs very seriously. I think Dr. Swenson actually gave it to them." Jenna looks down at my future ride. "And the wheelchair was just sitting in the corner behind that curtain," she tips her head toward the empty bed next to me. "I scoped it out earlier today. Do you think we can pull it off? Do you think anyone will recognize me?" she giggles, crumpling up the grocery bag.

"Jenna, you practically live at my house, and it took me a minute to figure out it was you, so probably not."

She wheels the chair right up beside me and begins setting up the poker game on the table next to my bed. As she begins dealing the cards, I become increasingly confused.

"What are you doing? Aren't we going to see Peyton?"

"I'm setting up the game in case someone shows up. Details are extremely important when it comes to pulling off a ruse like this." She smiles at me and winks, laying down the rest of the cards. "Now we're ready to go."

"Oh no!" I shake my head. "I want to see my hand first." I gently lower myself into the chair, and use my feet to scoot myself up to the table. I glance at the cards to see the crappy hand she's given me. Curiously, I take a look at hers. "Why do you get the good cards?"

"Because I'm the one who's in charge of this operation," she smirks.

"Fine, but when we get back to the room and play a real game, I'm dealing the cards." Putting on my best poker face, I grab a lucky chip for the road, and let Jenna know I'm ready to go see my girl.

CHAPTER 2

DON'T BLOW IT

"**W**AIT A SECOND, BUDDY! I know you're in a hurry, but Kaitlyn should be here any minute. This won't work without her."

"Why do we need to get my sister involved? Haven't you noticed how messed up she is? She's barely left the house by herself since she was released from the hospital. Not to mention, when she does come to visit, she hovers over me like a damn hawk. It makes me feel like I'm in a high security prison or something. Jenna, you know her guard is up right now. She's not going to let us go down there. She's already made it very clear that I need to stay away from that room."

"She's on board with this, Caden. I talked to her earlier. She knows how upset you are. She gets it. Brody's going to be with her, so it's all going to work out. They've thought of a way to distract Peyton's mom for us, unless you can come up with a better idea."

"Are you sure she's not just coming to stop us?"

"Cut her some slack. She's just worried about you, that's

all. She's only been HOVERING since they discovered the trail of shotgun shells at the scene of the accident, traced back to *your* stolen gun! She knows you can't protect yourself lying here in the hospital bed with your eyes closed. She's just looking out for you."

I gasp in shock at Jenna's revelation, "What are you talking about?"

She throws her hand up over her mouth. "Damn it," she shakes her head and mumbles through her fingers, "I'm so stupid sometimes."

"Start talking, Jenna. Now. Why is everyone keeping me in the dark? What's all this about shotgun shells?" *What is she keeping from me?* My mind fumbles to connect the dots between my shotgun shells and the accident. *That's right. My gun was missing from the truck when we got back with the Christmas trees.* "So that sneaky, little bastard is running around with my shotgun? He made it out of the wreck alive? Where is he? What, exactly, are you trying to protect me from?"

My breathing is heavy. Sweat begins to bead on my forehead. I hadn't thought about Pistol's whereabouts since the day of the accident. Naturally, I assumed that he was crushed beneath his truck or thrown into jagged rocks somewhere. His truck was tangled with mine when we went over the edge. I'm not sure where it went after we hit the first patch of trees, and I never saw him again after we rolled the first time.

The vision repeats itself on a speeding loop. It just doesn't make sense. *How could he have survived that wreck?* Anger wells within me when I realize that Jenna just let another secret slip. A secret that I should have been aware of since day one. A secret that could jeopardize all of our safety. I try not to call attention to my room by raising my voice, but the new information has my mind going haywire. Her blunder has confirmed that everyone knows more about what's going on than I do. My face flushes with fiery heat, "What are you not telling me?" I growl through closed teeth. "Where is that little punk?"

A tiny mumble sounds from Jenna's direction.

"What did you say?"

"I said I DON'T KNOW! Are you happy now? I DON'T KNOW! Nobody does. They haven't found Pistol anywhere. Everyone is freaking out, Caden. Your sister can't even sleep at night, and we think that's why Peyton's parents won't let anyone in to see her. Everyone is on full alert, thinking that he's running around somewhere with *your* gun! The one he stole from *your* truck while we were hunting for Christmas trees."

Jenna begins to shake. She's visibly upset, and it kills me that I'm the one who caused it. *Man, I can be an ass.* All I've been thinking about is how to get to Peyton, while my sister and our friends have been trying to shield *me* from an armed lunatic who could break in here at any minute. Now, more than ever, I need to get out of this hospital. I can't be in here. It's making all of us vulnerable. They shouldn't be protecting *me*, I should be protecting *them*. I need to find that miserable, little maggot and end this nightmare once and for all. *He could still be after my sister. Why have I been so focused on myself? T's still in danger.*

"Where's my phone?"

"Why?" Jenna fidgets nervously with the pen and clipboard she found hanging at the end of my bed. "Caden, please don't tell them I told you about the shells. I didn't mean to let it slip."

"I'm not telling anyone anything. I just need to talk to Brody. I have to know what he's doing to protect my sister."

"Don't worry. Protecting Kaitlyn is all he's been doing for days. In fact, he's with her right now. He hasn't left her side for one minute. He won't let her go anywhere alone. You don't need to call him. He'll be here soon, and then you can question him all you want." Jenna pauses as she bites nervously at the inside of her cheek. "But, I don't think he has any more answers than we do."

For the briefest moment I'm glad my friends have been

protecting me. The added stress of thinking Pistol might still be out there actually hurts. My pounding heart forces blood into my stitches. They painfully tug at the throbbing incision on my injured arm. The sheer panic I've yet to experience since I woke up in the hospital has suddenly come to visit, and it's awakening nerves I never knew I had. I'm completely on edge. When the door creaks open, I dart into the wheelchair, knowing it's time for our show to begin. She grabs a blanket from the bed and begins tucking it around me. Looking up, I find Kaitlyn and Brody standing in the doorway.

My sister's eyes meet mine before she begins to speak. With a hint of surprise in her voice, she apologizes, "Oh, I'm sorry, nurse. I thought my brother was alone."

"No need to apologize." Jenna finishes tucking in the blanket and turns toward my sister. "It's just me."

I watch Kaitlyn's eyebrows travel up her forehead. "What's going on here? Why are you dressed like that? Is this all part of your *big plan?*" One by one, the questions roll, as she makes her way toward me. When she reaches the wheelchair, her eyes zero in on mine. "Why does he look so pale? He's sweating, Jenna. You know, if a real nurse sees you in here, she'll pass right on by. He may not get the help he needs!" She lifts my chin, studying my eyes. "Are you okay? You look worse than yesterday. What's going on?"

"You tell me, T! What *is* going on? I want the truth, and I want it now."

"I'm sorry, Kaitlyn." Jenna rushes to my sister's side. "I didn't mean to say anything, I swear."

"What did you say to him? You know he's still recovering. He doesn't need any more stress."

"I know about my gun and the bullet casings. I know Pistol is missing, and I know we're all in danger."

Kaitlyn's eyes grow wide as she begins to slowly shake her head at Jenna. She's clearly upset with her lack of discretion.

Her glare pierces the room, and she bites at her thumbnail the way she always does when she's angry. I use her silence as an opportunity to continue my plea to get some answers.

"We have each other, but what about my girlfriend? She's going through this alone. I have to see her *now*. She needs me." Trying to contain my fury, I growl through my fastened teeth, "Now, will one of you please take me to her!?!"

Concern overtakes my sister's expression as she shrinks back toward the door. She looks at Brody as he protectively pulls her into his side. He kisses the top of her head and whispers something into her ear. She takes a deep breath and looks back in my direction. I can tell by the grimace on her face that I've taken her by surprise. When she came here to help me, she had no idea how worked up I'd be. I'm ashamed of the way I blasted her as soon as she walked through the door. I mentally punch myself in the face, angry with the way I treated her. She looks hurt. Hopefully she's still willing to help me after the way I just yelled at her.

"Look, I'm sorry. I didn't mean to take it out on you. I don't know what's gotten into me. I just can't handle not knowing what's going on. Enough secrets, T. I'm desperate. I need your help. Can you guys please take me down to see Peyton?"

The tension in the room is palpable. Pleading for help, my eyes bounce back and forth among all of my friends. Jenna looks to each of us, finally breaking the silence, "Okay, here's my plan. Kaitlyn. Brody. Did you guys come up with a way to distract Peyton's mom?"

Kaitlyn nods, "I think so, but are you sure this is a good idea? If we get caught, what will happen to us? Isn't there another way to see her? One that doesn't involve sneaking into her room? I'm sure her parents will come around if we just wait a couple more days."

"No more waiting," I shake my head at my sister. "Jenna, go on. This needs to happen today. What are we going to do?"

"I've stopped by her room a couple times, trying to get a look inside. There's an empty bed, and I don't think she's sharing a room with anyone. I scoped it out again before I got here, just to make sure. When I peeked through the window, the extra bed was still made. I've come up with a story to get you into it for a bit. That way, you'll be right next to her. The only problem is, in order to actually *see* Peyton, we need to get her mom out of the room for a minute."

Yeah, right. This sounds impossible. "There's no way. This is never going to work."

"Trust me. We can do this. I'm going to push you down there in the wheelchair. I don't think they'll recognize me in this outfit, but no matter what happens, just keep your face toward the ground. We can't let anyone see who you are. This will work, I swear. Once you're in the room, I'll get you situated on the bed and make sure the curtain is closed. You're going to need to wait until we can get Mrs. Carter away from the room. Promise me you'll be patient. We don't need security called on us. Do you think you can handle it?"

I take a deep breath, releasing it slowly as I visualize how to play my role. At this point, I'll try anything to see her. "I'm ready. Let's do it!"

"Kaitlyn and Brody, are you guys ready? You're a big part of this. I'll text you when he's all settled. That's when you guys will come down and get Momma Bear out of the room." Relief hits me when they begin nodding their heads in agreement. "Okay then. Stay here until you hear from me."

My stomach begins to grind and churn at the thought of sneaking down the hall into room 83. Maybe it's just the pain medicine I've taken mixed with the Gold Rush burger, but I think I'm going to be sick. My cheeks are beginning to quiver. Trying to swallow down the thick saliva, I continue fixating on the potential hazards that lie ahead. I have no idea what will happen if we're caught. *Does this small town hospital even have security? Why are they guarding her from us? Do they think we're the reason she almost died? Or, maybe they're trying to protect us from something they don't think we can handle. Is she missing a limb? Is she tragically disfigured?* My mind is plagued with "what ifs." I can't rationalize why they haven't let us in to see her.

Pushing all of the disturbing thoughts aside, I gather enough nerve to give Jenna the go ahead. "Okay, we can go now." Even though we're just five doors apart and we won't have to pass the nurses station, my biggest fear is that a real nurse or doctor will spot us. Or even worse, come into the room and see me in the bed next to Peyton. Jenna, on the other hand, doesn't appear to be scared at all. She seems to be enjoying her part in the risky, little adventure that she's orchestrated.

"Relax. I've got everything under control. Don't forget most of the staff is at the wedding. There aren't that many people to dodge. I've thought this through, and it's going to work. Trust me. Just remember, don't let anyone see your face. Are you ready?"

"As I'll ever be."

Concern etches itself on my sister's face, as she warns, "Be careful, guys."

Jenna nods, and begins to wheel me toward the door, when Brody steps in front of me. I watch him peek his head through the doorway to make sure the coast is clear. He turns to all of us and gives a thumbs up.

I watch the green tiles turn into a blur as Jenna rolls the wheelchair through the hallway. I have to remember to keep my face down. As we roll over each square of tile, I work to pull the grout lines into focus, counting each one. *Click, click, click, click,* the wheels of the chair roll rhythmically across the floor. Square foot by square foot, we make our way down the hall. I keep my mind occupied with the counting. If I allow myself to think about anything other than the lines, I may lose my burger all over the shiny, green tiles. Jenna gently nudges me as she whispers, "Walkin' the mile, walkin' the green mile." My stomach flips from the thought of the scene. She knows how much that damn movie upset me. I would totally elbow her right now to shut her up, but I can't move my arm. Leave it to Jenna to take a serious situation and make a joke out of it. *And what's with that reference anyway? Thanks for reminding me that someone down the hall probably wants to kill me.* My nerves flare once again.

The wheelchair slows to a stop as I listen to the knock of a wooden door. "Don't look up," she reminds me. When the door swings open, Jenna's voice drips with a sweet southern accent. "How y'all doing today? Sorry to disturb you, but I need to move this patient into that empty bed for a little while. His roommate just woke up from surg'ry and with all the moanin' and groanin' this sweet fella couldn't get any rest. Don't worry, we'll only leave him here for a bit, but this is the only bed left on this wing. How 'bout if I pull the curtain shut so you won't have to watch him snore? Hmm?"

Thinking about that black, bobbed wig swinging to the hilariously fake accent, I try not to choke out a laugh. I appreciate the fact that Jenna has completely submerged herself in the role and is taking on all of the attention while I get to hide under this blanket. My tension eases when I hear Peyton's mom reply, "No problem. My daughter's been sleeping most of the day. It should be nice and quiet in here."

"Thank you ma'am," Jenna replies sweetly as she rolls me through the doorway toward the bed. She turns the wheelchair around so I'm facing away from Peyton's side of the room. After pulling back the sheets, she helps me into the bed, slightly covering my face with the blanket. "I'll be back to check on you later, son." She bends down and squeezes my hand, leaning into my ear and whispering, "Good luck." Those are her last words before I hear the screeching metal sound of the curtain being pulled around to shield me from Peyton's mother.

The door opens and closes. My body tenses as I hear foot-steps slowly walk across the room and stop nearby. My stomach flips with the thought that only a thin piece of material separates the two of us. She's so close, I can sense her energy filtering through the curtain. One little, curious peek from Mrs. Carter could blow my entire world apart. I can't risk being exposed. I work to stay still, despite the fact that I need to shift my weight to relieve the pain in my arm.

Hold your breath. Stay still. I pull the blanket from my face, and notice the silhouette of Peyton's mom standing at the foot of my bed. *Why is she standing there? Is she suspicious? Breathe. Through your nose. Don't make a sound. Breathe.* I remain frozen beneath the covers as I talk myself through the anxiety. I don't know what I'll do if I'm discovered. *Why can't she just leave? I need to get up and see Peyton. Leave.* I pray. *When is Jenna's plan going to kick in? Hurry up, Kaitlyn. Come get Mrs. Carter out of here.* I repeat these words over and over in my mind.

After what feels like twenty minutes, I hear a knock at the door and thank God when Mrs. Carter walks away from my bed, allowing me the chance to shift positions and take in a much needed breath. I listen intently as the door creaks open, and I hear my sister's voice softly drift into the room. "Good evening, Mrs. Carter. We're sorry to disturb you, but we wanted to check on Peyton again, and ..."

With a low, stern tone, I hear Peyton's mom interrupt, "I thought we made it clear the first three times you came, that Peyton isn't taking visitors." There is a brief silence. *This isn't going to work. I'm never going to get over there to see her.* Dis-appointment stabs at my heart. I close my eyes and focus my attention back to Mrs. Carter as she pulls in an audible breath. When she begins to speak again, I hear her voice soften.

"Okay, how about this? You can let Caden and the others

know that Peyton woke up yesterday. She's still out of it from her brain surgery, but they relieved the swelling, and she is stable at the moment. She's on a lot of medication, and she hasn't moved or spoken. To tell you the truth, she's not out of the woods yet. Aside from drowning, she took a pretty severe blow to the head. It was a lot for one little girl to endure. The doctors don't know if she'll make a full recovery. It's just too early to tell. Look, Kaitlyn, we don't want to add any more shock or stress to an already volatile situation. I hope you understand. I'm sorry if this is hard on you and your friends, but I have to protect my daughter."

At the words *brain surgery*, adrenaline spikes through every nerve ending in my body. I gasp and stiffen, making the bed squeak and the covers ruffle. I see Mrs. Carter's silhouette flinch at the sound of my sudden movement, and watch her figure turn toward my bed. *Think fast.* I let out a small snore, trying to disguise my shocked movement as restless sleep. *Dear God. Brain surgery? What did I do to my girlfriend?* Now more than ever, I have to figure out how to see her. I have to make sure she's going to be okay.

"I understand, Mrs. Carter. Thank you for giving us an update. I know this has been awful for you, and we're praying for Peyton and your family. We also came to give you this." There is a pause as I watch the silhouette of Mrs. Carter's arm travel toward Kaitlyn's outreached hand. My sister continues. "This is my brother's pocket knife. It's pretty special to Peyton. She gave it to him for his birthday. She was holding it when I found her in the river. She insisted on keeping it. She told me she used it to cut herself out of the seat belt. I've been saving it for her until we could see her. I hope it brings her some kind of comfort to have it back."

I hear Mrs. Carter sniffle, followed by a long stillness. The deafening silence between the two of them allows me to focus on my own reaction to the heartbreaking image of a drowning

Peyton struggling to cut herself out of my submerged truck. It makes me sick to think I was too weak to help her myself. *I let her down. I let us fly over that cliff. I almost let her die. I wasn't even there to save her. What kind of a boyfriend ... no, what kind of a human being am I?* I listen to the greasy dinner grind in my stomach. The churning burger pushes a small amount of bile up my throat. I force it back down, covering my mouth to keep it from coming up. The heat of my body's furnace begins to roar. Sweat jumps from the flames and begins to escape down my forehead. *Oh no. I'm going to be sick.*

I try to distract my mind so I don't lose it all right now and blow my cover. My cheeks quiver. They begin to pucker as thick, bitter saliva fills my mouth. I've got to find something to throw up in. I don't think I'm going to be able to hold this back much longer. Slowly rising from the bed, I scan the room. My mouth is filling fast. I can no longer swallow. Ready to lose it any second, I find a pink, plastic bedpan on the table stand next to my bed and hold it under my mouth, just in case I'm not strong enough to keep it all down.

Think Caden, think. Clear your head. You can't blow chunks right now. Mind over matter. Scanning through my store of memories, I work to replace the horrifying image of Peyton struggling to cut herself out of my truck. Flipping through the last month, my mind stops at the beautiful picture of the two of us holding each other in the lightly falling snow. I'm taken back in time to the night we played truth or dare; the night we carved our names into the green, chipping paint of Mule Bridge. I wrap her in my arms, and see her looking up at me, before she leans further in and giggles into my ear. I actually feel the tickle of her whisper float across my skin. Goosebumps rise on my arms and back. I love her so much. I can't handle not seeing her for one more second. Maybe if she can just see that I'm here for her and feel how much I love her, it will help her heal. *It's worth a try.*

I sneak over to the edge of the curtain nearest Peyton's bed, and peek around the thin veil. My eyes follow the white tiles across the floor and down to the foot of her bed. They scan their way up and across the scraggly, tan hospital blanket and come to rest on her face. When my eyes take in the first vision of her since the accident, the tsunami of nerves flares once again. Seeing her pale, lifeless body hooked up to all those machines knocks the wind right out of me. I can't help but lose it.

The battle of elements within my body causes me to break. A low guttural, rumble grows inside my stomach. As hard as I've tried, there's no way to stop it. I double over. With a deafening growl, the burning, bitter chunks claw their way out of my stomach and up my throat, splashing into the pink container. I pull away from the curtain, making my way back toward the bed. Just seeing the hospital-pink, plastic bedpan makes the wave of vomit worsen. There's no way I can hold back the sound as I wretch over and over. I pray this thing is big enough to catch it all, but it's filling up fast.

"Are you okay in there, honey?" I hear Mrs. Carter's voice as the first wave hits the ground.

I'm busted. There's no way she's not coming in here now. "I'm, okay," I groan. "Just the pain meds." I try to mask my voice with a low grunt to buy myself some time.

"Can I come help?"

"No. No. No. Please don't. It's embarrassing. I've got it," I mumble.

Through my low moaning and groaning, I hear Mrs. Carter pick up the phone beside the door and call for a nurse. *Crap. A nurse? Don't do it. I shouldn't even be in here. I'm screwed.*

CHAPTER 3

BEAT IT

*S*HE CAN'T SEE WHO I am. I've got to hide my face. Setting the full bedpan on the table, I crawl back into the bed. The rancid smell overpowers the room and even if she is asleep, I feel bad that I've subjected Peyton to it. I tense myself in anticipation of getting my hide kicked by a real nurse or doctor. *Oh Jenna, what have we done?*

The door closes, as I listen to Mrs. Carter's footsteps back away from it. Again, the soft pattering pauses at the foot of my bed. "You're sure I can't help you in there?" The inflection in her voice makes her sound as though she feels sorry for me. *If only she knew who she was really talking to.*

"Uh uh," I groan, hoping she'll go away and let me hide.

I lie in the bed, releasing soft moans. It makes me feel better to release the groaning sounds and break the silence of the room. All the while I think of what I'm going to say to the nurse or doctor who comes to help me. As the door swings open, I tense again, anticipating the worst. *Here we go.* I hold my breath and pinch my eyes closed as the curtain slides open, letting the dim light filter in. That's when a familiar voice finds its way to me.

"Oh dear, God, what have you done?"

Footsteps grow louder as they approach my bedside. My eyes pop open in fear when her hand unexpectedly comes down on me. She begins to speak again, "Ca..."

"Shhhhh." I bring my finger to my lips. "She'll kill me."

It's Nurse Sarah. I'm pretty sure I have her wrapped around my little finger. Thank God it's her and not that cranky, old biddy that comes in after visiting hours are over. There's light at the end of the tunnel after all. I send up a prayer of thanks for this one.

"Sarah," I mouth. "Please. Help. I'm sorry, I just had to see her."

She closes her eyes and drops her shaking head as she pulls her hand up and pinches the bridge of her nose. I've really put her in a bad position. She knows, as well as I do, that I'm not supposed to be anywhere near this room. I stare up at her with a pleading and helpless frown, hoping against all hope that she can get me through this. When Sarah finally bends down to me, she whispers in my ear, "You realize you could get me in a lot of trouble for this, don't you?"

I nod my head slowly, acknowledging the risk I'm asking her to take by covering for me. I feel the desperation plastered across my face, and I'm sure she can see it. Raising my eyebrows apologetically I whisper, "Sorry, Sarah."

With her eyes steeped in contemplation, Nurse Sarah studies my face. I hold my breath anticipating her next move. Finally, she looks as though she's arrived at a decision. I watch as her head nods thoughtfully, and she disappears behind the curtain.

"Ma'am," I hear her say to Mrs. Carter, "I'm really sorry, but I'm going to need you to step outside for just a few minutes. I have to take care of a ... uh ... situation in here. He had more than one little accident. It's very embarrassing for our young patient, and I don't think he'd want you to see the extent of the damage he's caused."

I hear Mrs. Carter gag. "Yes, I thought I smelled something." Her voice grows stern. "I know you've got to take care of this mess, but my daughter is the primary concern here. I'm sure you know the circumstances that put her in this hospital. I don't want her left alone for a second."

"I'll make sure to look out for her. I promise." There's a brief pause. "Oh, and since I can't leave the room, would you mind running down to the nurses station in geriatrics? They keep extra diapers there, and I'm sure he'll be needing them again tonight." She's raising her voice and enunciating every word. It's clear to me that the extra care she's taking with her words is for my benefit. *She's paying me back for pulling her into this. Diapers? How embarrassing.* "I'm sorry for asking you to go, ma'am, but we're short-handed, and I don't want to take any chances leaving her alone."

"You've got it. It'll give me something to do while you clean up this awful mess."

"Take your time. I promise I'll keep good watch over your daughter. I'll be right here mopping and changing the sheets." She pauses again. "Our patient also needs to take a shower. You'll definitely want to get a little fresh air while we're taking care of all this. Give me about a half hour or so."

"Thank you, Nurse." I listen to her footsteps as Mrs. Carter walks out of the room.

The clanking metal sound of the curtain rips across the ceiling. "Wow," I smirk at the sight of Sarah's proud face. "Did you have to make it sound like I crapped my pants? That's so humiliating."

"Well, I bought you a little time, didn't I? It's all I could think of to get her out of the room for a while. You can say 'thank you,' you know. Now quit feeling sorry for yourself and get on over there and see your girl."

Feeling grateful, I bow my head. "Thanks, Sarah. I owe you one."

"I know. You can pay me back by getting over there and showing that pretty, little girl of yours some love. I'm a sucker for hospital romance. Now go." She tilts her head toward Peyton's bed, urging me to make use of my limited time.

As I struggle to swallow the lump in my throat, I stand up to make my way to Peyton. The fear of seeing her up close for the first time since the accident is terrifying. I'm a nervous wreck. *I already lost the entire contents of my stomach just glancing at her from across the dimly lit room. What makes me think that I'll be able to endure the sight of her up close? I've got to do this, and I don't have much time. Get over there, Caden. Now.* I convince myself to shuffle my feet across the floor. *Left. Right. Left. Right.*

I'm slow in my movement, but I'm doing the best I can to fight the combination of nausea, painkillers, and straight up fear. My pulse quickens as I zero in on the floor beneath the bed. When my thighs are nearly touching it, I shakily grab onto the cold metal rail and work up the courage to look up. Painstakingly, I force myself to find her closed eyes.

Thump. In one big free-fall, my heart nearly drops out of my chest. My lungs deflate instantly at the horrifying sight. My entire body crumbles from the inside out. A slight whimper escapes my trembling body. I can't stop shuddering. *Get it together, Caden.* The shaking is so bad, I'm pretty sure the tremors might register on the Richter scale. My anxious nerves slap and splash at the residual bile that has tried so desperately to settle in my stomach. I'm glad it's empty, or I could lose it all over again.

Looking down at Peyton's motionless body is horrifying. Tears well up and beat at the back of my eyes. She is barely recognizable. Her face is pale and bloated. Her blackened eyes are nearly swollen shut. Traces of iodine line the turban of white bandages that form a band around her swollen head.

My God. This is worse than I imagined. I want to erase the horrifying image I see lying before me. Is this the same girl who stole my heart with her contagious smile? There's a small resemblance. It has to be her. I move closer to the bed so I can get a better look. I need to see if there's any recognizable piece of her lying in the wreckage before me, to discern even one of her beautiful features. I know they are hiding somewhere beneath her swollen black eyes and pale, puffy cheeks.

She's too lifeless. Buried beneath the mound of blankets, I can't see the rise and fall of her chest. It sends a wave of panic through me. Careful not to tangle myself in the IV line and monitors, I wiggle my way through the maze of tubes and machines. I have to touch her. I need to feel her heart beating. I need to feel the breath coming from her soft, pink lips. Leaning in slowly, I allow my cheek to delicately graze the tip of her nose and mouth. At the same time, I gently set my hand on top of her heart.

For the briefest instant, I can't feel it beat. It's at that precise moment that a fierce spike of adrenaline rushes through me. I envision myself weeping at her graveside. I can't handle the thought of her lifeless body, surrounded by the silk, padded lining of that box. *I can't live in a world where her heart doesn't beat. Wake up, Peyton. Wake up.* I pray over and over, leaving my hand on her chest, wishing it to jumpstart her back to life. Pressing a little harder, I concentrate on the stillness of her body beneath my fingertips. And then I feel it. A tiny thump.

The monitor above her head, sounds a tiny blip, breaking the silence of the room. I jump reflexively. The sudden panic attack brought on by Peyton's missing heartbeat has me feeling dizzy. I need to sit down. I struggle to find something to hold onto before I pass out. Placing my hand on the bed, I steady myself as I slowly move toward the chair. I can't breathe. I gasp for air. I've got to calm down and fight this rush of adrenaline before I pass out. I feel the sudden increase of my heart rate as

I look down at my girl, bandaged, unrecognizable, and fighting for her life. *Why did I let her sacrifice herself? I shouldn't have let her get in that truck with me. It was dangerous. I knew that. I'm a selfish bastard. This is all my fault! It should be me in that bed. What have I done?*

I stare at the monitor, and then back to my girl. Leaving my hand on her chest, I check to make sure that the small zig-zagging lines followed by the long green line, are truly connected to her beating heart. They are moving so slowly. I watch the tiny, digital heart blink on and off, on and off. *So slow. I wonder what 38 means? Is that okay?*

Maybe if I just talk to her, maybe if she hears my voice, I can convince her ... God, please help my Peyton.

When I start to speak, my voice comes out in a whisper. I pull the chair right up next to her bed, sitting down and leaning into her so I don't have to raise my voice.

"Peyton, if you can hear me, I'm right here, babe. I'm so sorry." My shell of a voice cracks as it quickens and raises pitch. I shake my head and pull my hand up to wipe the tears that are starting to slip from my eyes. *Get it together. You don't have much time.* "Peyton, I'm sorry that I let us go over the embankment. I know better than that. I should've veered the other direction. I can't bear the thought of you stuck out there while I was passed out on the bank. I couldn't even get to you. I hate myself for this, Peyton. I'm weak. It kills me inside that I wasn't the one to save you. I let you down." I have to reach for the Kleenex on the table. The snot bubbles are suffocating. I can't breathe. I can't talk.

As I sit and blow, trying to clear my nose, I listen to the monitor beeping. The near stillness of the rhythm has me worried. The number next to the blinking heart has dropped to 30. *Why has it slowed? What if it stops altogether? At some point, an alarm is going to sound. If it doesn't, I'm going to get a doctor myself. I'm no specialist, but this can't be right. She's slip-*

ping away. I can see it. I have to let her know how I feel about her before I lose my chance.

I lean in, close enough for her to hear me. "Peyton, I need you to know the difference you made in my life. Before you, I was such a player. The only thing that mattered to me was football, baseball, and partying. Girls?" I let out an ashamed huff. "I know that you know, there were a lot of them. The numbers were a big, damn joke to me. It was all about having fun. I didn't care about any of them. All they wanted was popularity ... dating the quarterback, wearing my jersey to ball games and stuff. They meant nothing to me. They used me, and I used them right back. Every one of them. They made it so easy. I hate to admit that, but it's true. I thought all girls were the same. Until *you*."

The monitor continues to drop. I know I need to hurry. *How do I get this out right? She needs to know how much she means to me.*

"You changed all that for me, babe. You knew how I was, and you gave me a chance anyway. You never asked anything from me. But for some reason, I wanted to give you everything. You were the first girl that I ever wanted to call back. The first girl I was proud to *let* wear my jersey. The first girl I ever stopped myself from crossing the line with. You were too good for that, too good for me. Do you hear me, Peyton? You were just too damn good to be true. I loved you with everything in me. You were it for me, beautiful. You were my future."

Why am I talking to her in past tense? She's still here. She's still with me. Fight for her, damn you. Fight.

I move in closer, desperately pleading in her ear. "You've got to come through this, babe. I need you. I need us. I want to be the guy you deserve, and I *will* be that guy. I know I'm not good enough. Not now. But, I sure as hell am going to try to do everything in my power to be the person who is worthy of you. I promise you, Peyton." I look up toward the ceiling. "God, please wake her up. I promise I will take care of her this time.

I promise."

I reach for her hand once again. At the contact, I hear an alarm sound. The green line of the monitor begins to spike and flutter. The beeping and chaotic line have me panicked. I look around frantically, "Sarah," I call in an audible whisper. She must still be out of the room.

I look back toward Peyton. "I'm here for you, babe." The line on the monitor spikes again. Squeezing her hand, I mutter desperately through my shaking voice, "Hang on, I'll go get help."

Again, the little green heart flashes faster. The number has climbed to 120. "Sarah!" I raise my voice, releasing Peyton and stumbling toward the door. "Sarah!" I shriek out. She's not in the room. I pat a path along the wall, finding my way to the door. As I throw it open, the rapid beeping drifts out into the hallway. Thankfully, Sarah stands just outside holding a stack of fresh bedding. She whips her head around at the sound of the alarm.

"Go, Caden. Quick. I need to get help," she says as she tosses the sheets onto my newly vacated bed.

Nodding my head, I step into the hallway, catching a quick glimpse of Mrs. Carter walking rapidly toward Peyton's room. Quickly, I turn my head toward the wall, hoping to avert eye contact. I pause, feeling the swoosh of Mrs. Carter's racing air push past me. I can't have her recognize me, or this could get even worse. After she passes and the door closes behind her, I walk back to the window and take a look inside. Nurse Sarah is standing at Peyton's bedside. She's on the red, emergency phone. I hope she can get help before it's too late.

"Doctor Smith, Doctor Smith, please report to room 83A. Stat!" I hear Nurse Sarah's voice boom over the intercom.

What have I done now?

CHAPTER 4

HEARTFELT APOLOGIES

TURNING BACK TO FACE THE hallway, the weight of a thousand elephants pushes against my shoulders. I can't handle it anymore. I can't believe I've done this to Peyton. I'm dying inside. I can't move. I can't breathe. A low wail escapes my searing throat. Nothing can hold it back. Slowly sliding down the wall, I tuck myself into a ball, and weep like a baby. I bury my head in my knees and peek up at the sound of pattering feet. As the sound of footsteps slows to a stop, I hear a man's voice. His hand comes down on my shoulder, "Are you okay, son?" I nod my head and wave him off.

"Go help *her*! Fast!" I cry.

"Alright, I'll be back to check on you."

Moments later, I wince at Jenna's unexpected voice, "Caden, come on!" She tugs at my hospital gown. "I heard the alarm. You've got to get up now. They can't see us down here or we're done for." She nudges the foot of the wheelchair against my leg.

"I can't go! Not now!" I gasp, wiping the residual tears from my eyes. "I need to make sure they save her. I think I just

45

crushed her heart! It's out of control. It was pumping so fast I thought it was going to blow up the damn machine! I know I did it, Jenna. It was steady until I started talking. I just couldn't keep my stupid mouth shut."

She continues to tug at me. "You are not going to sit here and feel sorry for yourself. You and I both know that you're not the one to blame for this. Get your ass up! Now! I'm not going down with your sinking ship!" she barks viciously. Then grabbing the sides of my face she orders, "Look at me. She's going to be okay. But you have to let them do their job!" Her fiery glare pierces my vision, snapping me out of my pitiful state.

That's when I realize she has a point. I'm not doing myself, or Peyton, any good by sitting here distracting the doctors and nurses who need to get in there to help her. I slowly start to inch my way up and off the wall. I'm so shaky, I teeter back and forth like a toddler learning to balance for the first time.

"Get in!" she growls, pushing the wheelchair into my trembling calves. With one quick thud, I fall into the seat and pull my feet onto the metal footrests. Before they're completely off the ground, Jenna begins to barrel down the hallway. She takes off with enough speed that we skid out of control, leaving black marks from the racing tires. The wheelchair tugs right, and nearly takes out one of the decorative Christmas trees lining the wall. When she overcorrects, the metal footrest catches an abandoned IV stand that tumbles to the ground with a thud. At the thunderous rattle, I hear a lady's voice fade off in the distance.

"Slow down, Nurse! Do I need to report ..." Panic rises once again, when I hear footsteps beating at the floor behind us. Holding tightly to the armrests, I blink my eyes closed, trying to keep from getting sick.

"Jenna, move. Faster!" I desperately squeal. When I re-open my eyes, Brody and Kaitlyn are standing at the end of the hall. Kaitlyn motions left, calling attention to Brody, who is holding the elevator door open.

"Jump in! I'll distract them," he grunts.

At the open door, Jenna spins me around and pulls me through, slamming the DOOR CLOSE button, followed by the L1.

"What are you doing?"

"Buying us some time. We can't stay up there. Didn't you hear them trailing us? That place is like an anthill. Every nurse and doctor on duty is crawling around up there right now."

There is a long silence as the elevator drops to the first level. When the door opens, Jenna is quick to slam the DOOR CLOSE button once again. She turns, looking down at me furiously. Then panting, she screams, "What the hell, Caden?" Her eyes burn into me. "How could you be so careless hanging out in the hallway like that? You completely exposed us! And after all my planning and disguises and ..."

"Stop, Jenna!" I throw my hand in her direction. "Listen to yourself!" My voice booms from my hollow chest. "Peyton could be *dying,* and you're worried about getting caught?!? All I was doing was waiting to see if she's okay. As if brain surgery wasn't enough, now it's her heart. It's bouncing all over the place. If you won't let me go up there, then *you* have to go make sure they fix her. I won't be able to live with myself if they can't."

When Jenna finally pauses long enough to realize what a wreck I am, her demeanor begins to soften. She releases an audible breath, and then reaches out and wipes a tear from my cheek. "You're right. Peyton's way more important than staying out of trouble. What do you need me to do?"

"Take me back up there with you so I can see what's going on. I have to make sure she's alright."

"Absolutely not! We can't take that risk. Look, I'm still dressed as a nurse. They don't even seem to know that I'm not a temp. I'll go back and look through the window ... see if I can get a handle on what's happening. But first, we need to hide *you* until everything settles down up there." Jenna's eyebrows pull together as she bites at her lip. "Look, I care about Peyton too, but we have to act rationally. If we get busted, there's no way we're going to find out how she's doing. Trust me on this."

I look away from my friend, taking a second to think things through. *The doctors on staff tonight are pretty great, and I haven't heard a code blue come over the speaker. Things must be going okay.* "I guess you're right. I'm not thinking straight. So, where am I going to hide out if I can't go back to the room to wait?"

"I've got an idea. There's a perfect place down around the corner. You won't even need to hide. Actually, it may bring you a little peace while I'm up there checking on Peyton."

The elevator door opens, and once again, I find myself rolling through the halls of Jefferson Medical Center. We pass the gift shop full of colorful, stuffed bears and flowers, and come to a stop at a small, dimly lit room with no windows. Jenna turns the chair and begins to push me through the open archway. *Thank God nobody is in here.* At the front, sits an altar with a hanging cross. There are a few empty wooden pews up front. I hear the creak of the old wood as we roll past them, making our way toward the front row. When we come to a stop, I glance off to the side and notice a square table holding several rows of flickering candles.

"I want to light one, Jenna. For Peyton. Can you get me over there?"

She nods her head and pushes me over, leaving me at the table long enough to light a candle and send up a prayer. I stare into the glowing blaze, as everything in my periphery grows dark. I'm captivated by the light, as it gently sways back and forth. It seems to be dancing with the surrounding flames. In and out, back and forth. Just like Peyton, my little fire is too attractive to keep to itself. It reaches out and gently touches the flame to its right, quickly pulling away before the two small blazes fully merge into one. Watching the friendly flame has the warm memories of my Peyton burning inside of me.

God, she is beautiful. I think of my sweet girl, and how everyone loves her so much. I don't know how I'll live if she doesn't make it. It would destroy me. *God, I know I'm not much worth listening to. I've done some terrible things over the last eighteen years. Look, I'm sorry about the time I took my nana's pop bead necklace and gave it to Kali at Sunday School. I'm sorry about the time I kissed Carley in the coat closet when the teacher wasn't looking. I'm sorry about switching the signs on the spiked apple cider at our barn dance. And God ... I'm sorry I didn't take better care of Peyton. Look, I know that you are a forgiving God. Please don't hold my childhood sins against me. Please find it in your heart to let her stay here with us. I'll do anything. I'll do anything if you let us keep her ...*

My prayer is interrupted by a soft voice, "I'll be back. Take your time."

"Oh, hey, Jenna, I'm done here. Can you take me back over to the pew? I can't wheel myself out of here with one arm, and someone else may need to light one of these."

"You've got it." Jenna rolls me away from the light of the newly flickering candle. "Now don't go getting yourself into any trouble while I'm gone. Stay here," she winks.

Emotionally drained and exhausted, I rest my cheek on my hand. "I won't leave here without you. I don't have the strength to get out of this chair right now, anyway." I look around the small, empty chapel. "This seems like a great place to calm my nerves." I take in a deep breath and release it slowly, as Jenna pushes me across the room.

Once I'm settled next to the front pew, I'm able to take in the serenity of this place. It's dark, quiet, and relaxing. I feel safe here. Watched over. I haven't felt this sense of peace for days. Every time I close my eyes, I relive that horrible day of the Christmas tree hunt. I need this. I need the rest. The flickering glow of the soft candlelight lulls me into a dreamlike state. Before I know it, my eyes blink closed. Peace at last.

CHAPTER 5

GOSSIP GIRLS

I AWAKEN TO THE AUDIBLE whisper of voices behind me. There has to be at least three of them pecking away at the back of my head. *Don't they know this is a chapel? A Godly place where people can come for refuge? Peace?* I'm annoyed that they are being so disrespectful in my restful sanctuary. *Why do they have to sit so close to me? This is the first time I've slept without those atrocities haunting my dreams. I needed this time. I needed this break from reality. Why can't they just go away?*

"Yeah, I guess she drowned, and they brought her back to life."

My ears perk up when I hear the drowning reference. *How many people nearly drown at this time of year?*

I cock my head, trying to hear their whispers. I'm curious to see who they're talking about. Living in such a small community, odds are I know who it is. *Another drowning? Holy hell. Hasn't there been enough trauma for one Thanksgiving break? Poor people.*

"Who was she with?"

"I thought you already knew she was with her boyfriend."

"Yeah, he was driving way too fast and totally flew off the cliff."

"Really, did he make it?"

"I heard he had some minor injuries, nothing life threatening. What's really bad, is he didn't even help get her out of the water."

"Are you serious? How could he just sit there and watch his girlfriend drown? I bet he was drinking. If he was, they'd better charge him with attempted murder or something. I can't believe he didn't even go in after her."

The click of a tongue lights my nerves on fire, as the grating voice continues.

"He'll probably get off because of his family name."

"They always do. But he's still going to have to live with himself."

"I'm sure he was sloshed. Maybe they'll finally get a clue and learn something from this. Drinking and driving. I mean, I party, but I'd never drive afterward."

My boiling blood begins to awaken me from my grogginess. *How can they talk about a tragedy like this? In a chapel of all places? Don't they know God is listening?* I'm not sure who they're talking about, but I feel sorry for whoever it is. I know how it feels to suffer through this kind of trauma. *My own girlfriend almost drowned after flying over a cliff and rolling into a river. I couldn't help her, and it had nothing to do with drinking. I was knocked out on the ground nearly bleeding to death. They need to give this guy a break. Maybe he was facing the same kind of situation we were ... dodging a truck, fleeing gunshots, and ... wait a second. Cliff? Drowning? They can't be talking about Peyton and me?*

I shrink down into my wheelchair as the agony tears into my chest. The small town gossip has made it full circle, and I'm privy to hear what people are saying first hand. *See Caden, you were right. You're not the only one who thinks this is your fault. You did this to her. YOU did this to that beautiful angel.* I claw my fingers up both sides of my face, gripping my hair in my hands. Curling myself into a ball, I stuff the growing ache inside and rock back and forth, trying not to cry out. The pain burns as it slices its way down my constricted throat and finds its way into the pit of my stomach. Silently, I begin to weep.

The nasty gossip continues behind me when I feel a hand come down on my shoulder. I look up to see Jenna. I'm sure she feels me shaking, as I work to stifle an audible cry. She bends down beside me and lifts my chin. "What's the matter, Caden? Was this too much for you?" Rather than answering her question, I pull my index finger to my lips, trying to quiet her. Then I point discreetly behind me, trying to get her to listen to the conversation happening a few rows back.

"Was it just the two of them?"

"No, they were with those wine people too. I guess they were staying over there for Thanksgiving."

"Did anyone else get hurt?"

"I heard they all made it out with hypothermia and a little frostbite. They were all released the next day. Poor Peyton took the brunt of it."

"I knew she shouldn't have started hanging out with those idiots. They're reckless people. I mean, we all saw how they acted that night at the barn dance."

"Yeah, ever since she started dating Caden, she doesn't use her common sense anymore. Four wheeling, jumping off bridges, you name it. She'll risk anything for him ... I guess that includes her life."

"She just wants to be popular. I bet you're right about the partying."

This is just about as much as I can take. I mess up one time. One time. At my own birthday party nonetheless. And now

I have the reputation of the high school lush?

"Uh, maybe we shouldn't be talking like this right now. I kinda feel guilty."

"Yeah, do you even think she'll make it?"

"I don't know, but it doesn't sound good."

Jenna's hand finds mine. She begins to grip tighter and tighter, looking at me with disgust. "Don't listen to them! Don't do it. Nothing they're saying is true. They don't know what they're talking about. I'm going back there to set them straight." She releases her death grip on my hand and slams her fist against her palm.

"Not here, Jenna. Not now." I grab her pant leg, trying to keep her from leaving my side.

"So, it's okay for them to talk like that? And I can't put an end to it? Or, stick up for Peyton?"

"Peyton?"

"Yes, Peyton. Listen to the way they're trashing her ... saying she was partying? Saying she's just dating you for popularity? Stay out of my way. I'm going back there to smash somebody."

I can't handle it anymore. I release Jenna's pant leg and pray for the best. "Do what you need to do. I'm not going to stop you." I look back over my shoulder to see who she's up against.

"Oh, hell no!" It's Chelsea, Amber, and that slouche, Tiara. *I thought I recognized that clunky voice.* "Yeah, I'd wish you luck, but something tells me you don't need it. I've already watched you take Chelsea down once. Go get 'em!"

Jenna pulls off her wig and smock and throws them down into my lap. "If I'm not back in twenty, send a search party. It may take me a few extra minutes to scalp all three of 'em."

She marches down the aisle, stopping a few rows back. My body tenses as her sarcastic greeting rings through the chapel. "Hi there, ladies. Would you like some *true* gossip?" Jenna has perfected her snarky tone. "I overheard you talking, and I want to tell you what *really* happened. You know I had a front row seat to the whole thing. You won't want to miss this. I just don't want to tell you here, in the chapel. We should go somewhere, not so ... sacred, where we can speak openly and freely. You know, so I can fill you in on every last, gory detail, cuss words and all."

"Really?" Tiara sounds surprised, yet excited.

"Oh yeaaaah ... I want the *whole* town to know what *really* happened, and I can't think of *anyone* better to spread the news. Come with me, girls," Jenna purrs. "I know just the place."

Go get 'em, Jenna. I hear the creaking of benches and the shuffling of feet. If I know anything about my friend, it's that she's all about life lessons. And there's no way I'm not watching them learn this one.

Trying to move myself away from the pew, I find out really fast that I'm not going anywhere in this wheelchair with a bum arm. I pull my feet off the metal footrests and work my way to a standing position. I feel like I finally have enough strength to walk, but I can't take too long. I have no idea where Jenna is headed with those girls, and I don't want to miss this show.

Dropping the nurse outfit in the wheelchair, I begin to make my way through the chapel. It's too hard to push with one arm, so I decide to ditch it at the entrance. *I'll come back for it later. I'm sure one of those girls will need this more than I do when Jenna's through with them.* I shuffle my way out to the foyer and look down the long hall, only to catch the minute forms of Jenna and the girls rounding the corner. *She must be taking them out to the little garden on the west side of the hospital. No one goes out there at this time of year.*

I need to stop and take a break. I'm woozy and lightheaded. *Breathe.* As much as I want to see her teach them a lesson, I know I need to get out there to keep an eye on things. Sometimes that girl doesn't know her own strength. I back against the wall and scoot myself along until I reach the entrance of the intersecting hallway. The door to the courtyard is in sight.

Taking in a deep breath, I head toward the door. I'm fatigued from the long walk, and a little wobbly as I make my way across the wide hallway toward the exit. I hope I didn't miss the show. I'm a little worried Jenna may take it too far, but I'd love to see the looks on their faces when they see how wrong they were about the cause of the accident. They have no idea what really happened down river. Knowing them, they're going to be hanging on every word. They'll make sure the whole town knows about the shootout and Pistol's disappearance. Jenna's brilliant. She'll stop the drinking theory these girls are spreading all over town. She definitely knows how to set a backfire.

When I finally make it to the door, I peer through the glass to see if the girls are outside. My warm breath steams the cold window, blurring my view of the courtyard. I quickly rub out the fog with my hand and press my face harder against the glass, scanning left to right across the garden. Just seeing it again, reminds me of the time we spent out there during the fall when Kaitlyn was going through her shoulder surgery.

A sweet memory crosses my mind. It's Peyton and me snuggling on the wooden bench tossing quarters into the wishing pond. I'll never forget the look on her face when I told her I had a gift for her, and pulled out that old, brown roll of quarters tied up in a polka dotted bow. I'd been saving those treasures since I was eight. She's the first girl I ever wanted to spend them on. It was money well spent, too. There are some unbelievable wishes lying at the bottom of that pond. She still tells me it's the nicest gift a boy ever gave her.

I snap back to reality when the corner of my eye catches movement near the footbridge. Stealthily, I open the door and slide outside, losing my breath as an icy gale of wind blows through the courtyard. I have to wipe my tearing eyes so I can find my way to the path. Now that I'm out here, it feels so dreary. This place held a lot more life back in the fall. It hadn't yet lost its vibrancy. Now, it's almost unrecognizable. The spirit is all but gone. All that's left is the twiggy remnants of the rose garden, and colorless leaves lining the cobblestone path to the small pond.

As I near the water, splashing and screaming draw my attention upward. I pick up my pace so I can get a better look at which girl it's coming from. Caught off guard by the energy it takes to move in this condition, I double over to take a breath. Lord knows I don't want to pass out. Last time I fainted, disaster struck.

Seconds later, I look up to see it all unfold in slow motion. Jenna is standing in the middle of the bridge. She has a long blonde ponytail in one hand, while pinching a pointy chin with the other. I can actually see the white outline of her hand pressing into Tiara's cheeks.

"You think you're not going in there too?" Jenna spits in her face. "I'll show you exactly how it feels to drown in December! Let's hear you talk about other people's tragedies now, you gossiping slouche!"

There's a little wrestling around as I watch Tiara try to gain footing on the icy bridge. There's no way she's going to win this battle with Jenna. Just seconds later, one strong and final push, sends Tiara tumbling into the water. She lands right between Chelsea and Amber, who continue to bob and scream, clenching their chests as their teeth rattle wildly from their shivering.

"Jenna, let's get out of here, now!" I cry out, knowing that the commotion is likely to catch someone's attention.

"One second, Caden! I'm just starting to have fun here!"

"I think we've already pressed our luck enough for one day. NOW, Jenna!"

Of course she's going to ignore me. I watch her lean back over the bridge and laugh out, "And if you think you're going to rat me out for this one, you're gonna find out what I'm *really* capable of! From now on, you'd better keep your ignorant theories to yourselves. Before you go running your mouths about *my* friends and what happened down at that river, have your facts straight!"

She runs off the bridge brushing the filth of the gossip girls off her hands. Then stopping at my side she gloats, "Done and done! Let's go, Caden. I'll fill you in on everything back in the room."

It is certainly a sight to behold. The three sopping wet girls bobbing their way out of the green, slimy pond, while Jenna stands proudly untouched. "Jenna, would you mind stopping by the chapel first? I'm not sure I have enough strength to get back to the room on my own, and I have a feeling you're going to need that disguise after the stunt you just pulled." I wrap my good arm around her neck as she helps me walk back into the building.

Back at the chapel, Jenna pulls on the black wig and nurse's smock. Once I settle into the chair, she pushes me down the hall, nonchalantly. She starts in with a little tune she whistles when she's up to no good. Thinking of her in the black, bobbing wig I have to laugh. I look up at her with a nervous chuckle, "You know how we're gonna have to play this off, right?"

"What are you talking about?"

"I'm talking about keeping us out of trouble, Jenna. When we get back to my room, we need to settle in and act like we've been playing poker all night. And, make sure you're wearing that costume."

"Why is that? What are you thinking?"

"Tonight we're turning the tables on them. I'm pretty sure we need to call the front desk and make a report of three girls playing out in the wishing pond. Just imagine the looks on their faces when they try to pin the whole thing on you, and conveniently, Jenna Bailey wasn't even at the hospital tonight. If anyone comes to check out the story, the only thing they'll find is a black-haired nurse with a horrible southern accent." I have to laugh as the vision unfolds in my mind. "I can just picture the looks on their faces as security drags them through the hallways in their sopping wet leggings and sequined ugly Christmas sweaters."

Back up at the room, we sit down at the poker game. Now that I'm no longer sidetracked by the gossip girls, I'm growing fidgety and anxious, waiting for Jenna's report on Peyton. I know she has to be alive, or the skirmish down at the wishing pond would've never happened. But, she hasn't said a word, so it makes me nervous to ask. Maybe it's so bad that she doesn't want to say anything. *Is she hiding something from me?* I pick up my cards and hold them up to my face, peeking over the top. I scan her face for signs of deception. I press the cards against my lips, trying to give Jenna a chance to spill her guts, but I can't keep my mouth shut for one more second. *Oh, grow a pair.* "Well?"

"Well, what?"

"Are you going to tell me what you found out about Peyton? You're killing me here."

"She's alive. That's all I know. They moved her back into ICU. I tried to follow them down the hallway, but all I could hear was that they need to watch her fluctuating heart rate. I guess there aren't enough doctors and nurses here right now to have her in a regular room. There's no way we're getting back in there. I'm afraid we're at the Carter's mercy for updates."

"Great, they're the ones who won't let us see her. This sucks." I hang my head in defeat.

"It's gonna be okay. If your blood work checks out, you'll be out of here tomorrow morning, and we'll figure out another plan. She's going to be alright. It's better for her in there any-way. They can watch her more closely."

I can't stand the thought of being any farther away from Peyton than I am right now. My frustration builds until finally, my anger comes to a head. I'm furious that this happened to her. What's worse is that it's my fault. And, I can't even express my outrage that they're keeping her from me. I throw my good arm into the cards, blasting our poker game into the air.

Jenna surveys the mess of cards, scattered all over the ground. "You know what? Forget about poker. Let's just watch TV and relax. It's been a stressful day."

I feel bad about the mess. I work to mask my anger by helping Jenna pick up the cards. While I'm down on the ground, there's a soft knock at the door. "Hide, Jenna. In the bathroom. Quick." Jenna scampers off to the bathroom, leaving me on the floor alone.

"Are you okay, son?" It's my dad's voice. "You didn't fall, did you?"

I look up to see he's standing next to my doctor. "No. No. I just knocked some cards off the table while I was feeling around for the remote. I didn't want to give the nurses any more work tonight. They seem kind of shorthanded."

"That's what we want to talk to you about. Doctor Smith here, seems to think it's okay for you to go home a little early. He's checked over your blood work, and he thinks it'll be safe to release you tonight. They just don't have the staff for extra patients, so it looks like we need to get your stuff together."

Whoa. The news surprises me. It's a bittersweet moment. I am so ready to get out of here and back to my own bed, but it's hard thinking about being so far away from Peyton. The thought of her being stuck here indefinitely is especially hard.

Dr. Smith walks toward the bed, "I just need one last check on your vitals, and then we'll have you out of here."

My pulse quickens, and blood rushes to my head when I

stand up. Stumbling back toward the bed, I work to disguise my falter as a fancy skip. *I can't let this guy know that I feel way worse than I look.* "Just practicing my stellar footwork, Doc." I snap my fingers and throw up my finger guns. "My teammates don't call me Twinkle Toes for nothing."

"Well, if you can move like that, I'd say you're ready to get out of here. No need for this, I suppose." He dangles his stethoscope out in front of him and tosses it up and over his shoulder. "I'll just need your dad to come with me to take care of some final paperwork."

As soon as the door closes behind them I call out to my stowaway. "Time to leave, Jenna! Make the break while you have the chance!"

Jenna claws her way out of the bathroom, pulling off her scrubs and throwing them into her paper bag. "Meet you back home."

CHAPTER 6

WHAT A PILL

I SLOWLY TWIRL THE LAST pill in the little tan bottle, watching it roll around in circles. *How could one little tablet cause so much misery?* It's been a week since I got home, and I'm going out of my mind. I work to pull the blurry living room into focus. *Damn painkillers.* I should really try to get to the bathroom to relieve this nausea, but my heavy body changes my mind. At the slight movement of trying to lift myself from the couch, I groan and force the bile back down my throat. I hate feeling trapped.

The frustration of not being able to move has me crawling out of my skin. The worst part of this whole mess is having no control. I lie on the couch waiting for the side effects of my medicine to wear off. I need to get to that numb place. Helplessly, I watch Brody shuffle Kaitlyn into the kitchen. He's had her fused to his side since I got home. He watches her every move. It's a relief to know he's with her in case Pistol shows up, but at the same time, it's hard for me to watch him take on that role alone. I want to be able to jump in if he needs me. I also want to be there for Peyton. In the hospital, I promised to protect her. I hate that I'm breaking that promise. Guilt and worry eat at the back of my mind.

I still haven't heard from Peyton or her parents. I keep trying to call the hospital, but they won't release any updates. I wonder if I'm on a blocked list or something. I've got to get my mind off of it. I fiddle with the remote and surf through the channels looking for any kind of distraction. The unending flood of overplayed Christmas specials and infomercials leave my mind to wander once again. *I can't stand not being able to drive. One refill left and the pain should be gone. I can't wait til I'm off of these stupid painkillers. I've got to go see Peyton. I hate not knowing if she's okay. I hate Pistol Black. That bastard.* My scattered thoughts have my head spinning. *I need to get out of this place.*

My eyes drift across the room. Watching Brody with his forehead glued to Kaitlyn's is getting on my nerves. From what I've gathered, it's getting on Jenna's too. We've had a little adjusting to do, to get used to our "best-friend swap." The time I've spent with Jenna has been good for me, though. Thank God she's been around to help me work through my winter plans, and keep my mind straight.

Damn, my arm hurts. I stand up and stumble my way back to my bedroom to call her again. *I hope she gets here soon to help me get my medicine.* She told me she'd be here an hour ago, but she's taking forever, and I've got to get down to the pharmacy. My thoughts begin to bounce into overdrive. Bounce. *Does all pain medicine make you want to puke?* Bounce. *Thank God Jenna's willing to lug my lame, helpless ass around.* Bounce. *I should've just taken both of them, cutting the dosage isn't helping the pain.* Bounce. *I'd better get that medicine before Officer Marnia and the detective get here.* I'm dizzy from the ping ponging thoughts. I wipe a small trickle of sweat from my brow as I pick up my phone to dial Jenna.

"Hello?"

"Hey, are you coming?"

"Sorry I'm running late. I'm out of gas, and I still can't find my wallet."

It seems like Jenna's been losing a lot of stuff lately. She should probably clean her room. "Did you check under your bed? It's probably wrapped up in your dirty underwear." I chuckle.

"Funny. No, seriously, dude. I haven't been able to find it since our trip."

"Did you check your suitcase?"

"Believe me, I've checked everywhere. I'm getting worried. I had some stuff in there that I really need."

"Stuff? Like your credit cards?"

"Well, yeah … and never mind. I'll keep looking."

"Listen, do you have enough gas to get here? I can spot you the money. I just really need to get down to Cumming's Drug and talk to Gordy. I don't think my medicine is working right. My thoughts are bouncing all over the place. It's making me dizzy and sick to my stomach. I think it's the prescription."

"Yeah, I might roll in on fumes, but I'll pick you up in a few. Hey, Cade, thanks. I'll pay you back as soon as I find it."

"No prob. Hurry!"

I hang up the phone and hear that Mason has joined Kaitlyn and Brody in the front room. I guess I can go out there and see what's up before Jenna gets here. I grab my wallet off the nightstand and drag myself down the hall to find Kaitlyn sitting on Brody's lap. She's chatting with Mason who's perched on the couch opposite them.

"Hey ladies, sup?"

"Just kickin' it, waiting to talk to the officers."

Once again, Brody is cradling Kaitlyn like a doll. Watching them comfort each other hurts. I want to be able to do that for Peyton, and their constant displays of affection remind me of my broken promises. A rush of heat overtakes me, and I feel my cheeks flush red. I bitterly click my tongue and watch a confused look spread across Kaitlyn's face. She looks at me with a furrowed brow, "You okay?"

Stop being an ass, Caden. I remind myself that I'm glad they have each other to help get through the aftermath of Pistol Black. "Yeah," I force a half grin, then pulling my stare off of my sister. I glance over to Mason, remembering there was another person who was witness to the horror on the river. She hasn't been around either.

"Hey, Mas! No Marissa? Doesn't she need to be here to help with the investigation?"

"Nah, her parents wouldn't let her out. They've kept her under lock and key since the Forks. They say if the police want to speak to her, they can do it at her house."

Boy, those people sure did seem strict. It doesn't surprise me that they didn't let her come over, but I wonder if it's because they think we're at fault for what happened. "That sucks, dude. Do they blame us?"

"I don't know. They're just pretty uptight people. I don't think she gets out much."

"I get it. They don't know us well enough to trust us."

The room grows silent as we all look at each other not knowing what more to say.

"Well, Jenna's coming over to take me down to the pharmacy. If we're not home before Officer Marnia gets here, let her know we'll be right back."

I hear a car door close and look out the window to see Jenna down at the bottom of the driveway.

"K, ladies, she's here. See you in a few."

I slowly walk down the long, icy driveway to meet Jenna at the bottom. It takes me a minute to gain my footing, but the brisk air does me good. The nausea begins to subside as I make my way toward her car.

"Sorry, I'm all the way down here, didn't want to push my luck with the gas."

"I've got it covered." I hold up my wallet. "Let's go."

I bend down and stuff myself inside the little VW Beetle. After thirty seconds, I'm sweating from the heater, and my rear is on fire from the seat warmer.

"Uh, Jenna, I'm dying here. Can we roll down the windows or something?"

"Sorry. I haven't been able to warm up since that day on the river. Maybe it was the hypothermia or frostbite … I don't know." She shakes her head and stares out the window as a far-away look drifts across her eyes.

With the windows down, the icy breeze blasts into the car, sparking another flashback. It's that damn image of Pistol again. He's barreling toward us waving his hand frantically. Usually, this nightmare haunts my dreams. This is the first time I've had it while I'm wide awake. It looks a little different now that my eyes are open. I draw my focus to his hand, something I haven't been able to do in my countless recurring night terrors. It's empty. I hear gunshots, but Pistol's hand is empty. *I swore he was holding a gun. It's that awful medicine. It's messing with my memories now.*

"Earth to Caden. Where are you, man?"

"Sorry. I just keep having that messed up vision of Pistol flying toward us in his truck." I take a deep breath and let it out slowly. "Maybe I'm just worried because they still haven't found him. My mind likes to play tricks on me." I shake my head, trying to replay the image of gunless Pistol. "I hope the investigators have turned up something. I just can't wrap my mind around it. I feel like we're missing something here. Maybe they'll have some kind of news for us. Let's hurry up with that medicine so we can get back there, k?"

Just like always, the pharmacy is swamped. I tap my foot impatiently as I stand in line and wait with Jenna. As we move closer to the front, my eye catches a newsstand. "Hey, hold my place in line for a sec. I want to grab a paper. I haven't been able to keep up with football since Thanksgiving. I've gotta see who's got a shot at the Superbowl."

I snag a paper and walk back to the line with Jenna. "Here, hold half. It's kinda hard to do with one arm." Jenna helps me fumble through the paper trying to get to the sports section. When a familiar image grabs my attention, I stop turning the pages.

"What's that?"

"Take a closer look, Jenna. Don't you recognize it?"

"No way. Is that a picture of the cabins?"

"Pretty sure. Let's see what it says."

The headline reads, ***Who's Been Sleeping in My Bed?***

The unsettling thought of Goldilocks crosses my mind, as the cheesy title jumps out at me. That fairy tale always creeped me out. The only noises uttered between the two of us are gasps of shock as we read through the article. The story tells of several cabins at Forks of the Salmon that had been plagued by unexplained visitors during the week of Thanksgiving. No one was reported to be inside at the time of the break-ins. There were, however, reports of ruffled blankets, missing food and alcohol, and even a case of a broken chair. Oddly, there were no reports of stolen items of value. Investigators believe it was a homeless person looking for clothes, food, and shelter.

"See, I told you there was something in the creepy cabin. I bet it was him. So we're not crazy after all. Just wait til I get to rub this in Brody's and Mason's faces. Crap dude, we could've been killed!"

"Yep, it's all pretty crazy. What are the odds of those break-ins happening while we were there?" I'm finding humor in her reaction, so I decide to mess with her a little. "Maybe we should give the sheriff a heads up when we meet today. Let him know about your flying phone," I chuckle, knowing full well it was a raccoon that spooked Jenna into throwing it. I cough the word "raccoon" into my hand, laughing.

Jenna backhands me, protesting my continued taunting. *Thankfully it's on my good arm.*

We make our way up toward the register. *Thank goodness, it's Gordy. He'll get me all straightened out.*

"Aww. There's that beautiful girl that reminds me of my own granddaughter. How are you doing today, Jenna?"

"Hey Gordy. Just bringing this lug in to talk to you about his prescription."

"Oh, I've already talked to his doctor. We've got it all straightened out for you. Let me just go grab it."

Between the time Gordy leaves and returns with the bag, Jenna's already managed to give me two more noogies and a wedgie. "Take it back," she whispers in my ear, as she tugs my underwear higher. I fake a smile as Gordy begins to speak.

"Sorry about what happened down river to you kids. I'm glad you're doing better. These should help. Be careful, they're pretty powerful." He hands me the bag and looks at Jenna. "You make sure to keep him under control," he winks.

"No problem." she laughs, turning to me. "See, just doing my job."

Tugging at my underwear, we continue our banter on the way out the door. "Jenna, you can be such a little pill some-times."

"Guess that's why Gordy likes me so much."

CHAPTER 7

QUESTIONS AND ANSWERS

WHEN WE PULL UP AT the house, I see the police officer's and sheriff's vehicles are both parked in the driveway. I never thought I'd see those big, white SUV's marked with thick, black *Police* lettering lining my driveway. *This is so surreal.* I take in a deep breath, clearing my mind. I am ready for some answers, and hopefully today is the day I will finally get them. *Here we go.*

When we enter the house, everyone is gathered in the living room.

I instantly recognize the toned backside of my favorite cop. She turns, and flashes her gleaming, white smile. "Good afternoon guys," Officer Marnia greets us. She flips her long, brown ponytail over her shoulder. *Damn, I'd forgotten how hot she is.* I force my eyes to look at the guy standing next to her, so I can actually pay attention to what she's saying. "I'd like to introduce you to Detective Edward Ferrara. Since this all happened outside of my jurisdiction, he's handling the investigation. Though I am working closely with him because of my history with your case."

The tall, muscular detective stands up to shake my hand. *This guy makes the hulk look small.* "Nice to meet you. I've already told the others they can call me Eddie. I know we're jumping into this pretty fast. Do you kids need any time before we get started?"

Time? That's all I've had for a week. I don't want any more time. I need answers. "I think we're good. Let's get to it."

Jenna and I sit down on the long couch next to Kaitlyn and Brody. My parents look fidgety and oddly uncomfortable. We kept everything from them for so long that I think they're both still in shock at the criminal level of Pistol's activity. Even Jenna's, normally chipper parents, sit solemnly on the couch opposite us. The mood in here is intense, to say the least. All eleven of us anxiously crowd the unbearably quiet room, staring at each other, waiting for the officers to begin.

Officer Marnia speaks first. "Detective Ferrara and I have reviewed my previous documentation on all criminal behavior involving Pistol. He's up to date on the history of violence, drinking, and stalking behavior. Because they both involved physical attacks with injuries, I made sure to fill him in on the details of the assault after Kaitlyn's swim meet in October, and the second attack at the barn dance. Those offenses give us cause to believe this may not have been an accident. Eddie has been down at the site of the accident, investigating the possibility of Pistol's involvement with the crash being premeditated. He's also been investigating his whereabouts."

I can't get the questions out fast enough. "And? Where is he? Did you find him?"

"I'm sorry to say, his whereabouts are unknown at this time. That being said, Kaitlyn, you still need to be on high alert. I don't want you going anywhere alone."

I watch Kaitlyn tense, as Brody tucks her under his arm. She pulls her hands through her hair, and I can see she's terrified. "I'm so sorry guys, this is all my fault. I should've said something that first night when my room was trashed."

"What are you talking about, Kaitlyn?" I hear the shock bleeding through the hurt in my mom's voice.

Crap. We're going to get it now. I knew we shouldn't have kept that one a secret.

"It was after the homecoming dance. When I got home, I found my teddy bear from Pistol. Its throat was slit, and the stuffing was all over my room."

"Don't forget about the picture that was torn in half," Brody cuts in.

"Or the weird text about your pajamas the next morning," Jenna adds.

I watch the color drain from Kaitlyn's face. Jenna and Brody have just thrown her under the bus, and she looks like she just swallowed the bitter pill of betrayal. *They're gonna get it now.*

Officer Marnia lifts her perfectly sculpted eyebrows as she quizzes Kaitlyn. "Kaitlyn, do you have something more to tell me? I don't have any of this in my reports. What's this about a pajama text?"

"It's nothing. I think Pistol was just trying to scare me, you know, make me think he was watching me."

"What does that have to do with pajamas, T?" I snap, annoyed that I haven't heard about any of the crap that happened the morning after the dance.

My sister grows silent, clearly not wanting to talk about this in front of all our parents.

Jenna looks sternly at Kaitlyn as she finally speaks, "If you're not going to tell them, I will." She looks at Officer Marnia and then to Detective Eddie. "The night after the homecoming dance, Kaitlyn got a text from Pistol telling her he liked her new pumpkin pajamas. She was freaking out because it was the first time she'd ever worn them, not to mention, he's never seen

71

her in pajamas before. We couldn't figure out how the sicko knew about them. That's all."

"Jenna, he was probably watching me through the window."

"Yeah, but Kaitlyn, you and I both decided that the windows and curtains were closed all night. That's impossible."

A new look of concern crosses the officers' faces. Officer Marnia looks over to the detective. "That certainly throws a new monster into this case."

"Indeed, now we'll need to determine if Pistol's also a peeping Tom, or if he was actually inside the premises that night. Kaitlyn, I'd like to take a look around your room just to get a look at the layout. Maybe I can get better insight into how this character operates."

Kaitlyn breathes a deep sigh and lets it out slowly. She stands up steadily, addressing all of us, "I'm so sorry guys. I should've spoken up sooner." She shakes her head back and forth continuously, "I thought it would stop. I never, in a million years, thought Pistol could go to these lengths to get back at me." Her lips turn down and she looks as though she's fighting back tears. Then shakily she motions to the detective, "My room is this way, sir."

A minute later Kaitlyn returns to the living room alone. Both officers have stayed back to search her room. We all sit quietly. My eyes study the pattern of the carpet beneath my feet. I can't imagine what's going through her mind right now. Even *I'm* a nervous wreck. *What if they figure out that Pistol was in her room? How did I let him get past me and creep in on my sister like that?* I'm disgusted with myself that I wasn't a better bodyguard. I look up to find the adults peering back and forth from one to another, shaking their heads. "I thought we raised them better than this," my mom finally speaks up.

My dad reaches for my mom's hand and quietly says, "Shhh, now, Jacie. I'm sure they did the best they could to handle the situation. Nobody could've seen this coming. We raised ourselves country kids. Stuff like this doesn't happen around here. They're not equipped for it. You teach high school. You know that."

Jenna's mom, Cinda, looks toward my parents bobbing her head up and down in agreement. "He's right, hon. We work with teenagers all day long. We both know these small town country kids don't have any exposure to these kinds of situations. They're all too trusting of people."

"I know, but ..." my mom looks at both Kaitlyn and me, "I thought I've always made it clear that you kids could come to me with *anything*. I'm not that mom who you have to hide things from. I understand things happen to kids. You can always come to me."

My mom's emotional grilling stops when we hear the officer's footsteps make their way back down the hallway. Officer Eddie holds something in his hand. "What can you kids tell me about this?" He holds a small, white contraption in the palm of his hand.

A curious look grows on Mason's face. "Let me see it." He studies the object closely before handing it back to the officer. "I've seen something similar to that at my house. My dad used to have it attached to our computer when I was little. Can't say I know what it is though. He took all of his gadgets with him when he left," Mason replies quietly.

"I've never seen that before. It was in *my* room?" Kaitlyn sounds genuinely surprised.

"I was checking out your computer. My fingers grazed it when I ran my hand under your keyboard tray. I almost missed it. The color blended right into the white of the desk. I'm pretty sure it's some kind of a camera, but I've never seen another one like it. I'm going to have to send it to the lab to find out more. Look, I didn't see anything else, but just in case I may have missed something, keep your eyes open. If you find anything in your room, house, or car that you don't recognize, let me know immediately. I'll have it checked out. You'd be surprised to see what they can hide spy cams in these days. If Pistol is still out there, who knows what else we may find."

I'm sitting at the feet of Detective Eddie when he turns to Officer Marnia and whispers, "This seems a little sophisticated for a rodeo cowboy from the valley."

Without saying a word, Officer Marnia nods her head. I don't know if they realize I am within earshot, but a new level of worry finds its way into my head. *I might just keep this one to myself for a while.*

The detective turns to us and speaks once more. "Look, I know you kids have been through the wringer, and this discovery is a lot to deal with right now, but this just goes to show you how serious the threat still is. Was there any other interaction with Pistol before you collided on the mountain? Did you see him? Did you know he was out there? Did you get any phone calls? Texts? I'm looking for anything here, guys. All I know right now is the little bit of information Officer Marnia gathered that first night in the hospital when you kids were still pretty dazed. It's not a lot to go on. Have any of you remembered anything else?"

Determination fills me as my mind races back over the scattered memories of our time at the Forks. I note the intent looks on the faces of my friends and sister, too. I really can't think of anything I haven't already told Officer Marnia. She knows about the broken out windows, my missing gun, the bottle of Jack Daniels ... *Was there anything before that? Think.*

I shake my head and pull my fingers up through my hair, "Guys, I've got nothing. Maybe I have some kind of undiagnosed head injury, but I am having a hell of a time remembering anything that happened before we found my busted up truck. Do you guys remember anything crazy happening before that?"

Brody's eyes light up. "What about the footprints, Pip?

Remember, the ones we were next to when we were wrestling around in the snow? You were getting worked up because you thought someone else was out there. I convinced you that our secret spot wasn't really a secret, remember?"

Eyebrows begin to pop up all over the room, like sprouting buds of renewed possibility.

"Oh, Brody, with everything that happened down at the river, I totally forgot about that." Kaitlyn's face twists into a grimace. "Guys, what if someone was up there? I mean, before. Like the night before. Remember *Truth or Dare*? You might think it was a big joke, but I swear someone was in that cabin. What if they followed us up the mountain?"

"T, I'm sorry I didn't take you seriously. I thought you were just paranoid because ..."

"I should've never told you that old urban legend about *Jump off Joe*. It's my fault for getting you all skittish," Mom interrupts regretfully, then looks back at me so I can finish what I was saying.

"T, I know we gave you a hard time about being scared of the cabin. I thought your mind was playing tricks on you because you're so freaked out about ghost stories. But I'm starting to wonder if you were right about someone being in that cabin."

Jenna tugs on my shirt sleeve. "Caden, what about the newspaper at the pharmacy? It said there were several break-ins up at the cabins during Thanksgiving week."

Renewed interest spreads on the detective's face. "So, I'd like to know a little more about this cabin. What makes you think someone was in there?"

Jenna speaks up. "Well, the boys dared Kaitlyn to go inside because it was so creepy looking, all dark and screened in. I think they wanted to get her back for something. Oh yeah, for daring Mason to talk to Marissa. So we offered to go with her cuz it was way too scary to go alone ..."

I watch Detective Eddie hurriedly jot down notes as Jenna

speaks. "Go on," he prompts.

"Okay, so it was really creepy. Especially when someone kicked the beer bottle and the foam started oozing all over the place. I thought I was going to have a heart attack when that happened."

Kaitlyn looks up at Jenna and takes a deep breath, letting it out slowly.

Officer Marnia chimes in, "So, there was an open beer bottle, and it was still foaming when you kicked it?"

"Yeah, pretty sure."

Officer Marnia scans our circle of family and friends, looking at each of us. "Were any of you drinking beer up by the cabin?"

"No, we just had the wine from the vineyard." The adults all look at each other shrugging and raising their eyebrows.

"And were there any other campers in the area of the cabin?"

"Only the cabin down below," Mason answers. "Marissa's family was there, but they don't drink."

"And you know this for a fact?"

"Oh, yeah. It's one of their family mantras. *"Alcohol is your Adversary."* They live by it.

Officer Marnia begins writing now too.

"You getting all this, Eddie?" Marnia looks up at the officer through her long, thick lashes. Something about watching her gorgeous badass self, being all badass makes me forget some of the stress, if only for a minute.

"Okay, Jenna. So what happened after the beer bottle?" Officer Marnia prods.

"Well, we got to the cabin, and the girls were too chicken to go up the ladder, so I went. But then, something happened. When I got to the top, something hit my phone out of my hand. We were all so spooked that we made a run for it. I've never been so creeped out in my life … and that's saying a lot."

I can't help but laugh. The vision of those girls running away from that cabin was insanely hilarious. Bouncing and jumping over logs, darting around trees, I'd never seen any of them move so fast. It was a blurry mess of wild, screaming hair.

"Is there anything else you can remember? Or was that the last thing that happened before you went tree cutting?" Detective Eddie asks one last time.

We all stare at each other, raising our brows and lifting our shoulders.

The detective reaches down to check his phone as a text alert chimes. He raises his eyes to Officer Marnia, mumbling, "Good news, Peyton's been released. She's home. They're letting us know it's okay to head over now."

His words strike a match inside my chest, lighting me on fire. *Peyton's home? Why didn't they tell me? I've been calling non-stop for days. I've got to get over there.*

"Well, you've all been very helpful. You kids all have my number if anything happens, or if you need me. Eddie, I think we've got a good start with this new information. Let's go see if we can learn anything else." Marnia looks at each one of us, then focuses on our parents, "I'll be contacting you soon with any new leads." Nodding toward each of us, she reaches for the door.

She's followed by the detective, who looks back over his shoulder and speaks, "We'll be in touch."

The door creaks closed behind them. I look around the room. Every last one of us looks like a deer in the headlights.

CHAPTER 8

SAME HELL, DIFFERENT DAY

T HE SILENCE IN THE ROOM is too much for me. It's letting my mind go places I can't deal with right now. I need to get out of here. I can't believe Peyton was released today, and I had to find out by chance. *Why didn't she let me know? Has she forgotten about me?* My chest tightens and the fire reignites inside of me. My mind opens the door to the same hell it's visited a thousand times this week. *Why are her parents keeping her from me? Do they think I'm an irresponsible hellion? They probably want to throw the book at me. I can see their point. They trusted me to keep their daughter safe, and I damn near killed her. I deserve this.*

My throat constricts, and I fight the tug of my lower lip. I try to stop it, but the damn thing is too stubborn. I quickly look down at the floor, hiding my face from the crowd. *I will not cry in front of them. Snap out of it, dumb ass. Be strong. Just fix this.* I have to go over there to make this right. I need to explain what really happened. *The red truck. The gunshots. Do they know what led up to the accident?* I know I can't redeem myself for driving my truck over that cliff. I can't take back my inability to save her. All I can do is beg for forgiveness. With desperation, I glance up at Jenna, and secretly point to the door. I need her help getting out of here, but I can't let her know it's to go see Peyton. When her eyes meet mine, a faint smile crosses her lips. It's followed by a subtle nod.

"Whew, that was intense," she belts out as she bounces off the couch. "I think I need some fresh air. Anyone up for a drive?" *I knew I could count on her.* She turns her back to our parents, discreetly gesturing to Kaitlyn and the others that I need to be alone. I breathe a sigh of relief that she's recognized my anguish.

Brody stands slowly, stretching his arms over his head. After the exaggerated stretch, he reaches for Kaitlyn's hand and pulls her to her feet. "We're going to grab a bite to eat before heading back over to the valley to decorate for Christmas. Who's coming?"

Mason stands up quickly and says, "I'm in. I want to help with the grandparents' tree."

Thankfully Jenna turns down the offer. "I have a few errands to run. Caden, it looks like you have a choice to make. Do you want to go play Santa's elf or stay here with me?

How am I going to get her to take me to Peyton's?

"No icy, winding hills for me today. I'm staying with you. I have a few errands of my own. Do you mind driving?"

"Only if you don't mind dropping by the bank to take care of my missing debit card."

That catches Cinda's attention, "What did you say?"

"Oh, Mom, sorry I didn't tell you. I kinda misplaced my wallet." She looks down, shuffling her feet, "I've been looking for it since the trip to the cabins, but…"

Mr. Bailey leans forward, scowling at Jenna through his heavily wrinkled brow, "Why didn't you say something earlier, young lady? We've been back for nearly two weeks." He shakes his head as his voice becomes increasingly scornful. "How could you blow that off for so long, especially when I'm the one responsible for that account?"

"Dad," Jenna retorts, "I was hoping it'd show up when we got home. You know, maybe find it under my car seat or stuffed in someone's bag. I swore I never took it out of my suitcase the whole time we were on vacation. I didn't mean to lose it, I swear."

Mr. Bailey starts in again, "You need to be more responsible with your stuff. Last week it was your locket and now this?"

Jenna's face melts into a frown as she bows her head in defeat. Dead silence fills the air.

"Why did you have to bring that up? You know how much that locket meant to her." Cinda stands up and moves toward Jenna, pulling her into a hug. She sets her head down on top of Jenna's, scowling at Mr. Bailey, "We'll find it, don't worry."

"You're right, I'm sorry. I'm just so damned frustrated with all of the irresponsible behavior. Jenna, the next time something as important as a wallet comes up missing, you need to let your mother and me know. Now, get down to the bank before it closes. Have them run a report on any activity in the last two weeks. You'd better hope that wallet is wadded up in your dirty clothes somewhere," he shakes his head. "Go, now. We'll discuss this later."

I've never seen Jenna look so worried. I kind of feel bad for her. Her dad was really tough considering all she's been through the past two weeks. *Maybe he's reached his breaking point with all of this.* I've got to try and smooth things over for her. After all, she was just trying to help me get out of the house. "I'll make sure we get to the bank right away." I nod toward the adults in the room and grab her by the hand, "Mom, Dad, I'll be back in a while. Let's go, buddy. Your dad is right. We need to look into that debit card immediately."

Quickly, we run out of the house before her dad starts

in again. Jenna can't get the car door opened and closed fast enough. I can tell she's beyond upset. She's not saying much, but she can't even start the car. *This must be bothering her more than she's letting on.* She tries to stick the key in the ignition, but her trembling hand is fumbling for the keyhole. I lean over, holding her hand in mine, and help her start the car. "Settle down, girl. I'm sure he didn't mean to jump on you like that. This is just a lot for our parents to take in."

"I didn't mean to lose my wallet ... or my locket! My dad can be such a jerk!"

I'm quiet for a minute trying to let her cool down. *Mr. Woodley was right about that wallet. Who knows what someone can do with all that stuff?* I should defend him, but I don't want to say the wrong thing and piss her off even more. There's no way she's gonna take me to Peyton if she's fired up. I bite my tongue and focus my attention on Mr. Brownell shoveling his walkway.

"Well?"

"Huh?"

"Aren't you going to say anything?"

I shake my head, quickly back and forth. "I've got nothin'."

She turns up the radio and slams her foot on the gas, screeching away from the sidewalk and sliding through the first stop sign. I pull on my seatbelt and shift my weight to gain better balance in my seat. I forcefully swallow the bitter chunk of mid-afternoon snack that resurfaces upon take-off. "Ease off the gas, Jenna! This isn't Fast and Furious! It's icy out here, and you don't have your studded tires on."

"I can't hear you!"

I turn down the music, "I said, ease off the gas! I've already pressed my luck once this month." I can see she feels bad about making me lose my shit as she begins to slow down. "Do you want me to drive?" *Why did I ask that? What if she says yes? Please say no.*

"No, I've got this."

Phew. She slows the car to a normal speed for a snowy, residential area. "Sorry, I didn't mean to scare you like that. I'm better. So you don't mind going to the bank with me?"

"No. Let's get it over with. It'll give the officers time to finish with Peyton, and then we can head on…"

"Peyton? Is that why you wanted out of the house? So you could go get your heart broken again? Really? Caden, do you seriously think her parents are gonna let you see her? They didn't even tell you she was being released!"

"Yeah, well, I don't know, but I'm going to try. I can't handle this ostracism for one more day. You know how screwed up things are between us right now, and you know that in order for me to get past this, I need to go over there and straighten it out. I've got to know why she won't talk to me. I mean for God's sake, Jenna, maybe she can't even talk. And for whatever reason, her parents won't let me see her. Geez, is she dying? Disfigured? What is it? I need answers, and I need them today. You've got to take me. Please!"

Relief comes over me as I watch understanding replace her anxious sneer. "I will help you," she nods. "But, I don't have a good feeling about this."

CHAPTER 9

NO MORE CRASHES!

THE TRIP TO THE BANK went well. There was no sign of activity in the report. Jenna's dad will be happy to hear that she changed and secured her account. I'm sure she's relieved. I know I am. We crunch through freshly fallen powder as we make our way to the car. The latest snow-storm must've begun while we were inside. I guess we were in the bank longer than I thought because there looks to be a good two inches on the road.

Progress is slow, as Jenna is extra cautious driving her VW in these conditions. We painstakingly crawl from block to block. She's turned the music off. I know the soundlessness helps her concentrate, but it's grating on my nerves. I study her face in the rearview mirror, trying to take my mind off of the never-ending drive of doom. Her lips twist from side to side while her eyes squint and release. I take a deep breath and release it with an audible sigh.

"I can see the look on your face. You're scheming again. We're not playing with this one."

"What do you mean?"

"Just what I said. No more games. We're going to pull up to the house. I'm going to march down her front walk, knock on that door, and confront my demons. No more sneaking around. I already learned my lesson at the hospital. It's time to face the music like a man."

"You're pretty dense. You know that, right?" Jenna shakes her head and takes a deep breath. "Well, I'm not going to fight you on this. But you should probably know you're not getting in. Maybe you'll finally believe me when one of the three bears slams the door in your face."

"I'll take my chances."

As we approach Peyton's, I spot the tail end of the police SUV rounding the corner. I wonder how Peyton handled reliving the nightmare on the Forks. I feel horrible for her having to do that alone. I'm glad I'm here in case she needs me. Finally, I have a chance to help pick up the pieces. *Hang on, babe. I'll be right there.*

I grip the handle above my door, practically crushing the plastic beneath me. Being just moments away from facing the Carters has my stomach in knots, but it's something I have to do. *I've got to own up to what I did. I need to take responsibility for the wreck. I should've pulled my foot from the gas, not slammed on the brake. It's my fault we slid out of control.* The guilt is eating me alive. It's all I've thought about for days. Inside I'm a raging mess. My heart is racing. *I need to get in there and get this over with. I need to be there for her. I hope they'll let me see her.*

Jenna pulls up next to the sidewalk. "Want me to go with, or are you doing this on your own?"

I take a deep breath in through my nose, holding it in my cheeks for a few seconds.

Jenna raises her eyebrows with a half grin. "You plan on going in there looking like a chipmunk?" she giggles. "Breathe."

I look to Jenna, and begin directing the air slowly toward her. Watching her bangs blow from her forehead does nothing to relieve my stress. I'd hoped completely deflating my lungs into her face would calm my nerves and bring a little comic relief. Not a chance. I'm weak and shaky as I open the door and begin to step out onto the sidewalk.

"Wait! You may want a piece of this!" Jenna pinches her nose and holds out her extra-large jug of fresh mint gum.

I bend down, looking back into the car door. "Not funny." I take a piece anyway, just in case. "Wait for me here, k. I'm not sure if they'll answer." An image of Peyton's dad tossing me to the ground flashes through my mind. "I'm not sure her parents will let me through the front door."

"Well, not with that garlic breath anyway."

I shake my head and turn toward the walkway. I begin my long journey, listening to Jenna's snarky voice drift down the sidewalk. "Hey, knock 'em dead, huh?"

I continue walking toward the door, pulling my hand behind my back, flipping her the bird. Sucking as much minty juice from the gum as I can extract, I hear her laugh blurring into the background.

I have to admit, Jenna is a great distraction. You never know what's going to come out of her mouth. *Garlic breath. That little turd.* Now that I'm close to the door, I feel every vibration of my shaky quads. I darn near trip trying to lift my leg onto the first step. Grabbing onto the handrail with my good arm, I pull myself up the five wooden steps to the front porch. I jump as the wood creaks beneath my feet. I convince myself to shuffle across the deck to the door. *Left. Right. Left. Right. Breathe in. Breathe out.* I hear my heartbeat pounding in my ears, as I lift my hand to knock on the big wooden door.

I duck out of the way of the fancy window, hiding off to the side. *Maybe they'll actually answer if they don't know it's me.* I wait impatiently, listening to the roar of my heartbeat growing louder. *I should've brought a girl scout with me.* I scan the neighborhood trying to find someone selling cookies to use as a decoy. No luck. *Come on, open the door already.* I look back to the car and see Jenna lifting her hands, palms raised, mouthing something.

I squint at her, trying to make out the movement of her lips, shaking my head in confusion. I can't tell what she's saying. She drops her hands and pulls out her phone. I feel a buzz in my pocket and pull out my cell to find a message.

Jenna: Well????

Me: Not answering.

Jenna: I saw her mom walk past the window. Told you so! :P

Me: Shut up! Not giving up this easy. I'm knocking again. >:)~

I shove my phone back in my pocket. My heart jumps when I lift my hand to knock again and miss the door as it opens in front of me. I raise my eyes to meet Mrs. Carter's fatigued face. "Sorry, Caden. I didn't mean to scare you like that."

"Hey, Mrs. Carter. Is Peyton able to see me yet?"

She pauses momentarily, cocking her head to the side. "You know she's already had a long day. Those officers have been here talking to her for quite a while. I'm not sure she's up for any more visitors. She's pretty exhausted."

More excuses. "Please, Mrs. Carter. That's exactly why I need to see her. I want to help. I figure I kinda know what she's going through. A little anyway. I know I haven't been through half of what she has, but maybe I can make her feel better."

She bites her lip and twists her face into a painful grimace.

It's almost as though she feels sorry for *me*. Contemplation overpowers her face for a brief moment, and she finally speaks, "I'll see what I can do. No promises. You might want to prepare yourself. Peyton's not the same person."

"None of us are, Mrs. Carter."

"Well, you've got a point. I didn't mean to sound so insensitive. Come on inside where it's warmer. I'll see if I can get her to come out."

I step through the doorway and wait at the entry, watching Mrs. Carter head down the hall toward Peyton's room. She rests against the wall as her head disappears through the doorway. I can't hear what she's saying, so I slyly inch my way further into the living room. The voices are still muffled, but their sudden bursts of volume tell me that there is some tension. I lean in a bit closer.

"Peyton, you've got to give this a chance."

More muffled outbursts.

"He went through it too. Just let him talk to you."

I hear a crash.

"Peyton, you've got to stop doing that! I'm not sending him away again!"

Silence.

"You know, he's trying to work through this too. Maybe he needs your help as much as you need his. Can you try?"

Her voice is raised now, to the point I can hear the tail end of Peyton's sentence. "...get hurt!"

"He's hurting in more ways than one, young lady. Maybe you should see him so you know what *he's* been through. It might help you recover if you hear his side of the story."

Crash.

"Don't hurt yourself, young lady. Your stitches! Stop ... those trophies can't be replaced!" Mrs. Carter disappears through the door.

Crash.

87

"You know what? I'm sending him in. If you won't snap out of it for me, maybe you will for him."

Holy shit. What am I walking into? What's wrong with her?

I inch back toward the front door, panicked that I might not be able to defend myself if she chucks something at my head. I can't hear what she's yelling at Mrs. Carter, but the sound of metal crashing into her walls is scaring the hell out of me.

What the hell is happening in there? Realization hits hard. *She blames me. Hell, I can't even forgive myself. What right do I have to ask her to forgive me? I shouldn't have come. I really shouldn't have come.* I stumble backward, reaching toward the handle. *I've got to get out of here.*

"Stop, Caden. You can't go!" The desperation in Mrs. Carter's voice makes me loosen my grip on the handle.

"Mrs. Carter," I shake my head back and forth, "I don't … I … I don't think she wants to see me right now." I raise my sling, reminding her that I have no defense against flying trophies. "It might not be such a good idea. I shouldn't have come. I should've called first." I'm practically hyperventilating from the shock of Peyton's reaction to my presence.

"Calm down, son," her voice shakes. I watch the tears well up in her eyes as she begins to speak. "She might not realize it right now, but she needs you. Her father and I haven't been able to get through to her. The night she woke up in that hospital, she was like a different girl. She's angry and aggressive. She won't let anyone touch her. I feel like I sent my sweet, little angel down that river, and she came back without a soul. It's not the same girl in there, Caden. I need your help. You might be able to make a breakthrough. Just be careful."

Mrs. Carter begins to cry, inconsolably. "She's lashing out and throwing things. She wakes up in the middle of the night screaming. What you just heard, the crashing trophies … that fit pales in comparison to the last couple nights we've had her home. She's gone crazy."

I watch Mrs. Carter's face drop. Her voice softens to a whisper as she shakes her head. "Maybe you can bring her back. Please, will you try?" She moves toward me, grabbing my hand. She looks into my eyes, pleading, "Please, Caden. We want our daughter back, too. Try. For me."

I hear another crash. My ears buzz with the surge of adrenaline. I'm going in there to face a different girl. One who I don't know; don't understand. *I destroyed my Peyton. Ruined her, just like I was afraid of. Peyton has to be hiding somewhere in the fiery girl behind that wall. I have to try to get her back. If not for me, for her parents. I owe them that much.*

CHAPTER 10

DAMAGED

I'M NOT SURE IF I can do this, but I need to act strong for the broken woman in front of me. I don't want to be the one who took this mother's child from her. *I have to fix her.* I put on a brave face and look Mrs. Carter in the eyes. "I'll give it my best shot."

I take a deep breath as I step past Mrs. Carter and make my way through Peyton's doorway. I scan the room looking for my girl and come up empty. Instead of finding her, I observe what looks like a demolition site. The curtains are half hanging from the window. There are crumpled papers lying all over the ground. It looks like a photo album has been ripped to shreds. *Could Peyton have done all this? Where is she?* I continue to walk deeper into the room, looking behind the bed, hoping I might find her there.

"Peyton?" I whisper softly.

There's no answer.

"Peyton? Are you in here?" My nerves are getting the best of me, and I find it difficult to disguise my anxiety. The fear of not knowing what I'm about to face has my voice playing hide and seek inside my throat. I can't let her know how scared I am. I need to be strong for her. I fill my lungs with air and raise my volume slightly, working to keep the trembling at bay.

"Peyton, I know you're in here. Please talk to me. I want to help you."

"Go away." A tiny peep comes from the back corner of her room.

The floor creaks as I make my way toward the sound.

"I told my mom not to let you in. Go away," the aggravated voice pierces the tense room. A blue streak flies out of the bathroom.

Oh, there she is. My awareness heightens as I walk toward the bathroom. Being extra cautious of flying projectiles, I grab the blue hairbrush from the floor, carry it into the bathroom, and set it on the counter. "Are you decent?"

"That depends on what you mean." Sarcasm drips from behind the shower curtain. I've never heard my girlfriend sound so cold and detached.

"I need to talk to you. Are you dressed?"

"Like a damn mummy. Probably not what you're hoping for. Just go away, Caden. You don't want to see me like this. I look like hell." Her cruel, aggressive voice has me on edge.

"Peyton, that's not possible. You're the prettiest girl I've ever seen."

"Well, you haven't seen the damage you caused, have you? Your beauty queen died two weeks ago when you deserted her in your smashed up, sinking truck. You killed her! The old Peyton is gone. You don't want me. Not like this. And guess what else? I DON'T want you either. You're dead to me. You hear me? Dead!"

I deserved that. I was the one behind the wheel. I just wish I could remember how I made it out of my truck, and she didn't. Her words slice through me, but I know I'm the only one who can help her through this. *Take it like a man. Don't give up on her.* I swallow the lump in my throat as I tentatively reach out and slowly pull back the shower curtain that keeps her hidden from my view.

I brace myself as the curtain hangers glide across the plastic shower rod. Within seconds, the unknown is revealed. The hair stands up on my arms when I see her fully clothed body, nestled into the back corner of the tub. Clearly, she lost weight in the hospital. The bumps of her spine protrude through the knit fabric of her t-shirt. I need to see her face, but my only view is the top of the turban wrap. She's tucked into a fetal position. My eyes are drawn to the bruises that line the pale skin of her bony arms. An image of an ad I once saw about anorexia, crosses my mind as I watch her holding her knees, curled tightly into a ball.

"Please look at me, babe." She looks so tiny, so frail. *I need to fix her. I don't want to break her, but I have to touch her.* Gently, I reach out toward her hand.

I barely sense the touch of her cold skin when Peyton rapidly draws back from beneath my fingertips. She snaps her head back and stabs me through the heart with her deadly glare. I'm startled by the quick attack on my senses and stumble back into the toilet. *Holy shit.* Grabbing hold of the tank, I steady my shaking legs, and fall down on the seat. I can't hide the shock at the sight before me. S*o, this is what I did to her?* I pull my fingers through my hair, grabbing at my scalp. *Oh, grow a pair. Look at your girlfriend. You owe it to her to make her feel beautiful. Lie, Caden. Lie you bastard!* I finally dare to look up.

My eyes meet her blood, red stare. "So, this is what you wanted to see?" Peyton spits, throwing both bandaged hands up in the air. "I tried to hide from you, but NO! You just couldn't stay away, could you? Get out! I want you to get out!" Peyton pulls her bandaged hand up to her mouth, smothering a gagging sound.

My heart stops momentarily, as I take in the damage I've

done. Her face is still pale and swollen. The puffiness in her cheeks hides the roundness of her eyes. *My God, her eyes. What happened to them?* The blue of her irises has been smothered by her broken, draining blood vessels. Greenish blue bruising shades the bridge of her nose, traveling beneath her eyes. I follow the bruises to her hairline, where yellow iodine, stains the lining of her turban. The terrifying vision stops my heart. I open my mouth to speak, but I can't find my voice. It's impossible to hide my shock.

"See, you can't even look at me. Get out! Get out now!" Peyton abruptly stands, screaming and pulling her hands to her head. "Damn it," she shrieks, "My head! Ow, my head! Go! Please! I'm begging you! You're making this worse. Can't you see what this is doing to me? Move! Now!"

She struggles out of the bathtub, as I work my way off the toilet and stumble back toward the wall. I feel my way around the molding of the door as I hear the loud clack of the toilet seat. I close my eyes and back further into the hallway, running into something warm and soft. I jump when I feel hands wrap firmly around my shoulders. A familiar voice makes its way into my jumbled head."

"Caden, it's just me. What's going on in there?" Jenna starts to say, before she's interrupted by the sound of heaving and retching. She turns to me with her face twisted into a disgusted grimace, as a loud splattering wave meets the water below.

"Ewww, what happened in there? Did you make her sick?" Jenna is hesitant to throw out her half-hearted joke. By the concerned look on her face, I can tell she's not sure that her timing is appropriate.

The sad thing is, it's not really a joke. I think she might be puking at the sight of me. I grapple with the possibility. I reflect on the change in her face, as our eyes met for the first time since the accident. *I can't believe she was covering her mouth to stop herself from throwing up. I make her sick. Oh my God, it's me. I'm the one who's making her sick.*

Horror stricken, I answer Jenna's question, "Yeah, I think I might have."

"You think so?" Jenna's contemplative expression tells me that she's searching for a way to make me feel better. "Maybe she's still on painkillers from the brain surgery. I mean, look how sick they make you."

"No, I'm pretty sure it's me."

"Well then, I'm going in there to help her. Puking with stitches probably sucks. Wait here. I'll be right back."

Jenna disappears through the bathroom door. I hear her voice intermingled with the heaving sounds, "Peyton, it's me, Jenna."

There's a momentary pause.

Silence.

"You too!?!"

Another wave of vomit empties into the toilet.

"Get!" *Splash.* "Out! Haven't you guys done enough?"

A toilet brush flies through the door, followed by Jenna backing quickly through the doorway with her hands held high. "Let's go." She tugs on my good arm. "She needs more help than we can give her. A psychiatrist would probably work better. We're not trained for this." I stumble back, tripping into Mrs. Carter, who has made her way down the hallway to check on us.

"Are you leaving?"

Jenna answers for me. "We're sorry. We're making this worse. We don't want to cause any more damage. She clearly needs more time."

Mrs. Carter shakes her head knowingly. She grabs my hand and looks me in the eye.

"I know what she thinks, Caden. That you abandoned her in that river. She lost consciousness. There are huge gaps in her memory. We've talked to the doctors and several of the investigators." She sets her hand on my shoulder. "Her dad and I both know it's not your fault. You did everything you could under the circumstances. It looks like that damn Pistol Black caused this mess, not you." She shakes her head, looking down at the floor. "One way or another, we'll get Peyton back. I'll call when I think she's ready. Let's pray it's sooner, rather than later."

CHAPTER II

DROWNING IN GUILT

"WHAT THE HELL WAS THAT?" Jenna pants as she slams the car door. No words come. I can't think. I stare blankly at my frantic friend sitting in the driver's seat. My brain tries to prime my body to respond. With intense effort, I finally get my head to shake. Still, no words. My lungs spasm dramatically, as I struggle to catch my breath.

When I woke up this morning, it never crossed my mind that my world would be shattering today. I knew it wouldn't be easy to confront my fears, but in no way was I prepared for this. The face that used to bring me peace has been replaced by the haunting reality of one bad decision. My reckless driving didn't just ruin my girl, it destroyed all of my friends. I can't believe that a tiny twist of fate could tear apart everything we had. Everything we were looking forward to. Never in my wildest dreams, did I imagine that I would be looking death in the face today. And now, there's no turning back. Everything in my world has gone cold. Dead, cold.

I'm lost in thought when Jenna sets her hand on my shoulder. "Calm down. It's going to be okay. We just have to figure out what's going on with her. I heard banging and screaming outside her window. It scared the crud out of me. What happened in there?"

I continue to shake my head. Still no words.

"Caden, answer me. Did she hurt you? Are you okay?"

Flying hairbrush. Shredded pictures. Broken trophies. Screaming. Puking. Red eyes. Bandages. Everywhere, bandages. I stare forward, blankly, losing myself in the snowfall that pounds against the windshield. I wipe the sweat from my forehead. *Holy crap, I just got attacked by a vomiting mummy.* "That couldn't have been her, Jenna." I shake my head wildly. "There's no way. It didn't act like her. It didn't look like her. There's no frickin' way that was her. I'm not buying it."

"It was her, trust me. I recognized her voice."

I half chuckle, half grunt at her attempt to make me smile. Only Jenna could make light of something that terrifying. *Maybe she really did die in the river. Is this her parents' lame attempt at trying to replace Peyton? What kind of people would be so insensitive that they would find a substitute daughter like that? Are they crazy?* I need Jenna to help me make sense of this. "Where do you think they got that thing?"

"Not following you. What thing?"

"That thing that they're trying to pass off as Peyton."

"Get ahold of yourself. Listen to what you're saying. Whether you like it or not, that was Peyton."

I rack my brain trying to make sense of the girl in that bathroom versus the one I used to know. Countless images float through my mind. Images of her laughing, smiling, holding me. My mind fixates on one of my favorite memories of fall. I reflect on the night we were building the homecoming float.

I was working across from Peyton. She was on one side of the flatbed truck, and I was on the other. She kept sneaking under the truck bed to steal my paint and brushes. I suspected it was her from all of the giggling. Not to mention, her cheeks flushed pink as she batted her eyelashes at me.

"Missing something?" she giggled, fanning herself with my four missing brushes. "Sorry, I was getting a little hot over here. I needed something to cool myself down."

I remember laughing at her lame attempt at flirting. "Could you throw me at least one bottle of paint and one brush, so I can get something done over here? The advisor's going to kick me out for loitering."

"Well, I'm not so sure you're good enough to catch my rockets. I wouldn't want to hurt you. Maybe I should walk them around and HAND them to you."

I still remember the cute wiggle in her walk as she approached me with those brushes. She held them tightly, not letting go until I gently pried them from her fingers. That was the first time I felt the electricity. "Well played, Peyton. Well played."

What a stark contrast to the girl who just hurled a hairbrush at my head. "Well, it sure as hell wasn't *my* Peyton. My Peyton would have never acted like that." I whip my head around to look at Jenna. I need to see her face when I tell her everything I just went through. When my eyes meet hers, I can read the concern etched across her face. "She chucked a hairbrush at me. She screamed at me. She told me she didn't want me." I watch her concern turn to anger, as my volume increases, unleashing each of Peyton's blows. "She told me I killed her! *I* killed her!!!"

"Whoa, whoa, whoa, buddy. First of all, *you* did not *kill* her. She is very much alive, maybe a little dangerous, but alive. We just need to figure out what's making her act like a lunatic. I think we need to remember that she endured a little more trauma than the rest of us. I mean, you were out cold. You didn't really get to see how it all played out."

"Well, why don't you enlighten me? Nobody's told me the whole story. This is exactly what I was talking about before. The secrets just add to the nightmare. Out with it. All of it!"

Jenna pauses for a second. I can tell she's collecting her thoughts. They've all been so careful about protecting me from enduring more trauma. I'm sure she's trying to find the right words to lessen my distress when I finally hear all of the gory details about what happened down river.

"Okay, I'm going to tell you what I saw, but I don't think it's going to make you feel any better. There were gunshots, a lot of them. We couldn't tell where they were coming from. Within seconds, we watched your truck start to fishtail out of control. It was a blur for a second, and then I made out what looked like a red truck, flying into your passenger door. It wrapped around you and pulled you over the embankment. Brody pulled over fast. We jumped out, just in time to hear crunching metal and a loud splash. Brody and I ran to the edge. When we looked over, we saw your crushed truck submerged in the water. Kaitlyn wasn't doing well, so I headed down the icy shale alone. It was hell getting to you. Not knowing if you made it terrified me, but knowing you needed my help, motivated me to keep going. I slipped and fell at least a half dozen times on the ice. Halfway down the mountain, I spotted you lying in the snow, covered in blood. I almost fainted. You were screaming bloody murder. Not for yourself, but for her. She was all that was on your mind. It was only minutes before you went silent. I was bending over the top of you, trying to find your pulse, when I heard the first scream for help. I looked toward the sound. That's when I realized she was still alive. I could see Peyton's hand struggling to curl around the top of the cab. She grasped all over, hitting the roof frantically. She couldn't get out. She was pinned in there. By that time, Mason, Brody, and Kaitlyn were all down at the river trying to save her. I can't imagine how scared she was."

Crap. Why can't I remember getting out of the truck? I

swear someone helped me. "How did I get out? I would not have left her alone."

"We don't know. You were already lying on the ground when we found you. You were still conscious. Don't you remember? You were yelling at us to get her out."

"You said you saw her moving. So, she was still okay after the truck rolled into the river?"

"I'm not sure how *okay* she was after being shot at. And, we don't know how many times you guys rolled down the mountain. She could've been pretty banged up, but I know she was still breathing. Kaitlyn told me she was gasping at a pocket of air when she found her. The water was freezing. That poor girl. I don't know how she was breathing at all. They didn't give up though. Kaitlyn kept going under, time and time again. Brody started yelling at her to stop. I wondered why, but then I noticed the truck start to wobble back and forth. Just as Brody snatched Kaitlyn up, the truck escaped downstream. She was still in it, Caden."

Visions of my truck being taken down the river invades my mind. Anxiety hits me when I picture Peyton struggling to hold her breath in the icy-cold, rushing water. I can't handle the suffocating thought.

"We all thought she was dead. The truck was completely submerged. All I could see was the swift current, and a glimmer of metal tapping the surface. None of us thought she survived. It was too damn cold. The boys could barely make it out of the water to get back to you. I watched Brody struggle to breathe life back into you. By the time I looked up, Kaitlyn was gone and Mason disappeared after her."

"So they saved her? Kaitlyn and Mason?"

"Well, sort of. She used your pocketknife to cut the seatbelt. She got herself out, but she died on the beach. They did CPR on her, until the Forest Service got there and took over. They finally got her breathing again in the helicopter. After that, you know just about as much as I do."

"I'm sorry you guys had to go through that, and I'm sorry I was too weak to help. This whole thing is making me sick." I roll down my window to see if the cold air will help stifle my growing nausea. A loud belch escapes me, letting Jenna know that my stomach is ready to blow.

"I think you might need a break. Don't beat yourself up. The thing is, she was always your priority. I know you were swerving to avoid getting shot. I know you were trying to keep her from getting plowed into by Pistol's truck. The last thing out of your mouth before you passed out, were your frantic pleas to get her help. Not for yourself. For her. YOU did not kill her. YOU saved her. YOU kept her from getting crushed. YOU kept her from getting shot. YOU called attention to her whereabouts. Stop taking the blame, and get your mind off of it. You've had enough for one day."

"I'm not sure what to say." The thought of my girlfriend trapped has my heart racing. "My stomach is in knots right now. I can't wrap my mind around Peyton drowning in my truck. Gunshots. Pistol. It's a lot to process, but thank you for letting me know what you saw. It helps to know that I didn't go down without a fight. I just can't remember *trying,* and it's killing me to think I almost let her die."

"Well, remember what I said. You did all you could do. So, let's get you out of here, away from this place, so you don't have to think about it. I'm thinking coffee might get you perked up?"

"Perked up? Always playing with words, aren't you?"

CHAPTER 12

IT'S NOT ROCKET SCIENCE

IT'S BEEN TWO WEEKS SINCE I've seen Peyton. She continues to refuse my visits. I know her mom's embarrassed every time she has to send me away, but also feels the need to protect her little girl. Thank God for Jenna. She's been spending every spare moment with me, trying to cheer me up. Last weekend we played Xbox and chatted with people all over the world. Today we've already had two cups of coffee and watched six episodes of *Duck Dynasty*. It hasn't done a whole heck of a lot for my mindset, but it did give me an idea. I'm not sure how I'm going to pull it off with no vehicle and an overprotective best friend, but I could really use a break from my new normal. I roll over on the couch and look down at Jenna, who's currently perfecting a candy cane shank. She's pulled her red beanie down over her eyes, but I can still see her eyeballs peeking up at me through the holes. She looks like a gnome rolling around down on the floor. "Hey, nut-ball, what are you doing?"

She holds the pointer in my direction, jabbing the deadly treat at my face. "Trying to think of a way to stop you from watching another episode. Ugh, can I go home yet?" she groans.

"Well, I have an idea, but you've got to drop your weapon to hear it."

She shoves the poker back in her mouth and pulls it out with a pop, "You scared?"

"Of you? Nah, I just don't feel like getting impaled by a creepy, little Elf on the Shelf this afternoon."

"So, what's your plan?" she asks, biting the pointed tip off of her candy cane. She holds it up, crunching. "You said you'd tell me when I got rid of my weapon." Grinning sarcastically, Jenna flashes me with her painted red teeth.

"Wanna drive me to my dad's store to see if we can get the keys to his Arctic Cats? I've got to get out of here and blow off some steam."

She pulls her beanie off of her eyes and sits up with re-newed excitement. "Snowmobiling sounds like a good time. I bet Deer Mountain has some wicked snow."

And she bites.

"Wait a sec." She narrows her eyes looking me up and down. I can feel her pulling me into her full body scanner.

Crap.

She pinches her face to the side, twisting her lips into a gri-mace. "I'm not so sure about this. Can you handle a snowmobile with your arm?"

Can I handle a snowmobile? Me? Caden Woodley, the guy who's been driving equipment longer than he could walk? I try to hide the incredulous look that's pounding its way to the sur-face of my face. I raise my half-healed, slung arm, and smirk, "You're kidding me, right? This ole thing's not gonna keep me from a little snow therapy. It only takes one good arm to steer. I can still handle that machine like a boss. I just can't be out on *the road* while I'm on meds."

"The road. I didn't think about that." Jenna stands up and walks over to the window, pulling the curtain to the side.

"There's like six inches of snow on the ground."

"So," I shrug.

"Did you forget I drive a Beetle? We're not going anywhere with my tinker toy."

Crash and burn.

Damn it. Curse the river for eating my truck. I have to think about this for a minute. "You're right, we can't make it to Deer Mountain with your elf-mobile." *Who can I get to make this happen?* "I'll tell you what. Let's see if we can get a group together so they can help you babysit me."

"It's going to take a pretty experienced babysitter to keep you out of trouble. Any ideas?"

"Maybe Brody or Mason will take us. They both have four wheel drives. What do you say? Huh?" I nudge her on the arm. "Do you think they'd want to go?"

"Don't give them a choice. Text them and tell them to get their rears over here."

"Aye, aye," I salute and pull out my phone.

Me: You boys up for some fun? I need a distraction from my depressing life.

"Hey, boss," I draw her attention away from the window. "I just sent a group text. Hopefully they get back to us soon." My phone starts chiming almost instantly. "They must be bored too."

Brody: What're you thinking?

Me: Snow hogs!!!

Mason: What the hell are snow hogs?

Me: Snowmobiles, dumbshit :D~!

Kaitlyn: Good luck getting Dad to hand over the keys to his babies.

Me: Oh, he'll give 'em to me. I just need to grovel a little ... let him know how depressed I am.

Kaitlyn: Tell him it's cheaper than therapy. That line always works for me.

Mason: I'm in, if your dad lets us.

Me: Don't doubt me. I'll keep at it til he bends to my will. Haha >:)

Kaitlyn: Yeah, the evil twin always gets his way.

Me: My way? Right. Have you seen your closet?

Kaitlyn: Speaking of closets. If we're going to do this, we need to come get my riding gear.

Me: You've got to come anyway. We need someone with four wheel drive to get us down to Dad's store.

Mason: Ah, I see why we're invited.

Me: No, it's not like that. You know we have more fun when we all go together.

I look over at Jenna, whose thumbs are rapidly pounding at her phone. "They're taking a minute to get back to me. Why don't you text T and make sure she's convincing Brody to come? Ask her if you can borrow some of her extra riding gear while you're at it."

Jenna gives me a thumbs up. "Already on it."

Brody: Well, it looks like we're coming. When do you want us to head over?

Me: The sooner the better. I'll call Dad and hook us up.

It took a little convincing, but Dad finally caved, handing over the keys to his rig and four snowmobiles. With Brody at the wheel, we pulled into the park at about two o'clock. "Hey Bro, could you drop us off over by those bushes? I can't hold it any longer," Kaitlyn's shaky voice peeps out from the back seat of the cab.

"You're not going out there alone," he warns, watching Kaitlyn through the rearview mirror.

He's right, they still haven't found Pistol. Our first priority is to keep T safe.

"I'm not taking you to the bathroom with me."

I pull down the mirrored visor to catch Kaitlyn squirming uncomfortably, and rolling her eyes. "Well, we've got to send someone with her." A vision of Jenna holding her candy cane shank, enters my mind. "Jenna has some badass weapons in her arsenal." I pretend to pop a candy cane out of my mouth and jab it at the air. "She can handle it."

"You made me destroy the best one," she teases, "but I've still got these," she flexes her arms, kissing both of her biceps.

Looks a little scrawny to me. "Yeah, on second thought, Mason, maybe you'd better stand guard."

"Got it covered. I won't look, girls. Promise."

We let Mason and the girls out near the park entrance and make our way toward a prime parking spot. Just as Brody begins to make the wide turn into the opening, a jacked up, white F-250 whips in front of us like a bat out of hell. Brody slams on the brakes. We slide a good ten feet, just catching the corner of their snowmobile trailer.

We come to a screeching halt and sit quietly for a couple seconds, as shock settles over the cab. I try to look over the hood, but I can't see much. I shake my head, mumbling to a wide-eyed Brody, "We didn't hit it hard. I'm sure there's no damage. Let's get out and check."

Brody nods his head up and down, not saying a word. I can see he's shaken.

"Man, that thing came out of nowhere. Good thing you weren't going very fast." I try to reassure him that he didn't do anything wrong.

No sooner do we get out of the truck, than a little streak of hair, hands, and words, jumps in front of us yelling, "Damn it! Which one of you two jerks was driving that death trap anyway?"

Speechless, Brody, subtly raises his hand. My eyes travel from his stunned face back to the white truck, finally coming to rest on the squealing fireball.

Well, this is not who I was expecting to jump out of that truck. How does she even reach the gas pedal? I take a minute to survey the spunky character standing in front of me with her hands now resting on her hips. She's a tiny thing, all wrapped up in country girl camo. With her curly, brown hair sprouting out in all directions, she reminds me of the camo-wrapped Christmas package that's sitting under my tree at home. She certainly has my attention. *Olive skin. Rosy cheeks. Big round, mahogany eyes.* She's a cute, little thing, and I can't help laughing at my false perception of who just cut us off. I would've sworn a 200 pound redneck would've been behind the wheel.

"What!?!" She throws up her hands and looks me up and down. "What're you laughing at? I don't see the humor in this."

I watch her curly hair bob back and forth as she inspects my dad's truck resting over the top of her trailer. She looks up at

Brody, "I think it's fine, but I can't see under that clunky heap."

He nods his head up and down, "K."

I watch her eyebrows travel up her forehead. "Well, what are you waiting for? Move it!"

"Hhhow?" Brody stutters.

"It's not rocket science. Your truck is still running. Put the dang thing in reverse, and MOVE it! I need to see what you did to my trailer."

I'm still laughing at the nearly lifeless statue of Brody getting popped by this pint-sized firecracker. My mouth drops, when I watch her thrust her shoulder into Brody's chest as she streaks by, jumps into the truck, and backs it away.

We're looking at each other in disbelief when the hissing ground flower spins her way back to her trailer. She looks back over her shoulder and yells, "I guess if you want to get anything done around here, you have to do it yourself." She shakes her head, inspecting the corner of her trailer. "You're lucky it didn't do anything. I guess I can't expect city slickers to know how to drive in the snow. So where did you get your driver's license anyway, a Cracker Jack box?"

City slickers? Ouch. What gives? This is HER fault. "Hold on there, Tangles. Go easy on my friend. You're the one who wasn't watching where you were going. You cut *us* off!"

"Lame excuse for crappy driving, dude. You know what? You're wasting my time. Now if you'll excuse me, I'm tired of burning daylight." Just like that, the tangly ball of sass turns her back to us and grabs her helmet off the trailer. Pulling it over her head, I hear her call, "Jessie May, you chicken. Get out of that truck and help me! Let's go!"

The door opens slowly. I watch intently as a second hel-meted girl, slides down and walks toward the back of the trailer. Timidly, she raises her visor and glances in our direction. Paus-ing just long enough to shrug her shoulders and raise her eye-brows apologetically. Not waiting for our response, she turns back to her friend. Together, they lower the ramp. "You go first. I've got Bumblebee," I hear Tangles command.

Jessie May climbs on a green snowmobile and takes off first. I watch her speed off down the path, until she vanishes in the distance.

Girls on snowmobiles, that's badass.

I'm caught off guard when a yellow and black streak whips around us, throwing a sheet of snow in our faces. Before I have time to process the icy sting, she's gone.

"Must be Bumblebee," I chuckle, watching Brody spit out a mouth full of snow.

He scratches the side of his nose, looking down at the ground. "Dude, what just happened?"

"Not sure, Bro," I chuckle, amused by the audacity of that chick. I feel my forehead pinch, as I pull my eyebrows together, shaking the snow from my head. "Whatever it was, I kind of liked it."

CHAPTER 13

GAME ON

I SNAP MY HEAD AROUND, startled by the crunching snow behind me. *What's that?* My heart rate spikes, and I freeze long enough to scope out the parking lot. I'm relieved when three familiar faces peek around a nearby trailer. *Phew, it's just Mason and the girls returning from their potty break. Damn, I was kinda hoping it was Tangles, back for round two.* Jenna cocks her head, as her eyes roam my body. "What's up with you?"

That damn mood detector of hers. I widen my smile, "What do you mean?"

"You're smiling."

For the first time in weeks, I'm consciously aware that the corners of my mouth are pulled into a grin. "Guess I am."

"It's a good look on you. What brought it on?"

I shake my head, chuckling, "I don't even know where to start." I look over at Brody, "Your story to tell, Brody. Go ahead."

He scratches his head, "Let's just say, while you were

away, we had a *run-in* with a couple of spicy country girls, and this dumbass thought it was funny." He points over to the big, white F-250. "See that truck right there? It cut me off when I was trying to park, and I plowed right into it."

Jenna looks back at me open-mouthed and wide-eyed, "And you're laughing? How's that funny?"

"You'll see when you read the stickers on her window."

"I'm a country girl. We don't keep calm."

"Not just the camo one. Read the one with the fairy god-mother wearing a cowboy hat."

Kaitlyn reads another sticker,

"I don't need no magic wand to get you off my tail. Who needs fairy dust when you've got gunpowder?"

"Don't those stickers just say it all?" I look back at Brody, and snort through my laughter. "The girl who was driving was something else. Spunky, little runt. She didn't back down for a second. Bro looked so scared, I thought he was going to pee himself."

"Sounds like she's got an attitude to me. Beware of them country girls," Mason warns.

"Well, anyone who can hold her own with two crazy oafs like you is my kind of girl," Jenna winks.

"Where'd they go? Did you already exchange insurance info and stuff?" Mason questions, walking around the front of the truck, as he surveys the scene.

"We already checked it out. No damage to either rig. They took off a minute ago."

"Well, in that case, we should hurry up and find them," Jenna giggles.

I'm caught off guard by her enthusiasm. "What? Why?"

"I'd like to thank the girl who put that smile back on your face … and ask her where I can get those stickers," she jokes, nudging me in the ribs.

Brody still looks a little off kilter. "Well, I think we'd best grab the machines and head the other direction. That curly haired one was fired up!" He releases a deep breath and pulls his hand through his hair, "And I'm pretty sure she's not lying about those guns. Look through the back window. Her rack is loaded. Scary. Nope, not messin' with that one." He climbs up the trailer and starts the first sled, backing it down.

Kaitlyn climbs on the back of Brody's snowmobile, wrapping her arms around him. "Don't worry, it's my turn to protect you for once. Curly-haired, country girls don't scare me at all."

Me neither. I think to myself, traveling up the ramp, to help unload the rest of the snowmobiles. Distracted by the replay of the feisty encounter looping through my head, it seems like no time before we're all on the snowcats ready to roll.

"Which way, boss?" Mason asks, buttoning his helmet strap.

I scan the wide trail noting the two paths that diverge before me. One leads downhill to the west, the other uphill to the north. Despite my best effort to resist, my eyes are drawn in the direction I last saw the yellow and black streak. *Bad thought, dude. Bad thought. That way's trouble.* My conscience tells me *no*, but the little devil on my shoulder says *YES*. Against my better judgement, I point my snowmobile north. "I feel like going this way today." I raise my good arm and motion my friends forward.

I follow the tracks left by Bumblebee and her sidekick, Jessie May. They swerve in and out drawing figure eights in the fresh powder. It's mesmerizing to watch the intricate pattern weaving beneath me as I run through the middle of the circles, cutting them in half one by one. I thoroughly enjoy the mindlessness of following someone else's tracks. I'm tired of thinking. Tired of overthinking. Tired of guilt. Tired of pain. I don't have to lead this way. I don't have to think at all. All I need to do is follow the mind-freeing map that someone else created. I'm almost giddy inside, until I begin to lose sight of the design. The figure eights have become slightly harder to detect. The falling snow has begun to fill in the tracks. *I can't lose their trail. I've got to see how that chick rides.*

Instinctively, I press the throttle. The machine snaps forward. Unprepared for the intensity of the sudden thrust, I'm whipped to the back corner of the seat, barely holding on with my good arm. *Crap. It almost got away from me.* Aside from nearly flying off, the sudden, sharp pain in my arm, reminds me that I haven't fully recovered from my serious injury. I let up on the throttle long enough to readjust my position and collect my thoughts. *I'm not about to give up the peace I found in those tracks. This beast is not going to take that from me.* Determined to ride like the wind, I center myself on the seat, plant my boots on the foot holds, squeeze my thighs around my opponent, and hit the throttle one more time.

As I travel swiftly down the path, the exhilarating speed has me laughing out loud. My periphery is a blur of green, brown, and white. The icy wind whips through my jacket, sending a slight shiver down to my core. I cock my head back toward the sky and squeal, "You guys cold?" I can't hear anything through the buzz of my Arctic Cat and my padded helmet, so I shrug my shoulders and keep going. *They can handle it. We've definitely been colder than this before.* My senses are on fire from the gorgeous sights, mind-numbing sounds, and chilly late afternoon air. It gives me a gentle reminder of what it's like to feel something other than fear, sadness, and despair.

I decide to slow down a bit to see if I can't take in another dose of clean-air therapy. A pristine wonderland stretches out before me. I'm nearly surrounded by towering mountains. Off in the distance, the meadows are blanketed with fluffy powder. Staring up at the tree-lined ridges, I picture the hand of God holding a paintbrush. It's calm. Peaceful. Serene. *No man could ever create something so perfect, so beautiful.*

I continue to sputter along, looking up at Mt. Shasta. Distracted by the exceptional skyline, I don't see the large rut below me. As the sled dips unexpectedly, I find myself thrown against the handlebars. I come to a sudden stop, carefully scooting back in the seat. My stomach flips a little from the shock of the impact. *I'd better be careful. One armed driving is trickier than I thought.* I decide to wait for a minute to regain my composure.

Sitting in the stillness, my eyes focus on the falling snow. I've always loved sitting outside in the middle of a gentle snowfall. There's a certain feeling that comes with it. An unparalleled quiet. An insulating calm. I've relished this comforting feeling since I was a child, and I eagerly look forward to its return each winter.

Gazing into a gentle flurry, I follow a snowflake until it lands softly on my rounded visor. Then another. And another. A familiar vision comes over me. I'm not sure what it is, but I've had it before. My mind searches to make the connection, until it finally comes to me. The Thomas Kincade Painting. *Our Winter Wonderland painting.* A picture of Peyton flashes through my mind. We're standing together in the falling snow. I have my arms wrapped around her. We're carving our initials into the bridge. *Peyton. What am I doing?* I snap out of my trance and pull my eyes back to the ground. It's a brutal reminder of my search for the figure eights. My search for Bumblebee. Tangles. *I know I'm here to try to take my mind off Peyton, but what kind of a dog am I? Sniffing out someone else's tracks?*

I'm angry at myself. Angry for even thinking about being disloyal to Peyton. I close my eyes praying for forgiveness, but I can't focus long enough to speak an entire prayer. All I can do is picture her screaming at me over and over.

"You killed her! You don't want the new Peyton! And guess what else, Caden? I DON'T want you either! You're dead to me! You hear me? Dead! You killed her! You don't want the new Peyton! And guess what else, Caden? I DON'T want you either. You're dead to me! You hear me? Dead!"

Sick to my stomach, I turn the key and the engine roars back to life. *I've got to get out of here.* Furious about potentially destroying my relationship, I decide to take a different route. I don't want to think of what could've happened if I ran into that girl. *What the hell was I thinking trying to find her anyway? I'll take my own path. One that she's not on. I'm sorry, Peyton. Really, I don't know what I was thinking.*

Off to the left, a narrow trail catches my eye. *Perfect.* I hold on tight and press down on the throttle. I need to forget about the nightmare replaying in my mind. *She said she didn't want me. She said I killed her.* I can't handle the thought anymore. I search my mind for songs, television shows, anything to distract me from her cutting words echoing around inside my head. Finally, my senses clear, and I allow myself to refocus on my surroundings.

That's when I perceive it, another snowmobile nearby. I slow down to see if I can hear its motor. *Yes. That's definitely not my engine.* It's got a different buzz to it. *Alright. They found me.* I was worried about leaving the gang, but I just couldn't help myself. My trail sniffing, inner speed demon got the best of me. I can feel the second snowmobile pushing on my tail, so I turn my head to see who's caught up to me.

I can hear the high pitched buzz of the snowmobile, but I can't see it. It must be just behind the bend. I slow down to give my visitor a chance to catch up. The trail is so narrow, I need to face forward so I don't run off into the deep powder. I can definitely hear the buzz getting louder. I continue on slowly, making sure to close the distance between my friends and me. *When are they going to catch up? Geez, a guy can only go so slow before he starts going backward.*

The buzz of the second snowmobile sounds close now. In fact, it's so close I can feel it pushing on the back of me. The path has made its way to a narrow steep ridge, so I dare not look back to see which of my crazy friends is riding my tail. I hear the engine rev behind me. *Oh, that must be Jenna. She's the only one who would have the guts to rev her engine at me, and think she can get away with it. I think I'll drop my speed just a little more to mess with her.*

Gently, I back my thumb off the throttle, slowing to a near stop. Another rev. I can feel my grin stretching from ear to ear as I look around, pretending to enjoy the scenery. As I'm looking up to the cascading tree-line, I hear a double rev behind me, followed by what sounds to be a small squeaky voice. *Good thing I can't hear what she's saying.* I chuckle to myself, knowing that I'm getting her goat.

I'm having fun pestering the little gnat behind me, until the path begins to widen. *Game over. Shoot.* I can hear Jenna's snowmobile begin to pick up speed. I turn my head with a cocky grin, only to be pounded in the face by a sheet of snow. Wet slush drips down my goggles. Through the steam, I can faintly make out a yellow and black streak, passing me on my right. *What? Bumblebee?* My stomach flips when I realize it wasn't Jenna after all. I need to slow down to wipe my goggles. Working with an injured arm is tough. I can't get the goggles to defog, so I flip them up, and scan for the little shit that just killed my vision.

Not ten feet ahead of me, I spot the unmistakable brown curls, spraying out from beneath the helmet. She pulls to a stop. Looking back over her shoulder, I hear her voice flair, "Hey Grandpa, you really need to take that clunker to the golf course. It's more your speed. Plus, I hear they're giving away free Depends ... you know, just in case you mess yourself on the big kids' playground."

I don't have a chance to respond or react, before she raises her hand, shooting up what looks to be her middle finger, and then takes off. *No way. Who is this girl? What a biotch! You know what? It's time to squash the bumblebee.* I center myself on my snowmobile, lean forward, and tear across the snow like a bat out of hell. *Game on!*

Within seconds, I spot my prey. She's moving at a pretty good rate, but I know if I climb the hill off to the left, I can drop down and take her. I shift my balance knowing that I have to compensate for my injury. I rev my engine and climb toward the tree-line. *She won't even see me coming.* I stalk her for a few minutes, fascinated by her speed, as she weaves in and out of downed trees. This chick has nuggets. *So Tangles does have skill.*

I continue to sneak along, high on the hillside, ducking around bushes, and riding almost parallel to her. As soon as I see the path widen, I'll make my move. But for now, I want to stay hidden from view. It's entertaining watching her ride. I continue to stalk her as I see her begin to shift in her seat. She's moved into a kneeling position. *What is she doing?*

As I look down the path, I can see the large mogul she's spotted. I watch her pick up speed as she hits the huge mound and kicks her legs back away from her body into a full extension. A loud "Yeehawwwwww!" booms up the hill, as she slams back down onto her seat.

Maybe she doesn't have nuggets after all. I flash back to some of the freestyle tricks I learned last season. *I've pulled that one before. No man wants to land that one wrong. Ouch.*

It's time to get another look at this X Games princess up close. I make my move to drop down in front of her. *Too bad this bum arm is keeping me from flying by with my Superman Seat Grab, but at least I can show her my speed.* With the slope of the angle, I have to step off onto the left foothold, so I don't roll. I'm standing upright, trying to work out my balance without losing speed. It's tough to hang on with my arm tied up. *This stupid arm. I can't wait for my appointment next week to see if I can get this sling off.* My eyes cut through the trees, lining out a perfect path to pass Tangles. Quickly, I shoot down the hill, cutting right in front of the ice queen.

She whips her head around in such haste, that I know I've caught her off guard. Just as I pull in front of her, slide around to the hood, and jump onto the front skis, she whips her handlebars to the right. I try to maintain a hold on the throttle, but the play of events unravelling before me, brings my showboating to a stop. "Whoa there, baby," I call out. I release the throttle, and jump off, right in front of Tangles, who's lying in a heap next to her snowmobile.

I have to laugh when I see her struggling to move. She looks like a turtle flipped on its back. I bend down to give her a hand up, meeting her blazing, mocha eyes. A ball of fire burns its way into my chest, leaving sparks in its path. I jump back in shock by the force of the internal flare that caught me off guard. *Holy crap. Stop that, Caden.* I bend down again holding out my hand. Tangles stares it down like it's a snake, ready to strike. "Take it."

"You're an ass." She struggles to move on her own, dropping back down to the ground. She wraps her arms around her chest. "Owww," she wheezes, finally propping herself up on her elbows. "You knocked the wind out of me."

"I've been known to take a girl's breath away a time or two, but I didn't do it *to YOU.* How do you figure I knocked the wind out of you?" I pull my helmet off my sweaty head and toss it off to the side. Her eyes meet mine, and I hear a sharp, sudden breath. Her mocha cheeks blush pink. *Interesting reaction.* I can't help but smirk.

"You jumped out of the bushes and cut me off. Are you trying to kill me today?" Tangles mumbles a few more words under her breath. Her dainty eyebrows bounce up and down and her perfectly round lips babble away, popping her dimple as she mutters. At one point, I think I catch the words, "come in here with your sexy a…" as I watch a faint smile play at the corners of her lips. I struggle to hear the word that follows *sexy*, but she turns her head away a little too quickly. *Damn, missed it.*

It's funny watching her struggle to put on the tough girl act, but I can barely handle letting her go on in obvious discomfort. *My mom raised me better than this.* "I don't bite. Take it!" Exaggerating the movement, I extend my hand again.

She looks my arm up and down, "Are you sure you're strong enough? I do weigh 95 pounds."

I have to throw my head back and take a breath. I can't speak through my deep chuckling. I bring my eyes back down to meet hers. "What makes you think I'm a city boy?"

"Well, for one, you don't know how to drive in the snow …"

I don't hear another word. *She's right. I don't know how to drive in the snow. If I did, I'd be here with Peyton right now, not chasing down some spicy, spitfire country girl all afternoon. She's not even nice. She's the polar opposite of Peyton. Shit. Peyton.* Again, my girlfriend's crystal blue eyes haunt me. I think back to the day on the cliff. I can picture her face as we tumble down the canyon. Sheer terror. I couldn't stop us. All I could do was wrap myself around her … until the blackness came. I pry my mind away from the memory and look back at the mocha-skinned beauty at my feet. *It would kill Peyton if she knew how much fun I was having tangling with this girl.*

The sound of fingers snapping, draws my eyes downward. "Where'd you go? Geez, I was only kidding." Tangles raises her hand to mine.

I take it gently and tug her to her feet. "Let me get that sled turned back over for you. Sorry, I didn't mean to make you wreck."

An incredulous look comes over her face. "What? No kiss my ass? It's your fault? Nothin'? Yep, you're a city boy alright. A country boy would've never taken that kind of crap from me."

"Guess you've never met a *country* boy whose mama raised him right."

"Mmhmm." She rolls her eyes as I watch her struggle with

her chin strap.

"Here. Let me help you with that." I brush her hair away from the snap. At my touch, she pulls her lips together, and freezes in place. Her only movement comes from her big, brown eyes, which intently watch my hands as I work to secure her strap. *Are her lips turning blue?*

"It's okay, you can breathe," I chuckle.

Her piercing, brown eyes narrow in on my gaze, as a slight blush of pink softens the tan of her cheeks. I can see I've embarrassed her by insinuating that I took her breath away.

"I would breathe, but I don't like the smell of wet dog."

Not bad. She's quick. With the pop of her dimple and the upward tug of her lip, I can tell she's hiding a smile under her snide remark. Her combination of spunky, wit and country charm have left me bemused. I have no comeback.

"I've gotta get back to my friends, no more time for arguing. You want to lead the way?" My voice rattles, as I slip my helmet back over my head.

"If you think you can keep up," she laughs, as she mounts her snowmobile.

"Oh, I can keep up," I smirk, climbing on and starting my engine. I take off, passing her, but then ease off the gas so she can catch up. We ride for what seems to be hours. No words are spoken. No gestures are shared. Though we ride together, we are alone in our thoughts. It's comforting really, knowing she's there beside me. I don't know this girl. I don't even know her name, but I feel a deep connection to her that I can't explain. I needed this time, and something tells me she did too.

As the sun sets off in the distance, we take off back over the hill. As we near the main entrance, I catch a glimpse of Jessie May. She sits just beyond the trees, waving to Tangles to join her. I guess it's time for us to part ways. She doesn't say goodbye. Our sudden split leaves me feeling a bit empty. I kind of enjoyed my silent riding partner. She must not have enjoyed the same peace I felt riding side by side, or she wouldn't have taken off without so much as a wave goodbye. I can't put a finger on it, but I feel like a tiny bit of me just left with her. A bit unsettled, I continue on toward my friends, who are waiting in the parking lot.

CHAPTER 14

HAPPY, HAPPY, HAPPY

"**D**ID YOU EVER THINK TO check your cell phone once? You had us worried sick," Brody huffs as he opens the truck door.

Crap. I didn't even think about ditching my friends. I was too caught up in the chase. I feel bad. I know if it was one of them that disappeared, I would've been frantic. I should've checked my phone, it's just that I've been trying so hard to forget for awhile. Every time I look at it, I'm disappointed all over again. Peyton hasn't texted. Not once. It kills me every time I see her name missing from the list of recent messages.

"It's a good thing we ran into Jessie May out by Whale-back. I'm glad she saw that buddy of hers tailing you, otherwise we wouldn't have had any idea where you went."

"So, you talked to the friend?" *Tangles was chasing me?* "Then you knew I was okay."

"Guess so. Well, at first we thought you were fine. But then, we ran into Jessie May and she couldn't find her friend either." I can tell he's agitated. His hands move uncharacteristically as he speaks. "Just don't go pulling anything like that on us again. You could've gone over a cliff or something, and we wouldn't have known where to find you."

Brody's not the only one who's upset. The others look worried too. "I'm sorry guys. I guess I just got caught up in the moment. It's been so long since I felt ... happy."

Jenna's grimace melts into a smile. Eyebrows raised, she looks around at the gang. "Okay, let him off the hook. It made him *happy.*" Everyone else continues to stare at me, scowling in silence.

Very persuasive, Jenna. Good try.

Finally, grinning through her closed teeth, she snarls, "Happy... Let. It. Be."

"Happy, okay, happy." I hear ringing out in different voices as we continue climbing into the truck. Brody jumps into the driver's seat, while Jenna and Mason pile on top of each other right beside him. Kaitlyn and I spread out in the back, making wisecracks about the sardine sandwich up front.

As we drive away into the darkness, I pull my phone out of my pocket. "So, you guys tried to call?"

Kaitlyn answers dramatically, "Only a thousand times. Check your messages."

There are so many notifications on my screen, that I can't see them all. Hesitantly, I open my messages.

> Sadie: Christmas Party @ my place if you're up for it. Day after tomorrow ~> 7:00. Wear your ugly sweater!!! ;)

> Coach: Let me know if you can still make B-Ball Tryouts (Dec. 13).

> Brody: Dude, you lost us.

Lennart: Hey, Pres. Got some great video footage of our Christmas foreign ex-change party. Where should I send it for the JHS newscast?

Brody: Where are you, man?

Kaitlyn: Caden? Where are you?

Mason: It's about 1:30. Try to meet us at the Long Loop by 3:00.

Kaiya: Movies in Mt. Shasta tonight. Wanna come with our group? Text ME!

Jenna: 3:30. We're looking for you. Kinda scaring us Cade Monster!!! >;(

Officer Marnia: We've recovered your truck. No Pistol, but interesting news on that front. Call me for details.

Brody: Ridiculous! Meet us in the parking lot.

Kaitlyn: You're such a brat, Caden! Call us. This isn't funny!

Shoot. Missed the movies with Kaiya. That was two days ago. Wow, I've been neglecting everyone. I don't even know where to start with this list. I should get back to some of these people. Where to begin? "I'm really sorry guys. I just wasn't thinking. It won't happen again." *Check four people off my list.* I skim back up to the top. *Sadie? Hmmm. What a sweetie. She must be working with Kaiya on trying to get me out of the house.* "Did you guys hear about Sadie's Christmas party?"

"Got the message like two days ago," Kaitlyn chimes in. "You should check your phone more often."

"It doesn't matter. I didn't really miss anything." *Still no Peyton.* "Just a reminder that I can't play basketball this year, and some student government stuff that can wait til the weekend's over."

The cab is silent. Even though I try to stifle it, I know everyone senses my depression. It's weighing heavily in the air, and I can feel the brains around me fumbling for ways to fix it. Jenna is the first to speak. "Hey, I have an idea. I was thinking since you can't play basketball, you might be able to join the snow sports team. I mean, I know you have to use your arms for balance and stuff, but you don't have to shoot or anything like you have to when you play basketball."

My mind searches through any possible obstacle as to why this wouldn't work. *Got one.* I clear my throat. "Problem. Snow sports already started."

"I know they've already started *practicing*, but they haven't *competed* yet. Besides, cross country kids get to start late. I bet they'll make an exception for you too." I take a minute to process the idea. My lack of response has the others jumping in to help convince me.

"It's Coach Rico for crying out loud. He's always looking for new talent."

"Remember, he already tried to steal you off the basketball team sophomore year?"

"I forgot about that. Our team sucked so bad that year that I seriously considered it." *This snowboarding thing's not a bad idea. Throw another patch on my jacket?* "You think they'd let me on Varsity?"

"Why wouldn't they, dude? You already kick everyone's ass on a snowboard anyway. They'll be stoked that you can't play basketball this year."

"Guess I can talk to the coach on Monday." I look back

down at my phone and remember there's a message about my truck.

"Have any of you heard from Officer Marnia?"

"Not me."

"Me neither."

The only one who doesn't speak up is Brody, whose eyes pierce through the rearview mirror. He glares me down, with a silent warning to discontinue the conversation.

Kaitlyn's squinting eyes meet ours in the mirror. "What's going on? Have you heard from her?"

Brody clicks his tongue and shakes his head. I watch him curse under his breath.

"She messaged, saying they haven't found Pistol, but they did recover my truck. She wants me to call for details."

I watch my sister's face drop, as she clutches the seat in front of her. She bows her head against the forward headrest. My eyes reconnect with Brody's. He looks pissed. He's kept her in such a protective bubble since the wreck, that her response to the latest update has him agitated.

"It's gonna be okay, babe. I swear. I'll take care of you. Are you okay, Pip?"

She turns her head and looks out the window. Clearing the foggy glass with her hand, she softly speaks, "I will be when they find him. I just can't help feeling like he's out there. Watching. Not all the time, but, here and there. Jenna and I have talked about this. She feels it too. Don't you, Jenna?" I watch my sister reach through the seat and tug on Jenna's shirt sleeve. "Right, Jenna? Didn't you say you feel like someone's been watching you?"

"It's probably just cuz I'm still freaked out about the river. I don't know who'd be watching *me*, but I could've sworn that last night when I was leaving Ty's house, I was being followed. They didn't peel off til I was almost home. I took a different route, just so they didn't know where my house was."

She shakes her head. "I know it's impossible. It can't be *him*. It wasn't even a truck. It was a sports car with tinted windows. It doesn't make much sense."

"Maybe I should call Officer Marnia back and see what she wanted to talk to me about."

"Call now. That way we *all* know what's going on." Kaitlyn looks at Brody through the rearview mirror as she speaks. "Brody, you can't keep everything from me. I know you want to protect me. I get it. But please don't. We're going back to school the day after tomorrow, and you can't sit next to me in every class. I need to know what I'm up against. We all do."

I take out my phone and dial. As it's ringing, I hit speakerphone.

"Officer Marnia here. How can I help you?"

"Hi Officer Marnia. It's Caden Woodley. I got your message."

"Yes, Caden. I'm glad you called. There are a couple things I want to talk to you about. First, we've recovered your truck from the river. Sorry to tell you, it's a total loss, but your insurance should cover it. If your company needs pictures or a report, give them my number. They won't be able to see it for themselves. We already turned it over to forensics down in Sac."

"What kind of stuff are they going to be looking for? I mean, we need answers. Especially these girls. They're really on pins and needles here, thinking someone's still after them."

"Well, I have more to tell you." There's a brief silence. Everyone leans in. "We found Pistol's truck. It was hidden from view, wedged in a crevice between a huge rock formation. It looks like it took a pretty good roll down the embankment. The cab was completely smashed."

Silent gasps fill the cab.

Jenna whispers over her shoulder, "Ask about Pistol. Was he in it?"

"And what about Pistol? Your text said you didn't find

him."

"Well, we didn't find him in the truck. It was empty. Eddie and his team have been all over the place. They did find some traces of blood around the same area they rescued you. It was scattered along some rocks near the river. It could've been yours, could've been one of your friends'. We're still trying to get an ID on that. Worst case scenario, if it was Pistol's," Officer Marnia takes a deep breath, "he may be on the run."

I throw my head back, "Shit. What are you trying to tell me here? You think he's alive?"

"Hold on. Take a deep breath. Judging by the looks of that truck, it's unlikely, but I don't want to rule anything out. There's a remote possibility he escaped before the truck went over the embankment."

More gasps.

"Until we have a body, we're treating this investigation like he's still out there."

"So, where do we go from here? I'm not going to lie, this is pretty disturbing news."

"I know it is, Caden, but I can assure you that we are doing everything we can to find Pistol. In the meantime, keep doing what you've been doing. Stick together and stay close to home. It's unlikely he'd go anywhere we could be waiting for him."

"So basically, we're safe at school and at home. Fun."

"For now, yes. Just remember, I really don't think he could've made it through that crash. His body was probably thrown from the truck before it lodged itself into the crevice. It's pretty rugged terrain. When the snow clears, we may have a better chance of finding a corpse. I'll let you know the minute I get any new information."

"Got it. Thanks again, Officer. I look forward to hearing from you."

Our call ends just as Brody pulls into my dad's store to drop off the snowmobiles. When he kills the engine, silence permeates the cab. Once again, we're all shaken. A tiny sniffle comes from my sister's direction. Brody throws open the truck door and comes around to the back seat. "I need to help her, dude. Go see your dad so I can get a minute here."

I nod in agreement and slide out of the truck, allowing Brody to take my place. Jenna and Mason jump out and begin to unload the gear.

When I get back to the truck, all our bags are unloaded. I don't see Jenna and Mason right away, but Brody and T are sitting on the tailgate. He's holding her in his lap, rocking her back and forth. They look like they could use a little more time.

Not wanting to interrupt, I scour the parking lot for the others. I spot them near the big oak tree out in the middle. They look to be in an intense conversation. Their heads are close together, huddled over a glowing phone. I don't want to scare them, so I stomp my boots as I approach.

"Shhh. Not another word about it." I hear Mason's raised voice.

"Everything okay here?" I ask, as I walk up on my friends.

"Everything is just fine," Mason replies, looking sternly at Jenna. "Girl problems. That's all. Nothin' you need to worry about."

Something tells me there's more to it than just girl problems, but I've had enough for one day. *I don't even want to know.* "I'll take your word for it. Let's go."

We join the others back at Brody's truck. We all look at each other, secretly assessing one another's mental state. Smiles start cracking. Then a few giggles.

Mason looks at all of us. "We need to have some fun. Take our minds off this mess."

I look down at my phone, remembering all of our options. "So who's up for an ugly sweater Christmas party?"

Jenna's face brightens. "I'm in! I'll call Ty."

"Me too!" Kaitlyn grabs Brody's hand, smiling. He nods

in agreement.

"Sounds good to me." Mason jumps in. "I might be a little late. I'll probably have to sneak Marissa out again."

"Well, dig out the sweaters, boys and girls. We've got two hours to get home and make our sweaters shine!"

CHAPTER 15

BEST LAID PLANS

"**L**OOKS LIKE IT'S JUST YOU and me," Jenna links her arm through mine as we walk up to the front porch at Sadie's party.

"Well, we're not really alone," I say, pointing my thumb over my shoulder at Kaitlyn and Brody. "And Mason and Marissa should be here any minute."

"Yeah, I guess. I'm just bummed I couldn't convince Ty to come, especially cuz he's been after me for not spending enough time with him lately."

"He's been giving you a hard time?"

"He thinks I'm a little too consumed with watching out for my best friends."

"I'm sorry. You know you don't have to babysit me."

"I know I don't *have to* babysit you. I want to," she laughs.

I stop walking long enough to stun her with my pouty face. I watch her expression change when she realizes that I don't want her to feel obligated to take care of me. I especially don't want to come between her and her boyfriend.

"I'm just messing with you." She pulls on my arm to tug me forward. "Truth is, I feel safer when we're all together. We're on the same page. *On guard.* You know?"

"Yeah, I know." I feel my muscles tighten just thinking about how long we've been exposed since we left the safety of our car. A half dozen different scenarios have entered my mind about how Pistol could come jumping out of the bushes, swing down from the overhang, drive by with a gun, or ...

"I'm glad someone gets it," she pulls me in tighter and lays her head on my shoulder as we continue walking toward the house.

"Look, bottom line is we need *each other* right now. We've gone through some messed up stuff that not a lot of people are going to understand. It can't be easy for Ty to see us spending so much time together. You've just got to reassure him that he's your man. I'm just your best guy friend, someone you shared a horrible tragedy with. If I can do anything to help define our friendship, I will. Give him some time. Once they find Pistol, we can go back to our old lives, and you can spend every waking second with the guy."

"Just not tonight," her face drops. "Well, he can't say I didn't try."

"Guess we both failed tonight."

"What do you mean, *we* failed?"

"Peyton."

"You tried to get her to come?"

"I tried, but she won't even answer my texts or phone calls. *Damn it!* It's been a couple weeks since we went to her house. I figured she might be ready to see me by now."

"She's never responded?"

"No." *I wish she'd at least throw me a bone. Anything.* My throat constricts just thinking about it. "Pretty sure she's done with me." *God, I miss her.* The words, *"I don't want you ei-ther,"* begin hissing through my mind. Peyton's cutting remark is masked with the vision of red eyes and bandages. *No, I take that back. I miss the old her.*

"Okay, let's make a deal." I look over my shoulder to pull Kaitlyn and Brody in for a pep talk. "We're going to forget about Peyton, Pistol, the investigation, and everything else for one night. Let's go have some fun."

"Sounds like a plan."

The four of us pound fists and continue to the door. At least our conversation up the walkway has distracted me from my apprehension, if even for a few minutes. I seriously worried about coming out to this party tonight. Not only for our safety, but small town gossip can be rough, and I'm not sure how ready I am to face some of the people spreading it. I haven't seen anyone since the accident.

They probably think it was all my fault since I was driving. I think back to the chapel at the hospital. *Have those girls poisoned the high school against me? Do they blame me for what's going on with Peyton? I wonder if they've seen or heard from her. Do they even know what's going on? Maybe she's talked to them. They might know more about her condition than I do. Ah hell, I really shouldn't be here.* I turn to Jenna, "You know, this could be uncomfortable, right?"

"Tell them they can all kiss your ass. Nobody knows what really happened down river. If they give you any crap, come find me. I'll set 'em straight."

"She's right. We've got your back. We're all in this together," Brody says as he holds open the door.

When we step into the entryway, I take note of a few small groups scattered about downstairs. It's the usual party crowd, not too many surprises. Everyone seems to be engaged in deep conversation. *Nice, maybe they won't notice we're here til I get a feel for what's going through their heads.* No sooner does the thought cross my mind, than a cold breeze blows through, forcing the door to shut with a thud.

An abrupt silence fills the room. It's probably my imagination, but it sounds like the music has also come to a stop. A few eyes drift up and lock on mine. I can't help but feel a little defensive. I have no idea what these people have been saying about us. I scan the onlookers with a look of forewarning. *Go ahead, just try to start something.* After what feels like a solid minute, the eyes begin to drop away. The time warp slowly begins to re-seal itself. Motion in the room picks up, and the volume of the music begins to increase.

Snapping me from my garbled state, I hear a knock behind me. I gently nudge my group away from the door to allow more guests to enter. A group of jocks push past us, pulling liquor bottles from their jackets. They raise them in the air and roar, "Let's get this party started!" I recognize them as football players from South County. Behind them, another group of big hair and loud voices barrels through the door.

We let the herd clear our path to the kitchen, where we stop in our small circle. I take a moment to adjust to my surroundings. I want to see how many of my friends are here. I need to know what I'm up against. Looking back toward the living room, I take note of a short, pudgy girl standing next to a tall, skinny one. Scowling, they look us up and down a little, examining our group. I watch the shorter one lean in and whisper to her friend. Her eyeballs bounce back and forth between my sister and the tall skinny one. My face heats up instantly. I don't like the way they're looking at her. *They're talking about my sister.*

I make eye contact with the short, pudgy one, the one who strongly resembles Grumpy Cat. With a fierce death glare, I mouth, "Stay the hell away from her." She catches on to my warning quickly. I watch her pale face blush red, as she instantly snaps her head away from me. The incident lets me know that we are standing in the spotlight. We are definitely being judged by some of the partiers here. I've lived in this small town long enough to know how it works. One wrong move, and it's social suicide. I nearly killed one of the most popular girls at our school. That clearly falls under the "wrong move" category. I need to get used to the scrutiny, but right now I feel an intense need to protect my friends from the pain of judgement.

Shake it off, Woodley, I convince myself as I pull my group deeper into the kitchen. Over by the island, the herd of jocks has joined up with some of my teammates. They work to organize a grocery aisle's worth of bottles that were just smuggled in beneath letterman jackets and ugly Christmas sweaters. Behind them, I notice Tiara lying on the kitchen table with a lime in her mouth. Darryl is slurping tequila from her belly. "Hey, Woodley," Moose hollers from the corner. "Come take a body shot. Tiara's waiting for you."

He walks toward me on his way to grab another bottle of tequila. Pulling me into him, he whispers in my ear, "Trust me. The more you drink, the better she looks. You might want to give it a shot." He reaches around me and grabs a bottle, untwisting the lid. "Seriously, forget about her face. It's not what matters," he chuckles and burps from his obvious overindulgence.

"I heard that," Jenna looks toward me. I know that even if Tiara looked like Miss Teen Jefferson, that Jenna would still find her hideous. Beauty is only skin deep, and her stunt at the hospital chapel proved it. "There's not enough alcohol on Earth to make *that* look remotely appealing," she growls under her breath. "Is there, Caden?"

"Nope." I shake my head, continuing to watch the show.

I hesitate, as I watch the pack of jocks slurping from Tiara's body. It looks like they're going to devour her. The number of offensive linemen licking and sucking away at her has nearly tripled, when she calls out to her friends for backup. "Chelsea, CJ, which one of you wants to come help me out?" she giggles. "You've never felt anything like this." She yelps like a fox, "Ack-ack-ack-ackawoooo-ack-ack-ack, that tickles!"

CJ shoves Chelsea out of the way. "I'm in!" She throws

herself onto the table, raising her shirt.

"Oh, please," Jenna chokes. "This is gross."

They don't seem to think so. As a matter of fact, they look like they're enjoying the hell out of this. I find myself mesmerized by the squirming girls beneath the slathering tongues. My teammates are all over their bodies like lamprey on trout. I cringe. *Ugh. Not for me.*

"You coming, Woodley?"

I'm no double dipper. No way in hell I'm touching that. I've got standards. I raise my hand and cock my head. "Looks like you ladies men have it covered."

My thoughts of slimy spit swapping are interrupted when a whistle comes from above. "Psst. Caden, Brody, up here!" It's Sadie and Kaiya. *Phew, saved by the hostesses.* They're up in the loft, peeking over the rail. Sadie holds her finger up to her lips, as Kaiya motions us up. Poking her head through the rail, Sadie whispers, "Shhh, pool table's up here. Grab your sister and Jenna, and come play with us."

I turn to the girls, signaling them to look up to the loft. "You guys in?"

"Yeah, I'm done watching *Linemen Gone Wild.*"

"Let's go, but keep an eye out for my cousin. He should be here with Marissa soon."

Sadie meets us at the bottom of the stairs. "Don't tell anyone we're up here. We're keeping this place a secret."

The lighting dims as we approach the top.

"Welcome to the VIP lounge," she grins.

Looking around to check out the dark room, I feel like I've just walked into a first class establishment. There are a few simple strings of baby white lights, providing just enough glow for the disco ball to reflect. I notice a few of the elite crew, kicking back on the leather couches. "Wow, Sadie, you've really outdone yourself up here." I grab a jalapeño popper and stick it in my mouth.

"Well, I wanted someplace where my special guests could lay low. I know how tough it can be. Remember when my dad got in trouble? It was so awful I didn't feel like leaving the house for a year."

Without thinking, I shove another jalapeño popper in my mouth. *Poor Sadie.* I remember how she was ostracized when her dad got kicked off the police force for unlawfully firing his weapon. He thought his crazed attacker had a gun. Turns out it was just a magic wand prop he'd stolen from the local theater. He was waving it wildly, threatening the officer. When he lunged forward, the officer's reflex was to shoot. It was a mess, and Sadie took a lot of crap for her dad's mistake. My eyes begin to water.

"Oh, we're okay now. My dad's in a way better job because of it. You know what they say, 'When God closes a door, he opens a window'." Sadie stops and looks around the room, raising her hand to the lights, "And this, it was no big deal, really. You guys have been through a lot. I just thought you might want someplace to kick it that's a little more private. Not so many gawkers, you know."

I have to laugh. "I'm touched, really, but that's not why my eyes are watering. This thing is *hot.*"

Sadie laughs, "Veronica's jalapeño poppers. Here, let me get you a soda. Unless, you want a beer?"

"I'm good with a soda. Thanks."

"Well, there's an open couch. Make yourselves comfortable and watch the show downstairs. That's what I've been doing. When you're ready, the pool table's right over there." She looks back over the railing and laughs, "Man, some of these guys are going to regret this tomorrow."

We grab some food and sit down on the couch to watch the so called *show* unfolding before us. With the unobstructed view from the loft, the couch is in a great position to watch the party downstairs. I have a full view of the front door, and I can see into the living room to my left and the kitchen to my right. With all of the holiday escapades playing out downstairs, I soon realize this is better than television.

I look down into the living room to see Benny sitting on the La-Z-Boy with one girl on each knee. He's wearing a red stocking cap, imitating Santa. When he looks up toward the loft, our eyes meet. He belly laughs, "Ho ho ho. I thought Santa was the one who was supposed to bring the gifts." He lifts his eyebrows, and looks down, drawing my attention to Cindy's ugly Christmas sweater. Each of her breasts is covered in a shiny box. He lifts the lid and grabs inside shouting, "Surprise! Ho ho ho."

"Get a load of Benny!"

We all start laughing, watching him alternate between lifting Cindy's lids and twisting the flashing, red noses so conveniently placed on Charity's Rudolph and Frosty appliqués. I quickly break my fixed stare, when I hear approaching footsteps on the stairs. I curse myself for my jumpiness, but I'm hyper aware of my surroundings these days. I'm relieved to see it's a couple of the exchange students. Nobody that's going to give us a hard time. However, they do look a little lost.

"Can we help you?" Sadie asks the French guy.

"Ve are just looking for ze bazzroom."

"Oh, there's one just down the hall there," she points back behind the pool table.

He nods his head before bending over the top of Jenna, who's sitting on the edge of the couch. "Could you hold zis for me, please? It's really good. I haven't touched it yet, so you can drink some if you'd like."

He hands her a bottle. "Go ahead. I'll be right back. Try it."

As the guys walk off to the bathroom, Jenna opens the lid

of the unmarked bottle, sniffing the contents. "Smells like Kahlua."

Kaitlyn leans over to Jenna. "You're not drinking that, right?"

"Not on your life."

We have a conversation about the dangers of taking drinks from people at parties. I'm sure the Kahlua is fine, but I'm in protective mode these days, and I'm not letting my friends take any chances on anything. "You know I wouldn't let you drink that even if you wanted to."

"No worries there, cuz I don't," Jenna snarls playfully.

Brody leans into Kaitlyn. "You feeling okay about everything?"

"Yeah, so far so good."

"How about you, Jenna? You having fun?"

"Well, this is kind of awkward," she holds up the bottle. "But yeah, it's not too bad."

"I'm glad we came out tonight. It will make things a little easier before we head back to school on Monday."

Our conversation ends when the French guy comes back from the bathroom. He kneels down beside Jenna. "Did you try it? It's really good."

Jenna shakes her head *no*, and hands it back to him.

"Try zome. I inzeest," he whines, shaking the bottle under her nose. "Go on. Try it!"

This guy's a real gnat. I look at him, "Dude, she said, *no*. Back off."

I sense disappointment as I watch him slowly stand and turn away. Looking back over his shoulder, he grumbles, "Maybe later, huh?"

Kaiya pops up behind us, draping her arms over the back of the couch. "Is it just me, or is that guy a little strange?"

"Daemon? He swam with us this year," Jenna explains. "He's not too bad ... maybe a little socially awkward. It's probably a cultural thing. I think he's just trying a little too hard to make friends."

"Well, his accent is weird," she pauses. "I don't know, maybe I'm wrong. I don't know that many French guys."

"Hey, look!" Kaitlyn cries. "It's Mason and Marissa!"

I look down to see Brody's cousin escorting Marissa through the front door.

"I'll try to get his attention." Brody stands up and moves toward the loft railing.

"Sit down, you're blocking the show," Jenna commands, pulling back on Brody's pant leg. "Mason just caught view of the body shots, and I want to see the look on his face when he watches this for the first time."

"Fine," Brody sits back down on the couch.

My eyes are focused on Mason and Marissa standing in front of the doorway, when I notice something out of the corner of my eye. Movement. Slowly, but steadily, I watch a red stocking cap with blond curls move toward the couple. I know that gait. It's all too familiar. My stomach flips when I catch view of her profile. *Button nose. Ivory skin. Perfect pink lips. Sweet giggle.* The bandages peeking out beneath the Santa hat confirm my suspicions. *It's Peyton.*

Instantly, my heart pangs and all the blood in my body rushes to my head, causing me to jump in my seat. My breath hitches. *I can't believe she's here.* I feel a hand slide over mine. "Are you going to be okay?" It's Jenna. She's gripping my hand like a vise. She's noticed Peyton too. "You see her, don't you?"

"How can I not? She just attached herself to the back of Mason. What in the hell is she doing?"

Peyton has slung her arm over Mason's shoulder, her leg just peeking out around his. It looks like she's beginning to wrap herself around him from behind. Marissa stares forward, wide-eyed, clearly annoyed by the wedge that's just been driven between her and Mason. I watch Peyton's lips move, but I can't hear or tell what she's saying. She slowly raises her thumb over her shoulder, pointing to the kitchen. When Mason nods, she turns away and walks off.

"I guess she's giving them some space?" Jenna's drawn out statement comes out like a question.

In my periphery, I can see my friends' heads whip back and forth between Peyton, Mason, and me. It sickens me to form the third angle of a triangle. *Not that they even know that I'm sitting up here watching. Why is he letting her touch him? Why is she draped over his back? What's going on?* No one speaks. None of us know what to say. That's when I see Peyton move in over Mason's shoulder and whisper in his ear. My friends' banter has my head spinning.

"What's she doing?"

"I don't know."

"I'm so confused."

"You should get down there, Caden." Jenna commands. "Go let her know you're here. If she's well enough to be at a party, she might be ready to talk to you."

I feel my cheeks begin to heat. I'm mortified and embarrassed. *My friends are watching this happen. Hell, I'm watching this happen.* I have no interest in going down there right now. I want to see what she's doing with my friend. I watch as she drags him over to the wall. She leans against it, and spins him around to face her. His back is to me now, so I can't tell what's going on. Every few seconds, he shakes his head back and forth. Mason looks tense.

"What's going on now?"

"I don't know, but whatever it is, he doesn't seem to be agreeing to it," Brody assures.

I watch my girlfriend's hand, slide up over Mason's shoulder. His reaction looks uncomfortable. The back of his head twists from left to right, as though he's searching for a way to get out of this. *He must be trying to find Marissa.* She doesn't seem to be worried. I've spotted her over in the kitchen, taking up the table right next to Tiara and Chelsea. Apparently, so has Mason.

"I'm so proud of you, Marissa!" Tiara calls out. "I didn't think you would do something like this!"

That's got Mason's attention. He jerks his head around toward the kitchen, bobbing wildly as though he's trying to find Marissa. He subtly squirms out from under Peyton, setting his hand back down on her shoulder after he finally breaks free. I can see he's saying something, but I can't tell what. He looks back over toward the kitchen and begins to walk toward the table.

It's so quick I don't even see it coming. Peyton grabs Mason's sweater. "Wait!" Her yelp is so loud, I can actually hear it. I watch her point above her head. My eyes follow the direction of her finger. Mistletoe. *No.* I stand up and dart toward the stairs. I've got to stop this. She's making a fool of herself. She's making a fool of me. *Is she drunk? How can she do this to me?* I'm too late. By the time I get to the bottom of the stairs, she's already got Mason in a full lip lock. He's got both of his hands pressing against her shoulders.

I stand in shock watching my girlfriend make out with another guy. Not just another guy, but one of my good friends. I turn to Brody, who's clearly just as surprised as I am at his cousin. "Are you watching this?"

He squeezes my shoulder. "I'll take care of it. You can see he's not into this, right?"

"Looks pretty mutual to me," I choke, flabbergasted by the shocking episode unfolding before me. "What makes you think he's not into this?"

"He's clearly pushing her away."

"Well, he sure is taking his sweet ass time. I thought he wrestled animals. Isn't he stronger than that?"

"He's just trying to be gentle with her. She's still recovering from brain surgery."

"I don't get it. Is there something going on with those two that I don't know about? Have you been keeping this from me?"

"Look, he was there too. He has a lot of compassion for what she went through. He's the one who brought her back, you know."

"So I've heard. More than once, she's made sure to let me know it wasn't *me* who saved her."

Brody grabs my arm, "I'm sorry, Caden. For everything." Then letting me go, his voice melts into the distance. "I've gotta go help my cousin."

Help him? Screw that. I'm taking care of this myself. I follow behind Brody, swooping in on the scene, just as Mason pries her lips from his. He jumps, startled, when he sees me standing there.

He lifts his hands, "Sorry, man. I don't know what to say. I … I gotta go check on Marissa. She's going to kick my ass."

I feel the blood coursing through my veins, but I can't punch the dude. Not now. "Good luck," I growl, turning to my girlfriend. "Peyton, we need to talk."

She looks away from me, focusing her eyes on the ground. "What did you see?"

"Everything."

"Don't freak out. It was only a *thank you* kiss … for saving me. There was mistletoe, so it's okay."

"Seriously, do you really think so? I've tried to talk to you for weeks. You've been avoiding me like the plague. And now you think it's okay to go kissing on my friend? How could you? I haven't even kissed you yet. Not since the accident."

"You're right," she says, softly. "That wasn't fair to you." Then slowly, she raises her eyes to meet mine. When our eyes lock, she coughs out, "Oh God!" I watch her face contort as she covers her mouth and runs through the front door.

What just happened? I feel like I've been hit by a Taser.

My nerves are shaky and weak. I stand frozen in place, unable to comprehend Peyton's sudden disappearance. She was just here, standing next to me, and then poof. One look at me, and she disappears.

I'm surprised Mason is still behind me when I hear him say, "I'll go find her."

"Don't you think you've done enough? What are you trying to do, steal my girl?"

"Oh, God no. I've got Marissa. I'm just trying to help you out, man."

"You know, if you really want to help out, you'll stay away from her."

Mason lifts his hands in the air and backs away. "You've got it." He turns and walks off into the kitchen, leaving me to deal with the aftermath of the Mason-Peyton mistletoe make-out.

What the hell am I going to do to fix this? I run for the front door, searching the snowy street for any sign of her. I follow a set of fresh footprints out to the road. Scanning up and down the street, I scream her name. There's no answer. No sign of her anywhere. She's gone.

CHAPTER 16

WELCOME BACK

I FEEL ALL EYES ON me as I make my way to English class. "Welcome back, dude," Tyler smiles as he brushes past, suddenly stopping and turning around. "Hey, I heard you might want to join the snow sports team. We have a meeting at lunch today."

"Yeah, I've been thinking about it. You think Coach will still let me? It's a little late, isn't it?"

"Drought, man." He chomps his gum. "We got a late start, so I'm sure he'll be okay with it. You've only missed like two practices on the mountain. The rest was just running and ultimate frisbee and stuff."

"Sounds good. I'll be there."

I slip inside of Mrs. George's English class. She is that highly respected teacher who has a spitfire personality and just enough kindness that she can get away with a triple workload. All the students think she's pretty kick-ass. Not to mention, she's my mom's and Cinda's colleague, so she's known me just about all my life. Even though I hate reading and writing, this is one of my favorite classes. Mostly because Mrs. G gives me a lot of free rein. She understands my need for learning breaks and trusts that I'll get my work done, even if I don't finish it in class. Sometimes that means a trip to the vending machine and other times it means running downtown to Miner Perk for her coffee.

Needless to say, she puts me at ease almost instantly when she comes over with her endearing grin. "Caden, we've missed you so much. I talked to your mom about missing the week of school after Thanksgiving, and I know you kids have been stressing over it." That's just like Mrs. G. The first words out of her mouth are to take the pressure off. "I know you've been through a lot, and I don't want you kids to worry about all of your missing assignments. I excused most of them in the gradebook. I do, however, want you to start getting caught up. Here's a copy of the book we're reading. I think you'll like it." I look down at *The Way Around* and skim the synopsis. *I guess a guy might like this.*

"Uh, looks good. How far are you guys?"

"We're taking it slow, only five chapters a night. We should be done this week, and then we'll start our research project on our heritage."

My face drops. *Five chapters a night? Holy hell. Guess I'll get T's and Jenna's Cliff Notes version. They'll read it for me and fill me in.*

"You okay, kid? Like I said, I don't expect you to catch up right away," concern laces her voice.

"Yeah, this just, uh, reminded me that I have five other classes I missed. I hope my other teachers are as understanding."

"Well, pace yourself. We all talked during collaboration. Because of senior projects, we decided to lighten the load before Christmas break. Most of your work will come from English and Econ. Let me know how things are going. I can always extend your deadline if needed." She starts to walk away, when she turns around and comes back to my desk. "How about this? I'll make your assignment due the day before Christmas vacation. That gives you an extra week and a half." *Crap. Christmas vacation starts like two days before Christmas. With all this work, I'd better make a list for gifts. Guess it's online shopping for me this year.*

I shoot Mrs. G a thumbs up and mumble like Eeyore, "Sounds great."

Not wanting to waste any time, I pull out my phone and get on Amazon. I begin scrolling through images of electronics, car accessories, sports gear … "What are you doing?" It's Jenna. She's tardy, but finally here.

"Trying to shop for gifts, since I won't have any time outside of class." I hold up my book. "Did you get yours?"

"Mrs. George handed it to me on the way into the room. She said you'd fill me in."

"I don't know much. She just said we've got to read this book and do some kind of project *before* break."

"Oh, that must be what Daemon was talking about."

"Daemon? The French dude?"

"Yeah, that's why I'm late. He stopped me on his way to weightlifting class." Jenna rolls her eyes. "It was probably just some lame excuse to show me his muscles. He kept flexing while he talked." I watch her shake with heebie-jeebies. "Anyway, he just asked if I wanted to work on some heritage project with him."

"Hmm. Kinda weird. It didn't sound like it was a group project to me."

"Yeah, I don't know. He told me he wanted to meet me at my place." Jenna stops talking. I watch her face twist up like a pretzel. "Ewww. Do you think he was hitting on me?"

"Maybe. He seemed a little bit pushy with the Kahlua at the party. I suppose it could be his way of getting a girl."

"I have a boyfriend. Crap. I was there without Ty. Maybe

he thinks I'm single. I'd better start hanging out with my boy-friend a little more."

"Good idea." I continue to scroll through the pictures on my phone, tuning out everything around me. After several minutes, I zero in on a little voice pecking away at the back of my neck.

"Are you listening to me? You'd better put that away. Mrs. G will take it and put it in her June box."

"No, she won't."

"Yeah, she will."

"No. She loves me. Plus, you're going to cover for me. Unless you don't want a Christmas present this year."

"Well, in that case, I'll take an Amazon gift card. There's a new book I want called *When Fall Breaks*. I heard it sounds like our high school."

"One click, baby. Done." *Check Jenna off my list. That was easy.* "What about Peyton? I want to give her something mean-ingful."

"Oh, Caden. You've got to stop chasing her, especially after what happened at the party. I mean, she ran outside and puked at the sight of you."

I can still picture Peyton covering her mouth as she ran to the door.

"I really don't want to make you lose hope here, but the signs are pretty clear. She never came back. Please tell me you're not still trying with her."

My mind flashes back to the night before the Christmas tree hunt. Out under the stars, next to the fire. We were entan-gled. *Our souls were literally snuggling.* Everyone kept joking with us that they couldn't tell where one of us ended and the other one began. *They nicknamed us Cayton for crying out loud.*

"Cayton."

"What?"

"Cayton. I was just remembering when you guys nicknamed us Cayton. We were inseparable. It was like we were one person." I take a minute to reflect. I see Peyton on my lap by the fire. I feel the warmth of her arms wrapped around me. The comfortable curve of her body pressed against me. The rush of butterflies from that damn perfume she always wears. My mind jumps from image to image, in such a rush that I can't take it all in. My memory shifts to the bridge. We stand kissing under the gently, falling snow. The heat flows between us, warming our bodies. Peyton giggles as the flakes melt against our cheeks and noses. The contrast of the freezing snowflakes falling against our burning skin has exhilarating flames jumping through my body. I'm alive. More images. Football games. Homecoming dance. Birthday party.

"Nope." I shake my head in denial. "Jenna, I don't think it was me. We were attached at the hip. I can't make her sick. I'm sure she was just overstimulated. It was probably the first time she's been out of the house. I know she still loves me. I just have to help her remember it."

"Ok. I guess you could be right." Her words are slow and drawn out. *She doesn't sound overly convinced.* "It's just with brain surgery and everything else ..." the silence leaves me questioning her feelings, "I don't know."

"You don't know?"

"Well, I've been thinking, maybe something went wrong. Maybe they made a bad cut or something. She just doesn't act like *Peyton* anymore."

"She will. I'm gonna get her back. I just have to come up with a plan. Right now, that involves finding her the perfect Christmas gift. I have it all planned out. I'm going to recreate my favorite memory with her. There's gonna be a fire, s'mores, and I'm going to have our song playing on my iPhone. My only problem is, I haven't thought of the gift."

Jenna's face is all screwed up as she listens to my plan. She giggles silently and shakes her head, as she turns back to the front of the room. I hadn't even noticed that class has been in full swing for some time. Mrs. G hasn't said a word. *Proof that she loves me.* I glance back over to Jenna just as she whips her head back around to me. "Hey Loverboy, got an idea! Why don't you try something from one of those personalization stores? They have stuff that's meaningful. Plus, you can put her name on it."

"Good idea. I'll check it out," I whisper quickly when I notice Mrs. George's eyes coming down on me. Her eyes are warning me to pay attention. I drop my phone into my lap and look up. *I'd better at least listen for a minute.*

"I know we're only halfway through, but we're going to have a great research project to go with this story. I want you all to be thinking about your own family. Where you came from. How did you get to be where you are at this very moment? For some of you, whose families keep a family tree, this could be easy. For others of you, not so much. Start asking questions at home to see what you can find out. Learn a little about your family background. You'll be surprised what you might uncover."

Yes! I've got this. Thanks to my mom and my super awesome aunt, I know exactly where I came from. Ireland ... well, mixed with a sprinkle of Portugal and a few other Celtic nations. More Christmas shopping for me. I look back down at my phone, when I realize this isn't going to be so easy on Jenna. *What's she going to do? She was adopted from Russia. How's she going to do this project?*

My eyes meet Jenna's, "Are you okay with this? How are you going to do this project?"

"Same way you are. Work my tail off to figure it out. This is a family tree, not a genetic tree."

I'm so wrapped up in my conversation with Jenna that I don't hear the lunch bell ring. Everyone begins to stand and move out the door.

"Hey, if you need some help getting started on the project, I can skip the snow sports meeting. I kind of want to look for

Peyton anyway. She wasn't in first period, and I didn't see her at her locker this morning."

"No way. I'm fine. You are going to be on that team. I have a feeling it's gonna be the best thing you'll do for yourself this winter. I'll keep an eye out and let you know if I see Peyton. Now get to that meeting."

I step outside and spot everyone standing in the middle of the quad. "I'm on the team! I just can't compete without a note from my doctor."

Brody, Kaitlyn, and Jenna seem genuinely happy for me. "That's great! Do you think you'll be released soon?"

"Oh yeah. It's feeling good." I rotate my arm and stretch it out. "Ever since I got to lose the sling, I can feel the life coming back into this puppy. I'll probably have to miss the first race, but I'll be good to go for the next one."

"So happy for you, man." Brody slaps my back.

I'm totally uninterested in small talk. My mind has been on one thing all day, and I need to get it taken care of. "So have there been any Peyton sightings today?" I look around at my friends' faces. I watch their perky smiles drop to sullen grimaces. *T looks at the ground. She never does that unless she's hiding something.*

"Out with it, Sis. What's up?"

Hesitantly she mutters, "I've got a little bad news."

"Yes?"

"Well, during my TA period, I was running notes around for the office. They handed me a stack to put into the teachers' mailboxes. Normally, I wouldn't do this, but I saw Peyton's name, so I looked."

"Looked at what, Kaitlyn? Out with it."

"Well, they were unenrollment slips. I had one for each of her teachers."

Silence.

"She left school, Caden. Peyton doesn't go here anymore."

CHAPTER 17

MAY THE FORCE BE WITH YOU

"RISE AND SHINE, CADEN! IT'S race day."

I glance up at the large, red numbers on the clock next to my bed. "It's 6:30 on a Saturday, Mom. I don't get to race anyway. Can't I just skip this one?" I turn over and bury my face in the pillow, remembering how humiliated I am that I have to go up to the mountain as a helper and not a racer.

"Race or not, you need to get down to that bus. You made a commitment, and you're not going to keep them waiting."

I close my eyes, and before I know it the big red numbers are a distant memory. *I'm standing behind the starting gate. The buzzer goes off. Why can't I move? Why can't I move? I'm stuck. This is so embarrassing. DQ'd on the first race? What the hell?*

"Caden. Now! You're going to be late."

I pry my eyelids open and look back at the clock. 6:32. "Ugh." I untwist myself from my flannel sheets and jump down to the floor with a thud. I feel like a fork twisted up with spaghetti. "Coming, geez." I kick the covers furiously as I start toward the door, all the while whining at my mom. *She's got to be the most annoying alarm clock ever invented.* She doesn't even give me the nine minute snooze time afforded by most standard clocks.

"Step on it. You need to be down there in ten minutes. Here's a piece of toast."

I gag when I look at the dry piece of crispy french bread. I can't stomach the thought of eating first thing in the morning. "You know I don't eat breakfast."

"Shove it in there. I'm not letting you leave this house without *something* in your stomach." She's being excessively pushy today, but looking down at my watch, it's a good thing she is. I'm about ready to miss the bus.

Within ten minutes, I'm showered, have my gear together, and we're headed out the door. "Are you sure you don't just want to take my car?"

I fumble for an excuse. "Nope. I heard someone's been breaking into cars near the school. No use letting a perfectly good car sit in a parking lot all day just waiting to be vandalized." *There. That sounded reasonable, and it's true.* Even Jenna discovered she had a missing flash drive the other day. She swore she left it on the front seat of her car with her research project. *The crap high schoolers steal.*

My mom's eyes squeeze together as though she's questioning my sincerity, then sarcastically she mumbles, "It's nice to know I've raised such a thoughtful son." I'm sure she thinks I'm just being lazy, but she smiles and plays along, closing the door behind us.

It's a quick ride down the street. My mom leans over the seat trying to lay a wet, sloppy kiss on my cheek. I pull away, shoving my face into the icy window. "Gross. Your students are probably watching through the windows." One of the perks of being a teacher's kid is that you generally face embarrassment exponentially more than any of your classmates.

"You know I'm just messing with you. I know you're too grown up for mommy's goodbye kisses. Have fun today, honey. It's good you're not racing. You can see how everything works so you're ready for next time."

I roll my eyes and turn my head for a cheek to cheek goodbye. I know she was just trying to start my day out with a good laugh, so I humor her. "Yeah, thanks, Mom. It should be great." I don't let on how bitter I am that I don't actually get to race this week. The doctor said he would release me for the next competition, but this race, I'm there to play flag boy. *Lame.*

When my mom pulls up to the big gym, everyone's already loaded onto the bus. It's a little tricky carrying my gear with one arm, but I manage to get my bag and board over to the driver who loads it for me. Coach Rico steps aside so I can get up the stairs, "Hey Woodley, glad to see you made it. We almost left without you." He stops, looks around the bus, and then back at me. "Good luck finding a seat in there. Slim pickins' if you ask me," he laughs. "Hop on in."

I walk down the aisle looking at everyone, crammed in with their bags, blankets, and pillows. There's an open seat next to Tessa. *Hmm. Not enough room there, too many books.* Next open seat is Quenton. He stretches his leg across the seat and looks at me with his don't-even-think-about-it glare. *Moving along then.* About three quarters of the way back, I see a seat next to one of our exchange students. *This one will be good.* "Hey, Lennart, mind if I sit next to you?"

"Yeah, sure. Let me just move my camera."

"Cool, is that a GoPro?" *Yes ... More great footage for senior video.*

"Yeah, I just bought it. I was hoping we could get some good shots up on the mountain."

"Sounds cool." I say, squishing into the seat next to him. "You sure you don't mind if I sit here? It's a little tight."

"To be honest, I was hoping someone would sit next to me,

so that guy wouldn't." He tilts his head toward the front of the bus, just as the French guy is walking through the door.

I'm confused. "I thought you were buddies. Don't all exchange students hang out together?"

"Not all of us. Daemon's in a different program. He kind of does his own thing."

"Dang, I was hoping you could tell me if he likes my friend, Jenna. He seems to have a thing for her lately."

"The cute, aggressive blonde on the basketball team?"

I guess other guys would see her as cute. And definitely aggressive. I have to smile when I picture her barreling across the court, stealing the ball from another guard, and going in for a layup. "That would be her."

"Sorry. No clue." Lennart shakes his head and looks back up toward the front of the bus. Daemon makes his way down the aisle searching for a seat. When he finally spots one next to Lily, he plunks down across the aisle, one seat up. Lennart watches him sit down and take out a jar of peanut butter. He covers his nose as he turns toward me. "I don't know how people can eat that stuff. Thanks for sitting here."

I chuckle, "Any time."

It's a quiet hour long ride to the snow park. Most of my teammates have slept the entire way. Well, except for the AP kids, who did their homework by the light of their cell phones. "Make sure you have your bibs on and you're ready to go," I hear Coach's voice boom to the back of the bus. Everyone begins shuffling around, stacking blankets, and closing books. I glance up to see Daemon fumbling with his phone. I catch a glimpse of his background picture. It looks like a swimmer. It's oddly distorted. *Much too puffy to be any of our swimmers.* I look again, noticing it's been enlarged. *Oh I get it, he's so socially awkward that nobody will let him get near enough for a closeup.* I accidentally laugh out loud.

"What's so funny?" Lennart wears a smirk as he quizzes

me.

I look down and put my finger to my lips. "Shh. I'm trying to get a better view of something."

I strain to look back over his shoulder. *No way.* I squint to make sure I'm seeing who I think I'm seeing. And there it is, blown up large enough to cover the screen, a picture of Jenna cheering behind the diving block. *What do you know? He does have a crush on her. I'm going to have fun with this one.*

"Grab your stuff, and take a run. We'll be slipping the course when y'all get back down to the lift."

My attention snaps back to the front of the bus where our coach is giving instructions. *I wonder what he wants me to do while they warm up?* I need to have a chat with him. I walk up beside him, waiting for him to give a few of the skiers directions. "Hey Woodley, if you're up for it, you can take an easy run and feel it out. No tricky stuff. No black diamonds. I'm going to need you for the race next week."

Schwank! He's actually letting me strap in?!? A flood of excitement runs over me. I'll actually get a chance to show some of these people that I wasn't put on the team for my good looks. "You've got it, Coach. I'll stay off of Coyote for today. Nothin' but easy stuff."

"Right. I don't want to have to answer to your mother if I get you hurt out there. Meet us back here in about twenty. I'll be using you for flagging today."

As I'm grabbing my stuff from the bus, Tyler comes up beside me. "You want to take a run with me?"

I'm a little embarrassed that I'm not allowed on Coyote. Typically, that part of the mountain is no big deal, but it does have the most advanced runs in the park. "Well, I'm not sure you want to waste your time with me. Coach Rico told me to take it easy." I lift my arm, reminding him that I still haven't been released to compete. "I have to stay on Douglas."

"No worries. It's not about speed right now." A devious

grin spreads across his face, "It's more about *skill*. I spied some hotties from the Mount Shasta team over there." He points toward the direction of the lift, where a group of four snow angels are stretching on skis. "See what I mean? We're not going up to snowboard, we're going up to see who's under those kick ass racing suits."

I shrug my shoulders, "I can handle that."

"You sure?"

"Let's go Double 007." *This could be fun.* I'm up for a little detective work, even if it is just to help out my buddy.

As we make our way to the lift, I watch two of the four Lady Bears standing with their backs to the oncoming lift chair.

"Hurry, dude. Let's not get too far behind them," Tyler prods. He bounces around like a puppy waiting for a bone. He really seems to be excited about the view up here. I can't blame him. It's always nice to see fresh faces when you've been surrounded by the same small litter since kindergarten.

I nod my head and focus on the girls getting onto the lift. There are so many racers swarming this hill that I need to study their suits and helmets so I don't lose track of them. The two blonds hop on first. *Goodbye tight, shiny, blue suits.* Next up is the ginger in red and black, accompanied by a curly-haired brunette. Good thing for colorful suits and ponytails, or I wouldn't be able to tell the difference between these four girls. They're all tiny, little things, with similar frames, and those race helmets make it damn near impossible to tell who's behind them.

My eyes are drawn to the yellow and black suit. The one that the brunette is wearing. *Good taste, Curlicue. Sleek. Sharp. Just like a yellow jacket. Wonder how many people she's gonna sting out on that course today.*

I'm almost knocked off my board when the chair swings around and hits me at the back of my knees. *That came around quick.* I pull my stare away from the girls and look at Tyler.

"Do you think we'll find them up there?" He flips his goggles, visibly squinting to get a better look.

"How can you miss them? They look like Christmas ornaments. Just look for the shiny, blue and red. I'm going for the yellow and black. We've got this."

"So, you get one and I get three? Doesn't sound quite fair," Tyler laughs. "Are you sure you're okay with this?" he asks incredulously.

"Something tells me the one I'm looking at is enough."

"If you insist. Are you sure you don't want to take one more? I feel like the odds are in my favor, here."

I think about it for a minute. There's something about that suit and those curls that make the other three girls blur into the background. Her spunky glow definitely sets her apart from the rest. *She'll be the most fun to chase. Not that I'd do anything once I caught her. Just an entertaining fishing expedition. Catch and release.*

The lift hitches, as a beginner unloads a few seats up. We progress forward quickly. I scoot forward in the seat, lift my board, and prepare to get off. I'm eager to start tracking the girls, and I know it's the most fun I'll have on the mountain today.

I point as the yellow and black streak flies down the hill. "I'll put my money on the yellow jacket. That chick can move."

"Good luck catching her," Tyler laughs as he jumps off the lift. "She's already halfway down the mountain." He points his pole at the little black and yellow dot entering a diverging path.

I want to catch her, but I've got to be careful. *If I wreck, I'm screwed. I have to snowboard smarter, not harder.* I make up my mind to take a little riskier, but shorter path. *As long as I can control my board, I'll be fine.* "I know a shortcut. Veer left past this sign," I direct Tyler.

"Got it."

We fly down the first part of the run, tuck through some trees, and hop over a baby jump. I slow before I hit it, just to make sure I don't lose my balance and risk re-injuring my arm. I cut across the terrain park and plop down at the end of the run. I know that sitting smack dab in the middle is pretty much the rudest thing I could do, but I'm going for the win.

"That was quick. Are you sure you want to sit there, though?" Tyler looks a little nervous as skiers and boarders alike swish past us like speeding cars on a freeway. "We should probably move off to the side."

"And destroy my game? Not on your life." I pat the ground beside me. "Here. Have a seat."

"This is one of the busiest runs on Douglas. Someone's going to plow right into us."

I duck as I feel the wind of another passing racer. Then chuckling, I respond, "I'll take my chances."

No sooner does Tyler sit down beside me, than a sheet of snow pelts the back of my head. The force knocks me forward. I shiver as the powder seeps its way down the back of my neck, and into my jacket.

"Hey loser, move off the run. You're going to kill somebody!" The feisty words come flying from behind me.

That strong, feminine voice. It sounds familiar, but I can't place it.

I twist back and forth, trying to turn my head enough that I can see who it is. It's not working. Clearly, she's standing in my blindspot.

"Just taking a break. Didn't mean to get you all worked up, sweetie." Then coughing into my glove I add, "Good skiers know how to turn."

"Well, *good* skiers, don't sit down in the middle of a run." She pauses for a moment, as I feel her energy getting closer. "Oh, excuse me. I see you're a boarder. That explains a lot."

I'm surprised when I see the tight yellow and black suit slowly pass where I'm sitting. *It's her.* She doesn't turn around, but her leisurely speed tells me that she's up to something.

"If you want to sit around all day, you should go down to the lodge." She pauses. "You know, come to think of it, I hear they have free babysitting down there. It frees up the mountain for all of us big kids who actually like to ski." *So there's the little fireball that just pummeled me with snow.*

"Well, get a load of you." I study the pint sized princess in front of me. "You're not so big, yourself. Actually, I was thinking you look a little like Yoda." I chuckle. *Who is this shrimpy know-it-all, hiding behind all that black and yellow?*

Watching her slow to a stop and bend over in front of me, piques my curiosity. I'm intrigued as she drops her poles, and digs around on the ground like a kid in a sandbox. She *is one odd character. What is she doing?* In one swift streak, I watch as she spins toward me. Before I can comprehend the movement, I'm blinded by white powder. A huge snowball makes a thud, as it splatters against my goggles, completely blocking my vision. "Eat my snowball, you big, hairy wookiee!"

I love how she's so wittily turned *Star Wars* into *Snowball Wars*. But forget about all that. *I know that voice. Who is that girl?*

By the time I wipe all the snow from my goggles, and get them defogged, the girl is nowhere in sight. *Another disappearing act. Damn her.*

"That was rough." Tyler laughs. "How are my odds looking now?"

I can't help but laugh and sock Tyler in the shoulder. "No one said this game is over. I've still got a few tricks up my sleeve."

"Well, while you figure out your next move, I'd better get down to the team for warm ups. Coach Rico will pull me from the race if I'm late. I'm sure he'll go easy on you though, especially if I tell him you just got your ass beat by a little girl."

I shake my head, as we stand up, "She's not just a little girl. She's like a Jedi Master. And at least I got her attention. I didn't see any of your shiny, little suits coming after you at all."

"The day's still young, Woodley. Let's go."

Surprisingly, we're not too late getting back to the team area. Most of the racers are in position, and the rest of us are hanging out ready to assist where needed. I've never done this before, so I have absolutely no idea what I'm doing. Thankfully, I get a little one-on-one tutoring session. "I'm going to walk you up to your spot so you can see where you're flagging." Coach guides me up the hill. "It's giant slalom today, so if they miss a gate or go out of bounds, you know what to do, right?"

"Got it covered." I feel like such an idiot for not being able to compete. I'm the only guy not wearing numbers, and I stand out like a sore thumb.

"Skiers are up first. I know you're still learning, so I'm going to pair you with Tyler til boarders are up. That okay with you?"

"Sounds good. I appreciate the help." I fake a smile. *This is lame.* I can't help but feel humiliated by my newbie status. I'm used to being a starter, not a rookie. *I wonder how my basketball team is doing today.* This coddling stuff is hard to get used to.

A voice rattles over Coach's radio. "Okay, sounds like they're ready to roll up at the start. Here you go."

The announcer comes over the speaker, announcing the first skier. The radio's sound is muffled, but I can make out that it's a Mammoth skier. *She'll probably kick butt.* Not thirty seconds after I hear the buzzer, swishing skis fly by me. *Looking good.*

A couple minutes later. I hear the swishing again, and the hitting of gates. "Shiny, blue ... one of my ladies," Tyler raises his eyebrows and subtly waves as she flies past.

"Looked a little shaky on the turn. Seemed like she caught a bit of an edge." I mutter to Tyler.

Skier number three comes down. Again, when she nears our gate, she bobbles a bit, but catches her balance.

I hear chatter on the walkie talkies. "Looks like the girls are having a bit of trouble around Gate 13."

I survey the ground to see if there's anything noticeable that may be causing the trouble. "Looks okay to me," I say to Tyler, just as skier four runs over the top of the gate, and tumbles down the hill. I grab her skis and take them to her. I hate that I'm laughing, but it's this nervous thing I have.

"Not funny, jerk."

"Sorry," I hand her the skis. "I wasn't laughing at you. I swear."

"Whatever." She clips into her bindings and finishes her run.

I stand by and listen to several more minutes of swishing of skis and slapping of gates, before I spot her. The yellow jacket.

She flies around the gates, effortlessly. *She's got to be going at least 50 mph. Nice cross-blocking. This girl can ski.* And she's pouring it on, in and out, weaving beautifully, until ... she isn't. In that unexpected moment, time seems to stand still. I watch her ski clip the gate in front of me. Silently, I wish her a smooth recovery, but it just doesn't happen. Arms flailing, skis quivering, body squirming, I watch as her wide, brown eyes ... SLAM right into me!

I'm down on the ground, lying flat on my back, gasping for breath, wheezing, desperate to pull in air. I feel like I was just run over by a three hundred pound lineman. *Am I at football practice? What just happened?* My chest feels crushed. *My arm. My God, is my arm still there?* I try to reach around to feel for my arm, but I can't get to it. There's something in the way. Something on top of me. I open my eyes to get a look at my barrier, and find an unexpected surprise weighing me down.

There, looking down at me are big, round, twinkling, brown eyes. *Hold up. I've seen these eyes before*. I squint harder, trying to make out the face above mine. Curly, brown hair. Flawless, mocha skin. Suited up in yellow and black. Yellow jacket … NO… Bumblebee. With the recognition of her face, I feel the electricity spike through my fingertips. *Hell no. She skis for Mount Shasta?* My cheeks burn with heat, and an uncontrollable grin overtakes my lips. "Tangles?" I laugh out.

"What the hell are you talking about? Tangles? Get your arm off of me!" She looks around, patting at the ground. "Where are my skis? Where's my other pole?"

"Calm down a second. There's no rush. I'm pretty sure you're already DQ'd after that wreck."

"You don't need to rub it in." She pushes against my chest.

"Take it easy. Take it easy," I wince, still trying to catch my breath.

"Oh, sorry. Are you okay? I didn't mean to hurt you." She rolls to the side, trying to take some of her weight off of me. "I'm just pissed. I've been trying to beat Kenzie for three years, and I almost had it this time."

"It's all good, Tangles," I grunt. "Glad I could attend your yard sale," I half chuckle, half cough.

My laugh dies off with her taunting glare. Then gradually, the crinkling around her eyes begins to soften. She's looking at me strangely. It reminds me of that stupid movie my sister loves. The one with that Channing guy. Something about a wedding or something. She was in a coma and couldn't remember she was married to him. Then it dawns on me. *She doesn't remember who I am.* "You don't recognize me, do you?"

She leans in closer, squinting. "Oh yeaaaaaah, you're the jackass from the middle of the run who almost tripped me earlier. You seem to get in the way a lot." I watch the tiniest smirk play at the corners of her mouth. She turns her head away from me and pinches her lips to one side. I know she's hoping to hide her grin. *I made her smile. She must not hate me too much.*

"Oh, we've met before. Trust me, you'll remember, Tangles."

"I thought it was *Yoda*. Who the hell is Tangles? You must have me confused with someone else. I've never seen you before in my life." She pushes off my chest and kneels off to the side of me.

"Are you just going to lay there all day?" She looks down at me lifting her eyebrows, and pinching her lips. "Never mind. Don't answer that. I've already seen that you can't board."

"How do you know what I can and can't do?"

She pokes me in the chest. "Well, first, you sit in the middle of runs, so you're either an idiot, or you don't know what you're doing. Second, if you were good enough to board, you'd be wearing numbers, not holding a flag. Oh well, your coach has you in the right place."

"What do you mean by that?"

"You're good for softening a landing. You know, kind of like the Pillsbury Doughboy."

I know I haven't hit the gym since the accident, but, wow. "Harsh."

"I'm just playing." She pokes me in the tummy. "You're supposed to laugh, now. Haven't you seen the commercials?"

I look at her, silently. I refuse to play into her hurtful joke.

"The Pillsbury Doughboy thing, it was my way of apologizing." Tangles stands up, leaving me lying on the ground. She gathers her skis and snaps into her bindings. She faces the course, looking down at me over her shoulder. "By the way, it's not quite as soft as it looks … your tummy. Must've just been that jacket." She giggles as she begins to push away from me. "And for future reference, it's Avery, not Tangles."

Future reference, huh? I crack a smile. As she heads back down the hill, I can't help but shout out, "Later, Tangles!"

CHAPTER 18

THE GIFT EXCHANGE

AFTER WAITING FOR A WEEK, I run back up the long, icy driveway with a small box in my hand. "It's here!"

"What's here?" My sister looks away from her homework, long enough to see what has me so excited.

"Peyton's gift. Want to drive me over to give it to her?"

She stops writing and looks at me convincingly. "Caden, sooner or later, you're going to have to get back out on that road."

"I've driven."

"Really? What? And snowmobiles don't count. Dad has an extra truck, you know. You can't keep relying on all of us to get you around. Besides, I thought you wanted to do this whole s'more thing with a campfire and music. That sounds like it would be better done in private. You don't want an audience, do you?"

I think back on my elaborate plan with the right music and setting, and decide I just can't wait that long. "Changed my mind. I don't think she's ready for all that, and what about my arm? It's really hard to drive like this." I whine. "Can't you just take me and drop me off? You don't have to wait around or anything." She still doesn't look convinced. "Look, there's no better time than right now. Christmas is in seven days, and we're spending the whole week helping Dad's store get ready for the holiday parade and Night of Lights. I need to get it to her. Please." I work my puppy dog eyes and lift my arm one more time, reminding her that I can't do this alone.

Kaitlyn takes a deep breath and releases it in a huff. "Your arm? Sooner or later you're going to have to stop using that excuse. Your sling has been off for over a week, and the doctor released you to snowboard, yesterday. You can do this on your own. You don't need me."

I don't want to let on that the thought of driving a vehicle on the road makes me nauseous. If I never have to drive in the winter again, it will be too soon. Whenever I think about it, I can feel the tires sliding out from under me. The crunching. The rolling. I'm dizzy all over again.

"Are you okay? You look a little pale."

"I'm fine, T. I just need a ride, that's all."

Kaitlyn kneels down and looks me in the eyes. "You're my twin. I've known how to read the looks on your face longer than you have. I can see the way those two lines in your forehead are crunched together. I can see that little vein in your neck pumping in and out. And you know what? You're pinching your lips together like you're about ready to lose your breakfast. I know that look on you, brother. And that look right there … that look tells me you are *not* okay. You may be able to hide it from the rest of the world, but you can't hide it from me. You're scared to drive, aren't you?"

I really don't want to answer that. I stall by pulling my hands around my neck and cocking my head back toward the ceiling. *Crap. She's onto me.* My body is betraying me. I can feel the little vein she was talking about, pulsing under my hand. Even worse, the sweat is beginning to make its way through my fingers. Surely, that's going to give me away. I look back at my sister and try to explain.

"I don't know what's wrong with me. Since I got out of the hospital, the terror hasn't let up. I don't even have to close my eyes anymore to be thrown right back into the accident. I see it as clear as day. I feel every tug and roll of my truck. It's a never ending nightmare. It won't go away. It's worse when I'm in the car. I can't do it, T. I can't get behind the wheel on these roads. Please just take me. I have this really cool gift. I just want to get it to her. That's all."

I inspect my sister's face. She's deep in thought. I use my twin superpower to will her out of it. *Don't overthink it, T. Come on. Leave it alone.* I watch the look of intensity grow. *It's not working.* I've got to stop the wheels turning in that head of hers before her overthinking turns to concern. "I'm good, T. I'm good. Just one last time. I'll get back on the road after this. Besides, my gift is breakable and I want to hold it on my lap so it doesn't shatter."

"I guess this one time. But I'm worried about you. I know it's going to take some time to get through this, but it's been weeks." She pauses and runs her fingers through her hair, tugging her head back when she reaches the nape of her neck. I can tell she's thinking when she stares up at the ceiling and lets out a sigh. "Look, we're all alive. We're all moving around, breathing, feeling … We were given a second chance." She releases her hair and looks back at me. "We've been blessed. We can't waste this opportunity. You were made to do big things, Caden. The proof is that you're still alive. There *must* be a reason God saved you. Saved us. He's not going to rescue you, just to let you get in another car wreck. Don't be afraid. Get back out there and live again."

I have to admit, my sister makes sense. I mean the odds

that I would survive that crash are slim to none. I must have something left to do, and there's no way I can do that something without driving. *Okay!* I feel like I've been given a new lease on life. Lips pressed together, I bob my head up and down quickly. *I'm pumped. I'm ready. I can do this ... just not today.*

"I can see you're *almost* ready. How about this? I'll let you off the hook. I'll take you to Peyton's, but next time, *you* drive. Deal?"

Relief washes over me. "Deal."

I peek into the Christmas bag, where Peyton's present is nestled in between layers of candy cane tissue paper. It's beautiful. A perfect snow globe encasing a wooden footbridge, surrounded by an alpine forest. Atop the bridge are two tiny figurines embracing. The base of the globe holds a music box that plays *All I Want for Christmas Is You.* I've had it engraved to match our carving on Mule Bridge. Inside a heart it reads, *Caden Loves Peyton.*

I couldn't have chosen a more perfect gift. When I shake it, it reminds me of our night on the bridge and our time by the campfire. The night we became "Cayton." As we near her house, I pull the bag into my chest. I'm anxious to give this to her. It's my last effort to make her remember how much we love each other. How much we belong together. I can't wait to see the look on her face when she sees our most treasured place. When she relives our memory captured in glass, there's no way she's not going to feel something. *This is how I'm going to get her back. I know it.*

"Wait here?"

"Yep. I'll be here, Monster Man. Go get her back."

I'm a bit shaky as I walk up the sidewalk, back to that big, wooden door. It's been a while. I try not to think of the last time I was here. Things look a bit different now. There are several packages out by the garbage can. *Probably boxes from Christmas gifts.* My eyes trace the empty boxes to a mess of papers, surrounding the garbage. *Guess the neighbors left their dog out last night.* I ignore the mess and face forward. I'm on a mission. I'm going to get my sweet girl back.

I plaster a smile on my face as I ring the doorbell. *Here Comes Santa Claus* chimes out on the other side of the door. *Wow, the Carter's have gone all out this year to spread Christmas cheer.* A beautiful ribbon embellished wreath covers the stained glass window. Fluffy, green garland with scattered baby white lights adorns the railing. Daintily lit reindeer are scattered about the lawn. *After all she's been through, her parents must be working hard to make this an extra special Christmas for Peyton.*

As I look back down into the bag, I hear footsteps approaching on the other side of the door. I step back slightly when I hear it begin to creak open. When I look up, my eyes meet Mrs. Carter's. "Oh, hello, Caden. I … I wasn't expecting you today." Poor Mrs. Carter. She looks like she's been through a lot over the last few weeks. She looks tired. Worn.

I hold up the gift. "Yeah, uh, I just wanted to bring Peyton her Christmas gift. Is she home?"

She looks at me, and then at the bag. I can tell she's debating on whether to invite me in. "Yeah. She's home. Come on in, and I'll see if I can get her to come out." *Yes. Off the blocked list! That's a good sign.*

"Is she still having a hard time?"

"Some days are better than others. We'll see if this is one of those days. Come on in, son."

I step through the door to the smell of gingerbread. As I wait for Mrs. Carter to come back for me, I notice the Carter's tree. It's fake. I can't smell the scent of needles. It's not the one we cut for her in the forest. *That's odd. We picked the biggest, fullest one, special for her.*

When she returns from her room, Mrs. Carter notices me looking at the tree.

"Was the tree we got at the Forks damaged? I'm sorry we didn't do a better job of taking care of it." *I know that Brody said he delivered the Carter's tree. We made sure to put them all in my dad's truck.*

"Oh, uh no, Caden. Peyton's having a bit of a struggle with the smell of evergreens this year. We opted for the artificial one when we figured out that it was making her sick. I turned the tree you kids got into that beautiful wreath on the door. I just couldn't see letting it go to waste."

"I see. I'm sorry. But I'm glad you could use it." *That's the strangest thing I've ever heard. Everyone loves the smell of Christmas trees.* "So can I see her now?"

"She's in her room. She agreed to let you go in. I think she has something she wants to give you too."

I take a deep breath and walk down the hall. *When I get to her room, her door is open. This is a good sign.* "Peyton."

"Hey. I've been thinking about you." She's sitting on the bed, but she doesn't look up. "I'm sorry about the other night at the party. I feel kinda bad about the way I left things."

"Don't worry about it, babe." *What a relief. She's actually being nice this time.* "I brought you something. It's a Christmas present."

"Caden ..."

"Yeah?"

"Don't ... okay. You didn't have to get me anything."

I can't help but wondering why she hasn't gotten up to greet me. I want to see her face. I miss her so much. *Why isn't she looking at me?*

"I wanted to. It's the least I could do. I can't wait til you see it."

I watch her fiddle around with a cardboard box sitting next to her. "You might want to wait to give me that. I have something to give you first."

"Okay." My mind is spinning, wondering what on earth Peyton is going to give me. Slowly she stands, grabbing onto the cardboard box. My mind flashes back to the collage of pictures she gave me for my birthday. It was wrapped so beautifully. The card. The paper. The bow. Everything was coordinated. *Hmm, it's not like Peyton to leave a gift unwrapped. She's still not looking at me.*

In the thirty seconds it takes her to walk across the room, the heavy silence has my mind working overtime. *Does looking up still make her dizzy? Is she nervous about what's in the box? Maybe it's something that will spill or break if she's not careful. I hope it's not a puppy. I can't take care of any animals right now. No, she wouldn't keep something that big from me. Wait ... is she keeping something from me? Her face looks a little guilty. Did she do something she regrets? Maybe she did mess around with Mason at the party. Why won't she look at me?*

When she's finally standing within an arm's distance, she raises the box toward me. Looking down at the ground, she speaks, "Here you go." I set her gift on the nightstand next to me so I can take the package. I wonder if I should look in it now, or wait until Christmas.

"Should I open it?"

"Sure. It's your stuff."

My stuff? When I untuck the flaps and look inside, my blood stops cold. I'm frozen in fear of what the contents mean. *What the hell? Why is she giving this stuff back to me?* It's full of all the gifts I've given her ... souvenirs we've collected while we were dating.

I look down at the teddy bear I won her at the harvest festival, the ticket stubs to the homecoming dance, my football jersey, and some dried flowers from the bouquets I bought her when I was still trying to win her over. "What does this mean, Peyton? Are you trying to get me to remember our time together? You don't have to give this back to me. I still remember it all. Every last thing. It's sweet of you to remind me, but you can put the stuff back now." I'm pretty sure I know what this means, but I'm trying my damnedest to pretend I don't. I work to control my shaking voice as I set the box on her bed.

She's silent as I look at the top of her head. "Look at me, babe. Please." *Why the hell won't she look at me?*

"I can't, Caden. I'm sorry."

"What does this box mean, Peyton?"

"It means that I want you to have your stuff back. It doesn't belong here anymore."

"Oh no, no, no, no, no. It belongs here all right. That box is you and me. I gave it to you. Every single thing in that box is a little piece of me that belongs to you. You need to keep it." Silence. *She's not just getting rid of that box. She's getting rid of me.* "You need to keep *me*."

"I can't." She pauses, closing her eyes and shaking her head thoughtfully. "I just … can't."

What can I do? Shit. What can I do? "Here. Here. I have something for you. Take it." I grab the gift from the nightstand. "I bought this for you. It's really special. You'll love it. It will help you remember. You love me, Peyton. I love you. Here. Go ahead. Open it."

I watch the change in her expression as it turns from sympathy to anger. "I'm trying to be nice about this, Caden." She begins speaking through gritted teeth. "Just take your box. I can't take that gift. I'm giving your things *back* to you. Let it go. Let *me* go!"

"Why are you doing this to me? Won't you please just take the gift?" *If she won't open it, I will. I'll just put it under that stubborn face of hers and make her remember. As soon as she sees it, everything we had will come back.* Without further thought, I pull the snow globe from the bag. When she hears the paper rattle, she shuts her eyes tightly. I hold it just inches from her face. *There's no way she'll be able to deny what we have when she sees this.* "Open your eyes, Peyton. Open them, now!" I growl.

"I can't look at this stuff! I can't. Don't you get it?" she snarls back.

"No, I don't! I don't get why you're getting rid of our stuff. Why are you throwing us away like this? Open your damn eyes, Peyton!"

"Do you really want me to open my eyes? Cuz you won't like what happens if I do!"

"Yes, I want you to open your *beautiful* eyes. I want you to see what I got for you. I want you to remember what we had together."

"Fine," she huffs. She opens her eyes, and looks down at the ball that rests in the palm of my hand. She studies the scene I've had captured in glass. Her breathing deepens as she begins to shake her head wildly. I brace myself for whatever it is she's about to say.

"You Son of a Bitch!" Her volume increases until her voice begins to fly out in flames. "You just couldn't leave it alone. You had to force me to look back at that place. You feel like it's your job to make me remember, don't you? DON'T YOU?!?!"

"I'm sorry. I don't know what I did. Look at it, Peyton. It's us. It's the bridge. Read it." My voice becomes shaky, and I feel the first warm tear slip from the corner of my eye. "What's wrong? What is it?"

"What's wrong? What the hell is wrong? *You* are what's wrong! I can't look at you. I can't look at any of this! It all makes me *sick*! Didn't you notice? I can't even be in the same room as you without throwing up? Get out! Get out, now!"

"Peyton, please. I love you. I can't make you sick." By

now, the tears won't stop. *I can't leave. I won't leave. I will stand my ground until she loves me back.*

Peyton growls some of her last angry words through her gritted teeth. "I said get out! Now!" In a flash, I watch the beautiful glass ball being snatched from my hand, just before it flies from hers, and hits the wall with a crash. Shimmery water, gently runs down the wall, leaving a glittery stained path in its wake.

I look down at the snowflakes and broken couple lying on the ground next to the wall. They've been separated from the splintered bridge that's resting under her bed. Shards of glass lace the carpet, near the doorway. "Now take your stuff and get out!" She screams one last time. I'm frozen in place. I don't know what just happened. She picks up my box and throws it through her bedroom door, just missing my head.

I look down at the scattered contents, laying in the hallway. "You don't want to do this. You really don't," I sniffle.

"Oh yeah?" Peyton lunges for a shard of glass, swiftly grabbing it from the ground and gripping it tightly like a knife.

I've never seen her like this. The way she's holding that glass looks like she's about ready to strike. *Would she really slash me?* I picture it all in slow motion. As she begins moving toward me, I put my hand up to shield my face. *She's gone crazy. I can't leave her mother alone in the house with her.* "I'm not leaving you, while you're acting like this."

"Want a bet?"

I'm not quick enough to get out of the way. When she springs forward unexpectedly, I feel the tear of the dagger come down on my hand and make its way clean through to my elbow. Fire runs across my ripped flesh.

"Peyton, stop!" I hear Mrs. Carter scream from behind me. "Caden, go. Get out now! She won't hurt me. It's you that she has a problem with."

Holding my slashed arm, I back my way through the doorway. I grab my jersey off the floor to wrap around the wound.

Down on the ground, working on my injury, I can hear Mrs. Carter trying to calm her. "See, Peyton. This is why we're taking you down to that specialist. They said they can help with this."

"Mom, I tried." She wails. "He wouldn't leave! He doesn't get that he makes me sick. Everything about that day makes me sick! They keep shoving it in my face. They're smothering me."

"I know it feels that way, honey. They're just trying to help you, the only way they know how. We'll get you through this. You'll be in the city. Away from the trees. Away from the mountains. Away from your friends. Your auntie will take good care of you."

"Friends?" Peyton screams. "They're not my friends! They were *her* friends. And look what they did to her. I don't even know who that girl is anymore. They killed her! The old Peyton is dead, Mom. *Dead*!"

I look back through the doorway to watch the scene unfolding before me. Mrs. Carter has her arms around Peyton. She's swaying with her back and forth, back and forth, stroking her hair as she calms her. "Shhh. It'll be alright. You're alive, sweetie. Everything's going to be okay. You never have to see them again. Caden's leaving now."

As she rocks her, Mrs. Carter looks back over her shoulder and pleads with me. "Caden, please go. Take your stuff. It's the only way to help her. We need to get everything about that day out of her sight. I know you love her. If you want to help her get better, you'll do this for me. For her. Take your stuff. It's over. You have to move on." I bob my head up and down, knowing there's nothing else I can do. "I'm so sorry about your arm. Do you need me to call someone to take you to the hospital?"

"No, my sister's waiting for me outside. It's just a scratch. I'll be fine." I know damn well, it's not just a scratch. I can feel the blood seeping through the jersey I've wrapped around the gushing wound. I've caused enough damage, and I don't want to add any more trauma to this volatile situation. I try to man up and suck my threatening tears back in my eyes. "Before I go, could you just answer one thing?"

"I can try."

"You said she needs a specialist. *What's* wrong with her?"

"Post-traumatic stress. It's the worst case Dr. Curtis has ever seen. We're sending her to a specialist down in Palm Springs. She needs the change of scenery."

My heart sinks. *Peyton is leaving.* "When will she be back?"

"I'm not sure if she will."

"So we're really done?"

"I'm afraid so. It's time for you to move on, son. It's what's best for her. The counseling is not working. This is our last hope to get her better. None of us like the idea of sending her away. But you see her. She's dangerous. She's got to go."

I have nothing left to say. I bow my head, swallow the big lump in my throat, and gather my box of belongings.

I walk the box to the garbage, where I see the rest of the trash strewn around the ground. When I dump it next to the big green trash can, I'm able to see up close, all the papers I noticed scattered about earlier. One holds our grins, another our eyes. Piece by piece, I recollect every moment, all of them, now shredded on the ground before me. That's when I realize, *Peyton is gone for good.*

CHAPTER 19

DRIVING ME CRAZY

I STRUGGLE TO OPEN MY puffy eyes when I hear the vibration of the phone on my nightstand. My head is pounding as I struggle to read the small white number and missed call message. *Looks like Jenna's trying to get ahold of me.* I glance at the big red numbers on the clock. 8:50. *At least she let me sleep. If that's what you can call it.* As I try to block out yet another nightmare of crazy, shard-brandishing Peyton, clawing at the back of my mind, a text comes through.

> Jenna: T told me about what happened with Peyton the other day. You okay? :/

> Me: Guess so. Feeling a little sleep deprived lately. My arm is still pulsing where she slashed me.

> Jenna: There's no excuse for attacking you. PTSD? Are you sure she's not just crazy?

Me: Go easy. We both know the old Peyton would never do that. This one's been through a lot.

Jenna: Don't tell me you're defending her. I hope you're done with her after this.

Me: It *is* my fault. But yeah, we're DONE! I haven't talked to her for a week. It's time to let the relationship balloon go. O~ I'm a free man, Jenna. Free.

Jenna: Would it be inappropriate to celebrate your new status?

Me: Totally appropriate. You have an idea?

Jenna: Take me with you to that charity event you always go to. Ty's got family over, and I want to help out. Plus I want to put something positive out into the world ... and maybe help distract you from your fatal attraction.

Me: Honestly, I think the attraction's gone. The last few times I saw her, she scared the crap out of me. I'm really done this time. She's not the same Peyton anyway.

Jenna: That scary, huh?

Me: You have no idea. Feeling lucky to be alive. Change of subject please.

Jenna: Yeah, let's go back to tonight. You want to take me, or not? I'm begging you. I need a break from this project. It's driving me crazy.

Me: You're still working on your report? I thought it was due before break.

Jenna: Well, since I was having such a hard time with it, Mrs. George extended my deadline. She told me I could turn it in after break. Minor setback though. My report was on that missing flash drive.

Me: Crap. What are you going to do?

Jenna: Well, Daemon's helping me catch up. He heard me telling Mrs. G that it's missing and offered to help.

Me: Daemon, the French dude? Do you think that's a good idea? You know he's crushing on you. You're not sending him the wrong signals, are you?

Jenna: He knows I'm all about Ty.

Me: I hope you're right.

Jenna: So about Night of Lights?

Me: The Dash to the North Pole starts at 4:00. Can you pick me up by 1:00? We need to get down there early so we can sign up and get our list of tasks before the parade starts.

Jenna: Oh, I see how it is. I'm driving again?

Me: Just one more time. My arm is throbbing ;)!

Jenna: Better idea. Let's hitch a ride with your parents. My car is not good in the snow, and my weather app says Mt. Shasta is in for a big one tonight.

Me: Sounds good. I'll let my parents know they have two hitchhikers.

Jenna: It's a date.

Me: See you then.

We pull into Mt. Shasta a little after 2:00. The street is bustling with people getting ready for the Christmas parade kickoff. Floats block the road, while horses jump around nervously from all the commotion. Santa hats bob along as people make their way to any opening to view the parade. "Son, there's no parking on Mt. Shasta Boulevard. I've got to be at my checkpoint for Dash to the North Pole. The logging truck will be pulling in any minute. Take my keys and go park in front of the store."

I have to drive? With all these people. Hell no. "Seriously? I have to sign Jenna and me up for the Dash. Not to mention, you want us to walk all the way back up here in the snow and ice?"

"I'll sign you kids up. Being a sponsor does have its perks. Plus, you don't have to walk. There are trucks and sleigh rides leaving the parking lot every twenty minutes."

"But Dad, they have carolers on them."

He smirks. "It's not going to hurt you to listen to a little Christmas music. It's either clydesdales and carolers or hoofing it three blocks. Take your pick."

I can tell I'm not going to win this one. He holds the keys out in front of me. I grab them from his hooked finger. "I'll be back."

As soon as my dad slides out of the truck, I turn to Jenna, "Here."

"Here?"

"You've got to drive," I quickly mutter, shoving the keys into her hand. I can't handle the thought of driving these streets. *Why does it have to be so crowded?* I don't want to hit anyone. I'm not in the right frame of mind to be driving. Sweat begins to pool around my hairline.

"Seriously? You really don't want to drive your dad's truck? I thought you lived to drive this rig."

"I'm not feeling so good. It's my arm." I hope I sound convincing. I'm already having panic attacks from all the cars and people. It's a swarming ant hill around here.

"Well, if you don't want to, I have no problem taking her for a little spin."

"Thanks."

Jenna discreetly slides over my lap, switching me places. I'm so thankful that she's the badass that she is. What other girl would take on the challenge of driving a truck this size in these crazy conditions?

Cautiously, she pulls away from the crowd, crosses the railroad tracks, and heads down to the store. The crowding somewhat subsides until we get into the parking lot where everyone is gathering to start the parade. I scan the crowd, looking for an open space, when my sister's eyes meet mine. She's next to Brody, sitting on the flatbed of a caroling truck. Her eyes track us until we've parked and stepped away from the truck. *Why does she look so unhappy? Crap. She sees Jenna driving. I'm toast.*

I swallow the lump in my throat as I take the keys from Jenna and lock the truck. *How am I going to explain this to T? I'm just going to pretend I didn't see her watching me. I won't bring it up if she doesn't.* "We'd better get over to the caroling truck before it takes off without us."

The caroling truck begins to lurch forward as we scurry across the parking lot to try to catch it. It's moving slow enough that I can jump on. Jenna still gallops behind, waiting for my help. I lower my hand and grip Jenna's, pulling her up onto the flatbed.

"Wow, looks like your arm is doing better," she grins.

"I guess it is." *Wow.* I surprise myself. *That was the first time I haven't thought about favoring my arm in a really long time.* I rotate my shoulder a couple times, just to make sure I haven't re-injured it. Jenna watches my face closely. I can tell she's checking for signs of pain. It feels alright. "I think I'm good." I chuckle. I'm amused that I just used my arm without too much pain. "Come on. Let's have a seat." We climb up on the truck and sit down next to T.

She sits quietly for a moment, looking as though she wants to say something. She holds off for a few minutes until she finally decided to open up. "I'm telling."

"You're telling? Are we six now? What are you telling on?"

"Dad's truck."

"What do you mean, you're telling on Dad's truck? It didn't do anything."

"You know what I mean."

I know exactly what she means, but I can't let her know that. "What? He told us to bring it and park it down here. What's the big deal?"

"I'm sure he did tell *you* to bring it down here. So why's *Jenna* driving? You love driving Dad's truck. Like I said ... I'm telling."

"I don't see what the big deal is. Jenna's a good driver ... better than me."

Kaitlyn narrows her eyes. "The big deal is that you haven't driven since the accident. It's been over a month, and you still won't get behind the wheel. Something is wrong with you, Caden. Really wrong. I'm worried about you. Mom and Dad need to know. You need help."

I hate being called out on my weaknesses, and if anyone knows my Achille's heel it's my sister. "Screw this." I turn away from her and watch the carolers assembling for their first song. Their mouths begin to move in perfect O's as *Carol of the Bells* starts ringing out around me. It starts out slow, but as the rhythm and volume of the song intensifies, my nerves begin twisting into knots. *This was supposed to be fun, and here I am, stuck in the middle of The Nightmare Before Christmas.* I begin to rebel against the injustice of being stuck on this truck with eighty year old Christmas carolers and a sister who needs to butt the hell out. Plugging both ears, I begin to shout, *"La la la la la la la la!"*

I feel the heat creeping into my face. I push the grating voices from my mind. *Why can't they understand why I don't want to drive? The last time I got behind the wheel, I killed my girlfriend. Maybe not her body, but her spirit. Now, she's all but dead, and I have to live with the fact that it's my fault.* I momentarily lose focus allowing the continuously looping *la la la la's* and *ding dongs* to re-invade my senses. *Old lady voices. Ding dong, ding dong. Grating violins.* I want to take them and break them over something. I feel the anger rage inside of me. I've had it. I've had it with Peyton. I've had it with T. *La la la la. La la la la. Ding dong, ding dong. Why are they trying to out-sing each other?* "For the love of God, make it stop!" I yell.

"Caden, what's gotten into you? You're going to hurt their feelings!" Kaitlyn puts her hand over my mouth. *I don't have to take this. I don't deserve this. I'm here to help people, not be driven out of my mind.* At this point, I'd do anything to stop this nightmare. I grab my ears to cover any further assault of *Carol of the Bells. It's not working.* I look down at Jenna. "See you later." I stand up, climb over the hay bale, and jump off the side of the truck, making a mad dash for Mount Shasta Boulevard.

As I approach the Italian restaurant I feel a quick tug on

my shoulder. I jump from the sudden, unexpected touch. I turn around to see Jenna, "Holy Crap. You scared the hell out of me!"

"Good!"

"Good?"

"Maybe it will wake you up to the reality of this situation."

"What situation?"

"He could still be out there, Caden. What happened to sticking together? You know damn good and well we aren't supposed to go anywhere alone. You took off like a bat out of hell. What happened back there?"

"I was sick of it. That's all."

"Sick of what?"

"I just wanted to have fun today, and people are trying to force me to drive, force me to ride with old lady carolers, jump my shit for stuff beyond my control. I just want to have a good time for once, okay? We need to move on with our lives. I don't want to think about it anymore. I don't want to be reminded of it. I don't want anything to do with it. I just want peace. I want to watch the parade, go do my good deeds for the dash, and enjoy a traditional, family Christmas. Is that too much to ask?"

Jenna stares at me with a look of understanding. After a moment of silence, she nods her head. "You're right. That's why we're down here. We need to give you that Christmas. Let's watch the parade and then find your dad to check on our team."

I stare at Jenna for a minute. I've clearly upset her, and despite my ranting, she's still standing here in front of me trying to get me through it. "Thanks."

"For what?"

"For letting me vent. For sticking by me even when I'm an asshole. For making sure that I'm going to be okay. You're a great friend. I don't deserve you."

"You'll make it up to me," she laughs, nudging my shoulder. "Oops, hang on a sec. My phone is buzzing in my pocket." She holds her finger up to quiet me as she takes the call. "Hey

Ty. Really? Oh, no. Yeah, I think so. No, I'm down in Mt. Shasta. Maybe. I'll try my best. Sorry. No, I'm going to try. Okay. Give him a hug for me. See you soon."

"Everything okay?"

"It's Ty's little brother. He had some complications with his diabetes yesterday. He's still in the hospital. Looks like he's going to be there overnight. Caden, it's Christmas Eve. Parents usually have *a lot* to do on Christmas Eve. I need to get back up there to help Ty so his parents can stay at the hospital with Aiden. I didn't drive, and I'm supposed to do the Dash to the Pole with you. What should I do?"

Jenna sounds desperate. "It's going to be okay. I'll tell you what. We'll either let you take one of the store trucks or find T and Brody to get you back up to the hospital. Don't worry about the Dash. They can always put me on an open team. There's usually a handful that needs to pick up an extra person. Let's get you up there to help your man."

"Thanks. I'll call T."

"And I'll call Brody. We'd better work from both ends if we're going to get them to agree to missing all of the festivities down here."

"Something tells me when they hear we're helping give Aiden some Christmas cheer, they'll jump right on board."

CHAPTER 20

TEAM TANGLES

AFTER BRODY AND KAITLYN AGREE to drive Jenna back to the North County, I run to *The Fifth Season*, the sporting goods store where my dad is stationed. I walk through the door, peeking over the tops of what seems to be a hundred heads. The parade has just finished. I can barely squeeze through the herd of last minute Christmas shoppers trying to find deals on ski clothes and snow equipment. Finally, I spot him back by the snowshoes. "Hey, Dad, did you get us registered for the Dash?"

"Yep, I took care of it," he mutters, continuing to highlight and check off names on his paperwork.

"Well, I need you to change it."

He pauses long enough to raise his eyes and inflict a scornful glance. "Seriously?" I'm a little busy here, son."

"I know, but Jenna had to leave, so I'm sorta teamless."

"Oh, that won't be a problem. Pierre will hook you up with someone."

Someone? "I'm not going to be on a team with nine year

olds, am I?"

Dad shoulders bounce up and down from his silent chuckle. "Doubt it. Hurry back and see him. He's in the back fixing some girl's skis. Come to think of it, I overheard her talking to her friend when they came in. They want to do the Dash, but they need a third person."

"Girls? Like more than one? Do you think they'd be able to keep up with me? I kinda wanted that prize."

"Well, the one girl's a racer, so I'm guessing she has a little competitive fire in her."

Spitfire racer, huh? Could be fun. Sounds like someone I might like to go to the prize party with. "I'll go talk to Pierre."

"You'd better hustle. The paperwork needs to be turned in the next half hour."

Making my way through the store, and back to the ski shop, I raise my hand to catch Pierre's attention. He's behind the counter, fiddling with a binding.

"Oh hey, Caden," he cocks his head and dons his best holiday smile. "What's up?"

"My dad told me to see you about changing my team for the Dash. My friend had to leave, and I'm kinda on my own. Are there any open spots?"

"You have good timing. Those two girls over there were just asking for a third person."

Pierre snaps his head toward the boot wall, directing my attention to the two girls. My breath hitches when I catch view of wildly curly, brown hair. I follow her knit beanie down to her delicate profile. Long eyelashes, mocha skin, and button nose. *It's her.* A tiny ball of fire surges through my chest. I can't figure out what it is about that girl, but every time fate puts her in my path, a minor explosion of nerves sends my stomach flipping and my head spinning.

"What are the odds?" I whisper under my breath, amused that I've run into the feisty snow princess again.

Pierre looks puzzled at my response. "Something wrong?"

I bury my face in my hand, continuing to chuckle. *Seriously?* I pinch my lips to stifle the laughter, until I've composed myself. Then fixing my eyes on the curly head of hair to my left, I speak through my half grin, "You want to put me on a team with *Tangles*?"

No sooner does her nickname leave my mouth, than she whips her head around to catch my incredulous snicker.

Her eyes narrow in on mine. I watch her lips twitch. If I know anything about this girl, she's thinking of her next brash comment. Before she utters a word, her friend, Jessie May turns around beaming. "Hey, I know you. You're the guy from the snowmobile park."

I can't help but smile at the way her face lights up when she recognizes me.

Pierre steps out from behind the counter. "So, you girls have met Caden?"

"Caden?" She stares me down, studying what seems to be every inch of me. After a few seconds, a look of recognition crosses her eyes. *Maybe she didn't remember me while we were pinned together on the mountain.* But, I can see now, by her expression that she's finally put two and two together. "The snowmobile park? He's the benchwarmer from my last ski race." *She's not going to give me the satisfaction of acknowledging that we've met on more than one occasion.* I watch a small dimple pop in her cheek as her eyebrows smugly wander up her forehead. "The one who tripped me at Gate 13."

"Tripped you? Coming out of that turn, you looked like a Yeti on skis. All I saw was hair and hands, flailing out of control. You know, you're lucky I stopped you from snow plowing over a cliff." *Go get her, Woodley.* I nearly snort through my nose trying to stop myself from laughing at the image playing in my mind.

"Yeti? I thought it was Yoda?"

"Yeti, Yoda … take your pick."

Pierre's broad smile grows as his eyes bounce back and forth between the two of us.

"Well, at least I'm good enough to race," she smirks, locking her deep chocolate eyes on mine. For a brief moment, her mesmerizing gaze stops my heart from hammering out its next beat. *Boom. Got me again.*

I feel the heat pound its way to my cheeks. I'm powerless against this girl. I have to look away so I can think. Scanning the room, I catch a glimpse of the counter. The broken binding Pierre is fixing crosses my line of sight. *She probably busted it during the crash at my gate.* My instinct is to shut her down before she detonates my last shred of dignity. *Should I call her on her crappy race?* I take a deep breath. *No, I don't want to go there.* This banter between us is still playful, and I'm having a lot of fun with it.

When I decide to let it go, I look back toward the girls. Jessie May is eyeing Pierre with amusement. I watch him hand her a slip of paper. She nods with satisfaction. "This is going to be fun."

"What's that?" Tangles asks.

Pierre sounds amused. "You're all signed up."

"What do you mean, all signed up?"

"You three are doing the Dash to the North Pole together," he laughs.

Tangles and I look at each other with serious uncertainty as Jessie waves our registration slip in front of us.

The waving paper finally slows to a stop, when she realizes neither of us are smiling. "Are you sure this is such a good idea, Pierre?"

His eyes bounce around our triangle of faces, finally fixing on Jessie May's. "I don't know if you feel the electricity in here, but I sure do. This is perfect." He chuckles, nodding toward Tangles and me, "And when you figure out how to harness the voltage those two are generating, your team is going to be unstoppable."

Am I really that transparent? I swallow hard, shove my hands in my pockets, and look away from the girls. My eyes drift back over my shoulder toward my dad.

Despite the fact that I'm currently trying to tune out of the conversation, I can still hear Pierre talking to Jessie May. "If we can convince them to compete, something tells me they're going to need your help to succeed. You really want to do this?"

The sudden silence tells me that there's a cunning exchange happening between the two schemers. "You're in the driver's seat, young lady."

Ah, what the hell. I shrug and turn back to face the girls. *A shot with them is better than no shot at all.* "I guess I'm in if you are." I hold my fist out.

Jessie May smiles, bumps her fist against mine, and fades away with firework fingers.

"Hopefully you're better on the street than you are on the snow," Tangles grimaces, as she gently sets her fist against mine. My body reacts like a pinball machine. A fireball shoots from the point of contact, up and around my head, and finally exits my pounding chest.

After my brain has been rendered useless by the scorching streak of fire, I manage to fumble the words, "Let's go rock the Dash, Tangles."

Our fists are still connected when she looks me in the eyes and softly whispers, "It's Avery." I watch the pink blush spread across her mocha cheeks. With a softer, yet confident tone, she looks me in the eye and instructs, "Get it right."

A barely visible smile plays at the corner of her lips. Amused at her ruffled response, I assure her with a silent nod, that I know exactly what her name is.

"Well, if you plan on rocking the Dash, you'd better get out there," Pierre chuckles, mocking my awkward phrase. "You don't want to miss the start."

"You're right. Let's go win this thing." I finally peel my pulsing knuckles from hers. "Let's go, Jessie May. Let's go, Tangles."

I grab my partners' hands and tug them through the crowded store. "See ya, Dad!" I fly past, looking over my shoulder. His happy eyes widen when he watches my team sweep through the crowd. I turn away from his silly grin and ask Jessie May, "You got the paper, Jess?"

"Right here," she beams, waving them around in the air. "Let's do this!"

We step out into the brisk air and cross the street to the town hall where droves of people are standing around the town Christmas tree. The mayor has begun to speak.

"Good afternoon everybody. On behalf of the Chamber, I'd like to thank you all for participating in this year's Dash to the North Pole. It's our town's long-standing tradition to give back to our community in an event that serves those in need. As you know, you will be competing in a series of activities. These activities are meant to spread the joy of Christmas to those who are not so fortunate. This year, the top ten teams to successfully complete each task and cross the finish line will win season passes and coveted tickets to the Mt. Shasta Ski Resort New Year's Eve party."

Wild cheers fill the town center. Jessie May leans over to Tangles, shaking her head assuredly. "We're going to win this for you, Avery. If anyone deserves a little Christmas cheer this year, it's you."

I can't help but wonder why Tangles, of all people, deserves this more than the next guy, but I'm ready to do my part to make it happen.

I focus my attention back on the mayor. "Listen closely, take notes, do whatever you need to do. I will not repeat my directions." I remember how this all went down last year. We missed a station, had to run back and complete it, and ended up losing to the Schack family by just a half a minute. Quickly, I pull out my phone to record the instructions. There's no way I'm missing the party this year.

Glancing down at my phone, I see a notification from Officer Marnia. It's a missed call. *On Christmas Eve? She's probably just checking in. I think I'll call her when we're done here.* I quickly enter my passcode and open my recording app. I press the red button just in time to catch the first instructions.

"You will be given a set of seven tasks of goodwill. To avoid congestion at any given station, each team will complete these tasks in a different order. If you look at your registration paper, you will notice an address in the upper right hand corner. This is the address of your first station. Upon successful completion of your first task, you will receive a gift from the giving tree, a signed document stating you have completed the station, and a card by the coordinator with directions to your next activity. This will continue until you have completed your seventh and final task. Your last good deed is to deliver your bag of wrapped gifts to the assigned destination and rush back here to the North Pole.

The first ten teams to successfully complete this challenge will be declared our winners." He sets his hand on the pole, as if to assure us it can be done. "Good luck making the top ten," he nods. "Are my contestants ready?" The eager crowd roars around me. "Five, four, three, two, one." The words, "Now, dash away all," ring through the air in conjunction with the loud blast of a fog horn.

CHAPTER 21

WOOD IF I COULD

TEAMS HUDDLE TOGETHER. SOME WAVE their papers to their teammates. Others scatter about the streets, running this way and that. Tangles, Jessie May and I look down at our paper, searching for our first address. I look up at the top, right hand corner and recognize the street name instantly. It's in the same shopping center as my dad's store. "It's down by the movie theater!" I cry out, pumped that our first station is within running distance.

Avery scans the streets, "If we're lucky we can catch the back of a caroling wagon and hitch a ride down."

"Good call, Pey ... Tangles." *Crap. She's still seeping into my thoughts. "Get out of my head!"* I mentally scream at myself. *I can't believe I just slipped like that. Hopefully Tangles didn't catch it. I don't feel like answering any questions tonight.*

Jessie May's eyebrows draw together as she questions us incredulously, "The caroling wagon?" She shakes her head like we're out of our minds. "Yep, you two are lucky," she giggles. "You happen to have a true leader on your team."

"Why thank you." I tug at my jacket collar and wag my eyebrows.

She snickers playfully. "I'm not talking about *you*. I'm talking about *me*. Lucky for you, I'm going to get us ahead in this race. I know these streets like the back of my hand. Come on." She tugs at my sleeve. "I have a shortcut."

We jog down Mount Shasta Boulevard until we reach the railroad tracks. A few yards into our icy trek, my foot slips from beneath me, sending me stumbling into Tangles. "Careful there." She grabs me before I fall to the ground. For someone who doesn't seem to like people in her space, I'm surprised when she doesn't let go. "I've got ya, Happy Feet. You can do this," she giggles, as she helps me recover my balance.

God, she's cute. Holding her tightly, I work to regain my footing. I find myself securely locked to her arm, my feet dancing beneath me. We're close. So close I can feel her heat. *What's that smell? It reminds me of cupcakes.* I lean in closer and realize it's swirling from beneath her winter coat. *It's her. Vanilla.* Her scent unlocks my senses, and sends a warm explosion to my chest. I can't think. The combination of heat and perfume has me fizzy inside. The warmth continues to crawl its way up every vein in my neck. I feel the blood pulsing at the base of my ears. Against the freezing December air, my face feels like it's on fire. I haven't felt anything like this in a long time. I'm distracted by her touch. My thoughts are drawn to it like a magnet. She's warm. Soft ... but *strong*.

"What are you doing?" A hand to my forehead, finally frees me from my smell-induced daze. "Are you sniffing me?" I become aware of my position. I find my nose being pushed from the crook of her neck.

"My favorite dessert. Vanilla cupcakes. Have you been baking?"

Her mouth pulls down into a questioning grin. "Seriously?"

The next thing I know, my teeth clap shut as Tangles lifts

her hand to my chin and closes my mouth.

"Your tongue's hanging out. Don't tell me you're going to lick me next." She laughs as she nudges me on the shoulder. That's when I notice my heaviness pressing into her. She's still holding my balance. This girl is no weakling. She's been carrying my weight for who knows how long. *Quit being self-centered, Woodley. You don't want to wear her out before we even get to the first task.*

As the hill begins to flatten, I slowly ease away from her hold. Coldness begins to fill the gap where her body has separated from mine. The bone-chilling void has my mind preoccupied, trying to find ways to pull her back into me. *I can't touch her again. Not while I'm feeling those fuzzy things inside. It would be cheating. Wouldn't it?* I talk myself out of warming up to her again, barely noticing that we've reached the shopping center. Jessie May was right about the shortcut. We're here in no time.

"There!" Jessie May points, leading the way toward the back of my dad's store. "The paper says 160. That's past the pizza parlor. It's got to be the grocery store. We have to go all the way around."

I watch her brown curls bob beneath her knit beanie as she sprints along the back alley toward the store. We follow suit, wrapping around the back, rounding the corner, and making our way through the automatic doors. I bend over long enough to catch my breath. Hands glued to my knees, I raise my head just enough to scan the store. There's no one in sight. It's Christmas Eve. The aisles are empty.

Finally, a voice comes from behind. "Can I help you?"

"Dash to the Pole." Jessie May replies.

"Gotcha." She looks down at her watch. "This must be your first station." She takes a card out of her smock and reads the instructions. "Your job is to fill this box with Christmas dinner for a needy family. Here's a list. Check it twice. Don't miss a thing, or you'll pay a big price." Smiling, she adds, "That's what this clue says anyway." She hands me a slip of paper. "Come back to customer service when you've filled the box, and I'll give you the signature card and the first toy of Christmas. Remember, the gifts must be wrapped and delivered before you go back to the pole. Understand?"

We all nod and take the list.

"There must be twenty things on here." I grumble.

"Let's split up." Jessie May inspects the paper as she finds the perfect spot to tear the list. "Avery, you take this half. I'll take this half."

I feel a bit helpless as I stand by and watch the girls scour their lists. "What about me?"

"Grab a hand basket and go with Avery. She'll need your help."

I nod my head. "Okay. No time to waste. Let's go, Tangles."

As I chase her through the bread aisle, I can hear her voice drifting back. "You know you're a pain in the ass, right?"

"What?"

"You heard me. And you're not just slow on the snow. You're slow on your feet too."

She grabs some rolls and tosses them back over her shoulder. Thankfully I'm close enough to catch them.

"Can of sweet potatoes." She begins to pick up speed.

"What?"

"The next thing on the list. It's a can of sweet potatoes. Keep up, Grandpa!"

She runs down the main aisle, peering left and right. "Back here!" I yell, calling her back to the canned fruit aisle. "Lucky for you I'm *slow enough* to actually *see* what I'm trying to find." *I showed her.* I laugh to myself when I see her reaction to her useless speed.

She shakes her head, grabbing the can of sweet potatoes off the shelf and throwing it in the basket. "Why are you so slow, anyway?"

Should I answer that honestly and make her feel bad for being such an asshole? Guess it couldn't hurt. "If you must know, I'm still recovering from an accident."

"Ski accident?" She stops unexpectedly, and looks me up and down.

I shake my head, "Auto."

I watch her face change. She looks as though she's really contemplating what I've just told her. "So that's why you weren't racing?" She mumbles quietly under her breath, likely thinking I won't hear, but I understand her well enough to respond.

"Yep."

"Recent?"

"Thanksgiving."

A faraway look overtakes her face. "Sorry," she mumbles softly, shaking her head. She reaches out, setting her hand on the shelf, as she takes in a deep breath and releases it slowly. She's not talking. Not moving. I don't know what I said that seems to have her so rattled.

"You okay?" I ask, trying to shake her from her motionless state.

She takes a deep breath and pulls the list back up to her face. "Green beans and cream of mushroom soup," she looks back toward me, dropping her hand from the shelf. Her shaky voice sneaks through her dimpled smile. There's a bit of a glint shining in her eye. I can tell she's trying to pull back a tear, but I dare not ask. I know what it's like to want to hide my sadness, so I simply nod and point her in the direction of the soup.

"It's over here," I motion. I can see she's still somewhat distracted, but this is a fun race with an unbelievable prize, and I'll be damned if I'm going to lose this thing. I need to help her snap out of it. I sprint down the aisle, grab the soup, and run it back to the basket. "Catch!" I pant, holding the can above my head, poised to make the shot. Avery lifts the basket just in time to catch it midair.

She shrinks back, giving off a slight hint of fear, but something tells me she's not going to give me the satisfaction of saying I scared her. "Thought you were a boarder, not a baller."

"Oh, I'm only boarding cuz my injury kept me off the court this season." I feel my spirits drop as soon as the thought crosses my mind. I hate that I can't play basketball. I hate that while all my friends are on the court, I have to stand up on a damn, snowy hill, holding a *stupid* flag, for a bunch of *stupid* skiers, who don't even know that if it wasn't for that *stupid* accident, I'd be leading my team to the section championships this season. I hate that every minute of every day I have to fight to forget about all this crap. *The accident. Peyton. My arm. Basketball. Pistol. Pistol. It always comes back to Pistol. Where is that asshole anyway?* This race is supposed to be a distraction. It's supposed to give me something positive to do. So why isn't it working? *Push it out of your mind, Woodley.*

"Earth to, Caden." Her voice rescues me from my state of self-pity, allowing me to focus on her probing, brown eyes. "You okay?"

No, I'm not. But she doesn't need to know that. "One more item checked off the list. What else do we need?"

Avery scans the list. "Let's see. Brown sugar, marshmallows, butter, and a pumpkin pie." I stand in amusement as she begins jogging down the aisle, looking left and right. She stops, backs up, searches the aisle signs, takes a few more steps forward, and comes to a stop. Finally, she jogs back to my side. I watch her wheels spinning, when again, she looks down at the list, and back up at the aisle markers that hang from the ceiling. After a few seconds, she shakes her head and takes a deep breath. She's obviously flustered.

"Are *you* okay?" I ask, returning the same concern she'd just shown me just moments ago.

"Look, I'm sorry. I know you're counting on me to help you win this thing, but I'm not even from here. I don't know this store at all." Her tone becomes increasingly desperate. "I thought if I ran fast we'd find the stuff sooner, but my strategy sucks. I don't know where any of this is." She shakes the list in the air. "You probably know where to find these things faster than I can. Want to take the lead on this one? I'll make it up to you at the next station."

I look her up and down, examining her posture. I can see by her body language that it took a lot for this girl to admit she needs help. In fact, she looks like she just ate a huge slice of humble pie. She holds my gaze. Something in her eyes tells me that she's been through a lot recently. Maybe that's why she's so ballsy. On guard. Defensive. She's protecting herself. Well, if anything, it's clear I'm not alone in battling inner demons tonight. If I can't beat mine, maybe I can help her beat hers. Rather than give her a hard time about it, I decide to play nice. "Everything should be on this aisle and the next one over." I point around the corner.

"Got it. Let's grab the goods and beat Jessie May to the front. If we want a chance at winning this thing, we've got to get out of here."

We grab the last of the items on the list and throw everything in the box. Jessie May is waiting at customer service, jumping up and down. "Hurry, hurry. We need to figure out our next stop." She motions us forward.

The clerk checks our box, signs us off, gives Jessie May a toy puppy, some batteries, and hands us a card with our next destination. "Oh and here," she hands me a large cloth sack. "You'll want this for the gifts you collect at each station."

I open the sack as Jessie May gently sets the package inside. "I love the giving tree. It's pretty cool that we can be part of it this year. I'm glad you're with me for Christmas, Avery." I watch the corner of Tangles's mouth tug downward. She bites at her inner lip, and pulls it into a smile. It's funny though. The smile doesn't quite reach her eyes.

We read our card, which requires us to collect fifty dollars for the Salvation Army bell ringer, who's working outside the store. I laugh and pull out my wallet. "Done!" I cheer. "Best fifty bucks I ever spent." I throw the money in the pot, collect the second gift of Christmas, and gain access to our next task card.

A half hour stint at the Elderly Manor decorating one of their many Christmas trees has earned us another gift and passage to our fourth task, chopping wood for disabled vets. *Finally, something I can really put my heart into.* Luckily, I know a lot of people in this town, and they're crawling all over the place. I scan the street, finally spotting one of my favorite ladies. I wave my arms wildly, trying to flag her down. I'm not sure she sees me through the crowd, but her distinct, green Jeep slowly pulls to a stop beside me. "Hey Sandy Bear, we're competing in the Dash tonight. Mind dropping us off at the City Park?"

A huge grin covers her face. "Hop on in, Cade Monster."

I open the door to the back seat, letting the girls load in first. When I jump up front, I'm greeted by an inquisitive smile. "So, who are the ladies?"

Not sure how to answer that, I remain silent.

"Cat got your tongue, huh? Where's that little blond you run around with? Is she home with family tonight?"

Boy, way to pull out the challenge questions right out of the shoot. "Not sure, Bear. We're done."

"Oh. I see." Shock is evident on her face. She stays quiet for a couple seconds, then looks up in her rearview mirror. "So, how did you girls meet this little monster?"

I hear some giggling in the back seat. "Oh, we've had a couple *run-ins* here and there," I finally hear Jessie May's voice chime in."

"Run-ins? Do you mean run-overs?" Tangles jokes.

Sandy starts to ask another question, but I turn up the radio, trying to drown it out. I love this lady, and appreciate what she's doing for me, but I don't have it in me to sit through *The Today Show with Caden Woodley*. I just don't have the answers, and we need to get to the next task fast. "Step on it, Bear. This is a race."

"Okay," she singsongs, pressing down on the gas and nearly throwing me into the back seat. "Hey, if you need me to, I can be your driver. It might get you around a little faster. I know you're still not moving as fast as normal after that *terrible* accident. I'm just so thankful you weren't *killed*."

Heavy silence suddenly fills the cab. I look back in the rearview mirror and examine the girls' lack of expression. Avery's eyebrows are drawn together as she fidgets with her fingernail. Jessie May is turned into her, gently rubbing her on the back. I watch Jessie mouth the words, "You okay?" as Avery nods silently in response. I can't help but wonder what she's going through. Something's definitely not okay with this girl, but she's certainly fighting whatever it is.

Sandy's voice draws my attention to the park entrance. We've pulled in next to the Upper Lodge. "We're here. Want me to wait?"

I can't believe she's actually doing this for me, but I'm so thankful she is. "Sounds good," I say, hopping out and opening the door for the girls. "Not sure how much wood we need to chop. You don't mind?"

"Not at all. It'll give me a chance to catch up with my friends over there." She points to a crowd of middle-aged people huddled outside the senior dining hall.

"Be back soon. Come on, girls." We run toward the lodge to find out where exactly this wood is that we need to chop.

When we enter, we're greeted by the parade Santa, who directs us to the pile of wood behind the lodge. An old truck sits next to the pile. "We've marked a line on the truck bed.

Chop and fill the wood to here." He holds his hand up to the line. "No big air gaps either. I'll be making sure your stack is solid. When you're finished, you'll need to have me check it. I won't sign you off and give you your next task card unless you do it right. This wood is going to some of my best friends," he belly laughs. "Ho, Ho, Ho. Good luck."

He hands me an axe. I look around, trying to find the chopping block. As soon as I spot it next to the front tire, I grab the first piece of wood and balance it in front of me. I stare it down pretty hard before I lift the axe above my head. I haven't used my arm like this in weeks, and the thought of embarrassing myself in front of these girls has me sweating through my flannel. *Bite the bullet, dude,* I think to myself before I finally raise the axe. *One, two, three.* I count in my head before I finally allow myself to take the first swing. The heavy blade crashes down as two new pieces of wood fall to the sides of the block.

Did it. Phew. The axe is a lot heavier than I remember. Jessie May immediately starts grabbing the wood and handing it to Avery, who's now standing in the truck bed. I have to admit, these girls know how to speed things up. Avery has obviously stacked wood before. I grab another piece, repeating the daunting process. This time, as I lift the axe, a tinge of pain finds its way from my shoulder to my elbow. I have to convince myself to work through the pain. I've got to get this done, and I don't want to embarrass myself. *Come on, Woodley. You're two pieces in. This is nothing you can't deal with. You've got to keep up with these girls or you're going to look like a wuss.* I watch Jessie May carry the newly split pieces to Avery.

By the third piece, I have to take off my flannel. Sweat is dripping down my back from over-exerting my recovering arm. I start in again, grabbing the next piece of wood. As I raise the axe, I glance up at the truck bed to find Avery performing a full body scan. When her eyes meet mine, she looks away quickly. I laugh to myself. *She's embarrassed that I caught her eyeing me.* This time, I raise the axe and peek discreetly under my arm. I want to see if I can catch her again.

And again, I catch her watching me. "Like what you see?" I chuckle as I bring the axe back down through the wood.

She's silent for just a moment. As I watch her intently, waiting for her response, I notice her mocha cheeks blush mauve. "Just thinking about how much faster *I* could get that done," she laughs, jumping down from the truck bed. She disappears behind the truck and reappears with another axe.

Where'd that come from? I study the tool in her hand as she moves toward Jessie May. Then slowly, she leans into her and whispers. Jessie May looks over at me. She's close enough that I can see her eyebrows wander up her forehead and pinch together. Her lower jaw slackens. *What's going on here? Why are they looking at me like that?*

"Step aside, Hot Shot. I want to try." Avery lifts the axe and splits through the wood with ease. "Another piece, please." I bring her another piece, and watch her crack through it again. And again. And again. She's so fast, I almost can't keep up with the fetching and stacking.

Who is this girl? Superwoman? I know my mouth is hanging open, but I can't believe what I'm seeing. How's she doing this so fast?

"Don't just stand there and gawk," she chuckles. "Get me another piece. Don't you want to win this race?"

Bending down to get a bigger piece of wood, I find myself shaking my head back and forth. *Let's see if she can chop this piece.* I hate to admit it to myself, but that was impressive. "Where'd you learn to split wood like that?"

"Well," she lifts the ax and slams it down, slicing through the wood like it's butter. "It's what country girls do. We hunt, chop wood, ride horses, and show up people who call themselves country boys." She looks at me through her lashes, popping her eyebrows to signal that she's talking about *me*. "Now, hand me another piece of wood."

I grab another piece and hand it over. "I know what country girls do. I've seen lots of 'em. But none of them chop wood like *that*. What's the secret?"

"No secret. Really," she laughs, looking back at the truck toward her partner in crime. Jessie May is doubled over, covering her mouth. *Is she sick?* I take another look. *No. She's laughing too*. I shake my head, stupefied by how much better than me, this girl is at chopping wood.

"Am I being punked?" I look around, trying to find cameras. "Wait, where'd you get that axe? Let me see it."

"No, no. I've got this. We've almost filled our quota. I only need to chop a couple more rounds," she giggles.

By now, I hear noise coming from behind the truck and watch blond hair bobbing up and down.

"Sandy, is that you?"

She comes out waving with a huge grin on her face. "How'd it go over here?"

Avery looks at her and wags her eyebrows. "I showed him up. Just like you said I would." She gives Sandy a high five.

"Told ya," she laughs.

I'm totally embarrassed that I couldn't keep up with Tangles on the wood chopping, and I glare at the two of them, who have obviously schemed against me in some way.

"Okay, that about does it." Jessie May comes up behind us. "Thanks for letting Avery borrow your magic axe," she gushes. "Let's go have Santa check our stack."

"Magic axe?" I question.

The girls laugh. "Just looking out for you, Caden." Sandy sets her hand on my injured shoulder and winks. Then she leans in and whispers in my ear, "Word of advice. Don't let your machismo ruin your recovery. Now go get that stack checked!" She pops me on the bottom, sending me on my way.

"But, magic axe? I don't get it."

"And you never will." She winks at Avery. "Some secrets are only meant for us country girls."

CHAPTER 22

GOTCHA

WE GRAB OUR CARD AND jump back in the jeep. "You kids all done?"

"Yep, got our next task card right here!" I toss the toy over the seat, back to the girls, and look down to read the card. Before I can speak the first set of directions, Sandy's already screeching out of the parking lot.

"Hold up!" Jessie May squeals. "I'm not even all the way in!" I look over my shoulder to see Avery reaching across the seat. It's hilarious to see her attempt at keeping Jessie May from flying out.

"No worries! Step on it. Tangles ain't lettin' her go anywhere!" I have to laugh, watching the pint-sized princess pull Jessie May back in and slam the door in one fierce motion.

My voice strains to read the blurring card, as we fly over the ruts and bounce around the corner, leaving a heavy trail of dust in our wake:

"Now that you're no longer rookies, go and decorate some cookies! They're waiting for you at the school. Get there fast!

Just past the pool!"

"Which school are they talking about?"

Sandy shrieks, "It's a clue. *Just past the pool!* It's got to be the high school!"

"Well, what are we waiting for? Step on it!"

As I'm slammed into the back of my seat, I realize Tangles' command to *step on it*, was completely unnecessary. It seems as though Sandy is working with two speeds tonight. Stop and light speed ahead. The adrenaline begins to pump through my chest as we fly up McCloud Avenue, practically breaking the sound barrier. My lunch has found its way to my throat, and my cheeks begin to quiver as we rush past the long line of parked cars. Wide eyed, I feel my heart catapult as we rapidly approach tail lights on the corner of McCloud and Washington. The excessive speed has my nerves tied up in knots. When we nearly hit the back of the stopped car, I thump the dashboard with my hand and jump back in my seat.

"Shit!" I accidentally blurt out.

Tangles' giggle floats through the cab, and I swear I hear Danica Patrick's name being whispered in the back seat. I look up through the rearview mirror to see if the girls are okay. To my surprise, they seem to be rather amused by the driving.

"What's the matter, Caden? Can't you handle a little speed?" Tangles jokes.

I feel the heat spread through my cheeks, as I catch a quick glimpse of her laughing at her own wisecrack. I'm embarrassed by my reaction to the near fender bender and find myself a little tongue-tied. *She's right. I'm being a candy-ass. Other people are starting to notice. How am I ever going to get past this?* I scratch the back of my head out of nervous habit. I've got to come up with a way to mask my fear. *Come on, dude, think of a comeback. Say something.* Nothing.

When my silence becomes uncomfortable, Avery finally speaks. "You are scared, aren't you?"

I can't bring myself to look at her, so I glue my eyes to the road ahead of me. A momentary void fills the cab, until she breaks the thick silence.

"Well, it was a little scary," she pauses.

Did I hear her right? I glance back to gauge my read on her response. *Is she trying to make me feel better?* I watch her elbow Jessie May, "Wasn't it?" She raises her eyebrows and nods toward me.

"Uh, yeah." Jessie May giggles.

"Not funny," Tangles growls under her breath.

Jessie May tries to ease the situation. "Sorry, I laugh when I'm nervous."

While I try to figure out where the new, compassionate side of Tangles came from, Sandy pulls up next to the curb and unlocks the door.

"Well, go on," she encourages.

I can't move yet. I need a second to allow my stomach to fall back into place, and let my blurring eyes adjust to the stillness. Rather than get out right away, I roll my head and look at her in disbelief. "What got into you?"

"What do you mean?"

"Last time I rode with you, I could've gotten there faster if I'd saddled a turtle."

I hear Tangles snort-laugh from the back seat.

"What are *you* laughing at?"

"The turtle thing. It just reminds me of the way you ski," she giggles again.

I shake my head and huff. *I wish she could've seen me before the accident. Back when I was fearless.* Again, uncomfortable silence fills the cab. I have nothing to say.

"Don't worry, Cade Monster. You'll be at the top of your game again in no time," Sandy reassures me. "It's only been a month."

She must remember our conversation from the store, because Tangles leans over the front seat. "I'm just messing with you." She pats me on the shoulder. "What are we waiting for? Come on. Let's see if you can get some of your speed back. I'll race you to the school!"

All of our doors swing open at once.

"I'll wait here!" I hear Sandy's voice ring through the air, as I kick it into full speed and race across the lawn. I look over my shoulder as I approach the front door. The girls are a good fifty yards back. *Good job, Woodley. What are they gonna say to that?* Feeling a little guilty for the ruthless beat down, I run up the steps so I can hold open the front door. *I'd better show them that I'm still a gentleman.*

Between the two girls, Avery's much quicker than Jessie May. There's determination in her eyes, as she lunges into her stride. When she nears, I watch the gap widen between the two girls. *She's a competitor.* Her quads pop through her leggings, as she bounds up the sidewalk. *Wow, she's smooth.* That face. That look. *She reminds me of someone. She's got to be a racer... and not just a skier. Probably a runner.* I'm fixated on her movement. She's strong. Fast. Gorgeous.

I watch intently as her eyes meet mine. My heart jumps a little as I notice a smile play at the corner of her lips. I can't look away from her. That smile. It's rare. I don't want to miss it. *Aw, there it is.* Adrenaline washes through me, infusing me with the medication I've only found with her. *God, she really is beautiful.*

We watch each other intently as she moves quickly up the walk. I can't help but wear victory on my face. Her feet have barely found the steps when she begins to humbly laugh out, "You did it! Got meeeeee!" At the same time, she leaps forward, skipping a step, for an enthusiastic high five.

Unfortunately, we don't connect. She just misses my hand as her feet come back down onto the icy sidewalk. She's unprepared for the slick landing. I watch her arms swish through the air, grabbing for anything to steady herself. She comes up empty, as her feet dance below her, trying to gain their footing. There's nothing she's going to be able to do to stop herself from falling. Instinctively, I lunge forward, to save her.

In the nick of time, I catch her tiny body before she hits the icy ground. The feeling of holding her in my arms lights me up inside. I can't hide my smile. Then looking down into her big, brown eyes, I find myself whispering, "I got you alright."

My eyes are fixed on hers. As I hold her tightly, trying not to drop her, I can feel her quickening pulse beneath my fingertips, and I have to wonder if she can feel mine too. I pause to take her in. Every tiny piece of her. Her face, her feel, her smell. *Her smell. There's that sweet vanilla again. Is it really her?* The door to the gym is open, and I can't help but wonder if maybe it's the cookies we're supposed to be decorating. I've never smelled such a delicious scent on a girl before. I want to know for sure if it's her, so I can file it away in my memory as my favorite fragrance. I can't help myself. I lean forward.

Her response to my closeness catches me off guard. Her eyes grow wide with surprise, as my face nears hers. She swallows loud enough that I can hear her gulp. Then she takes a deep breath. *Does she think I'm going to kiss her?* I'm amused by the thought. As not to embarrass myself, I decide to run her through a little test. Slowly, I pull her in close until we're chest to chest. I move my mouth directly toward hers. Pausing, I smile down at her. Momentarily, I watch her eyes question mine. She squints at me, lifting her eyebrows, and pulling her face away. I'm positive she's warning me to back off.

There's the feisty Tangles I know. As adorably funny as I think her reaction is, I can't help but wonder if she's maybe a little overconfident. If she thinks she can get a kiss out of me this easily, she's in for a surprise. *I'll show her.* I decide to have a little fun with this game. Again, I move in closer, pausing just as my nose slightly touches the tip of hers.

For a brief moment, I think I'm going to fail my own test. I actually want to go through with the kiss. *Why does she have to smell like vanilla? Where's your self control, Woodley? You can't do this. Not yet.* Again, I look her in the eyes and smile. I slowly tilt my head to the side, allowing myself to close the space between us. Then gently brushing past her lips, I slide my cheek down hers and turn away at the last second.

I make an effort to tickle her cheek with a warm trail of breath, as I move across her blushing, mocha skin. I brush her hair away from her face and cup my hand around her ear. I feel her body tighten beneath me. It takes every ounce of restraint I've got not to kiss her, as I watch her gently bite at her bottom lip. *I'm actually making her nervous.* I can feel her heartbeat pounding against my cradling arms. *I'd better let her off the hook.*

Again, I lean into her, pushing my face into her ear. I want her to feel my smile. I wish I could see her face right now. *Let the games begin.* Again, I pull my face away, letting her watch me lick my lips. Then I look down at her, like I'm going in for the kiss. I have to laugh to myself. I spit my gum over her shoulder, and wipe my mouth on her collar. I know I'm killing the moment, and probably any chance I ever had of a real kiss, but for once, I feel like I have the upper hand.

Disgust covers her face. Her mouth drops. She shakes her head in disbelief.

"Gotcha!" I chuckle, pulling away, and bringing her to her feet.

"Got me? What the hell was that?"

"You thought I was gonna kiss you, and you know it."

"Whatever! You're a jackass! I wouldn't kiss you even if you tried. Especially not with those moves."

"We'll see about that. Challenge accepted."

Tangles doesn't even have time to react. Jessie May runs up, grabbing her by the arm. "Come on! Do you want to lose?

Stop flirting, and let's go do what we came here to do."

Silence lingers between us, but I still feel sparks flying from my chest as we run up to the school and find our way to the kitchen. I don't know why, but I feel bad about what I just did to her. *Should I have kissed her? Did I screw up?* The look on her face, when I pulled away was something I've never seen before. She almost looked … hurt. *Did she really want to kiss me?* I glance over at her, just to see if she's okay. No sooner does she catch my glimpse, than she looks the other direction. I want to say something, anything, but when we enter the building we're met by the principal and a huge pile of undecorated sugar cookies. There's no time to make things right.

"You kids have some work to do. Two dozen of those have your team's name on them. They need to be decorated and transported downtown in time for the holiday auction tonight."

Aside from a tiny frosting fight between Jessie May and me, we make quick work of the task. Tangles barely looks up. She looks flustered. I can tell that the attention I'm giving Jessie May has her on edge. "Let's do what we came to do, Jessie May," she barks out. "That's what you told me, isn't it?"

Jessie May apologizes, "You're right. I'm sorry. We're almost done, and I think we've got a good shot at that prize. All that's left after this is to wrap and deliver toys." She turns toward me. "Do you think your friend is still waiting for us?"

"I know she is. She'd never let me down," I say as I plop a bit of frosting on the last cookie. "Done!" I set it gently on the plate. We run to the principal for the check, and to collect our final toy.

He gives us our last task. It's directions for the toy delivery. "Looks like all you have left is to do is figure out a way to get these gifts wrapped and delivered to the resource center." He smiles and looks down at his watch. "I think a few stores might still be open. You kids have a real shot. Good luck making it into the top ten. See you at the pole."

We grab the toy, and run out to the jeep, where Sandy is waiting with a huge smile on her face. "What's got you so happy?" I ask, opening the door to find a seat full of wrapped gifts.

"Oh, I've played this game before. I know how hard it is to try to get the wrapping done, especially if the store is closed. This task could make or break you."

"But isn't it cheating?"

"There's nothing in the rules that says how to get 'em wrapped. Trust me, I checked into it after it cost me the challenge last year. I ran down to Eleanor's and wrapped them while you were decorating. Surprise! You can thank me later." She holds up a square of wrapping paper and some tape. "You can take care of the last one, while I get you back to the resource center." We barely have the doors shut, when she steps on the gas, racing to our last destination. We arrive in no time and run to the store entrance, delivering the beautifully wrapped presents. We practically throw the gifts at the employee and race back to the jeep.

"Done!" We jump back in the jeep after delivering the bag of toys. I can tell Sandy's surprised by our speedy return. "Let's go!"

Within three minutes, Sandy has us to the finish. "Go! Go!" she yells, pushing me out the door. "I've got to find a parking spot. Text me so I know how you placed!" She crosses her fingers and takes off, leaving us to run across the street to the pole.

"You got the proof that we finished our tasks?"

"Right here!" Jessie May holds up all the cards.

I grab the girls' hands so we can run across the line together. To my left, Jessie May wraps her fingers around mine. My right, however, is a different story. Tangles, tries to tug her hand from mine. "Do we really have to hold hands?"

Jessie May, uncharacteristically roars, "You have to be holding hands when you cross, or it doesn't count!"

"Fine." Tangles crunches my fingers in her tight grip, as we cross together.

Cheers boom out all around us. I can barely hear the judge over the roar of the crowd. He looks down at us from his riser, and holds out his hand. "May I see your cards?"

Jessie May releases my hand, so she can hand them over. The sudden release, allows me time to focus on my other hand. It still feels like it's being gripped in a vice. I try to let go, but Tangles won't release me from her death grip. I work to open and close my fingers. She looks over at me smirking, "What? I thought you wanted to hold hands."

"Yeah, hold it. Not be eaten by it. Do you mind?" I try again to pull my hand away.

"Fine. But only because I never wanted to hold it in the first place. Not because you told me to let it go."

Damn, this girl is a firecracker. It's clear that with Tangles, everything is on her terms. *Or, at least it used to be.* I smile, and grab her hand again, curling my fingers around hers. I look over, wink, and click my tongue.

"What are you doing?" she whines.

"Seems to me, my hand has a mind of its own. If it was up to me, there's no way I'd be doing this right now." Smiling, I hold our locked hands in front of her face.

"Your hand has a mind of its own, huh? Well, so does mine."

Before I know it, I'm leaping forward in pain. It feels like a fire ant has just bitten me right on my seat. I pull my hand from hers and rub at my bottom. "What was that?"

She holds up her tiny, left claw, pinching her fingers together. "That'll teach you not to mess with me."

My bottom is stinging, when I redirect my attention up to the judge. I watch as he flips through the cards, inspecting each signature carefully. "Well, it seems that everything is in order." He lifts a microphone and turns toward the crowd, "Ladies and gentlemen. We have team number three."

The crowd goes wild. "Yes!" We jump up and down. I grab Jessie May, twirl her around, and set her back down. Then I look at Tangles, silently asking her permission to celebrate with a hug. She shakes her head back and forth, but I grab her up in my arms anyway. As I swing her around, I feel her vibration. She's literally buzzing underneath me.

"Put me down!" she yells.

Slowly, I slide her down, dangling her feet just above the ground. "Sorry, I couldn't help myself," I smile, finally allowing her to step down onto the sidewalk. I don't want to let her go. For some reason, my hands just can't make the break. Instead, I hold her shoulders at arm's length. Looking into her eyes, my heart pops in my chest. *I'm going to the New Year's Party with Tangles and Jessie May?* "We won! I'm so excited! Aren't you?"

I slide my hands down to her waist, still unable to release her. Her breath hitches, as I pull her in tighter. *Is that her pulse?* "So you are excited. I can feel your heart beat!"

"You're kidding me, right? Are all city boys this overconfident?" Her dimple pops, so I know she's half joking. *She must have some idea by now that I'm not a city boy.*

"What? That's not your heart racing at the thought of accompanying me to the New Year's party?"

"No, silly. It's my phone!" she laughs out, grabbing it from her pocket. When she looks up, the mocha color has faded from her face. She gently grabs my hand from her waist, giving it a tiny squeeze. She looks at me once more, apologetically. "I've got to take this." She shakes her head. Something seems wrong. I watch intently as she walks away from the crowd.

I watch Tangles huddle in the corner, back by the gift store. Her face twists into a painful looking grimace. Her hand comes to her mouth, as she bobs her head up and down. I watch her slide down the wall into a fetal position. Worry crosses Jessie May's face.

This doesn't look good. Tangles looks like she's just entered her own private hell. "Is everything okay?" I ask.

"I don't think so. That could be the call she's been waiting for."

"Can I help?" I begin walking toward her.

Jessie May stops me. "No. Stay here. I've got this. She's a private person. Wait! There is something you can do. Could you collect the prize and get a hold of us later."

I nod. "I can do that. How do I get a hold of you?"

"Let me see your phone."

I pull it out. She takes it from my hand, and turns it on. "Uh, you have a ton of notifications on here. Don't you ever check your phone?"

I suddenly remember a missed call from Officer Marnia. *I'd better take care of that when I get home.* "Guess I've been a little distracted."

Before she says another word, Tangles's panicked voice interrupts. "Jessie May! Hurry!" I glance over to see her, still huddled in the corner by the gift store.

"I'll check 'em later. Go ahead and do what you need to do."

Jessie May clears the screen and starts tapping away. "Here you go." She hands me my phone. "Our numbers are in there. Don't forget about us."

"Not a chance."

I watch Jessie May scoop Tangles from the ground, as they make their way down Mount Shasta Boulevard. I'm unsettled, as I shove my phone back in my pocket, and collect our prize. *I wonder what's wrong with her. Must be something awful. She's too tough to break down like that for no reason.*

I follow behind for a few moments, just to make sure she's okay. I can still feel her warmth on my hands. I can still smell the scent of her perfume. *Damn. That perfume. Vanilla, my favorite.* It must have rubbed off on my jacket while I was twirling her around. I roll my head down to smell my collar, when my eyes catch a shiny piece of silver, glinting under the streetlight. There on my lapel, I notice a little sterling silver spur, dangling by a metal hook. I pull it from my jacket, hold it up to the light, and inspect it. It's an earring. Engraved inside are what looks to be initials. AGB. *A? Avery? It's her earring. A piece of her.*

I should run and catch up. Give it to her. But I can't. Something stops me. I don't know why, but it's comforting to hold this little piece of her in my hand. I stop right there. Right in front of the railroad tracks. The whistle blows as the train begins to move between us. I move left and right, trying to watch the tail lights through the blurring boxcars. It's too hard. The extra bows, bells, and garland, decorating the mock Polar Express, block her from my view. I look down at the earring, then back up through the passing train. It's too late to see her again tonight. But there's no way in hell I'm passing up a chance to see her again. I've got to give this back to her, after all. I shove the earring in my pocket, right next to my phone. It's time to go home and celebrate Christmas with the family. The way it should be celebrated.

CHAPTER 23

I LIKE BIG GIFTS AND I CAN NOT LIE

"**G**ET UP, SLEEPY HEAD!"

Here we go again. Every year for the past seventeen years, I've been woken up the same way on Christmas morning. *Bounce. Bounce. Bounce. Bounce.* "Enough already, T! Aren't you ever going to outgrow this stage?"

"But Santa came, and we have awesome stockings sitting out by the fireplace!" She grabs my t-shirt and pulls me back and forth, until I'm swaying like a ship in a storm. "And I have the biggest present under the tree, and you don't!" she giggles. "Come." *Tug.* "On!"

Ugh. It's the first time I can remember sleeping through the night without one of those damn nightmares, and I have to be woken like this? I flip the covers off and roll out of bed. "Okay, show me," I groan, shuffling my way down the hallway. "Wait, I have to pee."

"Make it quick. I really want to see what's in that box!"

I can't handle all the Christmas cheer so early in the morning. She needs to take it down a notch. Just to mess with her, I take a little longer than I need to. I can picture her standing with her back to the wall as I listen to her hand slapping against it. She keeps groaning, "Come on! Hurrrrry up."

I throw in a few extra grunts for dramatic effect.

"What are you doing in there? You hiding a new girl or something?"

"Wouldn't you like to know?" I joke through the bathroom wall.

A new girl? Yeah, right. As usual, brown curls, mocha skin, and a button nose, flash through my mind. A rush of excitement hits me. *She's been popping into my thoughts so much since the snow park. I can't get over how cute she is. Her smell. Her spunk. And, after last night, I'm practically sick from not being able to shake her from my mind. But, new girl? I don't know about that. She doesn't seem too interested.* I flush the toilet. "Be right there."

Why do I suddenly wish I knew more about her? I turn on the hot water and pump the soap into my hands. *Bubbles. Just like her personality.*

"Caaaa-den! Come on!"

This soap smells like vanilla. Just like Tangles. We need to go to Bath and Body to get some more of this stuff. Bath and Body? How do I even know about that store? Damn, I'm turning into a girl. The warm water continues to run, as I inspect my face in the mirror. *Not bad growth for one day. Yep, I'm still a man.* I dry my hands on the snowman hand towel. *Snow? I wonder where she lives. Must be somewhere in the South County. That's where I keep seeing her. Damn! Why can't she live closer? At least then I'd be able to accidentally run into her around town.*

A sudden thought occurs to me. I should text Tangles. *I don't want her to forget about me.* Besides, I should really check on her. *Mmmm, should I? I don't want her to think I'm desperate. Yes, I'm going to text her.* Adrenaline spikes through my stomach at the thought. *What the hell is happening to me? Are those butterflies? I'm seriously getting butterflies thinking about her? Shit.*

"Caaaaaaddddddeeeen! Fine, I'm just going to start without you." I hear T's footsteps walk away.

How can I get away with texting her without looking too obvious? Maybe I can send a group text about the tickets.

I hear heavy footsteps approach the door. "Caden. Stop messing with your sister and get out here." It's my dad, and he sounds serious. "Now!"

How can I get him to back off and stay out of trouble? I decide to play the bathroom emergency card. "Coming, Dad. Sorry. I don't know what I ate last night."

"Take your time, son." I hear him through the door telling my sister to give me some space.

I decide to hold off on the text and try to hurry through the present thing. When I get out to the front room, there's a mountain of gifts waiting for us. I know the only way we're getting through this at a decent pace is if I play Santa. *I'm a genius.* I spring my idea on the family. "I'll play Santa this year. Do you guys mind?"

After waiting for so long to get me out of the bathroom, my sister looks surprised. Her eyes close in on me, obviously questioning my motives. On the other hand, my mom looks ecstatic. "Aww, you found your Christmas spirit!" She claps her hands together and grins. "I can't wait for you to see what we got you."

Me either. I want to get through this and see if I can't start up a little conversation with Tangles. "Okay, let's dig in." I sit down next to the tree. "Here's one for you, T. Oh and you mom. Dad. Here you go. And another one. Oh, and another one." I begin tossing the gifts across the room.

My parents' eyes are spinning as they watch gifts streak

across the living room. "Slow down, son. We can't keep up."

We're almost through, there's no way I'm slowing down now. "It's okay, guys. The sooner we get them open, the longer we get to use them." I toss a few more presents out from under the tree.

I open some cologne, socks, and video games. Overall, it's been a pretty successful haul, but I wonder why my sister got a super big gift, and the biggest thing I got was a camo bean bag chair. My parents know I keep score, and usually they do a little bit better job with equal gift share. I shrug in disappointment, "Looks like it's time for your big present, T."

"Is something bothering you, Caden?"

I look at my parents, who are obviously delighting in my groveling reaction. I watch my mom look over at my dad and smirk. *She thinks it's funny that I have to look at a refrigerator sized box for my sister, while I'm holding socks.*

Kaitlyn climbs a step ladder and begins to unwrap her giant present. She looks up confused, pulling out a new comforter and bedding accessories. "This is awesome. Thanks Mom and Dad." She jumps off the step ladder, and runs to give them a hug.

"Get back up on that ladder, hon. There's more stuff in there."

After peeling off the top layer, she opens a second box. "Camera! Woo hoo!"

I look at the Cannon, she's holding in her hand. The same one I've been asking for since sophomore year. *What the heck? Did she get some of my stuff?* My mom laughs as she watches my mouth drop. "Wait. Um?" I point at the camera.

"It'll be perfect for you to take to college, T."

"Oh, yeah. I didn't even think about asking for this."

You're kidding me. I continue to watch as she pulls out a mini-fridge, luggage, some girly stuff, a wireless printer, and finally a brand new Macbook Pro.

And I got underwear and video games? Wow. I have no

words. I'm trying really hard to keep a happy face.

"So how was your Christmas, kids?" My mom beams.

I smile and nod, as Kaitlyn runs up and gives both my parents bear hugs. "It was the best Christmas ever! I'm all set for college! You guys are awesome! Thanks for everything."

I hold up my new Destiny game and try to act excited. "This is cool. How did you find it?" *At the second hand store?* "Can't wait to play it again. It's been a while. I think I was nine when this was popular."

"Caden, you sound very ungrateful. You're going to hurt your mother's feelings. She worked really hard to find you kids these gifts."

"Sorry, Mom."

My mom is snickering. She's trying to hide it, but she's not doing a very good job. "Oh honey, should we let him off the hook?"

By now, both of my parents and Kaitlyn are roaring with laughter.

"What's so funny?"

"Your face! You look like you just got underwear and socks, or something."

I hold them up. "Uh?"

"Well, we couldn't actually fit your big present inside the house this year."

Hmmm. Big present? My spirits begin to lift. "So, where is this big present you're talking about?"

"Outside. Are you ready to see it?"

"What are we waiting for?" *Yes! I got a big one too!*

When I step out into the blustery morning air, it doesn't take me long to see the big red bow. It stands out against the enormous black Dodge diesel that's parked out in the driveway. *Holy crap, a 2500! I've been wanting this truck since fourth grade. I got the truck. Holy crap. My dream truck?* I look up and down at the big gorgeous tires, the lifted frame, and the shiny black paint. *This beauty is mine? Wait. It's mine. That means I'm the one who drives it. Oh shit. I have to drive this monster.*

"Surprise!" Mom dangles the keys in front of me. "It's all yours!"

"A truck?" I'm shocked to see a brand new TRUCK waiting for me.

"Do you want to test it out?"

I look around at the snow on the ground. There are kids running around building snowmen. Our little neighbors, Danny and Megan, are running around with the Dancer kids, taking turns pulling each other on sleds.

There are too many people out here. Too much snow. I can't do this right now. I look over at Kaitlyn, who's eyeing me suspiciously.

"Yeah, sure I do! Right after I eat breakfast!"

"Not even a quick drive?" My dad asks incredulously.

I can hear I'm disappointing them, but I can't handle the thought of crashing my brand new truck ... or worse, running over one of these kids in the snow.

"Sure, dad. I'm just starving right now. I ran around so much last night during the Dash, that I didn't have time to eat dinner. I don't want to faint while I'm in the driver's seat."

Kaitlyn brushes past me, "Liar," she whispers. "I'm telling."

Heat rushes into my face, at the thought of my sister ratting me out. *How can I stop her? Act like you love it, Caden. Act like it's the coolest thing you've ever seen.*

"I love it! It's awesome!" I jump up and down hooting. Then, I run up to my mom, pick her up, and swing her around in circles.

"Okay, son. Okay. Put me down. I'm getting dizzy," she laughs.

I know I'm overdoing it, but I can't let them see that I'm scared to drive the truck.

"You know what? I'm hungry too. I can smell the quiche from here."

Oh, thank God!

"Let's go eat, and we can all take it for a spin later. Dad. You can do the honors. I want you to be the first one to drive it."

Kaitlyn's eyes close in on me. She shakes her head as we all walk back into the house for Christmas breakfast.

CHAPTER 24

WHAT A DOLL

W E CLAW OUR WAY INTO the kitchen, practically jumping over the top of each other to get to Mom's famous quiche and delicious pastries. I'm first out of the kitchen with a full plate. Looking over my shoulder on the way out, I think to ask, "Do you guys mind if I eat in the family room? I want to play a little Destiny before the football game starts."

"It's Christmas morning, son. We need to spend time together, as a family. It's our last Christmas before you kids head off to college. How about we all eat together? Maybe we could join you in the living room? Besides, it's warmer next to the fire."

"Sounds good to me," Kaitlyn agrees. "I want to charge my new laptop in there, anyway."

Mom carries an extra tray of food and sets it down on the coffee table. We gather around and strike up a lively conversation about last night's contest, and how disappointed Jenna's going to be when she finds out I was on the winning team without her. As I take a bite into an extra crispy pastry, our topic shifts to Aunt Jeanne and how much we miss her amazing scones. Before she moved out to the valley, she used to sneak a gift box under our tree every year, so that when we opened our last gift, we'd have a breakfast treat waiting for us. Remembering the good ole days, I glance back toward the tree and spot what looks to be an unopened gift. "Hey, looks like we missed one." I drop my remote and crawl toward the tree. *Aunt Jeanne hasn't been in town for a while now, so sadly, it can't be from her.*

"It's your fault, Santa. You were the one tossing the gifts at us so fast."

I pick up the small package. *Who's it for?* I roll it around looking for a label, when I finally spot Kaitlyn's and Jenna's names written neatly in permanent marker. "It's for you and Jenna."

"Seriously? Both of us? That's weird. Who's it from?"

"Doesn't say."

"Hmm. Let me see it."

I toss it to Kaitlyn. "You probably shouldn't open it without Jenna."

"I know. I just want to see who it's from."

I watch Kaitlyn roll the box around, looking closer at the cool pattern printed on the wrapping paper.

"Oh, it's right here. It says, 'Love, P.'"

"P?"

"Well, if it's for both of us, it must be from Peyton."

Peyton? I wonder if she left one for me too. "Do you see one for me?"

I crawl around the floor, searching for the gift Peyton must've sent me. *Nothing.*

My dad looks curiously at the gift, scratching the back of his head. "Oh, that's all there was, Caden. It was out on the wicker chair this morning when I went out to feed the dog. I brought it inside after I found it. I wasn't sure who it belonged to. Sorry, I forgot to tell you kids it was under there."

I feel the pain work its way up through my throat. I can't help but feel disappointed. *I can't believe she'd give the girls a gift, and not me ... her own boyfriend. Oh.* That's when I remember. I'm not her boyfriend anymore. I'm nothing to her. She's nothing to me. This proves it. *We really are done. Well, screw her.* A sweet little face crosses my mind. One that's been visiting me in almost every thought this week. *There must be a reason for what happened. Maybe she's it. Where's my phone?*

I grab my phone and search for Tangles's number. *Got it. How should I start? Well, first, I've got to change the name Jessie May put in my contacts.* I replace the name Avery with Tangles. Then I begin my first text.

Me: Hey there, Tangles. It's me, Caden.

Na. That's so cheesy. I erase my text and start over.

Me: What's up Tangles? Remember me?

Ugh. This is harder than I thought. I erase it again. *How am I going to do this without sounding desperate or cheesy?*

Me: Sup, girl?

Damn. I'm seriously out of practice here. Erase.

The doorbell rings, pulling me from my texting nightmare. "I'll get it!" Kaitlyn yells as she bounces out of the chair and runs to the door. "Oh hi, Jenna. Let me help you with those."

When I look up, Jenna is carrying an armload of packages. "Brought you guys some gifts."

"We have some for you over on the mantle too, but I've been waiting for you to open this one with me. I think it's from Peyton!" Kaitlyn's voice is full of excitement.

"Peyton? Seriously? She got us a gift? I thought she blamed us for everything."

Kaitlyn shrugs her shoulders. "Well, she's been in counseling. Maybe she's had a breakthrough."

Glad she's had some kind of a breakthrough. I look down so they can't see my bitter reaction to their gift. *It took long enough.* My desperate attempts to help her flood my mind. All the calls. The texts. The visits. I tried so hard to be patient. To bring her back. In my mind, I watch the snow globe shattering against her wall. I put so much effort into that perfect gift.

Her loss. I work to think of the only thing that's been making me happy since the accident. Instantly, my mind goes back to my happy place. It's her. Tangles. *I'm moving on to someone a little more my style. Someone who keeps me on my toes. A hot and spicy country girl.* I look back down at my phone, staring at the empty screen. *Hmmm. What am I going to say to her?* I hear paper ripping and look up.

"This looks … interesting. What is it?" Kaitlyn holds up a funny looking doll. "It has my name written on it. I thought this gift was for both of us."

"I know what this is!" Jenna lights up. "It's a nesting doll. I have a collection of them at home. My parents bought them for me as gifts from Russia. They give me a new one every year for my birthday. It looks just like one that I have at home. Look inside. They come in sets."

"When Kaitlyn cracks it open, a small slip of paper floats to the floor."

I crawl over and pick it up.

"Oh, this one has your name on it." Kaitlyn holds the smaller doll out to show Jenna her name scrawled in fancy script.

"Here," I hand them the torn piece of paper. "Looks like you dropped something."

Kaitlyn takes the tiny note and reads it. "Please accept this gift as my most sincere apology. Remember me when you wear them. You'll always have a piece of my heart."

My sister looks sincerely touched by the gesture, as she continues talking to Jenna. "Wow, that's so sweet of her. But, how do you wear dolls?"

"You don't wear them, silly. They open up. It's a set. Here, let me see. There must be something inside."

Jenna takes the funky looking doll back. *They sure are creepy looking things.* She holds it up to her ear and shakes it, then nods her head. "Yep. There's something inside." When she cracks it open a couple more times, she discovers some type of jewelry.

"Oh, look! Charm bracelets!" Jenna holds them up. "Best and Friends. They're labeled. Oh my gosh, Kait, your half has a saxophone, a swimmer, and a Beaver. Mine has a catcher's mitt, a basketball, and I'm not sure what this is? Do you know?"

"Looks like some kind of a castle." I watch her inspect her bracelet. "Cool."

"A castle? That's funny. She must be getting her sense of humor back. She always joked that I was a spoiled, little princess." Jenna laughs. "Here, help me put it on."

The girls gawk over their fancy new bracelets, holding them up to admire the bobbles. *They look a little bulky to me, but whatever. This is too much.* I continue to stew over the fact that Peyton gave the girls gifts and not me. *Aren't "Best Friend" bracelets like fifth grade status? Glad she didn't give me anything. Probably would've been a stuffed teddy bear or something lame. Guess I didn't know her as well as I thought I did. I need to go text a real woman.*

"Glad to see you've reconnected with P." I make sure to pop the "P." I want them to realize that they're being a little insensitive. *Geez, did they ever think once about how I'd feel? How can they be so excited to get a gift from the girl who attacked me and left without looking back?* "See you later." I say, raising my eyebrows and grabbing my phone and pushing off the chair.

By the looks on their faces, I can tell the girls realize they've made me feel bad. "Sorry, Caden. We didn't think …"

Before they can finish their apologies, I cut them off. "It's all good. I'm over her anyway. I'm working on someone new." I hold up my phone and smirk.

A wave of smiles takes over the faces in the room. "Care to share a bit more?"

"Maybe later. See ya." I walk out of the room, thinking of a way to text Tangles without sounding stupid.

Just as I make my way back to my room, it comes to me. *Group text! I can start out slow … talk about the tickets, and get her warmed up to me. Never gonna catch a fish unless I cast the line. Go for it, Woodley.* I pick up my phone and make sure to include both girls in the message.

ME: Hey girls. I have to admit, you kicked butt last night. I've got the tickets to the party, but you still need to claim your season passes. Text me for details.

JESSIE MAY: Sounds good. Yeah, last night kicked ass. YOU were amazing.

ME: Awww, shucks. You're such a doll! And, you weren't too bad yourself.

TANGLES: Gag!

JESSIE MAY: Oh, Avery. Snap out of your mood. It's Christmas.

TANGLES: Please forgive me. It was just a little hard to read your kissass texts back and forth. Besides, HE had nothin' to do with that win. Neither did you, Jes-

sie May. So why are you congratulating each other on
MY win? ;)

So sassy. Her text makes her sound a little jealous of Jessie
May. She did act funny when we were messing around down
at the school. I think back on the frosting fight when we made
each other's faces look like camouflaged hunters. Tangles did
not look the least bit impressed with our frosting makeup skills.

> JESSIE MAY: Yeah, sure. YOUR win. I'm the one
> who got us to the store in 5 minutes, and Caden threw
> in a whole 50 bucks so we didn't have to wait around
> collecting Salvation Army money.

> ME: Don't forget, we'd probably still be running
> around Mt. Shasta if MY friend hadn't picked us up.

> ME: And Jessie May did charm the socks off of the
> cookie decorating judge. If it wasn't for her sweet
> smile and adorable giggle we would've had at least
> another twenty minutes redecorating our gloppy icing.

> JESSIE MAY: Awww, shucks. I'm blushing.

The texting stops. I lie on my bed re-reading our conversation. Boy, Jessie May and I did sound a little flirty. Hope I didn't
give her the wrong idea. Or worse, piss off Tangles and ruin my
shot with her. I know how much girls hate watching a guy flirt
with their best friend. *Damn it. Did I blow it? I need to fix this.*

> ME: I have to confess, I've never seen another girl
> chop wood quite like Tangles. Wouldn't I love to learn
> your secret. ;)

There. A compliment. Hopefully that can get us back on track. I hate to admit it, but I'm bothered by the lack of messaging. *Come on. Text back already.* Frustrated, I throw the phone down on my bed and start to watch National Lampoon's Christmas Vacation. A light tap at my door pulls my attention away from Clark and the pool scene.

"Hey, Caden?"

It's Jenna's voice.

"Come in." I pick up my phone one more time. *Nothing.* I set it face down on the bed, and look up to see Jenna and Kaitlyn come through the door.

"Brody's here. He wants to take a ride in your new truck. You up for a little Christmas drive?"

Drive. Out there? In the snow? Suddenly I feel sick. "I'm not feeling so well. Maybe later, huh?"

"You're kidding right? You just downed three pieces of quiche and a cinnamon roll. You feel fine. I know what you're doing. You're trying to get out of driving. You're still scared aren't you?"

I can't answer her. Not in front of Jenna.

"Aren't you, Caden?"

Jenna's face shows a sudden look of realization. I watch her jaw slacken. "Oh, Caden. It's not your medication, is it? Of course it's not. You're not even taking it anymore." Jenna's mumbling so low, I can barely make out her words. "You're scared to drive. That's why you made me park the truck at your dad's store last night. That's why you made me take you to Peyton's … Why didn't I see it? I'm a horrible friend."

"You need to tell Mom and Dad. You need help with this. This isn't like you, Caden. You're strong and brave. Something's wrong with you."

I don't answer.

"It's okay to need help."

"Need help with what, babe?" Brody walks up behind T.

Great. This is all I need. On top of everything else, my best friend is going to think I'm a wuss.

"It's Caden. He's scared to drive. I think it's because of the wreck."

I can not believe she just sold me out to Brody.

"Shut the hell up, T!"

"Hey dude, don't talk to your sister like that. She just wants to help you out." Brody does that thing he does when he's being protective, and wraps himself around her.

It's great when he protects her from other people, but not me. He was my friend first! "Great. Now I can't even count on my best friend to have my back!"

The volume of my voice comes out just a little louder than I'd intended. I know it's because I'm feeling embarrassed and humiliated. *I knew my best friend had it bad for my sister, but I never thought he'd side with her on something like this.* I'm hurt. I feel betrayed, and I'm pissed about it. Everything I've been shoving down for the past month is boiling inside of me. The wreck. My arm. The nightmares. The pain. Not being able to play basketball. *And what kind of chump is afraid to drive his own truck?*

"You know what? Why don't you all just mind your own damn business? Leave me alone. You hear me? Leave me the hell alone! This is my thing, NOT YOURS!" I shout as I slam my hand against the door jam. I pause, and fiercely glare down not only Kaitlyn, but Jenna and Brody too. I'm telling them, with as much fervor as I have in me, that I am done with this. They'd better knock it off, or I'm going to lose it in a big way. As I try to squeeze my way past Brody, and out into the living room, I run straight into my father. He's standing tightly, next to my mother. He stops me from going any further, holding me firmly by my shoulders.

"Son, why didn't you tell us?"

"There's nothing to tell, Dad."

"Yes there is, Caden, and you know it!" My damn sister butts in again.

"Shut up, T!" I spit.

"Do not tell your sister to shut up. It sounds to me like she's worried about you. She's only trying to help."

"I don't need anyone's help. This is my thing! I'm the one who did it, and I'm the one who has to live with it! I'm sorry if it's affecting you!"

I have got to get out of here. I'm ready to break. The last thing I need to do is start crying.

"Kids, will you excuse us?"

Phew, saved by Mom. I start to pull away from my dad.

My mom's voice stops me. "No, not you Caden. We need to talk."

My sister, Jenna, and Brody all head out, leaving me standing there alone to face my parents.

"Let's go into your room, son." My mom's tone is soothing. It almost makes me forget that I'm about ready to face one of those life-changing talks.

"I've been talking to a few of my friends on staff at the high school. You know, just to find out if there's any way I could help you kids."

"Mom!" I interrupt. "That's so embarrassing. What did you tell them?"

"Caden, they all know about the accident. There's nothing embarrassing about it. I just wanted to see if there were any resources around here to help teenagers who've been through something like this."

I know my face is red. I can feel the heat pounding in my forehead. *How has my life turned into this?* One minute I'm a happy, healthy high school athlete, and the next, I'm a disabled head case.

"Well, what I found out, is there are a couple support groups in our area, for teens who have been through different kinds of trauma. It's just a place to talk, you know, connect with other kids your age who are working through some tough stuff."

"Oh no. Uh uh. I am not going to talk about this stuff with kids who go to my high school. No flipping way."

"I thought you might say that. The groups I looked into don't meet in our town. There's one in Medford and one in Mount Shasta."

"Well, I'm glad those kids are getting help. That makes me really happy. Can I go now?"

"Yes you can. To one of those groups."

I look at my mother in disbelief.

"I'm with your mother on this one, son. We're going to insist that you go. At least a couple of times, just to see if you get something out of it. If it doesn't work for you, then we'll look into a more individual plan of action. Maybe a counselor."

I throw my head back, and release the breath I've been holding. "You're really making me do this? What if I don't?"

"Then you'll be walking everywhere you go until you get better. No more rides from friends and family, Caden. You've got to do this. It's for your own good."

"I'm thinking you might want to go to the group in the South County. At least during the winter. It's not quite as bad as driving over the Siskiyous."

There's no way in hell I'm driving that mountain pass in the snow. How am I going to get out of this? Ugh.

"I'll go once."

"Once?"

I have to pull out my best negotiating skills. There's no way that I'm going to be spending my entire winter and spring with a bunch of messed up teenagers. If I know anything about myself, it's that I always want to fix the issues of the world, and I am not about to take on everyone else's problems too. "ONE time. To the one in South County. And if I don't get anything out of it, I'm done."

"We'll talk about that when the time comes," my dad retorts.

"When is it?"

"They're taking a break til after New Year's. Until then,
we'll let the kids drive you anywhere you need to go. Deal?"

I really have to think about this. Hopefully by then, I'll be
up for driving again. "Deal," I groan. *This is going to suck.*

CHAPTER 25

TEXT ME, MAYBE

I'M LYING OUT ON THE couch re-checking my phone, when everyone comes back into the living room.

"Hey, Caden." *Ugh, Brody.* I'm still mad at him for the way he teamed up against me with my sister. *Jerk.*

I can't help but lash out at him with my response. "What do you want?"

He pauses and looks at me apologetically. "Listen, can we just forget about what happened back there? I'm sorry for butting in like that. I should've stayed out of it."

Now I'm listening.

"Anyway, my cousin just messaged me. Seems the grandparents are asleep, and he wants to go check out his new snowboard. He wants to know if we'd be up for it."

"It's Christmas. Did you ask my parents?"

"They're cool with it. Said they wanted to go hang out with Jenna's parents.

I look down at my phone for the twentieth time in twenty minutes. *Still no text. I blew it. I know it. She thinks I like Jessie*

May. "Not sure I'm in the mood."

"Oh, come on, Caden." Kaitlyn steps out from behind Brody. "Look, I'm sorry I told Mom and Dad. You'll thank me later. I know you will. Just come with us. Jenna's going. You're not mad at her, are you?"

How could I be mad at Jenna? She really didn't do anything. Well, except for rub Peyton's gift in my face. "Where do you plan on going?" I grumble.

"We're thinking Ashland. It's a little less crowded than Mount Shasta on Christmas day. You in?"

I guess it's better than sitting here looking at my phone all day, waiting for a text that isn't going to come. I'd better try one more time. I pick up my phone and give it one more go.

ME: You girls do want to go to the party, don't you?

JESSIE MAY: YES! Sorry I didn't text back earlier. I was dealing with some family stuff. But, yes. I plan on going.

Phew. They got my text. But still no Tangles. "Okay, I'm in. When are we leaving?"

"Well, that depends on when we can find a truck that will make it over the Siskiyous. There's chain control right now ... unless you have a four wheel drive. Does anyone here have a four wheel drive?" Brody's devious smirk bores into me. "If we come up with a vehicle, I can drive."

I shake my head. Incredulously, I ask, "You want to drive my brand new truck? The one I just got this morning? Like before I do?"

Oh, this boy has some balls.

"Well, someone's got to drive it." I hear Brody's comment under his breath.

He thinks he's going to drive my truck before I do? Yeah, I don't think so. I'll just take it around the block when nobody's looking. I can at least do that. I have to be the first one behind the wheel. I have to.

"Well, go get your stuff together. We can take my rig. I'll be ready in a half hour."

While the gang goes to their houses to grab their gear, I decide to bite the bullet. *I'm going to do this.* I don't know how far I'll get, but I'm going to take my new truck for a spin. I grab the keys off the key hook and step into the cool winter air. Snow is coming down lightly. Except for a few snowmen standing in various yards, there's no one to be seen. Silence fills the air.

I grab my snowboard out of the garage, and slowly walk toward the truck. *It's me versus you, big boy.* I stare it down, like I'm ready to step into the ring with Mike Tyson. I swear I hear the engine roar at me. I bring the remote up to unlock the doors. *Click.* The sound rings through the quiet street. I flinch as it echoes out around me. I take a step back and survey the neighborhood once more. *Nope. Nobody's out here.* Again, I step toward the truck. This time, I lift my hand to the handle. When I pull back, it's locked. *Crap. I must've taken too long.* It's already re-locked itself. Again, I unlock the door with the remote. *Just do it.* I work to convince myself.

When I finally get up the nerve to open the door and jump inside, I jam the key in the ignition. *Ding. Ding. Ding.* I wince again. The alarm has me on edge. Something about that sound freaks me out. I pull the door closed and turn the key. My blood begins fighting its way through my veins the second I hear the engine roar to life. Trying to calm myself, I take in a deep breath and blow it out.

As I sit there, contemplating whether to shift into first, I recoil when out of nowhere, slush flies up and pelts the window. *I can't do this.* My heart is racing. My pulse is so strong it hurts. The window is beginning to fog up from my panicked breathing. *You have to do this.*

I push in on the brake and pull down on the lever. *Clunk. Clunk. Clunk.* I feel the shifter hitch into different gears as I move it down slowly. No movement. *You've got to take your foot off the brake, dumbass.* I decide to give it a go. Slowly, I release my foot from the brake and start to pull out into the road. Hhhhoooooonnnnk. *Oh my God. Oh my God.* I breathe in and out. In and out. *I forgot to check the mirrors. I can't do this. I can't.* I lay my head down on the steering wheel, trying to make my heart slow down. I can feel my pulse in my throat. This is a nightmare. *Okay, back to the basics. Pretend you're fifteen. Learning to drive. Nothing bad has ever happened to you. Get your head back in the game.*

A wave of courage comes over me. I check the mirrors this time. *All clear.* Finally, I release my foot from the brake and gently step on the gas. I look at the speedometer. I'm only driving six miles an hour, but everything I pass is making me dizzy. It reminds me of the first time I ever drove. I was nine, and everything was so big. So fast. Larger than life. I increase my speed to fifteen. It feels like the neighbors' houses are zooming by at warp speed.

I feel a bead of sweat trickle from my forehead. I start to hyperventilate, as I round the first corner and make my way up the next street. This road is pretty steep. *Glad this is an automatic, or I'd probably start rolling backward. Oh man. I sure hope Schuler's not home. He'd flick me so much crap if he saw the way I'm driving.*

By the time I make it to the top of Georgia Way, I have cramps in my calves and thighs. My back and neck have knots from stress. *Just one more corner and you'll be heading home.* Both sides of the narrow street are completely lined with cars. I watch a grey CRV come toward me. *This truck is wide. The road is narrow. What should I do?* I try to pull in as close as I can to the car parked on the side of the road. I step on the brakes and close my eyes, as I hear the sound of the car drive past. When

I open my eyes, the road is clear again. *That was a close one.*

I'm certain it's taken me a half hour to round our large block. *Everyone's probably back at the house, ready to go. I have to get there first. I can't let them know that I actually drove, or they'll expect me to do it again. Probably all the way to Ashland. You've got to get home, Caden. Now.* I press down a little more firmly on the gas. I accelerate to an uncomfortable level. I've got to slow down. Panicked, I stomp on the brake, and find myself skidding. Right through the stop sign. A family of deer try to make a run for it. I feel a thump. I watch his hooves spin out from beneath him. He rolls to the ground, but jumps back up and bounds off.

When I pull over and get out to look at my bumper I'm relieved that there's no dent. *I must've just tapped it. Thank God.* I can't imagine messing up my front end on the maiden voyage. I jump back in the truck, hoping to make it home before my friends get back. I round the corner, and take the road up to my house, just in the nick of time. Jenna pulls up behind me.

I open my door and step out. She's already beside me. "You drove?"

I can't answer her. I'm still sweating and out of breath.

"Oh man, you look like a ghost. Are you okay?"

I shake my head, no. "It's too much. Too soon. I can't do it. One block and I almost died three times. There were cars everywhere. And deer. Don't tell them. I don't want to do it again."

"I've got your back. Here, give me your keys."

"Why?"

"I've got to put your truck back. You didn't park up far enough. I can still see the tracks in the snow. They'll know you moved it."

I hand Jenna my keys. She jumps in and moves the truck forward about six feet. That's when Kaitlyn, Brody, and Mason pull up behind her.

Jenna jumps out, making kind of a big deal. "Great truck,

Caden. Thanks for letting me take it for a spin."

I know she's doing it for Brody's benefit. She's such a great friend.

"What? You let her drive it first?" I can tell by his face that Brody's messing with me. He really doesn't care about stuff like that. He shakes his head. "Wow, dude."

I smile and wink, trying to play off my near nervous breakdown. "You guys all ready? I'm kind of excited. I haven't been up to Ashland this season."

"Yep, let's load up."

"You want me to drive?" Brody asks once more, just to check and see if I've changed my mind.

"Uh, if you don't mind. I have a few things I'd like to take care of." I hold up my phone.

"Oh, the new *thing* you were talking about?" Kaitlyn questions playfully. "Any hints on who this new person might be?"

"No hints. I don't want to jinx it."

"Fair enough." Jenna smiles. "I'm glad you're moving on. Makes me really happy."

Curly hair and sparkly brown eyes cross my mind. "Me too." I look back down at my phone. *Nothing.* "I just hope it works out."

"T. Go ahead and sit with Brody. I'll take the back with Jenna and Mason. You okay with the middle, Jenna?" I look at Jenna, who's wildly tapping away at her phone.

"Oh yeah, sure. I want to spend some time texting Ty anyway," she says as we get in and close the doors. "He was going to come, but Aiden was released from the hospital this morning."

Brody starts the engine and begins to pull away from the curb. I clench my nervous muscles and look around the cab, trying to keep myself distracted from the road and weather conditions around me.

"This really is cute." Kaitlyn holds her arm up in the air,

dangling her new charms into the back seat.

"Yeah." I roll my eyes.

Jenna begins picking at hers. "This little castle is cute. I've never seen another charm like it."

For the love of Pete, will they stop carrying on about those charms? This is so stupid. I huff loudly, knowing that they might just recognize my disgust and stop glorifying Peyton's gifts right in front of me.

"Sorry."

I look down at my empty phone screen and glance up into the rearview mirror. Anything to distract me. I notice a sports car with tinted windows. It seems a little close.

"Some people are such assholes."

"What are you talking about? I'm sorry about the bracelet thing." Jenna sounds disappointed in herself. "I wasn't thinking."

"Not you. There's a car riding our ass. It's so rude."

"Well, it won't be for long. He'll have to stop to chain up in about a mile," Brody snickers, watching me through the rearview mirror.

"Want me to lose him?"

"Yeah." I forget about my new fear of speed when Brody steps on the gas and pulls out into the middle lane.

I find myself grabbing onto the handle on one side and Jenna's leg on the other.

"Ouch." Jenna whispers, "Are you okay?"

"I will be as soon as we're at the park."

"You look green. Do you need to pull over?"

I feel my stomach begin to churn. My cheeks quiver and sweat starts seeping from my forehead. "I think I'm going to puke."

"Seriously?"

"Yeah. We'd better pull over."

"Hey Brody." Jenna pats our fearless driver on the shoulder. "We need to pull over."

Brody slows and pulls off to the side of the road. I throw open the door and lean over the side. Quiche and cinnamon rolls splatter all over the ground beneath me.

I can hear my sister gag in response to the sound of vomit hitting the road. "Is he okay? Do you think he has the flu? Oh my gosh. We'd better take him home."

"It's not the flu, T. The back seat makes me sick ... especially the way this guy drives." I laugh, just so Brody knows I'm messing with him.

"Let me trade you places. The park's only about ten minutes away."

When I get out to exchange seats, I notice the little sports car making its way back up the mountain. *Hmm. That was quick. He must have those easy cables.* I get back in the truck. "Sorry about the delay. Let's go."

Within fifteen minutes, my stomach has settled, and we're up at the ski park. I clear my mind of all distractions and hike the hill, ready to conquer another mountain.

CHAPTER 26

NEW "THINGS"

THE RUNS ARE UNBELIEVABLE. THE powder is so thick, it's darn near up to my thighs. The girls are having a tough time keeping up. It takes a lot of strength to jump through this stuff. Kaitlyn's skis keep popping off, so she decides she wants to hit a different run. One that's been recently groomed.

"How about if we hook up in about forty-five minutes? That should give us all enough time to get a few good runs in." I look down at my phone to check the time. I have to admit, I'm pretty bummed that there's still no text from Avery. *Guess she's just not that into me.*

Kaitlyn and Jenna split off. Mason, Brody, and I decide to go for the hard stuff. We hit the terrain park first. "Careful with that arm," Brody warns. "You don't want to mess it up again."

"Oh, yeah. Seeing you out here like this, I forgot you jacked it up pretty bad. How is it?" Mason questions.

I lift my arm, spinning it in a circle. "Way better. I'm start-ing to be able to use it a lot more. You should've seen me chopping wood with Tangles last night."

"Tangles? Who's that?"

"Oh, just this girl I met." I turn to Brody and can't help but laugh at the image running through my mind. "Brody, you've met her."

"What? I've met her?"

"Yeah, you plowed her over at the snowmobile park."

"Oh shit! Oh shit!" His mouth falls open, as he booms with laughter. "You're hooking up with that spicy country girl? The one who called us city boys? How the hell did that happen?"

"I've just run into her a few times here and there."

Brody is still in awe of this new revelation. He slaps Mason on the arm, chuckling, "You should see her, dude. I mean the chick is *hot*."

"Oh, you haven't seen anything. You should've seen *her* chopping wood last night." I can feel my temperature rise in my face, just thinking about it.

"Are you blushing?" Brody laughs. "You must have it bad. Wait til I tell T."

"No! Don't tell her. I don't want anyone to know. They don't know her anyway. She lives in South County."

"So, how are you ever going to see her?" Mason questions.

Mason is so analytical. He's always thinking. Questioning. "Dude, she's on the race team. I'll probably see her every day next week during practice."

"Probably? So you haven't actually hooked up yet?"

I think about it. Think about the near kiss. The *group* text. There's not a whole lot there to show we've hooked up. That's for sure. "Well, not exactly."

"So, how do you know she's your new thing?"

"Well, I don't. Not yet. Umm. Let's just say, there's definite chemistry there. She flirts with me ... I think."

"You think?" The guys' faces look doubtful.

"I think it's her way of flirting. She challenges me. Like

all the time. It's so much fun. She's feisty as hell. Witty. I love it." *I can't believe I'm telling them all this crap.* It feels good to finally get it off my chest.

"So, you really think you found a new girl? She doesn't sound anything like Peyton."

"Good. I don't want another Peyton. This girl is different. She's more … like me. Ornery. Stubborn as hell. But in a good way. I love it. She's not like anyone I've ever met." *She smells like vanilla cupcakes. Looks like a rodeo queen. Rides like lightning.* My pulse picks up as the butterflies start to take flight inside of me. "I don't know, guys. I might've met my dream girl."

The guys start chuckling. "Have fun with that one. She sounds like she could be a handful," Mason laughs out. "But if that's what you're looking for, good luck to you." He pats me on the back and looks up toward the lift. "So you boys ready to hit it?"

"Let's go."

We take off and hit the rail first. My tricks feel pretty solid. I think I've got my balance back. I'm strong. Much stronger than even a week ago. I think I'm ready to move on. Test out my skills. "I'm feeling some jumps, guys. You in?"

"Let's do it."

We get down to the lifts and load up for another run. On our way up, I feel my phone ding in my jacket pocket. I don't take it all the way out. With my thick gloves I don't want to chance dropping it from the lift. I unzip my pocket and peek in, just to see if I can see the screen. Still lit up, there's a notification banner.

TANGLES: HI ;)

Hot damn. It's her. Should I chance it? Take my phone out? I can't. Not now. Maybe later at the lodge. Later, when we meet up with the girls. I zip my pocket, securing my phone, just as we get to the top to unload. Inside, I'm a blustering mess of hormones. I can't let the guys see me like this. I'm almost positive my face is red. It's going to give me away, for sure. *Holy crap. She texted! SHE! Texted!*

Come up with something to say. Something that doesn't involve the word Tangles, or vanilla cupcakes. "How's your board feeling, Ma?"

"Dude, it's sweet. I want to try the dog house. You think you can handle it with that arm?"

"Right now, I feel like I can handle just about anything." I glance down at the trail in front of us. Maybe some challenging jumps are just what I need to forget about the unanswered text waiting for me.

I stand in line behind both Mason and Brody. They do some pretty cool jumps. But me, I take it like a madman. I am pumped up. When I hit that roof, I fly into a 360, kicking my legs back and grabbing the tip of my board. When I land it, the boarders on the side of the run cheer. I can hear voices blending into the background. "Dude, did you see that gnarly turn? That boarder is rad."

Mason and Brody meet me at the bottom. "Well, looks like you're back to the old Caden." Brody pats me on the back. "Good to see, man."

"Speaking of good to see, I need to go see if Jenna and Kaitlyn are waiting for us at the lodge. We're probably late."

"Shoot, I'm just getting started. Mind if I take a couple more runs while you look for them?" Mason asks.

"Yeah, I want to hang out with Ma for a bit. Meet you back at the lodge in fifteen?"

"Sounds good." I take off down the hill, zigzagging in and out. *I have to pee.* I pull over behind a bush, lodged in between two trees. *No one will see me here. As I stand, taking care of business, I watch the skiers and boarders as they travel down the mountain. That one looks like Jenna. She looks like she's with a guy. Where's T? She must've gone down to meet Brody. There's no way she could be away from him this long.* I button up. *I'm going to sneak up on her and blast her with snow.*

I take off in the direction I saw her skiing. Just as I spot her, she begins to stop. It looks like she's with a guy. *That's weird.* I decide to go check it out. I want to make sure my friend is safe. It's not like her to hang out with random guys. And it's especially not like her to ditch my sister for them. She knows T's not supposed to be alone. I take it slow, until I'm within earshot. She's facing downhill. She doesn't see me. I unstrap, and push off to the side, so I can get a better look at who she's with.

I'm about four feet away, standing in back of them, when the guy turns toward Jenna. I can see his profile now. I have to laugh when I see who it is. It's Daemon. *Is he following her?* Seriously, I don't want them to hear me laughing, but now I know. He has it bad for her. I watch as Jenna slides her gloves off and drops them to the ground. *What is she doing?* I watch as she digs into her pocket and pulls out her phone. She leans into him, and holds it up. *A selfie? She's seriously taking a selfie with Daemon, the French dude? This is great. Oh, wait until the ride home. I'm going to rub it in hard.*

I continue to watch. This is too much fun to interfere now. He's taking her by the hand. "Ziz iz zoooo beautiful. Oh look. It'z zee Kremlin. I went there wiz my program. Before I got here. Where did you get zis?"

By now, I notice Jenna looks a little uncomfortable. Daemon is practically pawing at her hand. It's strange, the way he's lifting it up and twirling his head beneath it. He seems to be scoping out the charms on her bracelet. I could swear he would lick her like an ice cream cone if he could. *Should I let her off the hook? Save my bestie? Nah. Maybe in a few minutes.*

"It's from my friend. She gave it to me for Christmas."

"She?" His voice sounds oddly high pitched. *Is his voice still changing? It's a little late for puberty.*

"Peyton. You might remember her. She went to our school first quarter."

"Aww. Zuch a zweet friend. I would never take it off. The Kremlin. What a special place. It'z known for its miraculous powers."

I watch Daemon bow before her. *Oh shit.* I have to laugh. *This is the cheesiest, funniest thing I've ever seen in my life.* I literally fall to the ground. Jenna snaps her head over her shoulder.

"Caden! What are you doing here?"

"Apparently, I'm here to teach Daemon some new moves." I still can't stop laughing.

Daemon looks embarrassed that I witnessed his sorry moves. I can see him fidget and start to back away. "I'll catch up weez you later. Oh wait. Text me the picture. I want to show my host family."

"I don't have your phone number."

"Here, I'll do it. May I zee your phone?"

Jenna hands him the phone. "Very good. Zere we go. Zankz, Jenna. I'll zee you at zchool next week." He looks down at me and grunts. "By Ca-don."

"Oh, Jenna. How did you hook up with him?" I'm roaring with laughter. *That accent. Holy crap. I've never heard anything like it.*

"Hook up? Seriously? Geez. Give me a little credit. He skied up behind us when we were getting off the lift and asked if he could take a couple runs with us. Kaitlyn had to go to the bathroom, so I took a run with him. That's it."

"You took a selfie with him!" I clamp my lips together, trying not to laugh. "What's he going to do with that? Post it on Facebook?" I shake my head. "There goes your chance at Winter Court!"

I can't control it any longer. I'm doubled over laughing.

"I'm just trying to be nice. It's Christmas. He's away from his family. I wanted him to feel like he had someone. Have a heart."

"Speaking of hearts. You know who's in his?"

"What are you talking about?"

"Get a clue, Jenna. He's totally into you. As a matter of fact, I have a little secret I've been keeping from you."

"Really? What's that?"

"You really want to know?"

"Tell me." Jenna bends down and starts pawing at the snow. When she stands up, she's holding a big, round snow-ball. "Or I'll shove this down your pants."

"Okay. You're his background picture."

"What? I've worked with him on his laptop, and I am not. His background picture is one of the Rocky movies or some-thing."

"Not his laptop background. His phone."

She crinkles her nose and twists her face into a grimace. "How do you know? Is he your new BFF or something?"

Seriously, does she not believe me? "I know because I saw it. On our last race. If you don't believe me, ask Lennart. He saw it too."

"Lennart?"

"Yeah, our German exchange student. The really smart guy in our physics class. You know, he thinks Daemon is weird too. It's not just me."

Jenna huffs and rolls her eyes. "It's just his culture. You should give him a chance. He really helped me out with the whole heritage thing."

"So, it doesn't bother you?"

"What?"

"Having your picture on his screen?"

Jenna begins shaking her head back and forth. I can tell

she's curious, but trying to play it cool. "Well, what picture is it?"

"Oh, the one in your swimsuit." I don't look up to see her face. I strap back in. "Race you to the bottom." I hear her grunt as I swoosh past her. *Got her good!*

CHAPTER 27

POSSIBILITIES

MY PHONE IS BURNING A hole in my pocket. I couldn't text her back while we were at the lodge. Everyone was flicking me too much crap for checking my phone so often, and I didn't want to invite any more questions. I want to keep this one to myself for a while. She's too much fun to share.

When we pull up in front of my house, the first thing on my mind is replying to that, "Hi." *Hi ... with a winkie face. Is she flirting? I don't use winkers unless I'm flirting.*

I stick my hand in my pocket, just to make sure my phone is still there, ready to go. "See you guys, later, huh?" I practically skip toward the door.

"Going to check your phone again, huh?" Brody jokes.

"Be careful with that one. She sounds a little feisty to me."

"Don't you worry about me, boys. I can handle my own."

I don't see my parents. They must still be at the Bailey's. *Yes! Time to text.* I run through the door and jump on my bed. I open the text and inspect the messages. *What? She didn't mes-*

sage back on the group text. She started a new thread. Just to me. Interesting. A new wave of excitement overtakes me. *Oh, the possibilities.*

ME: Hi ;)

Smooth. I can't go wrong with that. I wait a couple minutes. *Maybe I waited too long. Dang it. I should've texted her while I was on the lift.* My feet are frozen stiff. I decide to hop in the shower to thaw out. I decide to bring the phone in the bathroom with me. I lay it down next to the shower door, hoping I'll soon hear the sweet chime of a text.

Oh, this feels good. The scalding, hot water runs over me, bringing life back into my toes and fingertips. *So hot. Like her. There's her face again. Thank you, God, for that face. Oh, stop it. Geez. Get out of my head.* I slap at my cheeks, trying to knock some sense into myself. *Guys don't fixate on girls like this. Maybe I should go get one of those magazines. Give my mind something else to work with. Maybe my dad has one hiding under his mattress. I know he used to have one.*

Ding.

I pop open the shower door, just wide enough to look at the screen.

TANGLES: I see you text just about as fast as you ski.

A smile spreads across my face. *Ahh, there's my girl. So, she has been waiting for me to text back.* I hurry to rinse the rest of the soap out of my hair, pull a towel around my waist, and pick up the phone.

TANGLES: You take forever to respond you know. Are you using a dictionary to look up spellings or something? What are you doing?

She's good. How do I answer her question and keep the banter rolling? Taking a shower doesn't seem like a fun enough answer. I know I've got to throw her off game to keep her interested. Something tells me I can't let this one get bored. *Let's see what kind of tricks I have up my sleeve.* I think really hard about my next text. Finally it comes to me.

ME: You really want to know?

TANGLES: I never ask a question I don't want to know the answer to.

I reach out and take a selfie. *Not a good enough angle.* I decide to take another one. I have to highlight my pecs. *I flex my chest, make sure I have a few water droplets showing. Oh yeah. There we go.* Snap. *Perfect.* I hit send.
Five seconds later, another text comes across the screen.

TANGLES: Awww, how cute. I didn't know you had a LITTLE brother. ;)~

ME: Ouch.

TANGLES: I'm just playin' with you. You look kinda hot.

Yes!

ME: You think so?

TANGLES: Yeah, like really hot. Is that sweat? Are you working out?

Oh, hot. She likes to play with her words, doesn't she?

ME: Nope. Just got out of the shower. What're you up to?

TANGLES: Do you really want to know?

ME: Yeah, and don't tell me. Show me.

TANGLES: You have to earn my picture. I don't send this face to just anybody.

ME: Are you saying I'm just anybody?

TANGLES: Oh, you're somebody. Just not somebody that I'm going to send a picture to.

ME: :(

TANGLES: Yet.

ME: Hmm. What can I do to earn it?

TANGLES: Take me someplace. Spend lots of money on me. Let me borrow your debit card for a day or two. You know, the usual stuff girls get from a guy who wants their picture.

ME: Haha. Well, I don't give out my debit card to just anybody. You know, you have to earn it.

TANGLES: Hmm. How do I earn it?

This isn't going so bad. Should I ask her? Heck, what do I have to lose? Besides my ego? Calm down, Caden. Quit being a wuss.

ME: Let me take you out. Spend lots of money on you. You know, the usual stuff guys do for girls who give them their picture.

TANGLES: Doesn't sound like a bad deal. What's your idea?

ME: New Year's. I want to take you. Not as my teammate, but as my date.

TANGLES: What about Jessie May? I thought you liked her.

My heart just about drops out of my chest. *She did think I was into Jessie May. How do I fix this? Think. Think.*

TANGLES: You're not texting back. You like my cousin, don't you?

ME: Well, I like her. She's a sweet girl. But I don't like her the way you like a girl when you ask for their picture.

TANGLES: Are you playing me? I could've sworn you and Jessie May were into each other while we were decorating those cookies.

ME: Nah. That was just me trying to get your attention. Jessie May was in on it the whole time. ;)

TANGLES: What do you mean? In on it?

ME: She saw the way I was looking at you. She wanted to help me out.

TANGLES: How were you looking at me?

ME: Like I just saw the most badass country girl in the county.

ME: And my life won't be complete until I have her picture.

TANGLES: Well, that's sort of a huge responsibility to live up to. Completing someone's life, and all.

ME: Yep. I wouldn't trust just anyone to do it.

TANGLES: Oh shoot. I've got to go. My parents are here. This isn't going to be fun. :(

ME: Tangles, it's Christmas. Is everything okay? Will I get to talk to you again? What about New Year's?

There's no response. Damn that girl is abrupt. She loves to leave me hanging. *All the time.* I take a deep breath and re-read our texts over and over and over. I could read her words all night long. *Damn, she's fun.*

I'm starting to get a little cold. *I should get dressed.* I walk over to my dresser to grab some underwear and socks. When I pull out my drawer, I see it. My stash of souvenirs. They remind me of Peyton. The soft, innocent Peyton. The one that existed before the accident. I look through the stuff. There really isn't much there. A couple tickets to the movies. A keychain from the homecoming dance. A polo shirt she bought me. I cringe. *I'd never wear this. Green and brown stripes? What was she thinking?* I laugh.

Memories come flooding back. Memories that, surprisingly, don't hurt today. They're good, but not great. Looking at the stuff, I realize, we were good. But face it, we were boring. There really wasn't a lot there outside of snuggling and movies. *Why didn't I realize it at the time? I thought I was in love with her. I thought I couldn't live without her.* Her screaming voice echoes through my mind. Her scathing face flashes in front of me. Peyton wasn't who I thought she was. For the first time, I know that I'm going to be just fine without her.

Ding.

I pull on my pajama bottoms and race back out to my bedroom to see if it's her. It's a group text from Officer Marnia.

> MARNIA: Hey guys. I've been waiting for you to get back to me. I'm powering down for the night, but I'll be back in the office on Monday. If I don't hear from you, I'll drop by for a visit.

I wonder what kind of update she'd want to give us on Christmas. Weird that she'd text this late at night. Kaitlyn's going to be on pins and needles. I'd better go check on her.

I leave my phone on the bed and go down to T's bedroom. She's in the bathroom, so I stop just inside the doorway. "Hey, T. You in there?"

"Yeah," her voice comes from around the corner.

"Did you get the text from Officer Marnia?"

"Um. I got one last night, but we were running Jenna back to town. I forgot to respond."

"She just messaged again. Did you see it?"

Kaitlyn walks out with her bathrobe on and a towel around her head. "She's tried to get a hold of us a few times this week. She must have something really important to tell us. What do you think it is?"

I take a deep breath. "I really don't know."

"Oh, God, Caden. Do you think he's still out there? Maybe someone's spotted him. The thought of that scares the hell out of me. What if he comes back?"

I can tell Kaitlyn's let her guard down the last few days. I watch the stress reappear on her face. *I shouldn't have said anything. I'm so stupid sometimes.* "It's okay, T. If he hasn't come back by now. I don't think he will."

"Just in case, can I sleep in your room tonight?"

"Why don't we just sleep in the living room? Like the old days. We'll make it a party. Watch all the 'Home Alone' movies."

"Yeah, um, two creepy guys trying to break into a little kid's house. That's gonna make me feel better about my stalker."

She does have a point. I'd better pick something a little less terrifying. "Okay, bad idea. We'll go for Christmas comedies."

I watch relief wash over my sister's face, and I can see she's been carrying more stress and fear than I'd realized.

"Alright. I'll be right out. Just let me get dressed."

I go back to my room to grab my sleeping bag and pillows. Just as I walk through the door, I hear another ding.

TANGLES: Okay. I'll go with you. Is your team practicing this week?

ME: Yes! To both.

TANGLES: Great. What day will you be up?

ME: Monday.

TANGLES: In that case, see you then. :)

Just a smiley? Something must be wrong. Hope it's not me.

CHAPTER 28

LIFTED

I CAN'T BELIEVE I HAVE boarding practice during Christmas vacation. At least I have a chance to see her up there. I shove my wool socks into my duffle bag and zip it up. "Hey, Mom, are you ready to take me down to the bus?"

My mom sounds a little put out when she responds from the hallway. "Are you sure you don't just want to take your truck down there?"

"I don't want to leave it down by the gym. Remember what I told you about Jenna's car? She still can't find that flash drive."

As I shove the last of my stuff into the duffle bag, I hear a voice behind me.

"What's up, Cade man?"

I turn around to see Jenna. "Speak of the devil." I greet her as she comes bouncing through my door. "What are you doing here so early? I thought you liked to sleep in on your days off."

"It's not my day off. I have basketball practice, remember? I'm here to see Kaitlyn before she heads off to her rehearsal."

"I see. So, did you ever find that flash drive?" I look behind me and notice my mom is listening intently. A curious look comes over her face. It makes me think she was questioning my story until now. *I hope she's not onto me about not wanting to drive.*

"Nope. But you know what else? You're right about not leaving your truck down there. The other night when I was at practice, I left my car in front of the big gym. I must've forgotten to lock it. It was open when I got back, and I could swear someone had been eating in there. It smelled like peanut butter and Fritos when I got inside."

I laugh. "Maybe you left your lunch under the seat. Or, it could've been your gym socks."

"Funny, only that's the day I ate lunch at Miner's Perk. Turkey and cranberry doesn't smell like that." She pinches her face and sticks out her tongue.

"See, Mom. Unattended cars aren't safe down there. You'd better give me a ride."

I pull my duffle bag over my shoulder. "Have a good practice."

"You kids are crazy," my mom laughs. "Peanut butter and Fritos, yum."

I barely register what my mom is saying. All I can think about is getting to the ski park. I can't help but feel excited that I'm on my way to see Tangles. I open the door and jump two feet when I darn near run into Officer Marnia. "Holy crap, you scared me."

"Sorry, kid. Do you guys have a minute? I can see you're headed out. I won't take long."

I glance up at the clock. I still have ten minutes. It's a good thing the gym is just down the street. "I can give you about five minutes. Is that enough time?"

"Sure. Is your sister here, too?"

"I'll go get her," my mom replies. "Why don't you come on in, Officer Marnia?"

I hear my mom's voice down the hall, as she beckons my sister out into the living room.

"Is your dad around?" Officer Marnia questions.

"No. He's already down at work."

"Okay, I guess I can do this without him here."

My mom, Kaitlyn, Jenna, and I have all gathered around in the living room when Officer Marnia looks at each of us. The expression on her face is serious. "I was going to tell you earlier this week, that they found a body. It hadn't been positively identified, so I didn't press getting ahold of you when you didn't respond to my texts. I just wanted to make you aware. But, with Christmas and family, I figured this could wait until today."

I hear Kaitlyn take an audible breath. I can see she's tensed from the news. I'm sure the officer is about ready to deliver some tough news, so I move to the other side of my mom. I want to be standing by T. I put my hand up to her back, so I can give her the support she might need with the next words Officer Marnia is sure to speak.

"It's him. The family identified the body the other night."

Kaitlyn's hand instantly comes up over her mouth. She gasps and folds in half. I tug her into me, taking her tightly in my arms. I can feel her shaking. She's holding onto me tightly. Brody's not here, and I hope I can be the support that she needs right now. "Are you okay?" I whisper into the top of her head. She nods up and down, not saying a word.

I know she's relieved that she doesn't have to worry about him coming after her anymore, but she must also be hurting inside. At one time, she really loved Pistol. I know she's forgiven him for everything he did. We've talked about it. She said there was a reason for the way he acted. We didn't get into it, but I know that my sister is full of forgiveness and understanding. More than I'll ever have. She wanted the best for him, despite the terror he caused in her life.

She's beginning to cry. I can feel her tears seeping through my shirt sleeve. This is going to be so hard on her. I hold her tightly. "Shhh. It's going to be okay, T. Shhh."

Officer Marnia speaks again. "I hate to tell you this, but there's more. Pistol's body was found in a completely different location than his truck. It was found by some snowshoers in a crevice away from the river."

What does that mean? "What are you trying to tell us?" I ask.

Officer Marnia looks around the room at each of us, as if she's trying to gauge our reaction to the next bit of information she's going to throw our way. "It means that there's no way the water could've carried his body downstream. And he was too far away from the vehicle to have been thrown there naturally. His body was actually wedged in between two boulders."

"I just don't get it," Kaitlyn sniffles. "How did he get there? What happened?"

"The forensics unit is looking into it. Right now, we know the body had to be dragged to the location. We're not sure if it was by animals, or something else. Snow covered any kind of tracks."

I'm trying to visualize the scene in my mind, and I just can't make sense of any of it. *He was there. In his red truck. Coming at us. Shooting. I heard it. I heard it.* "Did they find my gun?"

"I'm afraid not. There was no gun."

"But there were bullets in my truck, weren't there? You told me when they recovered my truck that there were holes."

"Oh, there was a gun. I'm afraid it just wasn't on Pistol Black. Not on his body anyway."

I'm sure sheer terror is covering my face right now, because it's for damn sure that it's plastered all over my mother's and Jenna's.

Officer Marnia speaks, "I know you kids have had a little time since the accident. Have you remembered anything else about that day? Anything at all?"

I scan my memory for anything but come up empty. "It's such a blur. It all happened so fast. But I'm just not sure."

"Not sure about what, Caden?"

"I just don't remember seeing Pistol with a gun, that's all. I heard it. I know that for a fact. I definitely heard it. I saw Pistol waving his arms. I just don't remember seeing a gun in his hand."

Officer Marnia looks down and begins writing on her tablet. She's shaking her head as she writes. "Well, I hate to do it, but I think I'm going to have to question Peyton again. Maybe she remembers something. She did have a different vantage point. I hope I can get her to talk this time."

I don't want to think about Peyton. I look up at the clock. *I'm going to be late.* I have two minutes to get down to that bus, and if I don't, it's going to take off without me. "Officer, I hate to be rude, but I'm going to miss my bus. If I remember anything else, I'll give you a call."

"Before you go, I just want to make sure you kids are still being vigilant out there. We're still piecing the puzzle together, and until we find that gun, and the reason for the body's location, we need you to be aware. Don't go anywhere alone. It'll just be safer that way."

I nod my head. "Thanks, Officer." I give T one more squeeze. "You going to be okay today?"

"Yep. I'm okay. Jenna, can you take Caden to the bus. I kinda need my mom right now."

"You've got it. Let's go." She leans in to give T a hug, and we head out the door with one minute to spare. *Good thing the gym is only four blocks away.*

We pull up to the ski park around noon. The entire ride was filled with visions of the wreck and Pistol's lifeless body lying on the bloody, snowy ground. I can't imagine what the scene really looked like, but I'm sure my imagination is making it far worse than it could've ever been in real life. At first, I visualize brains splattered all over a sharp rock. Then I picture his body impaled by shards of metal ripped from his truck. The images spin into worse and worse traumatic injuries, until I'm sick to my stomach.

I jump out of the bus and run to the side of the parking lot, where I heave over the side of the snow berm. I've literally made myself sick thinking about Pistol's traumatic death. *Was I responsible for that too? What if I'm the reason he went over the bank? I know my truck did crashed into his. Maybe there wasn't a gun. Did I freak out for no reason and cause him to crash? What have I done? Peyton and Pistol? I did this to them.*

Get a hold of yourself. I look up into the clear sky. I take a deep breath of the clean mountain air. *There was a gun. There were holes in your truck. You didn't do this.* I bend over, hands on my knees, and take in a few more breaths. *Water. I need water.* I pull my bottle from my duffle bag and take a swig. I take another, swishing it around and spitting it to the ground.

"You okay over there, Woodley?"

"Yeah. Just a little motion sickness. Be right there."

When I finally pull myself together, I head up to the lodge, where the team is gearing up. I've got to use the bathroom, wash my face off at least. I find my friend so I can give him a heads up. "Hey, Ty. Be right back, huh. Watch my gear, will you?"

Tyler nods, "You've got it."

As I stand up and move toward the bathroom, I see brown curls turning the corner. *Is that her?* Instantly, my mind changes stations from the Horror Channel to Hot Dish Network. I speed up and head down the stairs into the bathroom. There goes that hair. I decide to yell her name, maybe slow her down a little.

Otherwise, I'm not going to catch her. "Tangles." She keeps walking. "Hey Tangles!" The girl turns around. *Oh, God. Ohhhh. That's not her.* I raise my hand apologetically and duck my head as I round the corner into the bathroom.

I splash water on my face. That was so embarrassing. I decide I really should go to the bathroom while I'm in here. I know I need to hurry. We're going to slip the course in about four minutes. That doesn't give me a lot of time. I'm in and out. I don't waste any time fastening my pants while I'm in the stall. I turn my back toward the door, and begin to close them on my way out. When I turn around, mid-zip, there she is … looking down at my open zipper.

"Are those the same hands that are going to give me my ticket to the New Year's party?"

I smile. Unable to speak, I nod, "Mmmhmm."

"Well, not unless you go back and wash 'em."

Zip. I swallow hard as I feel the heat rise into my face.

"Pee right back. I mean *be* right back." *How embarrassing.* I'm a mess. *How am I ever going to face this girl again? She just caught me with my zipper down.*

When I return from the bathroom, Tangles is nowhere in sight. *Guess I chased her away.* I look down at my watch. *Crap. I'm late.*

I make a mad dash up the stairs. My gear is sitting there on the table where I left it, but the team is nowhere in sight. *I'm so busted.* I grab my board, pull on my gloves and run out the door. Thankfully, the team is still in line at the bottom of the lift. I push off and make my way down the small slope toward the back of the line. There's a whole group of people in line behind my team. Hopefully Coach will know I'm back here. I jump into the singles line, hoping I can get up there a little more quickly.

I look out toward the lodge, scanning the park, to see if I can spot my coach. I want him to see I'm here and ready to go. The last thing I need today is more trouble to worry about. I don't even look around to see who's in line with me. I'm gazing down the hill when I hear singing coming from the inside line. *What is that?* I listen to the lyrics coming from a dainty voice. I recognize the melody, but the words aren't quite right. These words are talking about a city boy on a snowboard. *Is that "City Boy Stuck?" No way.* I look forward, noticing the line has moved ahead. There's a four foot gap between me and the person in front of me. I begin to push forward, as I look over my left shoulder to see where the song is coming from. *Yellow and black flash before my eyes.* I turn and do a double take. *It's her.* She's smiling.

"You disappeared on me."

"Or you disappeared on me. It's all in the perspective, really. Actually, I thought the toilet may have swallowed you up. But then I remembered, you're just slow." She winks and pushes forward on her skis.

She's next to Jessie May in the doubles line. "Hey, Caden. Did you have a nice Christmas?"

"Yeah. Got a new truck."

"Nice. Does that mean you're going to pick us up for the New Year's party?"

I look down at my board. *How do I answer that?* Different excuses are rolling through my mind, when I see a ski pole fly up toward my face.

"We're meeting him there, Jessie May." She looks down at me. "Grab on, Grandpa. You're holding up the line."

I grab onto her pole as she pulls me forward. She winks at me and looks back at Jessie May. "I mean, we're still practically strangers. You can't expect Caden to pick us up. He doesn't even know where you live."

"Where *we* live, Avery. You live there now too, you know."

I can feel a shift in Tangles mood. Suddenly, she's quiet. Her face looks almost reflective. Sad.

I don't want to butt in, so I keep quiet too. I scoot along, minding my own business when we approach the lift. Our lines merge. As luck has it, we're on the same chair.

"You okay in the middle?" I ask quietly.

She nods.

It's uncomfortably quiet on the way up. Almost to the point where I can no longer handle the silence. *Is she mad that I'm on the same chair as her? Maybe I smell. Oh gosh. What if I smell?* I try to sniff at my armpits a little just to check.

"Are you really sniffing yourself?"

I can't answer that. Well, I can, but I'm not going to. Why does she always catch me at my worst?

She looks forward, not making eye contact. "It's not you. I know that's what you're thinking. But it's not."

Phew. "I was starting to wonder."

"Actually, I kinda like your smell. It reminds me of … pumpkin pie. Kinda sweet. Kinda spicy."

Pumpkin pie and vanilla cupcakes. Sounds like a sweet combination to me.

"Pumpkin pie, huh? I can handle that."

Silence returns. There's really no place to go from here. *Change of subject needed. Like now.*

"How was your Christmas?" *There. That one sounds safe enough.*

Silence.

"Okay, did you get any surprises?" *Everyone gets at least one surprise on Christmas.* "Good ones, I mean?" she shakes her head and looks down at her glove. "No."

I look over the top of Avery's bowed head. Jessie May is looking at me, shaking her head, and signaling me to cut the conversation. I nod my head and turn in the opposite direction to look out over the trees. If I don't say *anything*, I won't say the *wrong* thing. The chair stops, mid-cable. We begin bouncing up and down. Some jackass in the front of us thinks it's funny to swing his feet and make the cable bounce. At closer look, it's

Tyler.

"Hey, dude. Stop bouncing us."

He whips his head around. "Hey, Caden. Is that the girl you keep talking about?" He gives me a thumbs up and turns back around.

I try to cover my face with my gloves and look down. *This is the longest ride of my life.* Finally, the chair lurches forward. Thank goodness we're only three chairs away from the end. I can't even look at Tangles when we get off. I board right, and they ski left, stopping right next to Tyler.

"What was that?"

"I figured you needed a little help. She'll love it."

He can use some brushing up on his wingman skills. "Uh, look around. Do you see her?"

He pulls his lips together. "Oops, sorry, dude. Works with most girls."

"She's not most girls."

We take off down the face. I feel like we're already behind, and I want to take the short route down for my warmup. I watch for Tangles, but she's nowhere to be seen. Trail after trail, and run after run, I keep my eyes peeled for the one who numbs my mind and brings me happiness. I haven't found that feeling with anyone or anything else. I've got to find her. I just want to be close to her. She doesn't need to talk. She doesn't need to do anything at all. Just being in her presence gives me everything I want. Everything I need.

Ding.

My phone rings out from my pocket. "Hey Ty, I need to check this, k?" I pull over to the side of the run next to a tree and take out my phone.

> TANGLES: Hey, pumpkin pie. Sorry I had to run! Just couldn't wait around for you all day. ;) About the New Year's Party. I'll meet you in the upper parking lot at

7:00. Jessie May says if you can get an extra ticket, bring your friend. The hot one from the bouncing chair.

"Tyler! Tyler!" I wave to him about thirty yards downhill. "What're your plans for New Year's?"

I ski down, holding up my phone. When I finally reach him, I let him read the text. A huge smile grows on his face. "Guess I'm hitting the party with you and the hotties from the lift." He wiggles his eyebrows. "See, have a little faith, dude. I told you it'd work."

CHAPTER 29

MANLY BULLETS

"WELL, HOW DO I LOOK?" I struggle to open the top button of my suffocating collar, as I walk into T's room looking for some kind of reassurance. Tonight is a big deal, and I don't want to mess it up with a goofy looking outfit. I'm used to warm ups and tees, so I'm definitely out of my element trying to dress myself for a black tie event.

Relief comes over me when I hear the fox whistle. "Impressive." Kaitlyn gives me the once over, raising her eyebrows when her eyes meet my shiny, new tie. "I didn't think you knew how to tie one of those. Who has you looking so spiffy? I haven't seen you dress like for … well, I've never seen you dress like that."

"I've got a pretty special date tonight."

"Really. You've done a good job of keeping it under wraps."

"Well, I had to work pretty hard to make it happen. I wasn't sure it was going to pan out."

"It's New Year's Eve. Where are you taking her?"

"The party at the ski park, remember?" *Of course she's not going to remember.* I haven't talked about the party at all. I don't want to make anyone feel bad that I'm ditching them tonight. Not to mention, I can't answer the predicted onslaught of questions about "the new girl." Not yet, anyway.

"Oh yeah, the one I didn't have a chance to get into because you sent us home with Jenna."

"Yeah, sorry about that. She's a little bent out of shape too. I thought they'd at least give us a couple more guest passes, but we only got one per team, and ours is going to Tyler."

"Jenna's Ty?"

"No, Tyler R. We're going on a double date with my teammate from the Dash."

"It's okay. The rest of us are going to the Fear Factor party at Timmy's house. I hear it's a pretty good time."

"You're not kidding. Last year, I heard Lane and Trenton dared him to jump off of his second story balcony into his swimming pool. Little did he know, they figured out how to fill it with jello first. Besides snapping his collar bone, I guess he was digging slime out of every hole in his body for a week."

My stomach flips when I think of flying teenagers, wild animals, and tow ropes. *Crap. They're planning to run down to the city park and try out the merry-go-round dare this year. I hope she doesn't get herself killed doing something stupid.* "Do me a favor. Stay with Brody, will you? And don't lose your head. I think they're planning to do some outrageous stunts this year."

"Don't worry. I'll be safe. But what about you? Who is this mystery girl, anyway? I'd really like to get a thorough background check on this one."

I know Kaitlyn is still ruffled over how my relationship with Peyton turned out. I need to reassure her that I'm going to be okay. *Sound casual.* "You don't know her. She doesn't live up here. And, she's pretty cool. I think you'd really like her. She's cute, feisty, and country to the core."

"Really? How do you know her well enough to get that kind of info? Especially if she doesn't even live here?"

"Well, she was at the snowmobile park that one day. Then, I've run into her a few times at ski practice. And, I already told you, she was my teammate for the Dash to the Pole."

"Ah, the elusive snow princess. Always present, but never seen. I kind of want to meet this girl. Any chance you'll be bringing her home?"

"I'm working on it." I can't help but smile when I imagine my family seeing Tangles for the first time. She's like nobody they've ever met before. "Let's see how tonight goes first."

Kaitlyn looks down at her watch. "Well, you'd better get a move on it. Otherwise you'll only be spending half the night with her."

"Ty should be here any minute. He's probably double checking his pits. He hasn't had a date for a while, and he doesn't want to mess this one up. He's totally stoked to be going with the *hotties from the lift*, as he calls them." I air quote *hotties from the lift*.

Kaitlyn laughs, "That kid. He's so girl crazy."

"Yeah, he chased one of them all over the ski park the other day. I'm not sure he even realizes it's the same girl." I have to laugh at the thought that he may not know his date is shiny, blue suit. "It'll be worth the extra deodorant. She is pretty damn cute."

The doorbell rings. "Oh, here, let me fix you really quick. Stay right there." She runs into the bathroom and comes back in with a glop of green stuff on her hand.

"What are you doing?" I squint and pull back from the attacking blob.

"Trust me. She's gonna love it."

I close my eyes, and feel the cool jelly ooze into my scalp. She's tugging at the ends of my hair. *Is she spiking it? Seriously?* "T, this is how I used to do my hair when I was nine. Please don't do this to me. She already calls me a city boy."

"Well, it's too late to wash it out now. Take your chances. If she doesn't like it, it's only one night."

"Yeah, like the most important night of my life. I don't want to mess this up, T."

A funny look crosses her face. It's almost a look of amusement.

"What?"

"Oh nothing. It's just, I like what I'm seeing here." She stands away from me, smiling and nodding with approval. "You're moving on. You actually care about this girl, don't you?"

I hadn't really thought about it that way. *Moving on.* When I'm around her it feels good. It feels right. I'm excited about going on a date with Tangles. I try to bite the side of my cheek to hold back the smile, but it pulls itself away from my clenched jaw. I have to chuckle.

"You can't hide it, can you?" she giggles. "Well, it's good to see she's putting a little life back into you. That's quite a feat, you know … bringing something back to life in the dead of winter. She must be doing something right."

This is getting too deep. I can't think like this right now. I just want to have some fun with a pretty, funny girl. "Alright, alright. Thanks for your approval. But I gotta go." I throw my head back toward the door. "Ty's waiting, remember?"

"Be safe, big brother."

"You too."

My hand is shaky as I pull the handle to release the door. *I can do this. I can do this.* I have to convince myself to keep going.

My legs are shaky, but not only from the fear of the ride in the blustery snow. I'm a bundle of nerves. I've been clenching my muscles for an entire hour, trying to stop the insane butterflies from pounding an escape through the very core of my body. *Why does the icy air always seem to make them intensify?*

I can't believe I'm going on an actual date with her. I can't focus. I look up toward the glowing lodge, surrounded by fiery torches and twinkling lights. I see silhouettes of sleekly dressed ladies popping through the windows. *I wonder if she's already up there.* She's supposed to meet me at the Mountain Shop to get her ticket. I look down at my watch. *7:15, crap. We're late. She's still got to be outside. Waiting for me.* I rush to slide out of Ty's monster rig, nearly losing my footing. Luckily, I find the truck bed, just before my feet completely slide out from beneath me.

"You okay there, buddy?" Ty laughs as he pats me on the back. "I've never seen you so fidgety before. You were bouncing around like a jackhammer the whole way here. Reminds me of kindergarten, when we were all in the dugout, and you had to go to the bathroom. The coach wouldn't let you, remember?"

"How could I forget? I peed my pants right there on the first baseman's shoe. Most embarrassing moment of my life."

"Hey, but she still let you kiss her inside the jungle gym after the game. She must not have been too traumatized by it."

"That's a rumor, dude. A big fat rumor. It never happened." *I hope that sounds convincing.*

"Mmmhmm. Yep. Whatever you say. By the way, I was there."

I'll never live that damn story down. Change of subject. "It's hot out here." I pull off my jacket and toss it in the truck, then begin tugging at my button-up collar. I've already released a button, but I feel like I'm suffocating inside of this thing. *I hope I wore enough deodorant.*

"Are you sure you're okay?" Ty looks up in the sky and

opens his mouth to catch a snowflake. "You can't be that hot. It's cold enough to snow. You've got it pretty bad, don't you?"

"Wait til you see who's waiting up there for you. She's gonna warm you up real fast too. I guarantee it."

"Really? Well, now I'm intrigued."

We're interrupted by a text alert on my phone. I reach down and pull it out of my pocket.

TANGLES: Slow again. Should've expected that. Where are you?

ME: In the parking lot. Almost there. Are you always this impatient?

TANGLES: Only when I really want something.

My face heats up. It's hard to swallow. My manly bullets are pinging all over my body.

ME: And what is it you want?

TANGLES: Hurry your ass up here and find out!

Gulp. A new rush of blood finds its way to my face. I can hear my pulse beating in my ears. This girl's going to kill me, and I haven't even seen her yet. "Hurry, Ty. They're waiting for us." I walk faster. I'm sure I look like I'm trying to walk on a conveyor belt as my feet slip beneath me over and over again, trying to find traction on the icy surface.

We finally reach the corner of the building. I re-button my collar, run my fingers through my hair, and straighten my tie one more time before we round the corner.

"You ready?"

"As I'll ever be."

In the distance, I spot it right away. That curly, brown hair. From here, she looks dainty. She's dressed in a black peacoat, huddled next to little Jessie May. She's got to have the prettiest backside I've ever seen. From her shapely legs to her fancy boots, I can't take my eyes off of her. I take a deep breath and let it out. "There they are." I point.

"Where?" Ty asks as we get closer.

"Right there. Next to the shop. Black and blue coats."

I watch Tyler's face change as he squints to see them better. "Holy..." He looks at me, mouth agape. "Is that?" He looks again. "I get shiny, blue suit?"

I proudly nod, "Yep," popping my "p" with gusto.

"How the hell did you make this happen? I chased that girl all over the mountain the other night and never even got close."

I watch Tyler's face flush red. "How's the temperature now?" He doesn't answer, but I know when he loosens his collar, that we are both in trouble tonight.

I look back down at my phone to check the time. There it is, staring up at me, her last text.

TANGLES: Hurry your ass up here and find out!

When we finally reach them, the girls are huddled close. They look like they're freezing. I wish I could offer her my jacket right now, but I left it in the truck. *Guess that's what I get for having manly hot flashes.* "Tangles, Jessie May, right behind you."

Slowly the girls turn toward me. I can't be quite sure, but I think Tyler gasps just as loud as I do at the sight before us. Shocked by our lack of self-control, we grimace toward each other. Tyler whispers, "Did we just do that?" All I can do is pinch my face and nod.

I look up to see the amusement covering the girls' faces. *She's* going to have something to say about this. I can feel it coming. *Wait for it.*

"Oh come on. Seriously? You can't breathe? It wasn't that far. Time to hit the gym boys."

And she does it again. Why do I love it when she insults me like that? Probably because it's always accompanied by a dimple and a smile. Putting that kind of thought into me is her way of flirting. I know it. And I know she knows I know it. Time to knock her off guard.

"It wasn't the run that took my breath away," I wink and double click my tongue.

I study her reaction. *Did I just see her flinch?* She quickly wraps her arms around her waist. I watch as the mauve slowly creeps its way across her cheeks. Her jaw is clenched tight, but I swear, I can still hear her teeth chattering. *Either she's extremely cold, or I just made her nervous.* She takes a deep breath that audibly quivers on the way out. *Holy shit, she's not cold. I got her.*

Jessie May laughs. "I can't believe it! I'm standing in the presence of the first boys to ever stun my cousin into silence. Well done, boys. Well done." She nods, looking back at Tangles. "Well, since she doesn't know how to talk anymore, allow me to introduce myself." She holds her hand out to Tyler. "I'm Jessie May. We met on the lift the other day. Well, sort of. Okay, not really. But thanks for coming."

"My pleasure." Not letting go of her hand, he slowly pulls it to his lips and kisses it.

I watch Tangles turn her head and fake gag. "Alright Prince Charming. Let's take this show inside."

"Hey, I just remembered. I ran all the way up here because you wanted something. What was it?"

Tangles holds out her hand. "Those tickets. Hand 'em over. It's cold out here."

CHAPTER 30

HORMONAL FIREBALLS

ONCE WE'RE THROUGH THE DOORS, Tyler and Jessie May don't take long to disappear. Their instant connection is obvious, and we're both amused by how quickly Tyler has won her over. Tangles peeks through the crowd, watching the back of Jessie May's little black dress vanish onto the dance floor. "I don't think we'll be seeing them the rest of the night."

"It's okay. They look like they're going to be just fine without us." I point as Tyler picks her up at arm's length and spins her in a circle.

"Oh, I have no doubts Jessie May is going to have a blast with that one. But are you going to be okay without *your* side-kick?"

Trust me, beautiful. Tyler is not the reason I'm here tonight. "Awww, he was just a temp til I found a much better one." I hold my hand out to Tangles. "Shall we?" She looks down at my raised palm, hesitates for the slightest moment, and gives a quick nod. When she finally lays her hand in mine, I forget to breathe. With the gentle curl of each dainty finger around the side of my hand, a shock wave makes its way to my stomach. *How can the touch of one little finger do that to a person? I wonder if she feels it too.* I give her hand a slight squeeze, hoping for any sign that she's okay with this.

My hand warms as I guide her up the stairs to the party. The silence between us has me on edge. *Should I let go? Maybe she's not the touchy feely kind of girl. She does seem pretty feisty.* I look down to get a better read on her. She's watching our hands. Grinning. *She likes it.* Before she knows I've seen her smile, I slide my fingers and lace them through hers. *She's not pulling away.* I watch her tug her bottom lip into her teeth. I hear her breath hitch. The sound causes my chest to tighten. It's a proud moment, the moment I realize that I'm not the only one who's nervous.

As we reach the top of the stairs, I give her hand one more tiny squeeze. I want her to know how much I enjoyed our first touch before I release her to take her jacket. Slowly, I set my hand on the small of her back to steady her last step. I feel her movement freeze beneath my touch. "Sorry," I whisper into the top of her head. "The last step can be tricky." I chuckle. "No rail, you know."

"It's all good. But remember," she whispers, "you're the clumsy one."

I shake my head. "Where'd you get that idea?"

My eyes grow wide as Tangles unbuttons her peacoat, revealing her little, ivory dress. *Damn. How did I find this girl?* "Can I hang that up for you?"

She dangles the coat in front of her. I can't help but look past the black jacket. I'm mesmerized by the frilly, lace skirt that hits her just above the knees. My eyes follow the tight bodice up to her skin. *Tan skin. Lots of it. Do those qualify as straps?* She's magnetic. Every part of me is drawn to her. The crook of her neck. Her smell. I can feel myself leaning too far into her, but

I can't stop. I'm so entranced by her vanilla scent and the sight of the boots and lace in front of me, that when I step forward to take the jacket, I trip over my own feet.

She giggles, as she catches me and helps me find my balance. "Now you know."

"What?"

"Where I got that idea."

"What idea?"

She shakes her head. "Never mind. Let's see if you can dance with those feet?"

"Oh, I can dance … and I plan to. All night."

I take her by the hand. This time, I pull her into me. Again, my nerves light up at her touch. I feel every minuscule point of contact. Side by side, we make our way through the crowd and back toward the dimly lit dance floor. I look around, taking in the view. The ski park has gone all out this year. On top of hiring the band, Tapwater, to play us through the night, the atmosphere is magical. My senses are on high alert. Everything seems bigger, brighter, louder, larger than life. The music. The twinkling lights. The disco ball. The torches. Oh, and the mistletoe. It's everywhere. *Perfect.*

A slow song is starting. *Time to take her onto the dance floor and tell her how beautiful she looks in that dress.* I look down at her and smile, "You ready to dance?"

"Are you?"

"Oh, I'm ready." I chomp down on my gum and smile. I'm so excited for our first dance that I practically drag her to the floor. Our arms dangle between us, connected only by our tightly held hands. Instantly, the small gap between us has me feeling incomplete. I need her closer. I want her in my arms, tucked in next to me, but something tells me I need to take it slow. It takes everything in me to fight the urge to scoop her up and carry her off to somewhere private.

As soon as we find an open space, I give her hand a gentle

tug, slowly rolling her back into me. I carefully release her and glide my hands down to her waist. I stand still, looking down at her, taking in every bouncing curl. Every perfect eyelash. The soft curve of her rounded nose. Her pink lips. I take it all in. I want our first dance to be perfect. I don't want to make a mistake. All I want is a beautiful memory.

Give her time. Let her set the pace. I give her a moment to adjust to me holding her like this. Carefully, I feel her arms come up around my neck. She leans in. Closer than I expected she might. "You, okay?" she whispers into my ear. "Your arm, I mean. I'm not hurting you am I?"

I hadn't even thought about it. Nobody's really held me since the accident. My arm is still a bit sensitive, but no, this does not hurt. *She* does not hurt. *She* feels amazing. "Actually," I whisper into her head, "I was just thinking I wouldn't mind if you held on a little tighter." I smile, knowing I've just sent the ball soaring into her court.

She pulls me in closer. We begin to sway back and forth, our feet glued to the floor beneath us. For the first time, I feel her heart beating against mine. It's fast. Funny, our hearts have taken over where our words have left off. Like most of our conversations, they challenge one another. Hers beats and then mine. Back and forth like a ping pong match. Finally, the floor releases our feet, and we begin to move with the rhythm of the music. She looks up at me. When our eyes meet, I can't help but feel bad. I'm sure it shows on my face. "Sorry I haven't told you yet."

A worried look crosses her face. "Told me what?"

I can't take my eyes off of her. "That you are absolutely breathtaking."

She crinkles her eyes and nose, "me?"

Her genuine reaction says a lot about her. *She really has no idea how beautiful she is.* "Yes, you. I haven't been able to breathe since I caught sight of you tonight. And it's not just because of the rib cracking hold you have on me," I joke.

I can see that she doesn't know how to respond. She's not used to being told she's beautiful. *Where has this girl been hiding?* I have to let her off the hook. "I'm sure you hear that from all the guys ... that you're beautiful."

There's a long pause before she finally responds. "No. Not really."

"That's hard to believe."

"Believe it."

"The boys down here must be blind."

"The boys down here don't know me."

"Why's that?"

"They're not you."

Whoa. They're not me? What does that mean? I don't know, but it almost sounded like a compliment. From Tangles? My brain fumbles for a response, but words fail me. All I can do is smile down at her and pull her in closer. This time, something is different. I feel her begin to relax. She lays her head against my chest. We sway to the music until one song melts into another and another. She fits me perfectly. Our rhythm, our movement, our banter, even the way her head fits into the crook of my neck, is flawless.

Before I realize that three hours have passed, there's an announcement by the MC. "To all of our honored guests. We're opening the lift for the last few rides of the year. If any of you would like to go on up to the top, they've got a bonfire and food waiting for you."

"You want to go?"

How could I not want to go when those lips are asking?

"Are you okay in that dress? It's pretty chilly up there."

"I'm sure we can figure out a way to stay warm." Tangles pulls a trick from my bag and does the ole double tongue click and wink.

Again. How does she do that? Using my own moves against me? I don't know how she's managed to twist my stomach into knots with every touch, and every word out of her mouth tonight, but something tells me she hasn't finished with me yet. She grabs my hand and pulls me off the dance floor. "What're you doing just standing there, turtle boy? The line's not getting any shorter. Follow me."

After a quick search, we hook up with Tyler and Jessie May, and head down to the truck. It's a good thing I came to the mountain with a true outdoorsman tonight, because we return to the lift line with extra jackets and blankets. "Looks like we've got a bit of a wait," Tyler grimaces. "Here. Why don't you girls cover up in these?" I take one of the blankets from his hands and wrap Tangles inside.

When I'm finished, I realize the circumstances have changed. I'm not steadying her step, leading her anywhere, or dancing with her. *Is it still okay to touch her? Lord knows I want to.* I'm not sure what to do with my free hands, once I've finished wrapping her inside the blanket. I start to reach out, but decide to draw back before she notices. I convince my hands to stay put by shoving them into my pockets. Rocking back and forth seems to distract them a bit, but not for long. All I want to do is snuggle up behind her and wrap her in my arms. *Is that still okay?*

I decide to go for my "accidental proximity" move. I position myself as close to her as possible and begin telling stories with Ty. Each time I laugh, I try to accidentally brush against her, hoping against hope that one of these times she'll just decide to lean into me. A few laughs in, we are close. So close I can feel the magnetic connection between us. The nervous energy has me on edge. I can't take it anymore. I decide to take a chance and snuggle up behind her. Hands still securely tucked in my pockets, I lean over her shoulder and whisper into her ear, "You doing okay? Keeping warm?"

Unexpectedly, she lays her head back against my shoulder. "Now that you mention it, I could use a little help." She opens her blanket and motions me in. I literally feel the blood coursing through my veins as I slip in behind her. If I was cold before, I certainly can't remember it now. Little hormonal fireballs chase each other in and out every system of my body, leaving a sea of flames, and lighting my skin on fire.

Fastened by the tight hold Tangles has on the blanket, we move forward in the line, shuffling through the fresh layer of powder. There have been plenty of stories of ski team hijinks and capers exchanged between the four of us, each laugh giving me another opportunity to snuggle in tighter. By the time we get to the lift, it's an oven inside our blanket.

I look up to see only one more couple in front of us. *We can't ride like this.* Gently, I slip out and replace it around Avery's shoulders. The frigid night air hits me like a block of ice. I wrap my arms around myself, suddenly unable to speak. I don't like the sudden separation. It's leaving me with an empty feeling.

"You look miserable," Tangles laughs. "Why'd you leave?"

I snap my head toward the lift. "Wweee have to get on."

"So?"

"Ssoo wwee ccan't bbee wwrapped ttooggether."

"Yes we can. We're not on skis. Get in here." She opens the blanket back up to me.

"Hhhoww?"

"It's not rocket science. You let the chair come up behind you and sit down. Here. I'll hold your hand and show you how."

I can't help but laugh, as she takes my hand and pulls me up to the line.

"Now I can really see why you're just a flag boy," she jokes. "You don't even know how to ride a chair lift."

She can't tell me I don't know how to ride a chairlift. I grew up on this mountain. I've been skiing this thing since I was three years old. "Oh, I know how to ride a chairlift alright. In fact, I wrote the book on the proper way to ride a chairlift."

"Something tells me I'm about to be treated to an excerpt from your instruction manual."

"Only if you're lucky."

"Look, up there!" Tangles points up toward the night sky. "What is it?"

"A shooting star. Guess what that means?"

I shake my head.

"It's my lucky night. Sit down!" She pulls me onto the chair. "Put your money where your mouth is, big guy. You've got some teaching to do."

Why am I intrigued by, yet scared of, this girl all at the same time? I honestly don't know how to take her. *Is she joking right now?* Something tells me I'm about to find out.

CHAPTER 31

WEAPONS

WE SIT AWKWARDLY SILENT, AS the lift leaves the ground. I can't look at her. I don't know what to say. I look back over my shoulder to see Tyler already snuggled up next to Jessie May. When he sees me looking back over my shoulder he gives me a thumbs up. I watch him for a few seconds while I contemplate my next move. *I wonder what she's expecting me to do on this lift. I was just joking about that instruction manual thing. Crap. What have I gotten myself into?*

"You sure do take your time with things, don't you?"

"Oh, uh. Yeah, I don't like to rush into anything."

"That's obvious. But just because you're slow doesn't mean I'm going to forget. You're not getting out of it."

"Out of what?"

"My lesson. I believe it's titled, *The Proper Way to Ride a Lift.*"

"Oh, that. Yeah. Well, I didn't want to say anything. I was trying not to make you feel bad, but since you asked … you're already doing it wrong."

"Oh, I am, huh?"

"Mmmhmm."

"Well, correct me then."

"Okay. Well, first, you're sitting at the wrong angle."

I laugh as I watch Tangles sit up a little straighter and pop her neck back and forth. She looks back at me, grinning. "There. Better?"

I crunch my nose and shake my head, no.

"No? What am I doing wrong?"

"I guess I need to help you, but it's going to take a little work if you want to do it correctly."

"Work doesn't scare me. No one has ever called me lazy."

"Fair enough."

Once again, I slip out from beneath the blanket and slide away from her. Carefully, I turn my body sideways in the chair until I'm facing her. I lift my left leg onto the seat, and hold out my arms. "Slide on over." An amused grin spreads across her face. Then gingerly, she turns her back to me, pulls her feet up onto the chair, pushes herself closer, and snuggles up against my chest.

She pats the small opening on the seat next to her, and then reaches down and tugs on my dangling leg. I pull it under her, until I've carefully situated her on my lap, cradling her in my arms. Gently placing my chin on her shoulder, I whisper into her ear, "Someone's a fast learner." I can't see her face, but I can feel her butterflies swarming beneath my hand. "Now that we've corrected your riding angle, we need to focus on positioning."

"Positioning, huh?"

"Yes. Take your feet for example. They do have footholds for your comfort."

Tangles leans her head back, looking up at me. Giggling, she says, "Show me."

Deliberately, I position my feet beneath hers, securing her snuggly in my lap. I pull the blanket back over the top of us and wrap her back in my arms, whispering, "Don't forget the seat belt ... and then there's these." I find her hands beneath the blanket and begin outlining her fingers, one by one. "You should always make sure these are in the right place at the right time."

"And are they?"

I shake my head. "Not yet."

I lace my fingers back in between hers and pull them snuggly up to her chest, right on top of her heart. "There. Now they're right where they belong."

"Are you sure?"

"Cross my heart." I smile, amused by the erratic thumping my touch has ignited beneath our crossed fingers.

As we finish the lesson, the chair approaches the top. "I can see the bonfire. Time to get off. You ready?"

Avery's head rolls back and forth on my chest. "I think I changed my mind."

"You don't want to get off?"

"I just learned how to ride this thing. I'm not ready yet. Besides, you're keeping me warmer than any bonfire I've ever been to."

Once again, my heart beats a little faster, and my stomach contracts from the tornado of butterflies spinning out of control.

"Fine by me. I could ride this thing all night. After all, I did write the book on it."

"Guess what?" she gives my fingers a squeeze. "I'm starting to believe you."

The rest of the ride is relatively quiet. Aside from the subtle quivering I feel dancing across my chest and the few times she clings to me from the unexpected dips and bumps of the cable, the night is still. It gives me the time I need to reflect on how incredibly blessed I am to be here in God's country. Alive. Looking out over the towering evergreens and majestic snowcapped mountain. Watching the smattering of snowflakes blowing across the constellations. Seeing. Breathing. Feeling.

As I hold onto this beautiful, witty girl, I can't help but think of second chances. I look down at that curly, brown hair and sweet mocha face. She's the one thing that's brought me the healing I couldn't find anywhere else. She's given me something to look forward to. A reason not to look back. When I walk into that building tonight, I'm saying goodbye to the toughest year of my life, and hello to hope for a better new year. And it's all because of her.

As we approach the bottom of the mountain, it's time to come back into sitting position. I ease Tangles off of me and tuck her inside the warm blanket. Looking down at my watch, we only have a half hour before midnight. "Any last requests before we say goodbye to this year?"

"I'm thinking it's time to celebrate the fact that it's finally over." Tangles holds out her hand and grabs mine. "Let's hit the dance floor and stomp out some crappy memories."

"Yours was bad too, huh?"

"Oh, you have no idea."

"Tell me ab..." Before the rest of the word leaves my mouth, her finger is at my lips.

"Shhh." She shakes her head. "I don't want to talk about it."

I squeeze her hand and nod my head, fully understanding where she's coming from. "It's okay. I understand wanting to bury nightmares. I don't like to talk about mine either. When you think about them too often, it gives them too much power."

"Sometimes distractions are the only weapons we have to fight them."

"Distractions as weapons. Never thought about that."

"Well, start thinking about it. Cuz tonight you're mine."

We stop right there in the middle of the snow. I'm so thankful for the way she just opened up to me. I need to show her that

I'll be that distraction. With everything in me. I will help save her. I wrap my arms around her and squeeze her tightly. *I'm her weapon against her nightmare. The same way she's mine. Well, if that's the case, I'm going to be the best damn weapon she's ever had.* I can't help but bend down and hold my lips to the top of her head. As we stand there swaying back and forth, enjoying the serenity of the moment, an announcement rings out through the speakers, breaking the silence.

"This will be the last song before midnight. Anyone who wants to bring in the New Year on the dance floor should make their way back inside."

I pry my lips from her head and look down at her. "How about that dance?"

She takes my hand and leads me back inside.

The floor is crowded with all of the couples wanting to dance the year goodbye. As we move our way through the crowd, looking for an opening, I watch the ceiling. I need to make sure I'm in the perfect place for our special dance. *There it is.* I find the spot and pull her in close. As we dance, I think back on my journey with this beautiful girl. How we met at the snowmobile park. How I chased her for hours. Our chance meeting at Gate 13. Midnight texts. And the little stunt at the Dash when she slipped on the ice and ended up in my arms. I have to chuckle at the way I spit my gum over her shoulder and pretended I was going to kiss her. She was pissed.

"What are you laughing about?" she grins.

"Do you still think I'm a jackass?"

The countdown is beginning. Ten ... nine ...

"What're you talking about?"

Seven ... six ...

"The night at the Dash. You called me a jackass and said you'd never kiss me."

Three ... two ...

My eyes direct hers to look above our heads.

"Like I said before ..."

One.

"Challenge accepted," I wink.

An instant smile crosses her face. She sees it. The mistletoe. *I'm going to win.* I look her in the eyes and smile as I draw close to her. I hesitate as I lean in close enough to feel her breath tickle the corner of my mouth. Her smile curls against me, as her lips brush against mine for the first time. She whispers, "I guess you win."

"Best win of my life."

Gently, I take her lips in mine. *Vanilla. Damn. She couldn't be any more perfect. This is the best prize I've ever won in my life, but I need to show her that she's more than just a game. This kiss needs to be a thank you. Thank you for being exactly what I needed. Thank you for giving me something to look forward to. A reason not to give up on myself. On life. This kiss. It has to be unforgettable.*

I narrowly open my mouth as I move in slowly. Gently, I tilt my head, just enough to take her full lips into mine. Our tongues barely brush, when the feel of her soft flesh sets the first firestorm crashing through me. It starts at my heart and finds its way through every nerve ending, leaving a trail of burning heat in its wake. I hold her close, stifling the internal explosion that's sending sparks zinging and swirling through my core. We stand there, with reckless abandon, right in the middle of the dance floor, letting the world dissolve around us. It's going to take everything in me to pull away from this kiss, but when my senses start to come back to me, I realize that I'm about to lose it right here in front of everyone. My breathing becomes quick and shallow as I work to calm the reaction to her scent. Her taste. Her touch.

I need a second. I don't want to embarrass myself. I gently pull away from her, setting my chin on top of her head. Slowly she rolls her cheek down against my chest. She's giving me a chance to relax. I have to break the tension. "I won," I laugh. "I got you to kiss me."

"You got me to kiss you? Don't be so sure about that."

"Why not?"

"I can hear your heartbeat."

"What's it saying?"

"That it was tricked."

"Tricked?"

"Mmmhmm. I know how to get what I want. Now kiss me again."

Right there, in the middle of the dance floor, we move together for the next two hours. Holding each other close. Taking turns initiating kisses. Twirling and swaying to the music. It's hard to say goodbye to this magical night. Not wanting to forget how beautiful she is in this moment, I pull my phone from my pocket to capture a New Year's selfie.

"Smile for the camera."

I can tell she's not really into being photographed, but Tangles puts on her best game face. *Perfect.* This will hold me over until I see her again, and if I have anything to say about it, that's going to be real soon. There's no way I'm going to let this girl get away. I hold the picture up for her to see. "See. We look good together."

A flirtatious smile comes over her face. "I look good with everyone."

She giggles and shakes her head, just to let me know she's not being serious.

Well, I don't think she is anyway.

And something tells me, that this game has just begun.

CHAPTER 32

REVELATIONS

"CADEN, PUT THAT PHONE DOWN. You're going to be late."

"Almost done."

ME: Hey. I have this thing I have to go to today. Sorry, I won't be able to see you. I'll text you as soon as I'm done, k? ;)

TANGLES: Well, it all works out then, cuz I've got a thing too.

ME: I'll miss you.

TANGLES: I know ;P

I take a deep breath in. I don't know how I'm going to put her in my pocket for two whole hours. That will be our longest break since New Year's. It's too bad I have to be the one to break the streak, but my parents are making me go to the stupid support group. *"Son, this is going to help you get back behind the wheel. She's going to get pretty suspicious if you never drive down to see her."* My parent's persuasive words keep knocking at the back of my mind, reminding me why this is so important. As soon as snow sports ends, I'm out of rides. I'll only be able to see her if I drive myself down there.

A small rush of adrenaline courses through me, just thinking about it. *Crap.* The realization strikes again. *The only way I'm going to be able to see her is if I drive myself down there.* I take a deep breath and release it. *Maybe Mom and Dad are right. This is for my own good. And hers.*

I'm a bundle of nerves on the car ride down. "Do I really have to talk to strangers about it? Nobody's going to understand. They're going to think I'm a freak. What seventeen year old guy is afraid to drive?" I feel sick.

"Just give them a chance. You have no idea what those people have been through. They're all there for a reason. It's a trauma support group. They're going to understand. And, you're going to find out that you're not the only one who's been through a tragedy. Breathe, Caden. You're turning blue."

I'm holding my stomach, trying to settle the nervous ball of vomit trying to claw its way up my throat. The snowy road isn't helping.

"Do you need a soda or something? You really look like you're going to be sick."

"I'll be fine. Let's just get this over with. Where is it anyway?"

"It's in the old catholic church."

"The one they don't use anymore? Mom, nobody goes all the way out there. Is it safe?"

"Yes, it's safe. You've got facilitators and other clients. There's just no unwanted foot traffic. They hold it there because it's private. You'll be fine, son. Quit worrying. I'll be waiting for you right outside."

When we pull up outside of the church, there are a handful of cars in the parking lot. I turn to my mom, "Great, not only am I the new one, but I'm the late one too." I decide to sneak into the back as quietly as possible, and sit down in the last pew. That way, nobody will notice me.

The old wooden bench creaks as soon as I put weight on it. I have to look down so nobody sees how red my face is. If anyone's looking at me right now, I wouldn't know it. I'm not looking up. Not until I know they've forgotten I'm here.

"Welcome everyone," a voice echoes through the long narrow building. "It's good to see you've all decided to come out for our first meeting of the new year. I see some familiar faces," pause, "and a few new ones. I know this is going to be tough for some of you, so before we begin, I want you to know that this is a respectful group. We need to listen, but not judge. Please think about your comments, and hold your tongue if there's something you think could hurt somebody else. This is a safe place. You're all safe here. Respected. Shall we begin? For any of you who have been with us before, would you like to start us off by introducing yourselves?"

There's no sound. I look up to see nodding heads, covered in scarves and stocking caps. *It is chilly in here. Wish I was wearing mine.*

"Alright then, since I don't have any volunteers, allow me to introduce myself. I'm Bill. I started this group about ten years ago after my wife and son were killed by a drunk driver. I damn near went crazy. I turned to alcohol. Lost my job. I was down and out with nowhere left to turn. A pastor got a hold of me one day outside of a local coffee shop. He introduced me to a few other people who had sought him out for help. At first, we decided to meet up at the same coffee shop every Sunday after church. One thing led to another. The group grew, as more struggling people heard about our meetings. To date, this group has seen over two hundred faces come and go."

I bury my head in my hands. *Oh my God, is mom really making me come to one of these groups? This is something you'd see on television. What am I doing here? This is not going to help me. I should just text Tangles. Nobody knows I'm here anyway. They're not going to notice.* I pull my phone from my pocket and shoot off a quick text.

> ME: This thing I'm doing. Pretty lame. I'd rather spend time with you ... and those lips.

I search my phone for the picture we had taken at the New Year's party. I love the way the lights from the disco ball are scattered across her cheeks. It reminds me of how magical that night was. By the time I find it, I realize I've been staring at my screen a little too long. *I'd better look up so they don't notice I'm not paying attention.*

"You'd be surprised how much it helps to share your story with others who have faced hardship. I'm a prime example. Today, I'm back on my feet. I have a good job. And I get to meet here with all of you every week to help you through your struggles. I'd really like to start with getting to know you. If you feel comfortable, it would be great if you could come to the front and introduce yourself. Tell us a little about what brought you here. I know I've already asked once, but maybe we can start with some of you who have been here a few times. It might help ease our new friends in."

Speaking of new friends. I hit *send.*

I hear a little shuffling, and then a ping. *Weird. I just sent that text. That's not my phone already is it?* I look down at my screen. *Nope, wasn't me.*

"Before we begin, I have a few little housekeeping rules I forgot to mention. Please keep all cell phones turned off and put away. This is a secure environment." A few people in front of me reach into their pockets and purses fumbling around to shut down their devices.

Shoot. If she texts back, she's going to think I'm ignoring her. I should probably let her know I have to put my phone away.

ME: Sorry, Tangles. Got to go. I'll text you later.

Send.

Ding.

What? I look down, again. No message. I'm curious to see who's in sync with Avery's phone. I shift back and forth, trying to peek around the stocking hats and hooded jackets. I don't see anyone on their phone, but I do catch sight of a tiny, little figure moving toward the podium. When she turns around to address the group, she pulls her hood from her head.

My mouth drops. *It's her.* My mind starts spinning. *What is she doing here? Oh God. What if she thinks I'm spying on her? I didn't know you were here I swear, Tangles. I know you're not ready for me to hear whatever it is you're going through. You'd be mortified if you knew I was here.* I drop my head back in between my hands and sink down in my seat, hoping she won't see me. *I'm a good actor. She'll never know I was here.* I take a deep breath and curl into a ball.

"For those of you who don't know me. My name is Avery. I've been here for a few sessions, and I can say that Bill is right. It does help to talk about it with other people who are going through hard times too. I'm here cuz I can't talk about this with my family. To them, I'm the strong one. But I'm not. I'm not strong at all. I hide behind my humor. I crack jokes, talk back, and put on a fake smile every single day.

I knew it. She's masking her hurt. What is it? Do I want to know? I shouldn't be here. I shouldn't be listening to this. If she sees me, she'll be so embarrassed, she'll never be able to look at me again. It will break her. It will break us.

Tangles continues. "I don't want to let them down. Ever since my brother messed up, I feel like I have to be perfect. My parents can't handle any more stress. They've gone through enough. I figured if I came down here to stay with my cousin, it would give them a break. They wouldn't have to think about me or take care of me. But it's hard. It's hard to leave your parents when you're sixteen years old. Especially during the holidays."

She bends her head and starts to cry. I want to run up there. I want to run up there so bad, but I can't. It would destroy her.

"Avery. You don't have to say anything else, if you're not ready. You can stop at any time."

"No. I need to. I feel like I need to talk about it. There was a new development over the holidays. Something you guys don't know about yet. I know you were all praying that they would find my brother. Well, we finally got the call on Christmas Eve. Some snowshoers found him in a crevice, down by the river. He's dead. My big brother is gone."

Snowshoers found him in a crevice? On Christmas Eve? Just like Pistol Black? Avery Black? The swimmer? No. It can't be. My mind flashes back to the earring I found attached to my jacket on Christmas Eve. It was engraved with the initials AGB. My heart stops dead cold. I look up, fighting for air. I feel like I'm suffocating. My ears start to ring. I see a mob of people move toward the front, lavishing her with hugs. Her brown curls pop out around their arms. A vision of Pistol flashes before me. Brown hair. Brown eyes. Country to the core. *Son of bitch! Why didn't I put two and two together?* I'm frozen in place. Dazed by the realization that Tangles is Avery Black. In that very moment when I realize that my Avery is also Pistol Black's Avery, I see red.

Without thinking, I shoot my hand into the air as I jump up from my seat. "MY TURN!" I scream as I stomp down the aisle toward the podium. The group divides as I brush past the people who have gathered around that deceitful, little liar. *How could she pull this on me? She must've known. Something should've given it away. She knew. She played me.*

As I reach the front, her eyes meet mine. She gasps and falls back into Bill. Her hand comes up over her mouth. *Oh, cut the drama. Why does she look so shocked?* Is *she pissed that I found out her dirty, little secret? Well, in case she doesn't know, it's time she heard mine.*

I tap on the microphone. "Hello everybody." There's still mumbling. Again, I tap to get their attention. "I'm sorry if I took cuts, but I have something important to say." I'm breathing hard. I feel a hand come up behind me. It's Bill.

"Take a deep breath, son. It's okay. I can tell this is hard for you, but talking about it will make it better."

I hold my hand up to stop Bill. I don't want to hear his cheesy after school special right now. *This* is real. I scan the crowd to find her. She's shrunken back into a group of people, but I stop and wait until she looks at me. I know she can feel me glaring her down. When our eyes finally meet, I notice she's still crying, shaking her head, no. I don't care. I don't feel sorry for her.

"Allow *me* to introduce *myself.* My name is Caden. Caden *Woodley.*" I pause when I hear her audible gasp. *Time to get a taste of your own Black medicine, baby.* I squint my eyes and growl. "I am here today to overcome my fear of *driving.* A fear I never used to have until this past Thanksgiving." I look around at the crowd, and let the sarcasm drip from my voice. "Why, oh why would a seventeen year old guy be afraid of *DRIVING?*"

No answer.

"Well, let me tell you. There was this guy. A real ASS-HOLE. He beat my twin sister. Stalked her. Broke into my truck. *Stole* my gun. And used it to chase us over an icy cliff!" I stop and chuckle, shaking my head. "The irony is, this ASSHOLE, happened to be HER," I point at Avery Black, "BROTHER!"

I hear gasps firing out around the room, but I don't even

look back. I push away from the podium, stomp down the aisle, and slam open the front door. *I've got to get out of here. And fast. Thank God my mom is in the car waiting.*

"How'd it go, son?" my Mom's voice is coated with sugar. It makes me want to throw up.

"Let's just say, something tells me, I'm not going to be invited back."

CHAPTER 33

WORTH FIGHTING FOR

I GET UP TO RUN to the bathroom again. *I can't believe I fell for Pistol Black's sister. I kissed her. I liked it.* My mind won't stop battling itself. It's tearing me up inside. One minute I'm disgusted over who she is and the next I miss her so much it hurts. *I hate this. How could she do this to me? Doesn't she know how much I've already been through?* She was my last hope. My reason to move forward. *I miss laughing. I miss feeling good. When was the last time I was happy? It feels like forever.*

I think of the New Year's party. How exuberant she was. How we moved together with ease. She was beautiful that night. It was one of the best nights of my life. She's the one who made me happy again. It was her. Every bit of joy I've had since the accident was because of something *she* said. Something *she* did. Was it all a trick? I know she thinks she's really sly pulling one over on me like this. *How could I be such a fool?*

The thought of wanting the one girl in this world that I can't have, makes me sick. This feels like a cruel joke. Another roar escapes my throat. It's accompanied by a rush of yellow fluid. *I don't know how I can keep doing this. There's nothing left in me.* My throat hurts. My muscles ache. I can't breathe.

There's a knock at the bathroom door. My sister softly whispers, "Caden, I hear you in there. When you're done, come out and talk to me. Maybe I can help."

"Go away."

I hear thumping on the wall. *She's so stubborn sometimes. She's doing the same thing to me that she does to Mom when she locks her out of the bathroom. Standing with her back to the wall, slapping her palms against it til she drives me so crazy that I have to come out.*

"I'm going to wait here until you come out. You've got to tell somebody what happened at that group. It's been a whole week. Caden, Mom's in there crying again. She thinks it's her fault for making you go. What did they do to you in there?"

I rinse my mouth and brush my teeth. I lean my head up against the door, but I'm not going to open it. "Tell her it's not her fault. *They* didn't do anything to me. It was me. I made an *ass* of myself."

"I know. They called Mom and told her you're not welcome back. No details on why."

"It's hard to hear you through the door. Won't you come out and talk to me about it?"

I do not want to talk about this. I need an excuse, and it has to be one that T will relate to. I finally come up with a plausible reason for rejecting her counseling services. "It's a school night. I need to get to bed. I can't focus when I'm tired."

"You've been using that excuse all week, so that one's not going to fly with me. Besides, Fridays are easy. You don't even have to focus. Plus, you get to leave early for ski practice."

She's not buying it. I guess it wouldn't hurt to talk to her for a few minutes. She'd probably understand how pissed I am better than anyone. *This is so messed up.* I decide to open the door to face my sister and fess up to what I've done.

"You okay?"

I know she sees the pain etched on my face. There's no way to hide the hurt. The hate. The emptiness I feel right now. "Do I look okay?"

"You look like you should lie down. Why don't we go in your room for a minute?"

I'm relieved to get out of the bright, fluorescent light. My head is pounding, and all I want to do is close my eyes and forget about everything. As I sit down on my bed, Kaitlyn sits beside me, handing me two ibuprofen and a glass of water.

"Thought you might need these."

I don't respond.

"I can put them back if you don't want them."

"Oh no, I want them." I scoop the medicine from her hand and swallow it down in one quick gulp. I can see that despite my absence from the family room the last week, our twin telepathy is still intact. "Thanks, T." I raise the glass in appreciation for the much needed pain killers.

"So, are you ready to tell me what happened at the support group? You're killing us with the secrecy. You won't even come out of your room. What's going on with you?"

I struggle to find the words. This could affect Kaitlyn every bit as much as it's affected me. *How can I tell her that I've been seeing Pistol Black's sister without sending her into a tailspin?* I don't want to be responsible for destroying the progress she's made since she got rid of that bastard. Those memories might be more than she can handle right now.

I take a deep breath, and release it.

"Why are you so afraid to talk to me? We tell each other everything, remember?"

"Well, it kind of affects you." I look down toward the ground. I can't look her in the eyes when I tell her this. "It might anyway."

"What could've possibly happened at that group that would involve me? You're really scaring me, Caden. Tell me what's going on. Please."

I know she thinks whatever I tell her she can handle, but this ... this is different. How could she forgive me for getting involved with Pistol's sister? I can't believe I didn't see the family resemblance. I need to come clean. She has a right to know.

"Okay. There was someone there. Someone I wasn't expecting."

"Who? Who was it?"

I'm going to blow her world apart right now. I throw my head back and stare up at the ceiling, releasing an explosion of air.

When I finally gather the nerve, I mumble her name under my breath.

"Who?"

I decide to look at her this time. "His sister."

She shakes her head as a look of confusion covers her face. "Whose sister? What? You're not making any sense."

Again, I mumble. But this time I use his name.

"Stop with the games. Whose sister was at the meeting?"

"Pistol Black's sister ... alright? It was *his* sister. I didn't even know he had a damned sister. Did you?"

She cocks her head ever so slightly. "Avery?"

A look of curiosity crosses her face, as she pinches her eyebrows into a "v." It's not fury I'm detecting. *Why doesn't she seem angrier?*

After a few stunned moments of silence, she finally questions, "Avery Black? Why would she be at a support group in the South County, when she lives in the valley?"

Well, that one's easy. Maybe if she lived in the valley I would've been a little more suspicious of a little brown-haired, brown-eyed cowgirl. "Oh, she doesn't live in the valley. She's staying with her cousin in Mount Shasta."

"How do you know all this? Did you talk to her?"

"You're going to hate me when I tell you this."

"Caden, I could never hate you. What is it? You're really starting to scare me."

I take a deep breath, trying to gather the courage needed for the final blow. "T."

Pause.

"You know the girl I've been seeing? The one I was sorta keeping to myself?"

My sister freezes in place.

Oh, man. I knew I shouldn't go here. She's going to blow. She's opening her mouth. Here it comes.

"No."

Breathe.

"Way …"

Oh no. Oh no. I scrunch my eyes closed and clench my muscles tightly, preparing for the wrath of a teenage sister scorned.

There's an extended silence. *I'd better look.* When I crack open my eyelid to sneak a peek, she's shaking her head. *Huh. Does she understand what I just said? She doesn't look as mad as I thought she would. She looks more …*

"What?" she whispers.

This is it. She's going to lose it.

She straightens up, staring at me. Her mouth bobs open and closed, but no words come out.

"I didn't know, T. I promise, I didn't know. I'm so sorry. I never would've …"

At that moment, the most unexpected thing happens. My sister bursts out into a fit of laughter. "Avery Black? She's your mystery girl? My brother is dating little Avery Black?"

"This isn't funny, T. Aren't you pissed at me? Why aren't you yelling at me? Are you just laughing out of shock?"

"Oh, I'm shocked alright. Shocked that you had no idea about Avery. Why didn't I think of this before? She's perfect for you!"

She's being irrational. I think she's lost it. "Are you okay?" I study her face for signs of a mental breakdown. "Kaitlyn, it's *Pistol's* sister!"

"So."

"So?"

"Caden, it's not fair to hold someone's sins against their family member. I love Avery Black. She's nothing like her brother. She's a sweet, funny, amazing girl. I can't believe you didn't know about her."

"Why would I know about her? You never mentioned her." I am so confused right now. *My sister isn't mad at me? She loves Avery Black? And she's defending her?*

"Haven't you seen her at my swim meets? She's been swimming against me for like seven years."

"She's on your team?"

"No. She swims for the valley."

Well, that explains it. I hate going to those meets. As soon as T's done with her race, Dad and I take off to camp and fish. I never pay attention to anyone, but my sister. But, I'm not going to tell her that. I don't want to hurt her feelings, so I just come up with another line. "Well, people look a little different wearing caps and goggles."

"True."

There's another silence between us. "So, Avery Black. You like her?"

I swallow hard, hoping to control the sadness in my voice. "Did!"

"What do you mean, *did*?"

"It's over. She lied to me."

"If it's the same Avery I know, that's hard to believe. She's one of the most transparent people I know. What you see is what you get. How do you figure she lied to you?"

"She never told me she was *his* sister."

She pauses for a moment. I know by the way she's looking at me, I'm in for some sisterly advice. "Did you ever tell her you were *my* brother?"

"What's your point?"

"My point is, she could be thinking the same thing. Why didn't you ever tell her you were my twin?" There's a long pause before Kaitlyn starts in again. "Caden, I'm not sure how you and Avery ever hooked up, but why in the world would she start a conversation about her crazy, missing brother who may have been responsible for nearly killing two teenagers. It's not a great conversation starter, you know. Maybe the fact that she didn't talk to you about it tells you just how much she likes you. She probably thought if you knew what her brother did, your opinion of her might change ... and look what happened when you found out ... it did."

I begin to think through all of our conversations, and how I did know something was going on with her. Before I knew what it actually was, I felt awful for her. *This is what was going on with Avery?*

"Caden, stop and think about this for a minute. What did Avery do to you? She's just as much a victim as you are. I know it's easy to blame the family, but seriously, I don't even blame them."

I have a hard time understanding how my sister is so for-giving. *How can she not blame them? They let him get away with this. Didn't they?* I have to convince her that she's way off base about this. "T, listen..." I start to whine.

"No." She raises her hand. "You listen. Avery Black is one of the nicest girls I know. I've *always* liked her. She's sweet as pie and loyal to a fault. And if I know anything about that girl, she's dying inside right now. No matter what you or I think of Pistol, she looked up to him. He was her big brother. And I know for a fact, that he's done things for her that you can't even imag-ine. Caden, she just found out she lost her hero."

"Hero?" I'm sure she can detect the vomit gurgling beneath my words. *What?*

"There's more to Pistol than you know." She looks at me like she actually believes it. "Look, I know you don't like him. He's done some unforgivable things. But, Avery is *not* Pistol. She didn't do anything to anybody. Don't be one of those people. Just put yourself in her shoes for a minute." She stands up and pats me on the back. "I'm not sure how things ended with you two, but please don't turn your back on her. Fix this." She whispers as she walks toward the door. "For me?"

I think about it. I picture little, wild-haired Avery riding on her brother's back. I envision hide and seek, climbing trees, and swimming down river. Holding her arm proudly to take pictures for her first school dance. All the things T and I have done as brother and sister. Then, my mind flashes forward to what's probably getting ready to happen, if it hasn't already. I see her sweet face, sitting in the front pew at her brother's funeral. Bent over his casket. Dropping her last gift into the open grave. I hate the thought of seeing her heart break in two. Torn up over a nightmare that she had nothing to do with.

Oh my God, what have I done? How unfair was I to attack her? Not only attack her, but shame her in front of all those people? I'm such an ass. How could I put her through that kind of pain?

"T, I think I messed up."

She stops in the doorway and looks back over her shoulder. "Yeah, you did ... but I think you know what you should do to make it right."

"What if she won't talk to me?"

"She might not. You may have to work really hard to fix this. But, isn't she worth fighting for?"

CHAPTER 34

WHATEVER IT TAKES

ME: YOU PROBABLY HATE ME right now. Heck, I hate me right now. You didn't deserve what I did to you. I need to say that to you. But I want to do it in person. Please text me.

I hit send on one of the most humbling texts of my life. I don't expect her to text me back. I'm probably going to have to track her down at practice tomorrow and beg for forgiveness. I will too. I'll do whatever it takes to make her know that she didn't deserve what I did to her. I hope I didn't send her over the edge. Destroy her completely. She's probably already taking on so much guilt from what her brother did. And I'm sure I made her feel like it was her guilt to own. *How could I be one of those people? I've got to take that guilt away. Let her know that I wasn't thinking straight, and I don't even come close to believing it's her fault.*

> ME: Look. I can't wait. It's killing me to think I made you feel like you had anything to do with this. You

didn't. The only thing you've ever been to me was a lifeline. You were my light at the darkest time of my life. After the accident, I didn't even want to get out of bed in the morning. You made me laugh again. You made me forget about the fear. The agony of life after "the accident." I needed you. Nothing else. Nobody else. Every single day. I needed you. Please, Avery. Text me back.

I reread my text, line by line thinking of what else I can say. Anything else to make her understand how bad I messed up. *Please, God. Please have her text me. Please.* I stare at the unchanging screen. Hoping. Praying. *Wait, bubbles.* I see bubbles bouncing beneath my last text. As soon as they start dancing across the screen, they disappear. *Damn. She must've changed her mind about texting. At least I know she saw it.*

Again, I reread my words, wondering what she thinks of them. Wondering how she will react to me pouring my heart out. *Is there anything else I could've said, can say, to make her talk to me again?* The bubbles start, and disappear again. She's killing me. I wonder if this is how she's felt for the last week after I threw her to the wolves. I never even texted. *Was she waiting? Wondering if I'd ever talk to her again? Wondering if I would apologize for being such an ass? I can't take this.*

> ME: I miss you so much. I am so sorry, Avery. I know you're reading this. I'm watching the bubbles. Please say something. I need you.

> TANGLES: You're right. You do need me. More than you think. I have to show you something.

She has something to show me? Did she do something to herself? Did I push her that far?

ME: That's it? We need to talk? When? Where? Are you okay, Tangles?

TANGLES: It's Avery. And not really. I'll be at practice tomorrow. See you then.

Damn practice has to get in the way of searching for her. I do my darnedest to look for the yellow and black suit, but every time I get to a place I think she might be, we're re-grouped and shuffled to another run. The snow is coming down so hard they've got the groomers working double time. The strong winds are tearing at the flags and wreaking havoc on the course. Thankfully, the other ski teams are being re-located as well. My stomach is in knots thinking about the moment I spot her. And I will. I am not giving up. I couldn't even sleep last night thinking about what I need to say to her.

The wind pierces through my jacket, and the snow pelts against my face, stinging my skin as I ride the lift up to the top of Douglas. At least Tyler's on my right, blocking half the snow. He shakes his head, as another gust of wind rocks the chair. I can't remember a time I've felt so worried on the lift. It literally feels like it's going to blow off the cable.

I pull my hands up to my goggles, trying to block the snow from accumulating on the lens. *I have to find her.* I search the occupants of every chair for as far as I can see. Dusk is setting in, which makes it difficult. *Damn this snow.* It was really risky to hold practice down here, knowing there was a major storm forecast for later tonight. But, the team is preparing for States and we're running out of time. *Lucky for me Coach took the gamble to bring us to the mountain. At least now I have a chance to find her.*

Though the storm wasn't supposed to hit hard for a few hours, it seems the wind has ideas of its own. It's moving in faster than expected. We still have to get back to North County in a bus, and my bet is that he's going to pull us off the mountain soon. *I've got to find her before he makes us leave.* My desperation intensifies my search. Again, I strain to see the skiers and boarders unloading in front of me.

Finally, when we're nearly at the top, about five chairs up, I spot a flash of yellow. It's dangling right next to shiny, blue. *It's got to be her. That's Jessie May's suit color.* They're getting ready to unload. *I can't lose track of her.* I lean forward, willing my chair to go faster as I watch her travel over the small berm and down to the main run. *Hurry chair.* I've got to get there if I'm going to catch her. I have a feeling this is my only chance tonight.

I turn to my riding partner. "Ty, you've got to help me keep an eye on them. We can't lose 'em."

"But Jessie May told me things didn't work out between you two. Dude, if she doesn't like you, she doesn't like you. Leave it alone."

Great. Now I have to explain myself to Ty too. "It's complicated. I blew it, dude. I just have to go let her know how bad."

He shakes his head and points toward a small group of trees, just off to the left of the lift. "They're standing there. Next to the trees. Keep your eyes on them. It looks like they're ready to take off."

I jump off the lift. As soon as I catch a bit of slope, I strap in as fast as I can. I watch the girls start to move away from the trees and toward the other side of the run. "Hurry, Ty. We've got to catch up. I can't tell if they're hitting North Saddle or Highland."

Ty straggles behind me, but I can feel he's close. I tuck low to pick up speed, veering right on the main trail. I'm glad I know these runs like the back of my hand, because I'm damn near boarding blind. It's getting dark, and the snow is coming down in buckets. "Ty! Are you here?"

"About three feet back, but it's hard to see you."

"I don't think we'll be able to find them. Not unless we call for them. You've got to do it, Ty. Call for Jessie! Don't let her know I'm with you. They'll stop if they hear *you*."

Ty begins calling out for Jessie May. Instinct tells me they're going to want to get to Revolution. It's wider. Clearer. The wind is too strong. They're going to want to get out of this storm and make it back down to the lodge. "Follow me, but keep yelling!" We continue on to the right, trying to find our way over to the terrain park. "I'm sure they're going to Revolution. It's one of the best lit runs."

By now, any natural light is completely gone. It's dark, especially on the trails we're cutting through to make our way across the mountain. Tyler hasn't given up on calling. Just ahead, I hear crackling through the trees. It's got to be another boarder or skier. "Hey! Hey, over there."

"Yeah?" It's a husky voice.

"I'm trying to find my friends. I was wondering if you'd seen them."

The figure is still unclear, but I'm close enough to make out his response. "Who's that?"

When I get closer, I can see that it's another Mount Shasta skier. "Jessie May and Avery. You're on their team right?"

"Coach just called us all off the mountain. They should be headed toward Panther Creek. I just saw them by the rails. You're about a half minute back."

"Not anymore!" I raise my hand and kick off. "Thanks, pal."

With a blizzard beating at my face, I kick it into the next gear. I hear Tyler holler behind me, "Wait up, dude. I can't catch you."

"You know the way! Hurry your ass up! But, keep calling."

I'm so desperate at this point, that I start screaming out their names myself. I'm choking on snowflakes, screaming at the top of my lungs. I can hear Ty, echoing behind me. That's when I finally hear a tiny echo from the trees. "Over here." I recognize the voice. It belongs to Jessie May. "We're over here. We're stuck."

We ski toward the voices.

"Keep calling! We're trying to find you!"

"In the ditch! We lost the trail!"

"Stay there." I'm relieved that they're not moving. It gives us a chance to catch up, to be more careful about moving through this crazy storm. Slowly, we make our way toward the trees. When I'm about two feet away, I spot color, down in the ditch, surrounded by fresh powder. I slow to a stop and unstrap my board. "I'm here."

I turn back toward the run. "Ty, over here. They need help! I think they're down in the ditch."

"Do you need me to call for help?"

I try to peek over the edge. The ditch isn't that deep. I think I can get to them. I holler back to Ty, "Not yet." I don't want to worry him. "I think they just need us to pull them out."

"Are you girls okay?"

"We're okay. The powder is just too deep. We're not strong enough to get out."

"We're here. Hang tight. I have an idea."

I begin pounding at the snow with my board. Packing it down to make a small trail. "Help me, Ty. Pack it." The two of us make quick work of packing a small trail down to the girls. "Here, hand me the end of your pole." Tangles looks at me, untrusting. "Avery. I'm here to help you. Give me your damn pole."

Jessie May turns to her cousin, "If you don't, I'm going to. Get up there, now. Stop being stubborn. We're running out of time!"

"Fine," she grunts, hitting the handle of the pole into my hand.

"Hold on tight. I'll pull you up." Avery begins climbing, as I tug on the pole, backing away from the ditch. As she begins to slip back down, I begin to slip too. "Ty, help me. It's slick!" Ty gets in back of me, holding onto me as I pull. With one final tug, Avery comes up over the edge, falling right beside me.

I look down at her, panting and exhausted. She looks so fragile. The first thing I think of is how sorry I am. This poor, sweet girl is so undeserving of my anger. And now that she's lying right beside me, and I'm looking into those hurt eyes, the guilt begins to eat at me. I did this to her. I'm responsible for making her eyes look like this. A lump forms in my throat and I begin to tear up. I shake my head slowly, whispering, "I'm sorry. So, so sorry."

Her finger comes up to my lips. "Shhh."

"But ..."

"Not now. My cousin needs you."

Jessie May. She's still down in the ditch. Tyler is there now, pulling the skis up from below. "Can you quit making googly eyes at Avery and give me a hand? Jessie May's turning into Jack Frost down there. She's got icicles coming off of her hair."

I snap out of it and head over to help Tyler. Again, we form a train to pull her out.

With both girls sitting side by side now, we check to make sure they're okay. "Anything broken?"

"We're good. Except for this." Avery holds up her ski. "My binding is completely busted. It's the same one I had to get fixed after the last race."

Crap. How am I going to get her down there in this weather? We're still quite a distance from the lodge. I can barely fight the wind and snow on functioning equipment. I'm not sure how to get Tangles down on one ski. My mind flips through different methods. I'm determined to get her off this mountain, and I'll do whatever it takes. "Ty, take Jessie May down to the lodge. I'm going to help Avery get down the mountain."

"I don't know if that's such a good idea. Maybe I should help her down. Can I trust you? She's already been through enough."

I deserved that. After the way I treated Avery, I'm not sure I will ever gain Jessie May and her trust, but I'm sure as hell going to try. First, I need to convince her cousin I will get her down the mountain. "I promise you, I will take good care of her. I owe it to her. I won't let either of you down."

"Jessie May, I appreciate it, but I'll be fine. You need to go tell Coach we're up here. He's going to come looking for us. We should've been back down at the bus ten minutes ago. Here, take my broken ski. It'll make it easier for me. Now go!"

Avery gives Jessie May the ski and a hug.

"Take care of my cousin, will ya?"

"You've got my word."

And with that, Ty and Jessie May take off down the hill, disappearing into the gusty, windy snowfall.

CHAPTER 35

THE CHASE

"**G**OT AN IDEA."

And I do, but convincing her to trust me is going to be the tricky part. "Can you make it on one ski? You can use me to balance."

"You expect me to touch you?"

"No, I don't expect it. But, I hope you will."

Without warning, a strong gust of wind comes up, nearly knocking me to my knees. Avery drops, huddling to the ground, blocking herself from the pelting, wet snow. I lay myself across the top of her, trying to block her from the savage attack. As I shield her with my body, a loud crack booms out above us, drawing our attention upward. Swirling, darting sparks fly overhead. It's the last glow of light we see. When the light of the sparks vanishes into the night sky, complete darkness covers the mountain. The wind howls, the relentless snow pounds against us. I can't see my hand in front of my face. A whimper cuts through the blizzard. It's Avery. She's at her breaking point. *What am I going to do?*

Think. "Tangles. I know you don't want to touch me. But don't do it because you want to. Do it because you need to. I want to help you. We need to get out of here. The blizzard is getting worse. Face your ski downhill and hold on. I'll try to light the way with my phone. We need to stay low to the ground. Don't let go. We can't get separated."

"I'll try." Hesitantly, she wraps her arms around me, one foot on her ski, the other standing on my board.

As scared as I am, the feeling of her arms around me brings me renewed strength. *I will protect her. I will get us out of here.* "Hold on tight," I plead as I start us off down the hill. I shine the phone light down at the ground. As we pick up speed, the snowflakes fly in every direction beneath and around us. The movement against the snow is dizzying. That, mixed with the tug of Avery on one ski, has me off balance. We start to wobble. Her ski begins to move in and out in front of me, finally making its way across the top of my snowboard. Before I know it, we're wrapped up in a heap on the ground. "Tangles, are you okay?"

"Yeah. Sorry. This is harder than I thought. My boot is slipping off your board and the wind is throwing me off balance."

"We're going to walk. Let's leave a trail of equipment. If someone comes up looking for us, they'll see the ski and poles sticking out of the ground. Let's start with your ski."

"That would be great if I could find it. It popped off when we wrecked. I can't see."

Shit. My phone. I must've dropped it when we wrecked. "Tangles, my phone. We need it. We need the light. I can't find it."

We both pat around on the ground, blindly. *Damn it. If it would just die down for a minute, maybe I could think.*

"Found something."

"Is it my phone?"

"I think so, but I can't make it turn on."

What are we going to do without light? I'm frustrated and

find it hard to keep my cool. "Can this get any worse?"

"Let me try to get mine. It's in my pack."

Avery digs around her backpack. I swear I hear the words, "got to show ..."

"Did you find it?"

"Yeah, right here."

Once again, a small beam of light pinpoints our trail. "We need to call down to Jessie May. She needs to know that we're having a tough time. They've got to send up a snowmobile."

"Got it." Avery shuffles around, taking off her glove to text her cousin. We wait for a few seconds. "Oh, no."

"What?"

"My text came up with an exclamation mark. Message not sent. Caden, I think we lost service."

Lost service? Okay. We can deal with this. Just stay calm. There's no need to worry her. "Okay, let's just go. We've got to get down this hill. Stick your pole in the ground." As she buries the pole, the wind picks up speed, damn near blowing Tangles off her feet. "Here, take my hand." I hold my hand back to her, shaking at her to take it. As we stumble our way down, I see a large black mass off in the distance. *What is that? It can't be the lodge. We're not close enough.* After thinking through a few different possibilities, I remember there's another structure up on the hill. *I know what it is. It's the race hut.* I remember going there with my dad for the dedication. He donated some of the building materials so the coaches had a place to watch the racers compete. I was just a little kid. My team never uses it, so I'd forgotten all about it. *Why didn't I think of this before?*

"I know where we can go. A safe place to wait this out. They'll be able to find us there."

"Are you delirious? We're in the middle of nowhere. No place is safe. What are you talking about?"

I point to the large, black silhouette. "Look. It's the race hut. Come on. We can make it."

We battle through the wind and snow. It's freezing outside, but under this jacket, I'm a sweating ball of heat from pulling both of us through the intense storm. I can barely lift my foot onto the threshold when we finally reach the small wooden cabin. I pull on the door. It doesn't open. With disappointment, I have to let her know my idea's shot. "It's locked."

She looks at me and releases the breath she's been holding. "Here, shine the light into my pack. I think I have something that can help us."

I watch Tangles dig through her outdoor pack. I see some trail mix, a large thermos, and what looks to be a spiral notebook. *Interesting. She brings her homework up on the mountain? I didn't peg her for a bookworm.*

"Found it."

"Your homework?"

"No. We'll talk about that later. I found this."

She holds up a utility knife. Curiosity gets the best of me. I have to ask her, "Are you a girl scout or something?"

"I'm a country girl. You never know when you're going to need one of these things. Besides, it was the last gift I got from my brother. I carry it with me everywhere." I watch her willfully work away at the handle. "This one's not too tricky. I used to have to pick locks all the time out at our farm. We were always getting locked out of places we wanted to get into." I detect a smile playing at the corners of her lips. "Got it."

She pushes the door open, and we walk inside.

Impressive.

She walks toward the back corner of the room, shining her phone's flashlight down on the ground. When she sees an open spot in the back corner, she turns around and stares at me.

I can tell she doesn't know what to say. Now that we've found shelter from the storm, there's no reason left not to talk, and who knows how long we're going to be here. I've got to help her get through her anger. Her hurt. Give her a reason to talk talk to me.

I try to break the awkward silence. "Looks like you saved me."

No response.

"Tangles, I know you don't feel like talking. I know I'm the last person you want to be stuck in here with. This has been horrible for you, and I didn't make it any better. A good person would've taken the time to think it through. And I want you to know, I did. I thought through every last bit of it. The problem is, I took too long. Hopefully it's not too late. I can't imagine what you've been going through dealing with your loss, and my irrational behavior on top of it."

She looks down to the floor. I can tell she's thinking back to that horrifying scene at the support group. "That had to be the worst day I've had since my brother disappeared."

I feel like crying. I hurt her more than I knew. "If I could just turn back time, I would. I'd take it back. I'd take it all back. Look, I'm sorry. I messed up. I reacted without thinking. I lost control. I was a self-centered son of a bitch, and I hurt you. That's the last thing I ever wanted to do. You deserved better. I know that. And I will work my ass off to make it up to you. Please, just give me a chance."

The look on her face begins to change. *She's listening.*

"Caden, I'm Pistol's sister. Your family isn't going to accept me. This would never work."

"Do you see there?"

"What?"

"Do you see how easy that was? You're judging unfairly, just like I did to you. And you're wrong. I talked to my sister. She loves you, you know. She's the one who got me to see that I was looking at this all wrong."

I watch her face soften.

"T helped me see how off base I was. I was so unfair to you. Avery, I'm going to say it again, you are everything I needed since the accident. You gave me a reason to open my eyes every morning. You're fun. You make me laugh. And damn it, no one can challenge me like you can. Did you know I chased you for hours that day? Out on the snowmobiles. I couldn't take my eyes off you. And then again, up on the mountain at the ski park. I chased you down a half-dozen runs. You didn't even know I was there. And you know what else? Even if you never let me catch you, I'm going to keep chasing you. I'm going to keep chasing you because you're my reason."

"Your reason?" she questions.

"Yes, my reason. My reason to wake up every morning. My reason to breathe in and out. My reason to laugh. Smile. Look forward. You're my reason to live again."

No sooner do the words leave my mouth than an enormous crackle and crash boom out around us. The walls of the building shake. Avery squeals as she bolts into my arms.

I hold her tightly, thanking God that he just put her back there. "I've got you."

"What the hell was that?" she gasps out, trembling beneath me.

"I think something hit the building. It could've been a tree. The snow load's getting pretty heavy." *Crap. What if it damaged the roof? I'd better move her to a safe place.* "Sweetie, would you come over here with me?" *Next to the strong, sturdy beam...* "You're shivering. I think they leave blankets in the corner. It'll be cozy over there. It's a good place for us to sit down while we wait for help."

She closes her eyes. I can tell she's still contemplating whether she's going to allow my company. "Okay, I'm in." She whispers under her breath, nodding her head ever so slightly, "All in."

I pull my hand up, letting it rest against the small of her back as I guide her to the wall.

"Are you sure you're okay with this?" I ask, as we slide

down onto the floor, pulling a heavy, wool blanket around us.

"I think so."

I pull her into me, hugging her and kissing the top of her head.

She tilts her head back and whispers into my ear, "I missed you too, you know."

Instantly, an explosion of adrenaline hits me. I can feel the rush of blood racing through my core. *She's back.* I can't help but give thanks out loud. Not only so she can hear, but to make sure God knows I mean it from the bottom of my heart. "Thank you, God."

We sit there quietly, holding each other, tightly, not saying a word, until finally I can't stand not hearing her voice for one more second. I have to think of something to say, just to hear her talk. "You're starting to warm up."

She lifts her head and smiles, "You kinda do that to me."

"Even after everything I put you through?"

"Well, it was a pretty sweet apology, minus one thing."

What could I be missing? "Really?" I grin, leaning back into her head. "I worked really hard to get that right."

"Oh, you got the *words* right."

Is this real? What more does she need from me to make this right? My brain is on overload, running through a mental checklist of what I could be missing. All the while, I'm distracted by the feel of her in my arms. *Pounding heart. Rapid breathing. Snuggled in close, conveniently raising her mouth so near to mine that I can feel her breath against my lips.* Suddenly it hits me. *She wants me to kiss her. Oh, hell yes I can fix this apology.*

I lower my chin, moving in so close my lips graze hers as I begin to talk. "I'm sorry I didn't finish."

"Finish what?"

The movement of her lips against mine has me flustered inside. Everything in me wants to just do it, but I have to hold back.

"My apology."

"What more can you add? I thought you said it all."

I feel her smile growing. The warm tickle of her breath against my sensitive skin, sends me over the edge. "I told you I was going to make it up to you. I'd chase you to the ends of the Earth to do this. You ready?"

Her breath hitches as I move in closer, pushing past the last millimeter of space between us. Then carefully, without breaking contact, I pull the blanket over our heads. Encased in a warm, protective cover, I take in her familiar vanilla scent. I can't hold back any longer. Gently, I take her face in my hands and pull her lips into mine. *These lips. They're even softer than I remembered. This is more than I deserve.* I pull back and whisper into the corner of her grin. "Thanks for the chase." Again, I take her lips in mine. And just like our first kiss, the firestorm erupts within me. Every movement of her mouth and every brush of her tongue is a new memory I'm creating. A memory of the most perfect girl. The most perfect kiss. The most perfect season. I never thought I'd love the dead of winter, until this girl brought me back to life, right in the middle of it. When I pull back hesitantly, to let her feel the smile on my face, she giggles.

"Guess what?"

"What?"

"You caught me."

CHAPTER 36

UNEXPECTED ENTRIES

I FLINCH AS AVERY SUDDENLY stiffens in my arms. "What is that?" she asks. I can feel the movement of her head, and I know she's trying to see something. *As though that's going to happen in this pitch black hut.* "There it is again."

My heart skips a beat. "What are you talking about?"

"That sound."

My first thought is that the roof could be collapsing. I try to stuff my heart back in my chest and tame the beating so I can hear the sounds outside of my own body. I listen closer, until I detect a faint humming. "Oh, the buzzing. I hear it." I breathe a sigh of relief. "It sounds like snowmobiles."

"We've got to make ourselves visible. Let them know we're in here. Give me your phone."

Avery hands me her phone, as I scoop her up off the ground. "Hurry." We run to the door, yelling. "In here! In here!"

I shine the light toward the rumbling sound. "Down here!" I turn to Tangles, "I don't think they can hear us through the engines and wind."

"Keep shining the light. It sounds like they're getting closer."

A strong gust of wind howls through the hut, slamming the door shut behind us. The startling bang has Avery spinning toward the door. "Stay here with the light. I just remembered something."

I continue holding the light toward the sound, as Avery makes her way back into the cabin. I hear the roar. It's getting louder. The snowflakes in front of me begin to take on a shiny glow, as the skyline before me begins to light up. *Yes. They're close.* "Hey, Tangles! They're coming this way! Get out here!"

"I can't find it! It's too dark!"

She sounds frantic. *What does she have in there that's so important?*

"Don't panic. I'll be there with the light in just a minute."

"Over here!" I wave. "We're right here!"

Ski Patrol. Thank God. The beam of light, shines in on the open door of the cabin.

"Got it!" Tangles shouts, running to the front door.

A younger looking man, climbs off his snowmobile, holding up a couple pieces of our equipment. "Please tell me these are yours. I'd hate to think anyone else is still up on this mountain."

"They're ours."

"Good job on thinking to leave a trail. It's the only way we could've found you out here tonight. You must be Caden and Avery?"

We both nod our heads in confirmation.

He pulls out his radio, "Hey, Chicken, I've got 'em. We need to get the other sled down here. We're at the race hut."

"Be there in a few. Copy?"

"10-4."

He clips the radio back to his jacket. "When you didn't show up back at the lodge, your friends gave us the general direction of where to look for you. Sorry about the delay. A tree downed the power line taking out electricity all over the mountain. Your coaches waited as long as they could, but they had to take off before I-5 closed down. When we get back to the lodge, we'll use the landline to call your parents.

"Caden. My Aunt and Uncle are out of town. Jessie May and I are staying by ourselves this week."

"Don't worry, Tangles. We'll give you a ride."

"Well, let's get you kids down to my headquarters so we can check you out, and hopefully send you on your way. Hop on."

All goes well down at Ski Patrol. There are no signs of hypothermia, and my parents have arrived to pick us up. I tuck Avery under my arm as we trudge our way down the walk to Dad's waiting truck. I feel her trembling beside me. She's been quiet since my parents met us at the lodge. I can tell she's nervous about what they think of her. She said it herself, "I'm Pistol's sister. This will never work." As we load our stuff into the back of the truck, my mom finally speaks.

"Get inside, sweetie. I'll take care of the stuff. You're probably still freezing from being up there in the cold for so long."

"Thanks, Mrs. Woodley." She nods her head and jumps in the back seat.

My sister and I get in on each side of her, sandwiching her in the middle. T puts her arm around Tangles, pulling her in for a hug. "I'm glad you're okay, Avery. So did you and my brother get a chance to talk? I know he was awfully torn up about how he treated you."

I know my sister is trying to help me out right now, but I

really want to move past this. "T, I love you, but can we not talk about this right now?"

"It's okay, Caden." Tangle's turns toward my sister. "Yes, we worked it out, but there's still something I needed to show him. I'm glad you're here. I want you to see it too." Avery starts stirring around in her pack and pulls out a small spiral notebook.

"What is it?"

"It was my brother's. They brought it back in his box of stuff the other night."

"Brought it back? Where was it?"

"It was at the rehab center. He was going there, right before the accident."

The thought of Pistol Black in rehab doesn't make sense to me. I have to question Tangles to make sure I heard her right. "What? He was in rehab?"

"Yes. He checked himself into Sacred Heart in October. After the night he came home bleeding."

"October?" I question.

The doors to the truck swing closed, giving the pages of my mind, a chance to turn back to fall. *October, our birthday.*

As the truck engine starts up, Avery continues on. Her voice lowers, and Kaitlyn and I huddle in closer to listen. "Yeah. One night in late October, he stumbled through the door. It was obvious he'd been drinking again. Only this time, he was hurt. His head was gushing blood. He was muttering. Incoherent. None of us could understand him. We thought he was going to die. My dad went crazy. He'd had enough. Mom fought him off. She wouldn't let him take my brother down to the police station. Let's just say it wasn't a good night. The next morning when he woke up, I went in his room. He was crying. Talking about how he hurt you … again. That's when he decided to get help. Fix himself. He said this time it was too close."

Kaitlyn brings her hand to her mouth. I see the shock on her face. I watch her struggle, and know she's remembering the horrific attack in the barn. A tear rolls down the side of her cheek. I listen as Avery tries to comfort her.

"I'm sorry, Kaitlyn. I'm so sorry I brought it up. I thought I could make you feel better if you knew how sorry he was. If you knew he was getting help because of you."

Kaitlyn looks down, shaking her head. "Getting help? It didn't do much good."

"What do you mean? He stayed there for weeks, making sure he got sober."

"Well, he wasn't sober the night he came after us on the mountain. He left the bottle of Jack Daniels in the truck to prove it."

Avery shakes her head. Her disbelieving expression almost looks painful. "That doesn't make sense. He wouldn't have started again. He was doing this for you. It's the only way he figured he could make it up to you. He was going to go see you, to apologize, as soon as he finished his program. He wanted you to know that you're the reason he got help. We talked the night before he went missing."

The night before? But the night before I assumed he was down at the Forks. What with the accident and all. A vision of my sister running from the cabin the night of *truth or dare* crosses my mind. *So it wasn't him in creepy cabin after all.*

"I know him, Avery." My sister continues. "I'm not trying to make you feel bad about who your brother was, but yes, it does make sense. When he drank he went crazy. He didn't think straight."

Avery shakes her head in denial. "No." She continues to shake her head. "Read this. You'll see. There's no way he started back up. Look." She holds her phone light to the journal.

We begin reading through Pistol's entries. How he struggled during the first few days in rehab. About the withdrawals. The anger. The hurt. And how torn up he was over what he'd done to my sister. He hated himself. He couldn't live with it.

And then, the tone of the entries begins to change. I can see that in the last few entries he's sober. He's found clarity. Avery turns the page. It's the last entry.

> November 25
>
> It's the middle of the night. I'm drenched in sweat. I can't sleep. The last two months have been re-playing in my mind. Tonight when he came to visit, it brought everything back. I can't believe the crap I've done. What the hell was I thinking? I wasn't. The alcohol scrambled my brain. It fueled my jealousy. It amped my anger. It turned me into a monster. If I could go back, I never would've done it. This place has brought me clarity but along with that, I think I just inherited an even greater nightmare. Living with what I've done. I loved her. I loved her more than anything. I still do. Next to my little sister, she's the only one who ever saw the good in me.

"See, I told you. He loved you. I don't think he would've started drinking again. It just doesn't make sense."

I study the words over and over, trying to make sense of where his mind was, and why he would've driven down there the way he did. If he loved my sister so much, why did he come after us? As I hold the light of the phone up to the words, I notice faint letters bleeding through.

"Wait, it looks like these two pages are stuck together." I rub the corner back and forth, until the pages begin to separate. Then carefully, I peel them apart.

"Oh, wow, there's more. I didn't see this one." Shock is evident in Avery's voice.

> I know I was in a messed up frame of mind the night of the homecoming dance. The night he pulled me aside and offered me my ego back. It was jealousy. I was pissed off about Brody and her. I felt like they'd made a fool of me. All I wanted was revenge. Maybe I wanted to scare her. Pay her back for the way she made me feel. I don't know. I was too drunk to know what I was thinking. But how? How did it get so out of control? Helping him plant cameras? Watching? Stalking? How could I have done this? For a little cash, some booze, and a few pictures here and there? Why didn't I question him more? For weeks, I let him turn me into his puppet. Telling me what to do with that screwed up accent of his. What the hell did he want with her friend anyway? I can't believe the nerve he had showing up here, asking me to go with him. What is his obsession? Something doesn't feel right. I didn't like the look in his eyes tonight when he told me he was going down to see her. I don't trust him. Not one bit. I've got to go down to that river and make sure they're okay. All of them. I owe them that much.

I hold my breath as I look up at my sister. Her eyes are wide with fear.

"Caden, oh my God."

"Screwed up accent? I thought it was just an innocent crush."

Kaitlyn's jaw drops.

"Who is it? What's wrong?" Avery questions.

My heart stops cold. *Pistol Black was trying to protect us.* Turning toward my sister, the only words that escape my mouth are, "Oh my God, he's wasn't after you. He was after Jenna."

THE END

A Message from the Authors

When we first started writing *When Fall Breaks*, our dream was to write books as gifts for our own children. However, as the stories came to life, a message started to form. We realized, being teachers that we witness difficult situations that our students face every day. It is our hope that reading our stories will help teens make connections and seek help from professionals when needed.

Our first story, *When Fall Breaks*, dealt with underage drinking and substance abuse. Our message at the end of that story provided The Pathway Program as an available resource for help. We'd like to offer that information again. If you know of a young person who may need help, The Pathway Program is available by both phone and via the internet. You can call and talk to a representative Toll Free at 1-877-921-4050 or visit them on the web at www.thepathwayprogram.com. If you are a teen and find yourself struggling with drinking or substance abuse, please reach out to a parent, school counselor, teacher, youth pastor, or friend. As teachers, we are always open to help our students get the help they need. It doesn't matter if you were a former student, current student, or didn't even have us as a teacher. We care about all of you.

A second issue we addressed in *When Fall Breaks* was how teens and young adults struggle with domestic violence. This can happen to people of any race, age, sexual orientation, religion, or gender. Sometimes it starts out subtly and intensifies without the victim realizing how bad it has become. If friends are warning you that they see signs of control, verbal, or physical abuse, please listen. Many abusers are masters at manipulating their victims and making them feel like THEY are the reason for the incident. It's NEVER okay. It is NOT your fault. If you or someone you know is in an abusive relationship, there is confidential support out there 24/7. Please visit the National Domestic Violence Hotline at http://www.thehotline.org. Teens can go to www.loveisrespect.org, or call 1-866-331-9474, to speak with someone privately. It's a confidential online resource available to help young adults prevent and end abusive relationships.

As a follow up to the severe incident that occurred in our first story, *The Dead of Winter* focused on an issue that is extremely serious and often ignored. It is called Post-traumatic Stress Disorder (PTSD). This disorder is a mental health condition that's triggered by terrifying events. Some people have either experienced or witnessed catastrophes that may cause them to have flashbacks, nightmares and/or severe anxiety. The teen characters in *The Dead of Winter* lived through such traumatic events and did not receive the attention needed right away. Please do not ignore the symptoms of Post-traumatic Stress Disorder. Get help if you are having a severe reaction such as nervousness, fear, and even guilt after experiencing a traumatic event. If you believe you are experiencing PTSD, reach out to a professional. They can help you restore a sense of control in your life. Post-traumatic Stress Disorder can happen at any age. You are not alone. Please visit the National Center for Posttraumatic Stress Disorder (NCPTSD) at http://www.ptsd.va.gov or call (802)296-5132. It is a confidential online resource available to help adults of any age.

ACKNOWLEDGEMENTS

So here we are, just seven months after publishing our first novel, and we are finishing book two. What a whirlwind experience! We've had a lot of laughs and a lot of tears over the last year, but one thing is for sure, there were several people right there to help us through it. First and foremost, a special thanks goes out to our husbands and children who put up with our late nights, busy weekends, and our overbooked schedules. You guys stayed strong, encouraged us, and still maintained your amazing personalities. The same ones that inspired our characters. Because of your support and belief in us, you made this dream a reality. Thank you for encouraging us to follow our dreams.

We'd also like to send an enormous thank you to our mothers for all of your sweet, encouraging texts and comments that have helped us stay strong, stay brave, and persevere through one of the greatest challenges of our lives. We appreciate you more than you know. Thank you for the reviews, sharing When Fall Breaks with your friends, and never passing up a moment to promote our book. And to our Dads; we thank you for teaching us about country living, blessing us with half of our goofy personalities, our humor, and creativity. Though you're no longer with us, you inspire us every day to make you proud. We wish you were here to see us reaching for the stars and making our dreams a reality. We miss you!

To our close family and friends who have read our book

and given us support along the way, we are so thankful, and blessed to have you in our lives. It's really tough putting your work out there. We found much of our strength in the conversations we had with you. Just like when we were kids, you were there to protect us and cheer for us, and that is what made us continue with book two. There is one girl that has been like family to us. Our dear Sarah Jankowski, thank you for being such a great friend, heading up our support group on social media, decorating the halls of our middle school, and keeping us motivated through some stressful, tense times.

To our BETA readers, thank you for the time you put into helping us and your valuable input. Jeanne Burcell, Sandy Smith, Macy Smith, and Shanna Schack, we value all your advice and direction. To Marnia, our editor, thank you so much for your keen eye and honest input. This book would not have been the same without you. You mean the world to us.

To our beautiful Jada and Tori, thank you for giving us the inspiration to create Avery. Jessie May, you are right there too. We looked forward to your visits every single day for the past seven months, trying to get us to give up some secrets. We just can't get enough of you dolls. We don't even want to think of the day you leave our school. We love you.

To our formatter, Stacey Blake from Champagne Formats, we can't thank you enough for making the interior of our book beautiful. You have created masterpieces with both of our novels. Your designs blend together flawlessly, and we can't thank you enough for the beauty and magic you continue to produce.

To our promoter Erin Spencer from Southern Belle Book Blog, we are so happy to work with you and your enthusiastic personality. You make us smile. Rosie Snowdon, our beautiful friend from across the pond. We don't even know where to begin. You've been promoting for us from the beginning and we can't thank you enough. We always look forward to our messages and the times we get to chat with you. We are going to

England to meet you one day. That's on our bucket list. We love you!

To our author and blogger friends, we couldn't have done this without you. You made this dream a reality, and gave us the wings we needed to fly. Beth Flynn, K.A. Sterritt, Stacy Hendrickson, and Alyson Santos, we love you to pieces. Even though you are incredibly busy with your own books, fans, and promotions, you always seem to find time for us. Thanks for all your advice, your late night messages, and endless support.

To our amazing bloggers, Darlene, Rosie, Paula, Tracey, Tammi, Katie, Eli, Karen, Tesrin, Christina, Janet, Kelly, Erin, Kylie, Gloria, and everyone else who has shared positive reviews, supportive words, and blessed us with your friendship, we are forever grateful for your continued support and presence in our lives. You have added so much joy to this experience. We can't thank you enough for putting our book out there.

And finally, we want to send a bucketful of hugs and a huge thank you to our readers, especially those of you who have joined our Did Fall Break You? support group. What would an author be without readers who are willing to invest their time and energy into books? We rely on people like you who are brave enough to reach out and let us know your thoughts. You are the ones who share your enthusiasm with others, find us new readers, and make our dream a reality. We appreciate you taking the time out of your day to send us lovely, touching messages. Thank you for using your talents to write brilliant reviews, make beautiful teasers, and share your passion with others. You inspire and encourage us every single day.

This entire reading world would not be possible without you. We are forever grateful for all of you who endured the snowy cliff and continued on to give The Dead of Winter a chance. We have the best fans in the world. We love you.

.

ABOUT THE AUTHORS

Julie Solano has lived in far Northern California, nearly her entire life. She graduated from CSU, Chico, where she majored in Psychology and minored in Child Development. She later went on to Simpson University where she obtained her multiple subject teaching credential. Julie enjoys life in the "State of Jefferson," where she lives with her husband and two children. As a family, they spend their time tromping around the Marble Mountains and Russian Wilderness. They also take pleasure in rafting, skiing, snowmobiling, off-roading, campfires, and living it up in the great outdoors. When she's not with her family, Julie spends her days teaching next door to her co-author, fellow prankster, and partner in crime, Tracy. The most recent of their crazy adventures was to take on the challenge of writing this series of novels about what life is like in their neck of the woods.

Born and raised in Northern California, Tracy Justice is a wife, mother, and full-time teacher. She graduated from CSU, Chico, with a Bachelor of Arts Degree in Liberal Arts. One of her fondest memories growing up was herding cattle in the Marble Mountains with her family. She enjoys spending time with her family and friends, riding horses, running, hiking, swimming, and of course reading. After some encouragement from Julie, she decided to add "Co-author" to her ever growing bucket list. She never knew how much fun it would be to write a book with her best friend. She hopes you enjoy reading their second book in the "Seasons of Jefferson Series" as much as she enjoyed writing it with Julie.

Julie and Tracy hope you enjoy reading their stories, which were inspired by their small town, rural upbringing, and the personalities of their four children.

Remember to visit Julie and Tracy on Facebook, Twitter, Instagram and their Webpage.

https://www.facebook.com/JT-Authors-342478559284742/timeline/?ref=aymt_homepage_panel

https://twitter.com/jt_authors

https://instagram.com/jt_authors

http://www.jtauthors.com/